Village of Edgemont Cozy Mysteries

Book One

A Deadly December in Edgemont

Book Two

A Fatal February in Edgemont

Book Three

A Sinister Spring in Edgemont

Della North

Copyright Page

A heartfelt thank you to Darlene Hartung for her wonderful encouragement, it means a lot.

Book 1

First book in the Village of Edgemont Cozy Mysteries series

A Deadly December

in Edgemont

Della North

A Deadly December

in Edgemont

Della North

copyright 2023

publisher Lynda French

cover design by Dezynetek

Chapter 1

The body of missing teen Holly Lezinsky was found on December 19th, just two days before her fourteenth birthday. She'd been missing for one week and pregnant for eleven.

The discovery didn't affect Judith's plans for Christmas because she didn't have any, but she did have to rearrange the school's ruined holiday schedule. "Luckily there are only a few more days left, and the workload is light," she thought.

Although the news was sad Judith felt it was important that they learned the truth at last. It had been a very unsettling week for staff and students alike as everyone worried over Holly's whereabouts. She was a popular girl.

School Principal Patricia Johnson got the call from the police. They would be coming around later today or tomorrow with questions and to hold some interviews because it was a suspicious death. Well of course it was, the victim was just a child although Judith was quite sure Holly didn't see herself as such!

Pat answered the officer's call herself since Samira, the school secretary, was off sick with the flu. A nasty bug making the rounds had already affected staff and students. She called Judith and apologised for giving her the news over the phone but excused that claiming a pounding headache and a million things to do adding:

"I'll have to make an announcement but I'm hoping to get more information from the police first. Everyone's going to have so many questions. Ugh, I just can't think about it all right now."

Judith discovered that she wasn't shocked to hear the new, figuring she must have suspected that Holly was already dead. Holly did seem like the kind of girl to get into trouble. Unless it was suicide? How was she killed? Unfortunately, it wasn't a stretch to imagine Holly as a murder victim.

Judith did wonder "Am I being unfair to the girl?" but then an image of Holly in her school uniform came to mind: plaid skirt rolled up at the waist to shorten it, shirt unbuttoned to show the lace on her bra, and knee socks rolled down to her ankles to flash a lot of bare leg.

Holly Lezinsky was a brazen adolescent flaunting her new-found sexuality but the poor girl didn't deserve to die.

Of course, Judith felt terribly sorry for the girl's family. Holly was raised by a single mom and she was an only child, an upbringing similar to Judith's own. She started wondering about how her own mother would have coped in such a circumstance but forcefully slammed the door shut on such thoughts. The past was dead and gone. She had resolved a long time ago to move on.

Still, it seemed that somehow a death was made even worse when it happened so close to Christmas. Judith thought that the happiness of others would be unbearable to the bereaved. And then each successive anniversary would be another reminder.

Well, it's not my concern. It's up to the police now, thought Judith. Opening the scheduling app on her laptop she forgot about the girl and got to work revising the plans for the next few days.

Chapter 2

She got back to work thinking *No more distractions, I definitely want to finish the Accounts Receivable today. I'm not going to let this delay me starting my holidays tomorrow,* Judith decided. *I suppose that's selfish but honestly this girl's death is nothing to do with me.*

Her phone buzzed with another internal call from the principal. Judith sighed. Pat Johnson came straight to the point saying:

"Judith, I hope you haven't booked anything because I can't let you go on vacation yet. I need you here. I could have managed on my own without my secretary but not with Holly's death as well. The phone is ringing non-stop. In fact, I need you to come to my office now, can you do that?"

Frustrated, Judith banged down the handset. She definitely did not want to act as School Secretary for the day but she felt she owed Pat. So, she had no choice, she had to go to the principal right away.

But I will stand up for my rights, Judith asserted. *I'm determined to fight for my holiday time!* She smoothed her hair back from her face, it was brown like her eyes, and tended to frizz if not kept under control. Judith usually didn't much bother about her appearance – so long as she was clean and tidy – but right now it was important not to look frazzled. She wanted to present a calm but determined demeanour. Hurrying to the suite at the end of the corridor she planned her arguments along the way.

The moment she arrived in the principal's office Judith realized her time off was going to be cancelled for sure. It was obvious that Pat was sick, her face damp with the sheen of fever and her eyes dull. Judith was torn between sympathy for Pat's plight and her own self-pity. She resigned herself to hear disappointing news.

5

Lila Morelli, the school's nurse, entered the room a few moments later saying:

"You've caught the flu, Principal Johnson. And on top of the tragic news about poor Holly Lezinski, too. Your resistance will be really low."

Judith had met the new hire earlier in the month. As school bursar it was her job to put together Ms. Morelli's employment orientation package of passcodes, tax forms, and benefits. Afterwards Lila lingered but Judith had no interest in small talk or coworker gossip and hurried her on her way. Seeing Lila in professional mode was interesting.

"Professional except for the hair, that is." Judith amended, eyeing the turquoise streaks in Lila's blonde pageboy.

Nurse Morelli wore a white medical jacket over regular clothes, not scrubs or a uniform. She pulled a digital thermometer out of her pocket and checked the older woman's temperature at wrist and then at forehead.

"Normal temp, no fever," she announced.

Judith perked up at the happy news, saying:

"Great, not flu then."

But Lila shook her head answering:

"No, that doesn't mean no flu it simply means the virus can thrive instead of breaking with a high temperature. When the fever hits, and it almost definitely will, you'll be better off in bed. Principal Johnson is there anyone at home, or who could come to your home, to keep an eye on you?"

"Oh yes, yes really, I'm okay. There's no need to fuss. My husband took early retirement to pursue his hobbies from home. He'll look after me." She struggled to get up and both women hurried to give assistance. Frail and shaky – this was not the Patricia Johnson Judith was used to seeing!

"Judith, you'll follow the usual procedure and step in for me?" Pat pleaded.

Judith struggled to keep her thoughts from showing on her face. She hadn't want to take over the secretary's job and now it looked like she was getting the added burden of the principal's duties. She wanted to take her vacation break! However...

"Of course, Pat. Don't worry about a thing, just concentrate on getting better. We'll be fine," she soothed.

Turning to Lila Morelli she added:

"Well, Nurse Morelli, I'm afraid you'll have to help me while both Samira and Principal Johnson are absent." Judith resented sounding petulant. She spotted Lila Morelli's poorly disguised smirk and was surprised to find herself smiling back.

"Well, Bursar Taylor, since we've been thrown together, I suggest you call me Lila. Sound good, Judith?"

Chapter 3

Judith was busy studying the more extensive calendar, filled with appointments and class schedules, in the principal's office when Lila returned from helping Patricia Johnson into her car.

The principal had insisted on driving it home since she and her husband only had the one vehicle. Lila tried to organize one teacher to drive and another to follow in their own car, but Pat resisted getting anyone else involved. Judith had listened to the exchange without comment, she knew Pat was stubborn so there was no point arguing.

"Principal Johnson has given us a dozen things to do, most of which won't get done, but she had one very good suggestion," said Lila. "We can direct all the incoming phone calls to the staff room phone. That way everything will get picked up by the answering machine. She explained how it's done and it's a simple redirect."

"Yes of course, I forgot about that. It's something Samira does but not often."

Judith told Lila how the protocol had been established years before and was carried out whenever the admin office was unable to answer calls.

"Since the staff can't be expected to take down messages – some of which are quite lengthy! – while enjoying their well-deserved break every caller is asked to leave their information.

If someone in the break-room is expecting a call they are able to pick up the handset and have their conversation. The only drawback to the system is that anyone and everyone can hear the messages. People have warned friends and family about this and to be discreet, but people forget, and some calls are definitely amusing!"

"It sounds like a good idea and something we can definitely use for the rest of the semester."

"I think we're going to have to cancel classes and start the holidays a day or so early," said Judith. "So many staff and students are off sick. And now, with the news of Holly's death, I don't think the students will be able to concentrate. I'm sure even the teachers will be gossiping about it."

"Well, from what I remember of my school days not a lot got done in the time before Christmas anyhow."

"No, there are no exams or anything. The younger children make Christmas cards and chains out of construction paper. The middle group read Christmas stories, and the older girls are busy preparing for the play. Oh no, Holly had a starring role in the play!"

"This is my first Christmas here, so I don't know how important the play is--"

"It matters," interrupted Judith, "but with this flu bug going 'round we'll have to cancel the performance. Some of the cast are sick already and to sit in a closed room with a bunch of people who are sniffling, sneezing, and coughing... ugh! It will have to be rescheduled for some time in the New Year. Can't be helped."

"What play are they doing?"

"Their own. Noel Larkin – have you met him yet? – he's the Drama teacher and he gets them to write a script, play the parts, make costumes and scenery, everything in fact. It always has some sort of a Christmas theme. The parents love it."

"I do know Noel, he's invited me to his Christmas party, along with the rest of the staff, that is."

"Yes, it's a combination birthday and Christmas event. He was actually born on the 25th hence the name choice."

"I like the name Noel, it's unusual. And he seems like a nice guy, in fact considering how good-looking he is he's surprisingly nice."

"Hmm, never thought of him that way but you're right he is a nice man."

"And handsome too, remember," said Lila with a smile and a question in her voice. Judith wasn't paying attention; she was too busy studying the big calendar. She self-described as 'detail-oriented' and was reading every entry. She replied offhandedly:

"If you like the 'male model' type, then sure."

"Ha, that does fit him. So do you prefer the rugged he-man type?" Lila teased.

"I don't have a type," Judith retorted.

"'Okay Lila don't go there', I get it."

Judith rolled her eyes, saying: "I'm just not interested."

"So, is the party a fun thing? or does it feel like a work outing?"

"I don't know, I've never gone."

"Oh, sorry, I thought everyone was invited."

"Well of course I'm always invited, yes, but I don't mix with my coworkers as a rule."

Lila answered using a pretend-whiny tone: "Does that mean you won't go with me to show me the ropes, as it were?"

"I wouldn't know the 'ropes' if I tripped over them." Judith caught herself smiling, enjoying this unaccustomed banter. She found that she couldn't help but like Lila.

"Besides, when it comes to socializing with coworkers, I think you'll find the teachers consider themselves a cut above the rest of the staff. They seem friendly but they aren't exactly welcoming," Judith said with a shrug, "Maybe things will be different for you."

Lila sidestepped that comment by asking: "So how do we go about cancelling the rest of the school year?"

"We'll get everyone into the auditorium and make an announcement--"

"Yes, Principal Johnson wanted us to tell the girls about Holly and have a minute's silence. We can combine that with notice about the school closure."

"Well, that's the other thing. Many of the parents are at work during the day so we have to give them some notice before sending the girls home. The best thing to do is have the school open for the next couple of days, but attendance can be optional. For the students, that is, the teachers will still have to come in. Then, depending on how many students show up, we can decide to stay open or close.

For sure we'll close on the 24th. Usually, we're open for a half-day of snacks and socializing, card and gift exchanges, and then the school play takes place in the afternoon. This year we'll just have to tell everyone to stay home. I don't think even a small party would be appropriate."

"Oh, do you think Noel will cancel his party?"

"No, and nobody would expect him to do so. But it's different for the school. Holly was one of us and the parents expect us to observe the proprieties."

"You're in charge, Judith, so get on the PA system and call everyone to the assembly. I'll go organize the chairs into rows."

With Lila gone Judith took a moment to gear herself up. The announcement was no problem, she could easily speak into the microphone, but standing up to give a speech in front of the entire school? well... she'd accept her responsibilities but that sort of thing wasn't in her job description.

Chapter 4

As Edgemont village grew into a small town the local school needed a newer and bigger building. Thus, the old school became Edgemont School for Girls, which offered classes up to and including Grade Nine.

Graduating girls, usually finishing by age fifteen sometimes sixteen, went on to public or private high-schools. It served the community and surrounding area with at least one quarter of the students subsidized through donations and fundraising.

The elderly building was hard to heat in the winter, but for that season Principal Johnson had added leotards instead of knee socks to the dress code.

It was a day-school only, no one boarded.

Everyone admired the old school's style, character, and architectural details. It was built from sandstone in the Tudor/Gothic-Revival style sometime in the early 1930s.

There were no windows in the classrooms which were built in a circle inside the building. To get from one class to another the students crossed through a centre hub. One wall of windows was sectioned off to include the administrative offices, library, cafeteria, and auditorium. Indoor Phys Ed. classes were taken in the basement where a year-round chill kept the girls moving quickly in their exercises and games.

Judith shared her office with the librarian, a young woman called Cindy Callahan. Not for too much longer though since she'd received an engagement ring as an early Christmas present and would be known as Mrs. Thiessen in the future.

Cindy only worked in the library part-time since she also taught some English classes. While showing off her ring in the staff room, she'd shared her disappointment at Judith's lack of interest in the upcoming nuptials.

Cindy wanted to discuss ideal wedding dates and venues and look at Bride magazines for dresses and colour schemes, and rehash exactly Eric had said when he'd proposed... but Judith had been quite rude about *all this chatter*. The other teachers agreed that Judith Taylor was an unfeeling woman with a cold heart.

Full of indignation Cindy had repeated all of this to Judith only this morning, after brooding about it overnight, and Judith had looked at her saying:

"How do you expect me to respond to that?"

So, the two of them spent the rest of the morning in a silence that was frosty on one side and indifferent on the other until Principal Johnson phoned.

When Judith called everyone to assemble a few raised eyebrows were exchanged along with mutters of 'what's she up to?'

Lila told the older girls to help set out chairs and instructed the rest to be seated. Everyone was asking questions, some in whispers and some out loud. After a few minutes Judith came in and walked purposely to the front of the room. She looked at the notes she'd hastily written and addressed the audience which all of a sudden seemed huge and the room overfull.

"I have several announcements to make," she said.

"Where's Principal Johnson?" called out Marta Smith, a senior teacher close to retirement age. Judith suspected Marta was going to be trouble, it was in the older woman's nature.

"The first point I have to make is about Principal Johnson so please hold your questions until I've finished," was Judith's curt reply.

"Principal Johnson has appointed me in charge temporarily. She's sick with this flu bug that's going around and had to go home. As did her secretary, Ms. Kanji. Nurse Morelli is assisting me. That's the first item." She had to raise her voice over a mumbling of complaint from the teachers.

"Secondly, and this is very sad news, the police have been in touch to tell us they've found Holly Lezinsky dead."

Pandemonium as the audience gasped, cried, and shouted out in shock.

"It's an *unlawful killing* and that's all they've told us."

Everyone knew who everyone was at Edgemont School. They would all have known Holly.

The teachers often complained that Holly was always talking back but acknowledged that the girl added wit and humour to her cheekiness which made everyone smile. The youngest students idolized her. Questions were shouted out.

"I know everyone is upset. I'm upset by this news. It's terrible, but I'm sorry I don't know anything else. The police want to talk to Holly's family – her mother – before sharing details with us. When we hear more, I will pass on that information.

And that brings me to the final announcement: the school will stay open for the next couple of days, but classes are cancelled. Teachers will be in their rooms so any students who have to come in because of working parents will be looked after. We'll decide what to do on a day-by-day basis.

We will definitely close at end-of-day on December 23rd and remain closed until our return on January 2nd. Students, you must inform your parents about the school situation."

Somebody wailed, "What about the play?" and others repeated the question.

"It will have to be performed in January–"

"But it's a Christmas play!"

"Perhaps it can be adapted for Valentine's? Mr. Larkin will work that out with you. Besides, with so many teachers, students, and parents already sick we wouldn't have had a big turnout anyhow."

"To say nothing about cancelling it in honour of poor Holly!" exclaimed Marta standing up and turning to her fellow teachers for support. But students yelled her down with shouts of *the show must go on* and claiming, *Holly wouldn't want it cancelled, she has an understudy to take over her role.* Marta remained on her feet only to be shamed back to her chair when Judith announced:

"We will now have a minute's silence to reflect and pray for Holly. Again, once we're back in the new year the school will have a proper memorial service for her."

This was only a moment's respite before she was bombarded by the teachers asking endless questions despite knowing that she didn't have any further news.

Many of the girls were still sniffing away tears but one child was loudly sobbing. It was Bethany Penner. Of course, she was Holly's best friend.

They were two very different types of girl who proved the 'opposites attract' statement. Beth was quiet where Holly was loud, shy and content to follow Holly's lead. Now Lila was leading the girl out of the room with an arm about her heaving shoulders.

Marta informed Judith that she'd be speaking to Principal Johnson *right away*. Judith kept her *good luck with that* comment to herself, knowing that Pat's husband was more than capable of fending off unwelcome intrusions.

Chapter 5

"Let's go to the staff-room and see what phone messages have come in so far."

"I'll grab coffees and meet you there – how do you take yours?"

"Milky, no sugar," said Judith then added, "Thanks," as an afterthought.

Armed with paper and pens the two women listened to the dozen or so phone-calls. News about Holly hadn't gotten out yet, so the majority of calls were from parents calling in to excuse their children from class due to sickness. The flu bug striking again and again.

Once the messages were all listened to and return calls made where necessary, they decided to compose an email to the parents.

"I want to text it as well as send an email. I don't think we need to utilize the phone tree; it's only supposed to be for emergency use. Text and email should cover everyone," said Judith.

"Yeah, texting is a good idea because many parents skip over emails from the school. We send out far too many. This school follows the directives from both the Public and Catholic school boards, so it seems like we're nagging the parents about such-and-such a social issue every other day. I know because the boards keep coming to me for input on the medical issues."

"The next biggie is money. Parents are called upon to shell out for so much. Personal school supplies like pens, erasers, pencil cases – sure – but when we're asking payment to rent textbooks? and the insurance fee for Phys Ed. has more than doubled in the last couple of years.

And then there's the fundraising: *We want to plant trees, we want to have a year-end dance, we want to buy iPads, we want to sponsor a child in a Third World Country, we want a school trip to the Petting Zoo* ... it's no wonder the parents ignore our messages! So, we need a subject line that will grab them."

"How about *School Closure?*" suggested Lila.

"No, they'll think it's another email about our schedule for the holidays. What about, in all caps: *CLASSES CANCELLED.* That should get their attention, eh? and then we'll let them know the police have discovered Holly Lezinsky's body and are calling it a *suspicious death.* We'll add that we don't know anything else—"

"No, that won't work," interrupted Lila, "because they won't read that far, they'll already be dialling their cellphones. How about if we start off by saying something like *The school remains open until end of day December 23rd but there will be no classes and students do not have to attend.* Then we can word it like *When the police give us more information, we will pass it on immediately. They have discovered student Holly Lezinsky's body and are calling it a suspicious death. Please* – in uppercase again – *DO NOT PHONE THE SCHOOL. There is no one available to take your calls, we don't have answers yet anyway.*"

"That's good. But we'll leave out the bit saying we don't have answers because that makes it sound like we're to blame. They'll all call and leave messages asking: *why don't you have answers?*"

Lila laughed saying, "You're right, that's exactly what they would do! Hey, should we mention the school play? You said it was important."

"God yes, the stupid play."

Lila laughed and said: "How about: *There is no one available to take your calls and the mailbox fills up too quickly. We will give you the new date for the school play in January.*"

"Makes sense to me but they'll all assume the play will be held in January. It might, but we aren't sure. So, change that to *we're rescheduling the school play, date TBA* and we'll just have to hope for the best."

"OK, here's the revised script: subject line: *CLASSES CANCELLED*. Message body:

ITEM #1 The school remains open until end of day December 23rd but there will be no classes and students do not have to attend.

ITEM #2 When the police give us more information we will pass it on immediately. They have discovered student Holly Lezinsky's body and are calling it a suspicious death. Please DO NOT PHONE THE SCHOOL. There is no one available to take your calls and the mailbox fills up too quickly.

ITEM #3 We're rescheduling the school play, date TBA."

"That will do. Now, I'll handle the emails if you'll look after the texting. I've noticed that you're quick at it. I'm a typist trained to use all my fingers, not just my thumbs, even if the phone does provide a QWERTY keyboard."

"Sure, that works for me." Lila was agreeable as ever.

They smiled at each other, and Judith experienced an uncommon feeling of camaraderie, glad that Lila was working with her.

The women settled down to their respective tasks, pausing now and then to take a sip of coffee or to listen to yet another parent – some sounding quite frazzled – call in to say the household was struck down by the flu.

Chapter 6

"Hell of a day and that assembly was a truly horrible experience – very emotional," announced Lila, "So this medical practitioner is prescribing strong drink as a remedy to today – are you up for it?"

She was so surprised by the invitation Judith didn't even think before blurting out:

"I don't drink."

"Ever?" asked Lila with a grin.

"No, I never do."

"Not even at New Year's? or champagne at a wedding? or a frosty cold one on a hot summer's day?" Lila was smiling and not taking Judith's pronouncement seriously.

"No, I never drink alcohol or wine or spirits, cocktails, or beer – does that answer your question?" She regretted letting her annoyance show but Lila persisted.

"Why not?"

"That's none of your business." snapped Judith, reliving memories of coming home from school to find her mother passed out drunk. Mrs. Taylor was always found on the floor by the drinks cabinet where the sherry was stored. She'd gulp it straight from the bottle until she dropped to the floor in a stupor.

Judith could never bring schoolmates home and couldn't go out because someone had to take care of the drunken woman. The spectacle of her mother struggling and collapsing when Judith tried to lift her, slurring maudlin apologies, all accompanied by the stench of alcohol and vomit, combined to make Judith a committed teetotaller.

She wasn't worried that she'd become an alcoholic, she just couldn't bear the thought of becoming her mother.

"Remind me never to invite you to my parent's place, they would be totally offended if you refused a glass of their homemade wine."

"Why would you want to invite me to your parent's home?" asked Judith with a puzzled frown.

"They always like meeting my friends but I can't invite you anyhow because they live in Toronto."

"Well... that was a ridiculous... oh you!" Judith shook her head in exasperation but catching Lila's grin couldn't help but smile back.

"Okay so I know it's none of my business, but that doesn't mean I don't want to know why you don't drink."

"Hmm, but it also means I don't have to tell you."

Lila shrugged off Judith's refusal saying,

"Another time, maybe."

Judith marvelled at the other woman's persistence. Lila's strong personality and frank curiosity were like weapons. Judith would have to be careful with what she said around Lila, at least if she wanted to try to keep her – as she did with everyone else – at arms-length. She put on her coat saying,

"I'll see you tomorrow morning."

Chapter 7

Lila managed to get out successfully, but Judith was waylaid at the front door by a rather large and very determined woman. Judith had no difficulty recognizing Andrea Sealy, mother of a nine-year-old student called Margaret.

"I got in the car the absolute moment I got your text because I knew I couldn't sleep a wink if I didn't come and see you."

"Why?" Judith stayed in the doorway, not inviting the parent to come inside, because she wanted to end this conversation and go home.

"Whatever do you mean, why?"

"If you read the whole text, you'd know that it has already told you everything. Every. Single. Thing. That's all we at the school know at this time. You've wasted a trip because there's nothing more to say."

"Oh, Ms. Taylor it's so obvious that you're not a parent."

Judith couldn't resist saying: "Apparently what?"

"What?! Oh, this is nonsense. You must have more information like was the child assaulted... you know, sexually? or beaten up? how exactly did she die? and where?"

"Mrs. Sealy this isn't a whodunit on the TV. I do not have any of that information because the police haven't shared it with me. They want to speak to Holly's mother first and quite right, too. Our school is grieving and I don't want to speculate.

The police haven't even come to the school although they did say they hope to come by at some point tomorrow. I will be here to meet with them. If they give me more information, and I very much hope that they do, I will send out another round of texts and emails to all of the parents right away.

I do understand your concern, but I hope you will understand that I've had a very long and difficult day and now I want to lock up and go home."

Andrea Sealy looked like she wanted to rehash everything that had been said and then say it all over again but was thwarted by the determined look on Judith's face. She felt it would be unwise to push the other woman too far, after all she didn't want to be 'accidentally left out' of the communication loop.

Forced to live with her dissatisfaction she decided she'd leave now but would definitely have a word with Principal Johnson later on.

"Oh, very well," she said ungraciously, "I suppose I don't have any choice. Of course, I won't sleep a wink, not a wink!" When she saw Judith eyeing her fur coat she hastened to add:

"This isn't real, you know. It's a very good quality faux fur."

Judith bit her lip to hold back her comments. She didn't want to offend Andrea Sealy and she certainly didn't want to prolong the conversation. Though she wondered to herself: "Then what's the point?"

Andrea stood back to watch Judith lock the door and they each speed-walked through the chilly evening to their respective cars. Andrea Sealy stayed in hers until Judith pulled out of the parking lot and then she followed.

"Huh! no doubt she thinks I'm going to sneak back inside to gloat over some juicy tidbits that I refuse to share with her," Judith just shook her head. "What a battle-axe, I'll bet dollars to doughnuts nobody has ever gotten away with calling that one *Andy*".

Chapter 8

Lila was right, that was quite a day! thought Judith. She was tired, emotional, and anxious to get home as quickly as possible. She thought about Lila's offer of going for a drink and wondered why the other woman had made the suggestion. *Does she know something about me? I've always wondered if people do know about my background. I mean, it's not a secret but it's also not something I advertise.*

Judith had an uncomfortable moment imagining Marta and the other teachers laughing behind her back in the staff room. She tried, but failed, to picture Lila being a party to such behaviour and conceded that the invitation was probably just a friendly gesture.

Andrea Sealy had swung her SUV around into the other lane to pass Judith once they were on the road. She would have missed seeing Beth Penner at the lot's entrance hanging around, weighed down by her bulky backpack and looking forlorn. Judith spotted her and when their eyes met Beth gave a half-wave and a hopeful smile.

Judith felt imposed upon. She could stop and offer the girl a lift, but she didn't want to. She felt that the last thing she could deal with right now was non-stop questions from a weepy adolescent.

Work was over – this awful day was finally over – and she yearned to go home and forget about everything and everyone school-related until tomorrow morning. Tomorrow, which was actually supposed to be the start of her holiday now postponed.

Choosing to misunderstand she gave Beth a cheery wave back then turned her head away as she drove off, determined not to look in her rear-view mirror in case the teen tried to flag her down.

A light drizzle began but only enough to need the interval setting of the windshield wipers. Driving along Judith found herself wondering why Beth's backpack was so full since there were no more homework assignments for this semester. *I hope she's got one of those telescoping umbrellas packed inside*, thought Judith.

She had no idea where the girl lived, or how far she'd have to walk. She really had very little to do with the students themselves. The rain was turning to sleet as temperatures dropped even further and Judith needed to concentrate on her driving.

Chapter 9

As soon as she got to the school in the morning Judith moved her laptop and assorted files to the principal's office. She'd just settled in with the coffee she'd picked up in the lunch-room – the school's resources didn't run to a full-service cafeteria – when Marta confronted her with the snide remark:

"Hasn't taken you long to get your bum in the big chair."

Judith tilted her head at the *bum* comment but made no reply. In the silence Marta blurted out the reason for her visit:

"I want to meet with the police when they come."

"That will be up to the police, of course. I can't – and won't – tell them what to do, and neither would Principal Johnson."

"Hmph, well I don't know about that but anyhow, when are they coming?"

"No one has told me."

Marta thought about this a moment then turned to go saying:

"You better let me know when they get here."

Again, Judith said nothing, and the older woman flounced out of the room almost colliding with the young woman who had arrived and was lifting her hand to knock.

"Annalise! what are you doing here?" Marta demanded to know.

"I wanted to see Judith if she's not too busy..." Annalise's voice, always low-pitched, trailed off in uncertainty.

"Please come in, Annalise. Sit down and tell me what it is you wanted to see me about." Seeing that Marta was still hovering in the doorway she added: "Marta is leaving now."

Judith had a chance to study Annalise while the girl – it was hard to think of her as a woman – removed her outdoor things and got settled in a chair. She was very fair, very feminine, slender, and youthful. She could pass for sixteen, but Judith knew she was eight years older than that.

Annalise Sutherland came from enormous wealth and Judith was certain that a chauffeur driving a luxury car was waiting at the front door.

Annalise and Noel Larkin were engaged to be married in the coming year, and it was on his behalf that she said she was visiting:

"Noel is so upset by what happened to that girl, Holly. He knew her, you see, because of the school play. She had the leading role and so they were thrown together a lot and he told me he quite liked her." Annalise sounded surprised. "Naturally he's devastated by her death. Or should I say her murder?" she asked in a questioning tone.

Judith had no idea what kind of response was expected of her, so she made a non-committal *mmh-mmh* sound and that was all the encouragement Annalise needed:

"He's such a sensitive man. I'm the first to admit that Noel will turn his back on any unpleasantness and that's okay because I'm not confrontational either. We're both gentle souls – that's what he says – and our hearts are easily bruised."

Judith was growing more and more confused by the conversation: she couldn't see any point to it.

"Do you think there's something I can do to help you? or Noel? or both of you together?" she offered.

"Yes, actually. We would so, so appreciate it if you could see that both of our names are kept out of the papers. Daddy would be awfully upset. Also, Noel tells me that this Holly is a bit of a fantasist. Well, that's how he puts it but to me it sounds like she's a little liar.

I met her you know. A few times I've dropped in on rehearsals – to give Noel my support, you know – and Holly seemed to take the playacting to heart. She was very dramatic and, frankly, overly familiar with him, the little minx. She had a huge crush on Noel. I wouldn't like anyone, like the police, to get the wrong impression."

"In other words, if anyone connects Noel to Holly, I'm to put a stop to any talk of that kind."

"Exactly. You understand me completely," the young woman gave a sweet smile.

"Yes, Annalise, I do understand you." Annalise didn't notice Judith's dry tone as she continued:

"This is such a weight off my mind, and it will be for Noel too. He'll be so relieved, and so will his mother. You see, Holly had even started phoning him at home!

His mother told me she had the nerve to ask to leave a message for him to call her back. Now, you and I wouldn't think that's a big deal, but Audrey Larkin was beside herself! She complained that it was awful behaviour and so rude to expect her to write out a message. You do know Holly Lezinsky is – was – one of the girls they sponsor, right? Anyhow, because she considered it such an imposition Noel had to speak to Holly and tell her not to phone again. After that Mrs. Larkin said she started to get lots of hang-ups whenever she answered a call. Of course she put two and two together. It was all very unpleasant. Teenagers do have such a difficult time with all their emotions running rampant and wanting, so desperately, to be grown up."

"If they only knew, eh?" replied Judith.

"Too true! Anyhow, I won't keep you a minute more. Only this morning I was telling Noel that it's wonderful the way you've stepped into Principal Johnson's shoes at this difficult time."

Annalise put her fur coat back on, *This is definitely a real one*, thought Judith, although the waiting car would be toasty warm. They said their goodbyes and then Annalise was gone leaving nothing but her expensive perfume lingering in the air.

Noel and Holly had been staying after school quite a bit recently while they finished rehearsing their play. Under those circumstances Judith had never given their behaviour a second thought. Now that Annalise had drawn attention to the relationship, and commented about the police, it framed everything in a different context and Judith found herself wondering.

Chapter 10

Marta had been hanging around outside the closed door to the principal's office waiting for Annalise to leave. When Judith realized this, she couldn't help but wonder how much poking and prying Marta had indulged in at the secretary's desk.

It was satisfying for her to know that the snoopy teacher could find nothing since Samira kept her drawers locked, with no key lying about.

As soon as the young woman left Marta immediately came into the office, not even bothering to knock.

"Well, what did she want?" she asked, not bothering to mask her impatience.

"Marta, what do you want?" said Judith, feeling exasperated.

"I want to know when the police are coming because I need to speak to them, they should know that--" sensing someone behind her she turned around to see a man and woman standing outside the door.

"Are you the police?" Marta demanded to know.

"Are you in charge here Mrs.--" replied the man before Marta interrupted with a correction:

"Ms. Smith, Ms. Marta Smith, and I'm the Senior Teacher here at Edgemont School for Girls."

"Well, I hope you can spare some time for us later but right now we need to meet with the school's Acting Head a.." he glanced at a notebook in his hand before continuing, "Ms. Taylor."

"I'm Judith Taylor," announced Judith stepping forward to greet the officers who manoeuvred Marta out of the doorway and into the hall while moving forward to shake hands.

"I'm George Grant, Senior Investigating Officer, and this is my partner, Suzanne Mirteau."

"He's tall but aren't all police?" thought Judith as they exchanged greetings and business cards. She continued commenting to herself, "She's tall as well. They make me feel quite short but I'm not, I'm a bit taller than average height."

The three of them then moved into the sitting area of the room. Judith's offer of coffee was declined and when Suzanne brought out her notebook Judith produced her own asking if she could get a quick re-cap of the facts since many people were asking questions.

George Grant looked to be about forty years old. Judging by the laugh lines around his mouth and eyes he had a sense of humour, and his frank gaze spoke to an open, friendly demeanour. He answered saying:

"I expected as much and have thought about how much we can share with you."

"Since you're only a member of the public," interjected Suzanne. She was about a dozen years younger than him and a good-looking woman. George gave her a brief look then resumed saying,

"Here are the basic facts: The body of Holly Lezinsky was found by a woman named Kellogg walking her dogs in the wooded area that borders the school property but at the far side of it. The trails there are popular with joggers and dog-walkers. She told us she'd taken her animals to the same area early in the morning and there definitely was no sign of young Holly then. Based on this, the second walk of the day, we concluded the actual discovery must have happened between 11:00 – roughly – when Mrs. Kellogg arrived until 11:10 when she phoned the Emergency Services."

"Holly was killed in School Woods?"

"I didn't realize the area had a name."

"Well, it's what we've always called them. The girls are often in the woods: taking pathways home, playing at 'forest bathing', Natural Science classes... It's horrible to think of Holly dying there. And so close by to us, too. I hope she wasn't lying there dying and we never knew!"

"We don't think that's the murder scene, actually," said George. Suzanne made an annoyed sound at his revelation at the same time Judith gasped:

"Murdered? For sure? We thought it might have been some sort of accident or... well, suicide."

"Was Holly-- you did know her, right?"

"Yes, yes I did."

"Would you consider her at risk of committing suicide?"

"Not at all but I guess it just seems well... a teenage thing and somehow better than being murdered... oh, that doesn't make sense."

Suzanne's snort indicated she agreed but George's voice was soothing:

"It does make sense. Murder belongs in the pages of a book or on the big screen, right? We do understand what a shock it is for the average person."

"Members of the public," put in Suzanne again before turning to George and saying: "I'm not sure you should be telling her all this, Grant."

Judith found Suzanne Mirteau abrasive but even so thought it odd that she'd call her superior by his surname.

Judith had noticed that with him being white-blond and her having wavy black hair the two of them made a striking, good-looking pair, but it was obvious they weren't a couple. Despite the fact that Suzanne's gaze kept turning towards him, George Grant was all business.

Although Judith did notice him looking at the bare fingers of her left hand. When she looked up she saw that Suzanne noticed this as well and her face wore a sour expression.

"Ms. Taylor I'm giving you the same facts I discussed yesterday with Holly's family. Actually, it's just her mother, Dana, and her boyfriend." He paused and Suzanne supplied the name:

"Billy MacNeill."

"Yes, thank you. I know that once the family has been told word starts to get around and sometimes things are exaggerated or misunderstood because, understandably, it's such a very difficult time for a parent. It's hard for them to absorb everything."

"How did she die?"

"We can't be certain until after the autopsy, but she had received a severe blow to the back of her head that is likely to be the cause of death."

"Couldn't she have fallen and hit her head against something?"

"We're not here to speculate with you, Ms. Taylor," snapped Suzanne. Judith was puzzled at the woman's antagonism and George ignored the comment replying:

"We won't know anything definite until we hear back from the Medical Examiner. So yes, it could have been an accidental fall or even a push with fatal consequences but moving the body was a deliberate act to conceal evidence and that's a crime.

In our opinion, murder is most likely the answer."

"Yes, I see. Thank you for being forthright."

George stood to go, and Judith was taken aback by the warm smile he gave her. Glancing over at Suzanne she saw from the angry expression on the woman's face that she hadn't missed that exchange either. Judith didn't understand all the tension happening underneath the surface remarks and actions.

"That's all I can tell you right now. When people ask questions you can let them know that the police are treating the death as suspicious but that the actual cause hasn't been determined yet. We'll have more information by tomorrow and I can give you an update then."

"I appreciate you explaining this to me and thank you Inspector Grant. I will be here at the school all day tomorrow, but we might not have any students. If there are no classes the front door will be locked and you'll have to phone first so I can let you in."

"Okay, I've got the school's phone number."

"No, um I better give you my cellphone number. The school's phone is switched over to the staff-room and I won't hear it. For example, I'm sure there have been plenty of calls already today and we didn't hear any ringing from here."

"I'm certain you've got a busy day ahead of you, so we'll leave you to it. I'll take note of your number and if you can point us in the right direction, we'll go to the staff-room now to see Ms. Smith. I hope she won't be too annoyed at the delay."

Judith returned his smile saying: "As long as you call it the Teachers' Lounge instead of the staff-room, you'll be fine."

He copied down her phone number then followed Suzanne. He stopped in the doorway and turned back to Judith saying:

"Just 'Grant' is fine, that's what everyone calls me, you don't need to give me a title, and I don't use my first name."

Judith wondered why he was telling her this and, once again, was puzzled by Suzanne's glare.

Chapter 11

Lila came into the office the moment the police left it. She was full of questions about what they were like, what had been said, and what would happen next. Judith started from when they'd met Marta and recounted the whole interview.

"The body was moved? Poor Holly. So that happened by mid-morning. When did she die, by the way? She was gone a week or more."

"They didn't say how long she'd been dead for, and I didn't ask. Actually, I didn't ask any questions, that female officer was so mean and angry and resented every scrap of information Grant gave."

"Grant?"

"Mmm, Senior Investigating Officer George Grant who said he only goes by 'Grant' so that's what I'm to call him."

"Oh, I thought you were on first-name terms already," said Lila was a grin.

"Certainly not! He calls me Ms. Taylor." Judith ignored Lila's chuckle and continued:

"I figured he'd tell me more if I didn't ask questions so although it's not much we now know that Holly was likely murdered, not sure when, and her body was moved to School Woods this morning where it was found by a Mrs. Kellogg and her dogs."

"She was in our woods? Had she been raped? Was she naked? Strangled or stabbed or..."

"Nothing was said about any of that. What a vivid imagination you have! They did say that there was evidence of a 'severe blow' to her head and that's all that was mentioned."

"Aha, the infamous blunt instrument."

"Lila it's no laughing matter," cried Judith. Right away Lila drew closer and reached for Judith's hand saying,

"I'm so sorry. Most of us in the medical profession use humour to get us over the bad bits. But I'm sure it sounds ghoulish and unfeeling to non-medicos, and I truly do apologise."

Judith pulled her hand out of reach and told Lila she understood.

"So, an autopsy. Well, I guess the truth will come out then so I will tell you now what Holly told me in confidence the last time I saw her, which was the day she disappeared: she was pregnant."

"But she would just be turning fourteen this week!" exclaimed Judith.

"It might not be true, but she said she was and I have no reason to doubt her. She didn't come right out and announce it to me but when I noticed she was very pale and drawn looking – I wondered about anaemia – she said she figured it was her condition, being pregnant and all, and that she felt fine."

"That is shocking. It means she was thirteen when..."

"I barely knew her and I might have misjudged based on appearances but I wasn't floored by the revelation. I mean, thirteen is shockingly young but Holly doesn't, I mean didn't, seem like a thirteen-year-old girl."

"I know what you mean. Any mother, of girls or boys, would be worried about Holly being a bad influence but they'd still find themselves liking the girl despite it all. I wonder who the father is?"

"Isn't that the $20,000 question!"

Chapter 12

The trailer park was a surprise. Judith couldn't say what she'd expected but it wasn't this. There was nothing transient-looking about the place. No rusting-out vehicles or abandoned broken toys. The trailers were trim, and the yards were tidy. Most had hanging baskets for flowers, and one even had a quaint white picket fence. Strings of Christmas lights and inflatable lawn ornaments indicated it would be festive at night.

The trailer where Holly lived with her mother wasn't as nicely kept as those around it. The windows could do with a cleaning and the metal steps leading to the door were flaking with rust. However, inside the air was fresh and warm with the appetizing smell of home baking.

When Dana Lezinsky saw Judith sniff she turned and pointed to a wire-rack piled high with iced cookies.

"I always make them for her birthday, and I went ahead and made them as usual before I remembered. These pineapple cookies were her favourite." She opened the cupboard above the counter and pulled out a plate. "I've made coffee," she announced, "Go ahead and take a seat and I'll bring everything over."

There was a small table with attached bench seating, similar to a booth in a cafe. Everything in the trailer had a compact, space-saving design. Judith could imagine herself living quite cozily and comfortably in such a home.

Judith studied Dana while the woman filled up the plate with cookies and moved back and forth from fridge to counter to table with cups, a carafe of coffee, milk jug, sugar bowl, and spoons. Laying out the dishes with almost ritual precision.

She looked to be in her late 20s or early 30s which meant she had been a teenager when she had Holly. Judith knew from the records she kept for the school that Dana was a hairdresser and her income qualified Holly for the subsidy programme.

There was no money coming from the girl's father – he wasn't even given a name – and no mention of a boyfriend in the file.

Dana looked devastated by Holly's death and Judith realized the trauma actually had begun a week earlier when the girl went missing.

Dana looked like she hadn't slept during that whole week. Her hair was dirty enough to stand on end where she'd raked her fingers through it, the trails clearly showing. Her face was gray and sagging with a drooping mouth and swollen red-rimmed eyes. She must have been given tranquilizers because she was slow-moving and had trouble focusing.

The woman oozed sadness and despair. Judith felt terribly sorry for her but didn't know how to express her feelings. She thought it best to sit in shared silence until Dana was ready to speak. She ate a cookie murmuring 'mmm' sounds.

"I asked to see you because you were always nice to me. You spoke straight when we met about my finances, and you didn't talk down. Not like most of the mothers at that school do. That's why I don't, um... didn't, like going to those get-togethers and the parent-teacher meetings? they were always an ordeal." Dana's voice held little inflection, but she didn't mumble, and her meaning was clear.

"I'm not a parent, do you think that makes a difference? maybe makes it seem easier to talk to me?" asked Judith.

"I don't know... maybe. The police were here again this morning. They were here twice yesterday, to break the news of find... finding Holly and then they had to come back again later because I was too upset to talk first time.

Anyhow, they were good. A man cop and a woman and she didn't say much but he was nice. But this morning they came back and after what they told me well, I felt utterly destroyed. They said my baby was going to have a baby: Holly was pregnant!"

"Oh no."

"Yes, and that means some bastard got her pregnant when she was only thirteen years old! That's illegal, that is. It's interfering with a child, child endangerment, stuff like that. I mean, I was young when I had her, but I sure wasn't that young, and her Daddy was the same age or thereabouts."

"Is he around, her Dad? can he give you some support while you're going through this?"

"Naw, I'm not even sure who fathered her. I meant that there were a few boys, several of them, and we were all at school together, so we were all the same age."

"Holly was a very popular girl—"

"Oh, I know she had boyfriends, she was a pretty girl who wasn't backward about coming forward – have you heard that expression? it might have been written for her.

So, I know the boys were hanging around, but I told her and told her to be careful and she always said she didn't waste her time on 'kids', that's how she put it, called the boys who came by 'kids' and said they had no money, no car, and she wasn't interested in them.

They'd be out sitting on those picnic tables in that bit of a park across from us here and I could see them from the window.

I'd see kids smoking – probably drinking too – making some noise but not causing trouble. The manager of this place is pretty strict in dealing with problem people but he's a good guy and knows kids have to let off a bit of steam.

So, things were always under control and it seemed like Holly treated everyone, girls and guys, the same. They were all friends hanging out."

Dana became more animated as she spoke. Judith could see in her face that she was recalling images and conversations, and these were good memories. All of a sudden her mood changed and with it her body language too. Shoulders drooped and her head sunk down towards her chest. The next words were spoken in a low voice and Judith had to strain to hear.

"That's when I wondered what if Billy had done something to her? Or not him but friends of his? he was always teasing Holly and depending on how she was feeling she flirted back, or she shut him up quick. That's all I ever saw between them, the two of them talking shit, you know? but what if I missed something? what if he saw her away from here?"

"Well, he sometimes picked her up from school in his truck," said Judith.

"I knew about that, yeah, that was OK."

"And then there was the fight they had two or three weeks ago."

"A fight?!"

"Not a fight... more like a boyfr–uh brother-sister type of quarrel," Judith was quick to amend her poor choice of words.

"What happened?"

"I don't know what it was about or anything, I could hear their voices but not the actual words, it was the yelling that got my attention and when I looked out I saw Billy grabbing Holly by the arm and flinging her in the truck."

"He took her against her will?" cried Dana.

"No, because he slammed the door but her seat-belt or something must have caught because the door sprang back open. He didn't notice, he was already marching round to his door, but she then moved whatever was blocking and pulled the door closed herself.

She would have gotten out and run back to the school if she'd thought she was in danger. So no, it was just a very heated argument between the two of them. Otherwise, I would have done something."

In truth Judith doubted she would actually have done anything. At the time, listening to the screeching and swearing she'd thought 'trailer trash' to herself and dismissed the incident.

"Well, I'm not so sure. This is why I called you to come talk to me – and that was before I even knew about this fight they had. But anyhow after the cops told me about her being pregnant and asking who she was seeing and me telling them there was nobody in particular I got to thinking. If she thought the local boys were kids was that because there was a man she was comparing them to? A man who had some spending cash and could drive her places.

I got thinking that maybe Billy MacNeill was that man and, well... this is the hard part, you see I lied to the cops when they were checking up on us, on where we were and that. So, I was hoping I could tell you and you could tell them?

I know what I did was wrong but I never in a million years suspected Billy of having anything to do with Holly disappearing and then being killed so I figured it was okay to go along with his story. I still don't think he hurt her but now that I've found out she was pregnant I don't think I can cover for him anymore and I don't want to.

If he got my baby pregnant.... I don't even want to see his face even if he wasn't the one who hurt her. I'm done with him."

Dana sat back, nodding to herself and repeating that last statement. Confessing had done her good, she sat straighter and topped up both of their coffee cups. She even ate a cookie.

"I can tell that to the police if you like, but they won't be satisfied taking my word for it. They'll still want to talk to you."

"I know, but now that I've admitted it to someone it will be easier to admit it to them. And I knew you wouldn't tell me I was a bad mother for lying. I honestly wouldn't have lied if I'd thought for one minute that he had anything to do with Holly's death. I'm sure he didn't, and really? I don't even think he's the one who got her pregnant. I don't see how they'd have managed it."

Judith accepted her statement having had a similar experience when she was a girl. Her mother, Maureen, only had the one boyfriend, and he never showed any interest in Judith. That was the only thing about him that she liked.

Her mother thought they should feel thankful and be grateful that he took care of them but not Judith. She figured he got what he wanted and nobody owed anybody anything.

She was six when her father died. He and her mother had been very happy and very much in love, and Judith had wonderful, though hazy, memories of the three of them together. When the news came about the car crash, they were both devastated. A multiple-car smash-up but only one fatality.

Her mother never recovered from the shock with only alcohol numbing the pain of her loss. Judith had nothing to help her through her grief.

Maureen kept on with her job as secretary to the man she inevitably welcomed into her bed. Judith decided it was payback for all the times he covered up for her hungover mornings. No doubt there were afternoon problems as well after a liquid lunch. He also helped out financially although the house was paid for by an insurance payout of the mortgage.

Jack was married, of course, and that suited Maureen who didn't seem to want anything more from life.

He did notice Judith and sometimes paid her compliments, but she never felt threatened. When he came by, which occurred less and less as the years progressed, often as not he and her mother would sit in front of the TV. She'd make a fuss about fixing him a drink and finding him a snack. Sometimes they'd go into Maureen's bedroom, but they didn't stay long.

Judith grew to understand that what happened then was the sex she learned about in Health class. She would listen carefully but only ever heard murmuring voices and then a sharp yelp from Jack. Immediately afterwards her mother would hurry out of the bedroom and into the bathroom. Judith was not intrigued by any of it.

When Jack retired Maureen was out of a job. She sold the house, so she and Judith had something to live on which they did as cheaply as possible. Judith was an orphan by her senior year of high school when Maureen's damaged liver finally gave out.

Judith's grades got her into a university accounting programme and her status of no family support meant a full scholarship. She mourned the mother of her six-year-old self – she had always missed her desperately – but she had long ago stopped loving the woman Maureen had grown into.

These thoughts flitted through her mind as she finished her coffee and prepared to leave. Admitting to her lie had given Dana some sort of catharsis and after a huge yawn the woman looked like she could finally sleep. Judith wished her well and left.

Chapter 13

When Judith returned to the school Marta was waiting for her, sitting in Principal Johnson's chair. She didn't get up and Judith wouldn't give her satisfaction by sitting in the visitor's chair. Before she could say a word Marta complained that the phone had been ringing non-stop.

"That's why we switched it through to the staff room, so that the machine could take messages."

"Well in my opinion it's unprofessional for a school phone to be answered that way. Also, the Teachers' Lounge is for the teachers to refresh and relax in, not be pestered by the constant ringing of the phone."

"Do you have anything to report?"

"As a matter of fact, the police came back here because they had news. They were surprised that you weren't around, in fact the 'handsome detective' looked disappointed."

"Hmm, what did they have to say?"

"I don't know, do I?" retorted the teacher in a savage tone. "That woman detective just cut me off mid-sentence saying Grant preferred 'communicating' with one person only which means you since you're the liaison between the police and this school. That's an utter joke because I should be the school's second-in-command, not you!"

"What time did they stop by?"

"I'm not your secretary, you know."

Judith wanted to shake the older woman but instead she rudely replied:

"Well then get out of the office and go do your own job. I want to talk to the police, and I'd like privacy to do so."

Marta sputtered in rage, but Lila arrived before she could spit out whatever she wanted to say.

"Lila, grand! Marta's leaving so please close the door after her I need to have a confidential talk with you about your patient."

"Certainly," Lila replied crisply, holding the doorknob and gesturing Marta out of the room. The teacher left in a temper.

"Phew, you've made an enemy there," said Lila, sitting down while Judith took the recently vacated chair behind the desk.

"Oh, never mind her, that's an old grudge. Anyhow, I wanted to talk to you about my visit with Dana Lezinsky. She had a few interesting items to report. Oh, but you know what? she'd baked cookies for Holly's birthday tomorrow before she remembered. Isn't that awful?"

"It sure is. Poor, poor woman. I can't imagine what she's going through. I've never lost anyone close to me. I mean, there were a couple of elderly aunties, but I'd never met them so the only thing their passing meant to me was getting a pendant with an opal. They lived in Australia you see, which is why we never met, and of course I didn't go to their funerals.

Anyhow, I'm babbling, I get this way. What were you going to tell me about Holly?"

"The autopsy did reveal the pregnancy, so the police know and have told Holly's mother. She was shocked by the news and she's right; you know, Holly would only have been thirteen at the time so it was a criminal act unless the baby's father is also thirteen or fourteen. Is that likely?"

"It's possible but not too likely. Does Mrs. Lezinsky have any ideas about who might be the father?"

"Well, there's a mystery there. First off, Dana had no illusions about her girl. She knew Holly was outgoing and outspoken, but she also knew that Holly wasn't interested in any of the boys who hung around her. Holly said they were 'just kids'. That's led Dana to believe Holly was involved with some man and, well, the first man who comes to mind is Dana's own boyfriend Billy MacNeill."

"Oh, eewww. She must feel awful about that."

"More like angry, even though she says she doesn't think he was the one. However, she did lie for him and that's why she called me to come over. She wants me to tell the police that she faked an alibi for him but, now that she's discovered about the pregnancy she's recanting."

"If he asked her to lie, he must have something to hide."

"But that something might not have anything to do with what happened to Holly. Unless the police pick him up first, he's going to get quite a reception when he comes home! For starters he'll find out that it's not his home anymore."

"Serves him right!"

"Agreed, but actually Dana doesn't think Billy is the father. It might seem like Holly went her own way, but Dana kept a pretty close watch on her. She knew Billy sometimes picked the girl up from school and knew what time they'd be home. I don't think he had much opportunity."

"Yeah, but she works, right? There were times when she couldn't be there herself."

"True, but Holly usually stayed late at school because of rehearsals for the play and then she and Beth Penner would walk home together. I don't think Holly had a lot of spare time between leaving school and her mother getting home from work."

"Perhaps not but somebody got that girl pregnant, and this Billy seems like a strong possibility. It only takes one time."

"What a mess this is. As if poor Dana Lezinsky doesn't have enough pain right now."

"True, and she could use some support because she's got to bury her daughter and plan a funeral and all that stuff. It's a lousy time for her boyfriend's true colours to show. I should visit her in my role as School Nurse and see if I can help her out."

"She might have taken him back by then, but it sounds like a good idea. And it's nice of you. Better you than me!"

"I can tell you're not a hugger!"

"You've got that right! Anyhow according to Marta the phone has been ringing off the hook so I wonder if we should call a parents' meeting to give an update? Something informal, basically an opportunity for us to pass on the little that we do know and then to let them have their say. What do you think?"

"Good idea, but it will have to be soon. It's already the 20th and people have plans at this time of year."

"Oh, I don't care if anyone shows up – in fact I'd like it better if they didn't! but I want to make the offer."

Lila laughed at that. "When I came to the office, I heard you telling Marta Smith that you had to call the police so I will leave you to it. Let me know what they say, okay? and then we can send out another round of messages to the parents inviting them to join us for a chat."

"Sounds good to me, and please close the door after you."

Chapter 14

Judith was well-organized, as always, and located Grant's business card right away. Once she got him on the line she started to explain about meeting with Dana Lezinsky and her revelations, but Grant interrupted to say he'd come right over to get a statement from her in person. He arrived quickly but unfortunately had Suzanne Mirteau in tow.

"Good afternoon, Ms. Taylor."

"Good afternoon, um, Grant," Judith replied. Suzanne stood beside her boss smirking. "Please sit down, both of you. We're all busy so I'll get straight to the point. Holly's mother, Dana Lezinsky, told me about–"

"Sorry to interrupt but can we start at the beginning? How did you come to be speaking with Ms. Lezinsky?" asked Grant.

"Oh, I see. Yes, well she called me. I know her, of course, as I know all the parents of our students although some only by the names on their cheques. Anyhow, Dana called and asked if I could go see her. She was teary and sounded needy and frankly I wasn't keen to go because I'm not good at dealing with that sort of thing, but I knew Principal Johnson wouldn't have hesitated for a moment, so I went.

I'd never been to their home before, she told me you were there earlier, so I don't need to say anything about that."

"No, but how did you find Ms. Lezinsky?" At Judith's puzzled look Grant added, "In her person, how did she seem? I don't want to ask leading questions," he explained.

"I guess she was normal for the circumstances, I mean I didn't think about it. She looked terrible, but you saw her yourself. I'm not very good at describing people and I never wonder about how they're feeling or what they're thinking. Why would I?" Judith wasn't happy to hear that her voice sounded shaky.

She couldn't understand why she found Grant's questions disturbing. He seemed to sense this and told her to continue relating the conversation. Back on safe ground Judith regained her composure.

"Dana told me your autopsy revealed that Holly was pregnant. Dana has no idea who the father might be. Holly hung out with the boys in the trailer park, but she didn't show any interest in anyone particular, and Dana kept a watchful eye on her."

"Huh, not watchful enough!" interjected Suzanne.

Judith studied the woman's face for a moment trying to understand why she was so contemptuous. Suzanne herself was startlingly handsome with an athletic figure. She had a good job with the police and was now a detective. Judith thought Suzanne should be a much happier person than she appeared to be.

"Based on things she said, Dana is convinced that Holly was involved with some man. She spoke from intuition, not fact, because she didn't have any details," she added seeing the Grant was about to ask for more information.

"She also told me that she lied to you about Billy MacNeill and now wishes to recant her statement that gave him an alibi."

"Does she now!" exclaimed Grant, and Suzanne said:

"That's obstruction and it's a crime."

"She's a grieving mother, I doubt if you're going to convict or even charge her!" retorted Judith. She had little patience for Suzanne's negativity.

"Dana is quite definite that she doesn't think Billy MacNeill is responsible for Holly's pregnancy. However, now that her girl has been killed she couldn't care less about protecting him from whatever nonsense he's been up to."

"Hmm. Overall it's likely Ms. Lezinsky's judgement of her boyfriend is sound although plenty of women – and men – are often unpleasantly surprised at some of the things they learn about their mates.

Nevertheless we need to find Billy MacNeill and investigate whatever it is he was doing when Holly disappeared and again when she died."

"Do you know when that was?"

"The autopsy report suggests she was killed soon after she vanished. Again, we're waiting for the final results."

"Should we be discussing this with a civilian?" complained Suzanne. Grant ignored her comment and continued saying:

"After all, there's no evidence of any issues between Billy and Holly."

"Except for that fight they had at school a couple of days before she went missing," put in Judith.

"What fight?"

"Well, it was more of an argument, but he did yank her back when she walked away from him–" Suzanne interrupted her exclaiming:

"Why weren't the police informed about this incident?"

"I guess no one else saw what happened?" said Judith.

"But you did!"

"Oh, yes. I heard loud voices and looked out the window. From my office I can see the front driveway where he'd pulled up to get Holly from school. That happened quite often and her mother approved it. Anyhow, Holly got into the truck but a moment later she jumped back out again and started walking away. Billy MacNeill went after her and grabbing her arm he pulled her back to the truck and pushed her inside."

"That's kidnapping! Assault and battery at the very least!"

"No – and I already told all this to Dana Lezinsky – Holly's door didn't close properly so she opened it, moved whatever was in the way, and then closed it herself. Whatever it was that Billy said she accepted. If she'd wanted to get out the truck she could easily have done so. She could have run back into the school if she'd had any concerns, but she didn't."

"You should have mentioned this sooner," said Suzanne angrily.

"Why would I?"

"It's evidence."

"Evidence of what? I'm not privy to what was said, and I could have misinterpreted what I saw. I'm not a cop, it's not my job to make a report."

"It was your duty to tell us about Billy MacNeill."

"First off, I didn't even know you people existed so I could hardly tell you. Secondly, I didn't even remember this until today, and thirdly Holly's mother had alibied him. He was in the clear. The incident went right out of my mind."

"I can see how this all came about," said Grant in an effort to smooth things over but neither woman was admitting fault. To mollify his partner, he added:

"But it's disappointing to only be hearing about this incident now. We should have been informed about it sooner."

"Really? How about you should be doing your own job and I'll stick to mine. That's all I have to *report* to you." Judith stood up, flushed and angry, and the officers were forced to go.

Chapter 15

After the police left Judith remained on her feet. She started pacing back and forth, counting each step in a whisper:

"One, two, three, four, five, six, seven. One, two, three, four, five, six, seven."

Judith didn't realize Lila had come into the room until she said: "Oh! Is that an OCD thing? I know a bit about that."

"No, well at least not in my case. I don't have OCD. I mean I don't have to count but when I do it soothes me, calms me down."

"Why do you need calming down after a visit from the police? What happened?"

"He's so infuriating! and that woman hates me."

"No doubt she hates the fact that her Inspector Grant likes you. And if only he could see you now with your high colour and flashing eyes... Oops! I should probably have kept that thought to myself. But he is interested in you."

"No, he isn't. He was nicer than her, but as a matter of fact he was smarmy because he basically said the same thing she did, which was to complain about me not telling them about something I'd seen between Holly and that Billy MacNeill."

"Okay give me a second to untangle that sentence. Right, they're accusing you of withholding evidence."

"It's not evidence it's hearsay. Well, see I heard them yelling and oh forget about it. It wasn't the kidnapping Suzanne Mirteau tried to make it out to be. It was actually a nothing incident and I forgot all about it when I heard Dana had cleared Billy. Anyways, I did report this afternoon's conversation with Dana, and I guess the police will head over to her place now to confirm what she told me. I hope they treat her more kindly than they did me!"

"From my position on the sidelines I have to tell you I find all this fascinating. This is real drama like you see on TV. Although I'm crushed about a young girl being killed – have they confirmed yet if it's murder or suicide?"

"Not yet."

"Hmm, well that part is terribly sad – I did like Holly – but I have to confess the rest is pretty exciting stuff. Guess I lead an awfully boring life!"

"Oh, if only Pat hadn't gotten the flu, I wouldn't have had to deal with any of this. I'd be on the sidelines too. No, I wouldn't I'd be at home with my feet up enjoying my annual vacation."

"That's right! You were supposed to be off this week. But then you'd have missed all of this."

"I would be very pleased to give 'all of this' as you put it, a miss. Anyhow, since you're here you can give me some advice: do I go to the staff room to tell Marta and the rest of the coven about Holly's condition?"

"Oooh! Did I hear you call the teachers witches?"

"Oh God, I never meant to say that out loud. It's your fault, for some reason I can metaphorically-speaking let my hair down with you."

"I'll take that as a compliment! and yes, you should tell the Wicked Witch of the West about the pregnancy because it's going to get out and this way, with luck, you'll hear what the rumours are and then you can squash any innuendo."

"Good idea. Are you coming with me?"

"I wouldn't miss it!"

Chapter 16

Judith and Lila headed to the staff-room to meet with the teachers who gathered there at the end of the working day to chat and unwind. Judith turned to Lila and asked:

"I know the Good Witch of the North was called Glinda but what was the name of the Wicked Witch of the West?"

"Marta," was Lila's quick comeback, then she snorted a laugh. That made both women dissolve into giggles.

"You're a snorter!" exclaimed Judith.

"Ha! I've been known to honk!"

They were still smiling when they entered the staff-room. The room was L-shaped with the doorway blocked from the main part by the cloakroom and row of lockers. What they heard took the smiles off their faces.

"Omigod this is awful! Play it again."

"Yes, replay that message and turn it up too."

Coming round the corner Judith and Lila looked at the circle of people who turned shocked faces towards them.

"Listen!" cried Jennifer, the young Maths teacher. She pointed to the answering machine and they all fell silent to hear the message.

"M-M-Miss Taylor, please, I need you to help me I don't know what to do and I'm so scared," wailed a young voice. "It's Beth, Beth Penner and I need to talk! I've got Holly's diary and I don't know what to do... do... do... about it. It's... it's awful." She broke into sobs and the rest of the message was her hiccoughing voice stumbling over the words 'please help me' and 'I'm frightened'.

Everyone started speaking at the same time with questions like "what does she want?", and "what could be in Holly's diary?" and "why would Beth call Judith Taylor of all people?"

Lila and Judith moved closer to the machine and Lila pressed the Replay button. They waited in tense silence for the message to play again.

Listening to that tearful voice made Judith feel hot with embarrassment then goose-bumpy cold and nauseous but she closed her lips tight and inhaled through her nose to slow her breathing. She needed to calm down and think but her finger hovered over the Delete button and she really wanted to press down hard.

Chapter 17

"The police will want to know about this!" declared Marta.

Her voice seems to break the spell Judith has been under. She desperately wants to ignore the message but too many people have heard it and she is forced to act.

"Yes, you're right, for sure I must contact them right away. This diary could provide vital evidence, it might tell us who..."

"That's right," picked up Lila. "We actually came to the staff-room to share the news Judith had from Dana Lezinsky, Holly's mother. The police told her that Holly was pregnant when she died."

Other than a collective gasp of "Pregnant!" no one spoke until Marta said to Judith:

"But that doesn't explain why it's you Beth wants to talk to."

"I have no idea either. I mean, of course I know Beth, but she's never wanted to confide in me before."

"I can believe that," an unidentified voice muttered. Judith suspected it was Xiao, he was always very critical of everyone, and he was Marta's puppet.

"That doesn't matter, Judith," said Noel eagerly, "What's important is that you get over to Beth's place right away. I'll drive you. I know where she lives because I took her and Holly home after a late rehearsal once. We should go now; we shouldn't waste any time."

"No, we should leave it to the police. They've made it crystal clear they don't want civilians butting in."

"But Beth called YOU, not the police. What if she won't talk to them?" said one person.

"Right! What if it's the police she's afraid of?" exclaimed another and everyone joined in to agree.

"When did this phone message come in?" asked Judith.

"It must be fifteen or twenty minutes ago now. We've listened to it a couple of times and as new people came in, as you did, we listened again."

"Well, the police ought to be told." Judith knows she's stalling but she's struggling against the opinions of everyone crowding round her.

"Look, I'll go with you and Noel," offered Lila so Judith had to agree.

"Hurry up," urged Noel. "I don't think there's any time to lose."

Chapter 18

The drive to Beth Penner's home took about thirty minutes and Judith spent that time struggling with her feelings. She desperately wanted to maintain her usual arms-length stance but knew she no longer could.

Forced to deputize for Principal Johnson meant she was being pushed into liaising with the bereaved family, the friends, police, coworkers, and now students, as well.

She must deal with this phone message. Beth sounds very clingy and is demanding attention that Judith is loathe to give. But she knows she can't abandon the girl, even though she wants to. Silently she berates herself for even thinking such a thing. Yet it's true. Nobody cares that I didn't ask for this!

Lila and Noel have both been talking while all these thoughts were chasing around in Judith's head. She hasn't been paying attention, and didn't even realize that the three of them left the school without their coats and it's cold out. Judith doesn't even have her purse or her phone. Ever since she heard Beth's message on the answering machine it's like she's been cocooned with her own thoughts. Thoughts racing through her mind like a hamster exercising in its wheel.

The Penner's house is a white brick bungalow with blue shutters matching the colour of the garage door. They pull into the empty driveway and hurry out of the car to the ring the doorbell. They can hear it chime but no one answers. They ring again and knock harder but still no answer. Noel lifts the flap of the letter box and calls "Hello? Beth? Hello?" however there's no reply.

"Does her mother work? Would she go there?" asked Lila.

"Her mother passed away, it's only Beth – no brothers or sisters – and her Dad. He'll be at work. I don't have his number, but I'll have it on file at the school. We should go back and I'll phone him."

"No!" said Noel. "No point worrying him until we know more. We should wait here for a while."

Lila shivered and in that moment Judith felt the cold as well.

"I don't want to hang around here. It's cold–"

"Not in the car it isn't, we can wait in there," pleaded Noel, but the women wanted to leave.

The empty house was a letdown after their rush to get there, but Judith was secretly pleased, it felt like a reprieve.

Chapter 19

"Judith why would Beth phone you for help?" asked Noel as they headed back to the school.

Judith wasn't interested in cars but enjoyed the comfort of the luxurious vehicle he drove. The heat was blasting out the vents and the car was even equipped with seat warmers. She felt far more relaxed now that she was warm and the confrontation with Beth averted. For the time being, at least.

"I don't know why she would."

"Yeah, well no offence but you're not exactly the warm-and-cuddly type. You're not very maternal."

"Noel, I'd be offended if you said I was that type!" laughed Judith. "But no, you're right, it doesn't make sense."

"It's because you're not the motherly sort," said Lila from the backseat. "I mean, ever since her mother died there will have been relatives, neighbours, and other women hanging around wanting to smother her in hugs and urging her to cry and 'let it out'. Hearing enough stuff like that would turn any sensitive child off. Then there's you, somebody who isn't going to fuss her and will listen instead of saying 'don't think about that, put it right out of your mind'. Does that make sense?"

"Actually, it makes a lot of sense to me," said Noel. "Knowing that someone will give you an honest, straightforward answer is a comfort. Too many people tell you what they think you want to hear, or what they think you should hear. They try to protect you from the truth and that can be so frustrating."

Judith and Lila exchanged a look at Noel's comment, each wondering what particular memory he was recalling.

"But still, there must be more to it than just that. Think Judith! what have you and Beth talked about in the last while?"

Judith breathed out a gusty breath saying she'd have to cast her mind back. She definitely had spoken to Beth when they first discovered Holly was missing. In fact, since Beth was Holly's best friend she'd been questioned by the police and Judith had sat in on the interview as the Appropriate Adult. That happened about a week ago and Judith had been preoccupied with her own discomfort. She knew that she wasn't good with people and their emotional messes.

"I was called to accompany her when Holly went missing and the police came to the school. I didn't want to go to the interview because I was busy with my own work. I was trying to get most of my new year set-up completed since I was taking my vacation and didn't want to come back and have to hustle. But for some reason, if I'm remembering it right, there was an unavoidable Trustee meeting, Pat Johnson couldn't be present so she asked me to sit in.

As it turned out it didn't take long. Beth had very little to say to the two policemen – two different ones than now – she could only tell them when she'd last seen Holly and if Holly had said anything about going somewhere, or if she'd fought with her mother, or anything like that.

I got the impression that the police believed Holly had left of her own free will. I didn't get any sense of real worry from Beth or urgency from the police, although looking back there should have been."

"Hindsight, yadda-yadda."

"True."

"Had Holly run away before? Did she have a reputation for doing so? or for staying away overnight?" asked Lila.

"No!" Noel said loudly. "Holly wasn't like that at all, not a bit. She was a really sweet girl, very tenderhearted and kind. A gentle soul."

Again, Lila and Judith exchanged looks. This wasn't the Holly they knew, and Noel's sentimentality came as a surprise. Judith remembered that Annalise claimed he'd called her a 'gentle soul' as well. Was it some sort of pick-up line? Surely not, Holly was just a child.

"Well, you saw a lot of her with the play and everything so I'm sure you knew her much better than we did," answered Lila.

Noel dismissed that idea saying: "I wouldn't say I knew her that well," then qualified his answer by adding: "but I probably did see another side to her."

Chapter 20

"Where could Beth be? All the children left school ages ago," wondered Judith.

"Do you think she's gone out for dinner with her father?" asked Lila.

Noel had left his car running at the school's front driveway – a no-no in the 'No Idling' zone – but said he'd only be a moment running up the steps to grab his coat and briefcase. The women made their way to the principal's office and sat down to discuss this new turn of events.

"That's possible, or when you think about it she could be anywhere at this time of year: shopping or out at another friend's place."

"So, you think worrying about her is premature."

"Oh, probably but.." Judith hesitated a moment to think about this. Was it normal to worry about the whereabouts of a young teen? Judith didn't know but Beth was obviously in distress. Unless that was teen drama? "I have to say I don't know. What do you think?" she asked Lila.

"You should tell the police about the message left on the answering machine, and explain that you tried to get in touch with Beth but there was no one at her home."

"And then leave it in their hands! Yes, that's a good idea." Judith hoped she didn't sound too eager but Lila was following her own train of thought:

"Or we could go back to Beth's place later? We could have a meal and then drop by again just to be sure."

"No, if we bring in the police we have to leave them to do their job. Anything else would be interfering. Besides, they've got the resources."

Lila seemed doubtful but didn't argue, instead she replied:

"You could ask them to let you know what they find out. Beth called you so it's only natural you'd want to know that the girl's okay."

"Yes, I could ask them to do that. Not sure if they will tell me but I can ask."

"Okay then, let's get the announcement out about tomorrow's meeting."

"Good idea. I honestly don't know if anyone will show up. Do we want the teachers to attend?"

"No, but they might want to do so. How about we tell them a meeting is scheduled but say that attendance isn't mandatory."

"Yes, that's good. Also, I'm not planning on serving anything, so we'd better let them know that."

"Right, they might expect coffee."

"Oh, our parents expect much more than that! Whenever we have a meeting the girl's get to practise their baking skills, laying out trays, and serving. It's always quite the affair. Of course, we usually ask the parents to RSVP so we know the numbers and can cater accordingly."

"Something to look forward to at some future date!"

"Yes, it is always nicely done. Now if we make it six o'clock that will give everyone the opportunity to eat early or go out afterwards. So, we could say something like 'December 21 at 6:00 pm an informal meeting at the school for parents with questions about recent events. RSVP not required and no food or drink will be served.' How does that sound?"

"Yes, it covers everything. Same deal as before: you email and I text?"

"You got it."

"This won't take us long and then we can go get a bite to eat."

"Oh, not me, no but thanks anyhow. I've still got some work to do here, things I was planning to get on with when I got the call from Dana Lezinsky."

Lila looked mildly disappointed but only commented: "That seems like ages ago!"

"Only a few hours but yes, a lot has happened since then. I'll walk to the staff room with you to grab my coat as well. That'll save me a trip when I leave."

"Remember and make sure you do call the police – I think it's important and you don't want to give them any reason to complain."

"I agree! and I'll call for sure. I'm a bit concerned about Beth myself, I mean that phone message was..."

"Yes, it was definitely a cry for help."

Chapter 21

"Well, that was easier than I expected," thought Judith, smiling to herself. She reached Grant's voicemail when she called so was able to leave a message and avoid having a conversation. "Now I can get back to doing my real job."

Opening her laptop to get to work on her books Judith ignored the first guilty twinge but eventually the nagging of her conscience was too distracting. Against her instincts she picked up the business card again and looked for a main phone number to the police station. Sighing heavily, she dialled the number.

"Edgemont Police Station is this an emergency?"

"Uh no, no it isn't but it's important, well it is to me... Sorry I sound ridiculous..."

"Go ahead and explain, ma'am," said the dispatcher's bored-sounding voice.

"My name is Judith Taylor and I work at Edgemont School for Girls. One of our students phoned and left a tearful message on our answering machine and she sounded frightened by something. I've been unable to get hold of her since. I don't know her cellphone number..." Judith paused a moment to jot down a reminder to make a directory of all student's cellphone numbers, "but I went by her house and there was no one home."

"What time was this phone message left, and what's the name of the girl?"

"I'm not sure what time, hmm... it was about 3:30 to 4:00? Students left early today. We aren't having regular classes because of our other student, Holly Lezinsky, who was found dead after being missing a week.

I guess that's why I'm concerned about Beth, her full name is Bethany Penner, in case something's happened. Also, her message says she's scared but not why she's scared."

"I'm initiating a call out for the girl right now. You say there's a connection to the Holly Lezinsky case?"

"The two of them are... um, were, best friends and Beth claims she's got Holly's diary but I'm not sure if that's important. Detectives Grant and Mirteau have been here twice talking to me and the rest of the staff so I called them first but couldn't get hold of them, I had to leave a message. I don't know when Detective Grant will get it and Beth is only fourteen so..."

"You're doing the right thing Ms. Taylor. We'll start searching for the girl, and someone will follow up with you tonight or tomorrow."

"Thank you, I appreciate that. I don't like to fuss or waste time but..."

"Not at all, we appreciate your concern. Thanks again, good-bye."

After ending the call Judith found she was unable to return to her work because now she couldn't stop wondering, even worrying, about Beth. For a moment she considered calling Lila to give her an update but decided that would be intruding since Lila said she was going out for a meal. They could catch up tomorrow.

Judith switched off her computer, gathered up her belongings, and put on her coat. She didn't turn out any lights since the school custodian would be in sometime later to check up and would deal with the lights and the heating then. As she approached the front door she was clearly outlined against the darkness outside. She hesitated a moment with an eerie feeling that she was being watched.

She was.

Wrongly, she decided she was being fanciful and so she shrugged it off and locked up, walking at a fast pace across to the parking lot and into the safe haven of her car.

Until a body smashed against the driver's side door, grabbing at the door handle. Judith had locked that the moment she got in so the attacker was stymied but he, for she could see it was a man, started pounding on the window and yelling obscenities and threats. She pushed away from the door, fright turning to terror. Frozen in fear while this wild-eyed, raging and ranting man fought to get into her car.

In a split-second Judith recovered enough to blast the horn, over and over again, which startled the man into falling back from the vehicle. She sped away with her hands in a painful grip on the steering-wheel and her breath coming in gasps.

From what she could see and from what he'd said she figured that must have been Billy MacNeill. Complaining about what she'd said about him and Holly to his wife – although Judith knew he wasn't married to Dana – and vowing to get even with… well, she didn't need to remind herself about the insults.

Her first burst of fearful emotion soon gave way to anger. "How dare he! He has no right…" she was outraged and her thoughts were a bit jumbled.

Judith realized the man, Billy MacNeill, had been very drunk and most likely she hadn't been in any danger. She figured he'd have shouted abuse in the hopes of making her cry. She didn't need to be afraid of him. The fact that he'd come to the school meant it was doubtful he knew where she lived.

"Oh, of course he doesn't know that. I bet he doesn't even know my surname." She exclaimed, exasperated with herself. "Get home and make a cup of tea or better yet, a hot chocolate. The sugar will help. Then call the police. No, I've already got a call in to the police, so I'll just wait until Grant phones me back. Billy MacNeill will not be a problem, I won't allow it!" she declared.

Chapter 22

In the wintertime especially, Judith liked that her building had underground parking. Her spot was close to the inside door and she could see the overhead garage door in her rear-view mirror. She always watched to make sure no one sneaked in while she was waiting for it to close.

When a new building manager had told her she'd have to change parking spots she'd flat out refused. He tried to argue claiming he needed that space for crews coming in to work on the building but she suspected he wanted it for his own car. She told him it was a safety issue for her and that she was prepared to take it up with owner of the building. That hadn't been necessary because she heard no more about it, and that manager hadn't lasted too long.

Once she was locked inside her own apartment, feeling a little sheepish at how she'd almost run from her car to the door, Judith wanted to review the incident and get it all straight in her mind. Lila had added her contact info to Judith's cellphone so Judith called to update her on the Billy MacNeill incident.

"Omigod that must have been so scary!"

"It was. I mean I'm locking the front door of the school, it's quiet and dark, nobody's around but you know I had this creepy feeling that someone was watching me. And I'm not imagining that in light of what happened, I did feel something was dodgy. Anyhow, turns out I was being watched by Billy MacNeill of all people."

"What did he say?"

"It's hard to recall exactly... he was hollering and cursing and it was obvious he was very drunk. I mean, too drunk to be a problem because if I'd had to I could easily have outrun him and I'm not a runner! but when he suddenly loomed up beside the car door and started pounding on the windows, yeah he startled me and I was frightened."

"I would have peed my pants."

Judith laughed at Lila saying: "You'd have been out of your car with your fists up, I know you've got a fiery temper!"

"I prefer to call myself 'feisty', it's the Italian way. So, what did Grant say when you told him?"

"I haven't talked to him yet."

"You've got to let him know; I'm positive you'll find he's very concerned. This might be important evidence and your personal safety might be on the line."

"I don't think that's true, MacNeill was acting out in a stupid-drunk way. But I did call Grant and left a message for him to call me back."

"Well then I won't keep you on the phone. Thanks for letting me know and Judith if you start feeling scared or anything on your own call me. I can come over there or you can come over here."

"Thanks, that's nice of you, but I'll be fine, and I'll see you at school tomorrow."

They said their goodbyes and hung up. When the phone rang shortly after Judith expected it to be Grant but instead if was Annalise calling.

"You don't mind me phoning you at home, do you Judith?"

"Well, actually–"

"I got your number from Noel, he's got a directory of all the staff. He's so organized."

"I don't mind so long as you make it quick, Annalise. I've had a very long day already." Judith felt she'd already put up with enough of Annalise's dithering when the younger woman had visited the school. Now she just wanted her to get to the point.

"Oh! Well, that's easy because it's a simple request. My in-laws-to-be asked me to call and invite you to tea tomorrow. At their home."

"Why?"

"Why? Oh, I expect they want to pick your brains about what's going on with the murder and everything. They like to get the facts firsthand and of course as you're acting on Pat Johnson's behalf you're the man-of-the-hour, so to speak," she ended with a giggle.

"Well, that's very kind but my time isn't my own right now so I can't be sure if I'll even be free in the afternoon."

"Oh, you don't have to wait until four o'clock, in fact they'd rather have you come early. The sooner the better, actually. They'll be home all day and since Cook will be baking the goodies bright and early just drop by as soon as you can. They'll be waiting."

Judith couldn't see any way out of the invitation. She knew Pat Johnson would want her to accept because Eleanor Frampton did so much for the school financially. The woman's support meant funding came from her social circle as well.

Also, since Judith wasn't going to be attending Noel's birthday and Christmas party this was her chance to see the house. "It is an estate after all," she thought to herself, "and no doubt worth seeing 'how the 1% live'!" Aloud she said:

"Well. please pass on my thanks, Annalise and say I'll be delighted to take tea as early in the day as I can manage."

"Oooh that's wonderful news. We'll see you tomorrow, then. Byeeeee."

Judith considered her wardrobe while wondering what to wear for the appointment then decided she'd go ahead with the outfit she'd already planned on. She didn't feel obliged to dress up, in fact she was a bit resentful at having to attend at all. She was interested in seeing their home but she didn't like being summoned, it made her feel imposed upon.

"On the other hand," she thought, "I can use it as a practice run for seeing the parents at tomorrow night's meeting."

She meant it when she'd told Annalise that it had been a long day and she felt like relaxing in hot bubble-bath. She took her cellphone with her in the bathroom but Grant never did return her call.

Chapter 23

Why am I so stiff today?" wondered Judith speaking out loud although she was alone. She always spoke to herself; she hummed and sang out loud as well.

Each morning she counted her way through twenty-five toe touches but today she didn't make contact until attempt number four. She performed this routine in the shower figuring that if she lost her balance and fell the distance wouldn't be far. She was lucky that her bathtub/shower combo had proper doors instead of a shower-curtain.

The toe touching was to stretch. Judith didn't participate in any formal kind of exercise – no sports teams, jogging, or gym membership – but she did enjoy a good walk.

Year-round, so long as the weather was dry, she walked to work each day. Snowfall didn't deter her, but rain did. Walking in the rain made her feel very stupid, worrying that people would think she was 'too dumb to come in out of the rain'. The fact that there was no one to think that didn't matter – Judith herself would think that.

"I expect I'm achy because I tossed and turned so much last night. That idiot Billy MacNeill gave me quite a scare and I guess I'm feeling the aftermath of that. Also, I've had Beth on my mind, she's a worry; and my trip out of school – to Dana Lezinsky's home – was unusual. Then I got thinking about how much I enjoy Lila's company, and after that I rehashed that argument with Grant. Of course, I always think of much better comebacks when I'm writing the script! He never did call me back so it's just as well I called the police station main number too.

I hope I haven't gotten Beth into trouble with her father, I'm sure things are difficult for both of them with no mother in the house. And then that surprise call from Annalise inviting me, as if I have a choice! to join her at the Larkin house to *drink a cup of tea and discuss the unfortunate situation*. How can she think of the murder as an *unfortunate situation?* Unless she means the cancellation of the play? that would make her even more shallow! but it could be she's concerned after all the time and hard work Noel put into it. I don't know. With all this going around in my head it's a wonder I got any sleep at all.

Today's forecast is rain turning to snow and that overcast sky looks ready to fulfill it. Ugh, I hate driving in sleet but it's better than walking in it. It will be best if I take the car all week anyways in case I get called out in addition to this tea drinking with the school's most generous supporters. I expect Beth has turned up by now, so I'll have to go out to her home again if she asks."

Walking down the stairs to the parking garage Judith felt the odd twinge of pain. *Maybe I've got a touch of this flu bug that's going around? If so, at least it won't be severe since I've had my shot.* She didn't realize that when she violently jerked her body away from the car door last night that she wrenched a few muscles. These minor aches would plague her all day.

Judith drove slowly since the promised precipitation arrived and made the roads slick. Fortunately, there was very little traffic. This close to Christmas meant the shoppers would be out in force but both malls were in the opposite direction from where she was headed.

There were several intersections to get through and she kept an eye on the pedestrians' WALK/DON'T WALK signal to get a warning when the light was about to turn red. The actual driving was okay but stopping could be a challenge under these conditions.

As she got near to the school she noticed the car behind was following too closely, especially in this weather. It didn't have its headlights on so she couldn't get a good look but it appeared to be a dark-coloured car that was bigger than hers. She changed lanes to allow the driver room to pass but instead he – or she – moved into the lane behind her and stayed right there whether she sped up or slowed down.

Judith was getting annoyed, the road conditions required concentration and she couldn't keep looking in her rear-view mirror. What was the other driver doing? Were they sticking close because they couldn't see very well themselves? they might not realize their lights weren't on. Regardless, it was annoying to have someone tailgating her, she was concerned about being rear-ended.

With relief she spotted the school and was almost at its driveway when the car behind roared to life and clipped her left bumper as it raced past.

Judith's car began to spin out of control heading towards the wall of old trees that lined the road. Without thinking about it she threw the car into neutral and was able to slow it down enough to regain control. Popping it into a low gear she managed to drive into the skid and straighten out. Her heart was pounding, and her chest heaved with shallow breaths, but she was okay, and the car was still running.

That stupid, stupid person driving so dangerously, she thought. What a lousy way to start my day!

It didn't occur to her that the near-crash wasn't accidental.

Steering onto the school grounds she spotted an unfamiliar sports-car parked in the lot and suspected it belonged to Suzanne Mirteau.

"A second lousy thing to ruin my day. If it turns out that bad things do come in threes I'm done for," Judith grumbled.

Chapter 24

The office staff usually got to work before the teachers arrived but today Marta and a few cohorts were already at the school, waiting. Judith gave Marta's triumphant expression a puzzled look before noticing the grim faces on Grant and Suzanne.

"What's going on?" she asked, while nudging her way past Joanna, Jennifer, and Xiao, and walking up to the detectives.

"Let's take this into your office, Ms. Taylor. It's an informal interview but still best done without interruptions."

Grant didn't look towards Marta but Judith felt they all knew exactly what he meant. Without a word she marched to the principal's office, hung up her coat behind the door and sat in Pat's chair after putting her purse and briefcase on the credenza.

The silence extended until Suzanne broke it with an accusation: "You've withheld evidence from the police again!"

"No I haven't!" retorted Judith.

"Ms. Smith told us all about a phone message that was left to you on the answering machine. A message from a frightened, crying girl who claimed she had some evidence from the victim and you didn't tell us. And you—"

"I did I–" but Suzanne didn't let Judith interrupt, she was angry and continued:

"Went off playing detective! Instead of contacting us immediately you and your pals drove out to see this girl Bethany Penner on your own. Why? Do you think you know better than us? Do you think you're smarter than the dumb cops? is that it?" She was working herself up and Judith wondered how much of this tirade could be heard through the office door. She didn't doubt for a moment that Marta and the other teachers would be lurking nearby.

Judith refused to engage in a noisy argument. She turned her attention to Grant who gestured to Suzanne to stop. Judith took that opportunity to say:

"Several of the teachers urged me not to contact the police until I spoke to Beth in case she was afraid because of something she'd done or for some other reason, whatever it might be, that she didn't want the police involved. However, if you check at the police station, you'll find that I did call. I called there after I couldn't get hold of you," she held Grant's gaze adding, "The phone message was to me, that's correct, and so I responded to it. I wanted to see Beth to find out what she needed from me. If there was any reason to call the police after I learned what she had to say I would have done so."

"That's not up to you!"

Judith continued speaking to Grant as if Suzanne hadn't said a word.

"Since I was unable to reach Beth, and because I was concerned about her phone-call to me, I did leave a message for you. When you didn't phone me back I called the station and they took my report over the phone. There was an incident after that which I was going to tell you when you returned my call but... you didn't."

Grant sat up looking concerned: "What incident?"

"A man tried to attack me when I left the school last night. He was waiting in the parking lot here-—"

"Stop trying to deflect us with this fabrication!" exclaimed Suzanne.

"Who, to the best of my knowledge, was Billy MacNeill. Drunk, but coherent enough for me to know he was very angry and making wild accusations."

"You know MacNeill?"

"I've seen him from a distance on those occasions when he drove to the school to pick up Holly. Last night I thought I recognized him and also because of what he said."

Suzanne threw up her hands and fell back into a chair. She crossed her arms and legs, swinging one of them, and looking like a petulant child furious at being ignored. Judith and Grant continued to ignore her. He said,

"I'll need a full statement with all those details – you will press charges, won't you?"

"That depends. I don't want to add to Dana Lezinsky's troubles. She might have changed her mind and be willing to forgive him and take him back. If that's the case, I won't upset her further.

However, that man has no right to go around scaring people just because he can't control his temper or handle his drink. I hope you, or if not you some officer, shakes him up a bit. Not actually shaking of course but let him know that his behaviour has been noted as part of the official record or whatever you call it."

"Any other personal chores we can attend to for you?" Suzanne was sarcastic and snarky. Grant shook his head and told Judith not to worry, the incident would be logged and investigated. He glanced back at Suzanne and added that he would take care of it himself.

"Actually there is something else. We've called an impromptu parents' meeting for this evening and it would be great to have a police spokesperson to answer their questions. It's very last minute, I know, and it could be that no parents actually do show up but it would help us and it would look good for the police, too."

Suzanne got up and left the room without answering.

Judith felt herself relaxing a bit now that she and Grant were alone. He had such a calm manner whereas Suzanne seemed to buzz with negative energy. It crackled off her. Without considering her words beforehand Judith blurted out: "You two do make an odd couple."

Grant gave a slight smile saying: "That's because we aren't a 'couple'. We're work-mates and yes, we have different attitudes and different ways of looking at things, but that helps each of us get a broader viewpoint. To be honest though I've never seen my partner act with such aggression. I can only think it's because the victim was so young and with the holidays so close, well... it's a heartbreaking situation."

"I thought the police had to put their feelings aside."

"Oh we have to and we do, otherwise we couldn't work our job. But that doesn't mean we don't feel it, only that we have to compartmentalize in order to get on with it. We have feelings too, you know."

"I didn't mean to offend you."

"You didn't, and I'm sorry if I made it sound like you had. Actually, I am feeling a bit prickly myself, so I guess this case it getting to everyone."

"Either that or Suzanne is rubbing off on you."

The smile left his face and she realized it wasn't much of a joke.

"I'll talk to my boss about this meeting with the parents, there's very little we're able to share at this time so I don't know how worthwhile it would be."

Judith shrugged and said if he or anyone could make it great but not to worry. As Grant turned to go he said he hoped she would get in touch with Ms. Lezinsky soon and for Judith to let him know what she'd decided regarding pressing charges against Billy MacNeill.

"I'll leave you a message with my answer, you won't need to call me back."

Grant looked like he wanted to reply to that remark but after a pause he nodded and left the office.

Judith watched when the two of them appeared outside the window. The principal's office gave a better view of the front area than her office did. She briefly wondered how 'Chatterbox Cindy' was managing on her own at their shared room in the library. Judith figured she'd be spending most of her time in the staff-room.

Grant and Suzanne were arguing about something. Their body language showed that both were angry and neither was trying to placate the other. Judith wondered what it was all about. With the windows closed to the December cold she couldn't hear a thing.

Once the police drove away Judith should have settled down to work but she felt unable to do so. She blamed it on her poor sleep from last night, her overall acheyness, and the lack of physical exercise recently. That and the constant bickering with the police combined to make her cranky and restless.

She decided to put her things away in the staff cloakroom and fetch a coffee, hoping to find Lila in one of those locations so she could catch her up on the news.

Chapter 25

Lila was in the hallway hurrying towards Principal Johnson's office.

"I was just coming to look for you," began Judith but Lila cut her off whispering:

"Don't talk, super-cute guy who is SO mad coming right up behind me." She broke off as a deep voice called out:

"I want to see this Judith Taylor woman right now!"

The man, wearing a hi-viz vest over work clothes and safety boots, appeared beside Lila, and he was very angry.

And yes, he was also handsome in a rugged, outdoorsy way with his dark-red hair and bright brown eyes, an unusual combination. But Judith brushed that thought aside. He was a big man and in this mood he was intimidating. She lifted her chin stating:

"I am Judith Taylor and you had better come into my office and explain your business in our school." She signalled to Lila to join them.

Once in the office, with Judith seated behind her desk and Lila standing by the door, the man's anger turned to anxiety. He clutched his head in both hands and gasped out:

"I am frantic with worry. I don't know what's going on around here, but my little girl is missing." Judith met Lila's eyes and saw recognition there.

Lila guided Brian Penner, both women realizing that this was Beth's father, into a chair and sat down herself beside him. Judith came round from her desk and perched on the edge. This more intimate arrangement seemed to comfort the man.

"Mr. Penner, we are both terribly sorry to hear this about Beth. We went to your home looking for her yesterday right after school. No one was in and we thought the two of you had gone out. However, Beth is very young, so I called the police station to report our concern. You see, Beth left a tearful message on the school's answering machine, and we haven't heard from her or been able to get hold of her since."

"What message?"

"She said she had found her friend Holly's diary and something in it upset her very much because she was crying and saying she was scared."

"Scared? Scared of what?"

"That's all she said. You do know about Holly Lezinsky, right?"

"Holly's missing, yeah I heard all about it from Bethany, she's been beside herself."

"Oh Mr. Penner--"

"Brian."

"Brian, thank you, I'm afraid that Holly has been found dead by the police."

"No! Oh no, not Holly! Oh, poor Beth. Now she'll be devastated. But the police never said a word to me. I spoke to a woman called um, Suzie? I've got her card here somewhere." As he searched his pockets Judith and Lila again exchanged a look.

"Was the policewoman's name Suzanne Mirteau?"

"Yeah! that's it, I remember she had a French name."

"What exactly did Detective Mirteau tell you?"

"She said that Bethany would be here at school with you, that my daughter went home with you yesterday. I guess that sorta makes sense since she'd been upset about Holly missing and now, knowing she died, but I mean, who are you? and what are you to Bethany?" He looked puzzled but Judith could sense his anger simmering below this surface calm.

"Mr... Brian, I have no idea why Detective Mirteau would say that. I have never taken a student home with me and if, for some unimaginable reason, I ever feel called upon to do so the first thing I'd do is notify her family. I'm the school Bursar and I have very little to do with Beth or any of the students. I know who the girls are – for the most part – but I deal with the parents. And the bureaucracy."

"Then why did Bethany try to get hold of you? and why was she crying?"

"That's what we're all wondering. Lila here, who is the school Nurse, and I have been trying to figure that out." All of a sudden he jumped up saying:

"I'm wasting time sitting and talking with you. It isn't doing any good. I've got to find her. I need to know what the police are doing. If they think she's here at school with you then they won't be out looking for her. I'm going back to the station."

"I will call your home and will keep trying. Does Beth have a cellphone?"

He thrust his own phone at her saying: "I don't remember the number but it's in here." Lila took the phone from him and quickly found the number which she wrote down.

"We'll both keep trying to get hold of Beth all day. Tell the police to let the school know when they have news. Actually, I'm putting Judith's number into your phone – that will be much faster since you'll get through right away. I don't want to hold you up now but try to think of the names of friends Beth might be staying with because the police will want that information."

"I always thought Holly was her only friend. They've been best friends for years. I never saw any other girls come by the home or heard them mention meeting up with anyone else. I've gotta find Bethany, she needs me, and I wasn't there for her."

"Brian, we're having an informal meeting with parents tonight and you might want to come to see if anyone knows anything or, if you can't make it we'll ask on your behalf. With it being last-minute and, of course, a busy time of year we might not get much of a turnout but nevertheless..."

"Yes, unless the police need me I'll be there. There was a text, I guess, but I don't remember."

"It's scheduled for six o'clock here."

The two women walked with him to the entrance, giving assurances that they would all keep in touch. Judith told Brian that at school Beth preferred to be called 'Beth', not Bethany, so that's how her classmates and their families would know her. He said he'd try to remember that, then walked away.

It was too cold to stand outside but they watched from the vestibule as he drove off in his pick-up truck. It was snowing now, and the lawn had a covering of white. The school had hired a landscaping firm to create a drive-through by cutting an arc from the road to the front entrance and back to the road again. Alumnae had protested the change, but it prevented the girls from ruining the grass, in addition to being much safer for pick-ups and drop-offs to happen off the road and on school property.

"Judith why are there so many hot-looking men involved in this case? Teacher, Cop, Parent... wow!"

"Gee Lila, I was thinking about what that poor man is going through, not rating him on a 'hotness scale.'" said Judith.

"How could you not be? Oh well, stick with me and you'll catch on, kid. So far as Beth is concerned we need to keep thinking positive thoughts and hope for the best," replied Lila.

"Why did you give him my phone number?"

"Because I couldn't give him mine – I'm married."

Chapter 26

Lila's statement was a shocker but before Judith could speak Noel came up to them in the foyer to say a ton of messages were piling up on the answering machine.

"I answered one of them because the caller was the mother of one of my girls but boy was that a mistake! I couldn't get her off the line even though all I said, over and over, was 'we don't know, the police haven't said, I have no idea' – it was so frustrating. I let the rest pile up. Anyhow, Judith I did want to talk to you..." his voice trailed off as he looked at Lila. She took the hint saying:

"I'll head to the staff-room now and see it I can't make some headway with those messages," and gave Judith a wink.

Judith had never cared for Noel's affectation of calling his students 'his girls' but she didn't comment on that, she wanted to hear what he had to say. He took her by the arm and pulled her in close so he could speak in a low voice.

"I want to let you know that there's quite a bit of back-biting going on amongst the teachers and it's directed at you. The main complaint seems to be that Pat Johnson should have put Marta in charge, not you, since you aren't even a teacher. Also, that phone message..."

Judith waited for more then realized that was it. She sighed inside thinking Noel was very young after all. This Christmas Day was either his 26th or 27th birthday, she wasn't sure which. The fact that his and Holly's birthdays were only days apart, and that each of them had Christmas-related names, had been yet another bond between the two of them.

"Noel, understand that I do not care what the teachers think. The decision was made, and they must abide by it, regardless of their opinion. I know I'm not a popular person, that's part of the reason why Pat knows she can trust me: I won't play favourites, in fact I won't play games of any kind."

"Nor should you! I totally agree with everything you're saying! but I thought it was important that you know what's going on. Boy, I wish I had your guts! I care way too much about what people think about me," he said with a half-laugh.

"Why? You've got it all, Noel. You're great at your job, you're a good-looking man, your family is well-off, you've got a beautiful fiancee, and you're a nice guy to boot!"

"Aww, it's so kind of you to say all that! You're right, I'm lucky in so many ways. I should be more self-confident."

"That's right. We've only got to get through the next few days and everything will be back to normal when we return in the new year."

"Well, not everything." said Noel with a sigh, looking forlorn. Judith wasn't sure if he meant Holly or his play. She decided not to ask. For such a handsome, manly-looking man Noel Larkin could be quite needy.

"I'm sure that's a tactic that works very well with plenty of women," she thought, "but not with me."

Since Judith didn't react Noel settled for giving a sad little smile saying:

"You're right, of course. Somebody's stirring things up. It will be Marta behind it all but she's got plenty of acolytes to do her bidding while her hands stay clean. I thought you should know.

Friends need to stick together." He moved away then turned back saying:

"I hear you're having a goss with my ladies today?" adding, when Judith looked puzzled, "A gossip, 'tea and scandal' with my mother, auntie, and Annalise," he explained.

"Oh right, yes. Feels like a command performance," Judith replied, wondering if he'd named the women in order of importance to him.

"Not that bad, surely!" Noel laughed.

"Actually, I was thinking it will be like a trial run for tonight. Did anyone tell you about the parents' meeting we're having? Teachers aren't required to attend but of course can if they want, if you want. We're not serving any food or drink so we figure no one will stay too long!"

"What's the agenda?"

"Nothing formal, a Q and A except we won't have very many answers! No doubt it will turn into a venting session. I'm not expecting to get much of a turn-out. It's short notice and it's such a busy time with social, shopping, and family stuff.

Unfortunately, the ones most likely to show up will be those people who love to hear themselves talk. Wow, I'm really not selling it, am I?"

Noel laughed and told her to definitely take the opportunity of her daytime visit with his family to practise for her nighttime meeting with the parents saying:

"The idea will be to pump you for inside information, politely of course! although I'm sure my ears will be burning, too!" He gave a little wave and this time did walk away.

Judith hadn't been looking forward to the *tea party*, even less so now that she knew she'd be grilled.

It annoyed her so she decided: *Now I'm just in the mood for a chat with Suzanne.*

Chapter 27

Judith returned to her office to make the call but before doing so tried both of Beth's numbers again. She'd left a message at each earlier so didn't bother doing so again.

Picking up Grant's business card she entered his cell number into her contacts. Easier than looking it up each time. When he picked up, she immediately launched into her attack:

"I've just had Beth Penner's father in here accusing me of abducting his daughter because – apparently – that's what you detectives told him happened."

"Judith? What are you talking about. I haven't met the girl's father—-"

"No, but Suzanne has. She told him I took Beth home with me last night and he could find both of us here at the school this morning. What the hell is she playing at? Does she think it's a joke or something? We're talking about a fourteen-year-old girl who is missing, you know!"

"I do know she's missing and I hope you're not interfering again, Ms. Taylor," his voice cold as he replied.

"Again?" Judith was equally frosty. Grant softened his tone saying:

"I'm sure this Penner guy has got it wrong; Suzanne wouldn't say something like that."

"Is she there with you now? Hmm? ask her. Go ahead, I'll wait."

Judith heard Grant's exasperated sigh, but he must have covered the phone because the rest of the conversation was a mumble of noise. She could identify Suzanne's higher pitch and it sounded like they were arguing. That wasn't Judith's problem, she interrupted the quarrel loudly calling: "Hello? Hello? I'm still here."

"Sorry. It seems there has been a mix-up of some sort. Anyhow, Beth's father came back here and has filed a formal report about his daughter's disappearance so we're on top of that--"

"I made a report last night that Beth Penner was missing. Check with your dispatcher. Did Suzanne cancel that or something?"

"Well, not to say cancel but since you aren't the missing minor's legal guardian–"

"So you're telling me that the person who answered the phone at the police station yesterday only pretended to take down my report? Because I did mention I was from the school, I didn't masquerade as a parent."

"No, that report was filed but... oh hell, as I mentioned things are a bit mixed up."

Judith didn't reply and after a minute of silence Grant said:

"We've got all of our resources out pursuing this now. We will find the girl. I'm certain of it."

Oh, I am too," replied Judith, "After all you were so successful with Holly."

Chapter 28

Judith immediately regretted what she'd said to Grant but she'd already hung up and wasn't about to call him back. Instead, she had the ordeal of tea at the Frampton residence ahead of her.

Annalise was staying with her fiancé's family for Christmas, her own parents having flown to one of their island paradise vacation homes.

It meant Judith would have to travel there alone. This felt like another thing straining her nerves and pushing her out of her comfort zone. She resented being manipulated but knew how much the school and Pat Johnson relied on the benevolence of this family.

Their annual donation covered the costs of most of the sponsored students, one of which had been Holly Lezinsky. If nothing else the family was entitled to know what had happened to its protege.

Judith realized her resentment was fuelled by the discomfort and apprehension she felt around meeting with people, especially rich people. She wished she had some of Lila's ease of manner and then thought: "Why not take Lila with me? It might be rude to bring along an uninvited guest but they're rich so I'm sure they can fix another plate."

She hurried from the office to find Lila who jumped at the chance when asked.

"Of course, I'll go with you! I'm dying to see their place; I've heard plenty about the Frampton estate. Will we really be served tea? I'd much rather try a sherry, although it's not even noon yet so I guess that's out of the question. I thought tea was a four o'clock thing?"

Judith couldn't help but laugh at the other woman's enthusiastic response. "Oh, who knows what they'll serve us. Go grab your things, we'll have to leave right away before the phones blow up again with calls and we get stuck here. I'll go warm up my car and meet you outside, it's the burgundy Subaru."

Within ten minutes they were on the road. Lila asked about the Larkin-Frampton set-up and Judith passed on what she'd learned from Pat Johnson after the principal's years of charitable association with the family.

"Audrey Larkin was widowed young due to a flying accident. Her husband was an adventurer and died flying his own plane that he kept near here at Springbank Airport. His family had money but it seems they tied it up in a trust for Noel, their only grandson.

No one knows if it was for lack of money or for companionship, but Audrey chose to move herself and Noel, who was a toddler at the time, into the home of her elder sister Eleanor. Eleanor was married to Basil Frampton. The Frampton's never had any children of their own and they helped Audrey raise Noel. This estate has been Noel's home his entire life, and he's expected to inherit everything someday.

Basil Frampton was a very wealthy man and Pat confided in me that Eleanor said he had never liked Audrey. Pat never actually met him; he'd already passed away by time Noel joined the school.

Bas, as they called him, was older than Eleanor who herself is quite a bit older than Audrey. Pat doesn't care much for Audrey either. Told me she's one of those people who let their innate racism show through even though they never say anything untoward. She said Eleanor is the exact opposite. That's the scoop on the Larkin and Frampton families."

"So, Noel has been raised as the spoiled darling in a wealthy household. He's never actually needed to get a job so it says a lot about him that he's not satisfied to live as one of the 'idle rich'. In fact, he's awfully nice considering that up-bringing."

"I agree."

Edgemont was quaintly picturesque but the enclave of estate homes on the outskirts was magnificent. They were at the opposite end of the village from the trailer park, and half the distance from the Penner household. Judith felt she was seeing the whole financial spectrum of Edgemont residences. Judith had never been to the Executive Estates subdivision before – she'd never had reason to hobnob with the wealthy!

The house was built in the English Tudor style of off-white walls and blackened cross beams and it was huge. Plenty of trees were planted throughout the property and would look lovely in the summer.

It was as pretty as a Christmas card in the winter. The windows were shuttered against the dull gray winter sky but a warm glow escaped from designs cut out of the wood. With the snow falling the whole scene was inviting and welcoming.

The two women looked at each other and Lila whistled.

"I agree, again!" said Judith.

"Seriously, though: why does Noel even bother to teach?"

"It's his vocation. His love of teaching makes him a great teacher. If he'd gone into some other kind of work the family donations would have gone to that business instead of the school so we're doubly grateful to have Noel."

They parked in the front and by the time they reached the steps a manservant had opened the double-doors and was welcoming them inside. Judith, whose coat was new two years ago but now felt distinctly shabby, was heartened by Lila's apparent lack of concern when she handed over her own duffle-coat. The butler led the way to a large room where three women sat in front of the fire.

It was a beautiful room with tasteful and expensive decor and that same wealth was reflected in the occupants.

The oldest woman wore some sort of robe in gold and red brocade, her sister – the family resemblance was striking – wore a velvet dress in winter white, and Annalise was shiny in moiré silk. Judith felt that her plain shirtwaist dress and Lila's sweater and skirt looked very casual in comparison. She lifted her chin and decided she didn't care.

Annalise began the introductions but she'd never met Lila who greeted her hostesses with an apology for tagging along but said she 'couldn't resist gatecrashing to see their beautiful home'.

Eleanor Frampton was gracious, replying:

"How refreshing! We're delighted to have you, Miss Morelli."

"Oh call me Lila, please."

Audrey Larkin raised her eyebrow and looked snooty. Noel had once complained to Judith that his mother was 'awfully possessive and her behaviour towards any women of marriageable age was terrible'. Judith battled the temptation to put Mrs. Larkin's mind at ease by saying 'Neither of us are interested in your son, he's way too young in age and personality' but wisely kept silent.

"Besides", she thought, "We're obviously no threat to young Annalise who has both beauty and wealth."

They had settled into their chairs and watched as a laden tea trolley was wheeled in when a cacophony of barking erupted through the open door. A frenzied melee of snarling, snapping dogs violently entered the room and Judith was frightened as the dogs raced about fighting each other.

Lila laughed at their antics and voluntarily joined Annalise in separating the animals from what turned out to be their mode of playing to drag them out by their collars. Mrs. Larkin complained at the noise, but Mrs. Frampton was indulgent. The barking diminished as the dogs were removed further and further away from the drawing room.

Audrey Larkin started the conversation by quizzing Judith about Patricia Johnson's illness. Lila answered in her capacity as nurse to explain that the principal had a bad bout of the flu.

"I understand her secretary got it first and since the two of them are together so much it was only a matter of time before the principal got sick too."

"And you have had to step in, Bursar?"

"Judith, please, and yes I've been Principal Johnson's deputy for a number of years now. I don't have to cover for her often, but some engagements can't be scheduled outside school hours and on those occasions Pat will ask me to take her place. I will be delighted to resume my usual position when she returns."

"Do you find leadership that challenging Miss Taylor?" queried Mrs. Larkin with a sniff, refusing the familiarity of first names.

"Yes, I do when a student has been murdered and another has disappeared, and I'm supposed to be taking my annual leave."

"Who's disappeared?" asked a startled Annalise.

"Beth Penner. She didn't go home last night, and she hasn't turned up at school today. Her father's gotten the police involved. He's especially worried because Beth was best friends with Holly Lezinsky."

"Holly is the dead girl, correct?"

"Yes, that's right."

"And is it true she was murdered?" Mrs. Frampton had dropped her voice while saying the word 'murdered'.

"The police haven't come right out and said so but they are calling it an *unlawful killing* now whereas before it was only a *suspicious death*. I'm not sure what the distinction is but I expect it makes sense to them."

"Well, none of it makes sense to me," complained Mrs. Larkin. "I'm all confused about missing girls, and Noel said something about missing diaries, and the school play having to be cancelled for some reason. I was looking forward to seeing it on Christmas Eve day."

"They had no choice but to cancel the play, Holly had the starring role!" explained Annalise.

"Well there must have been an understudy to the lead part!"

"Audrey," intoned her sister, "think of how it would look if the play had gone ahead. These girls aren't professionals so there's none of this *show must go on* attitude. It would be highly improper."

"And the seats would be half-empty since so many of our families are suffering from this flu bug."

"Nasty thing, the flu. You have to be very careful. We are inoculated against it every year."

"I do wish everyone was as sensible!" said Lila. "It would make my job much easier."

"The shot always makes me sick with a touch of flu for at least a day," stated Audrey Larkin.

"Oh, but you can't get the flu from the virus–" Lila started to explain but was cut off when Audrey replied:

"So, they say. But I know differently."

"Noel is the one who will be getting sick if he doesn't start taking care of himself," said Annalise with a pout. "He looks like he's hardly slept, he's lost his appetite, and have you noticed how pale he is?"

"Of course, I noticed, he is my son after all, but when I commented he snapped my head off."

"Well, he's a man, Audrey, he doesn't like to feel babied."

"A mother's concern is nothing to be ashamed of! Sometimes it's like I'm navigating a minefield, it's very tricky when you have a deeply sensitive child. Motherhood can be very trying at times."

Since none of the other women present were mothers no one responded to this.

"I hope to find out someday," said Annalise looking at Audrey Larkin. The older woman was ready to reply but her sister cut in first saying:

"Noel will make a wonderful father, and I hope he gets to have a daughter since he's so good with the girls. Now ladies, is there nothing more at all that you can tell us about this investigation?"

"There is something that isn't general knowledge yet, although I'm sure it's only a matter of time, and that is the fact that Holly was pregnant when she died." Judith's statement caused a shocked moment of silence while they mulled over this news.

"But she was just a child!" exclaimed Mrs. Frampton at the same time Mrs. Larkin burst out with:

"That's disgusting!"

"This news will knock her off the pedestal Noel has her on," put in Annalise. Again, the women were silenced while they contemplated her words.

"He's so softhearted, he'll be terribly upset when he hears about this."

"It's about time he had his eyes opened."

"I hope knowing this makes it easier for him to move on. He'll realize she wasn't the girl she made herself out to be, and that he wasn't the close confidante he thought he was."

"Holly took her troubles to Noel, did she?" asked Lila.

"All those girls do, but that Holly was the only one who ever had the nerve to phone him here at home," complained Audrey.

"Well, my dear, it will be up to you to distract him from his unhappiness, and the holidays will provide lots of opportunity." Eleanor Frampton was smiling at Annalise and didn't notice the sour look on Audrey Larkin's face.

Judith stood up and Lila hurried to her feet as well. They both felt the tension between the women and were anxious to escape. After giving fulsome thanks to their hostesses, and again admiring the beauty of the house and praising the festive Christmas decorations, they were able to leave.

Once they were in the privacy of the car Lila expelled her breath in a whoosh saying:

"Amazing visit – started with a dog fight and ended with a cat fight."

Chapter 29

Judith drove Lila around the Executive Estates subdivision so they could admire the Christmas decorations on the stately homes before heading back to the school. The places that were set too far back to see from the road usually had some holiday ornamentation at the end of their driveway. Lots of lanterns held by snowmen or Santas or even religious figures, and plenty of light bulbs and *hanging icicle* lights strung along the fence.

The snow that had fallen unseasonably early this year still lay on the lawns and in the trees but the roads were in good shape for driving. Judith voiced her thought out loud:

"Considering the property taxes these homeowners must pay I guess it's only right that they get top-notch snow clearance."

"There sure are plenty of rich people living in Edgemont," said Lila, her head swivelling from one side of the road to the other.

"Especially when you add in the ranchers. They might not go for these fancy homes, but they've got money all right. Often, they look just the same as regular working-class folks with the way they dress and the vehicles they drive but many have substantial wealth, and most are very generous donors to a variety of causes."

After touring for about fifteen minutes they had their fill and Judith headed back to the school.

"When we get in can you check the answering machine for messages, especially for anything related to tonight's meeting? I want to call Dana Lezinsky."

"To invite her to the meeting?" questioned Lila, doubt evident in her voice.

"No, no. I'll tell her about it of course and if she wants me to pass on a message on her behalf I will do so. No, I need to talk to her about Billy MacNeill. Grant wants me to press charges but I want to run that idea by Dana first. If they're back together I've decided that I'll drop it."

"Oh, I do hope she doesn't take him back. He sounds a selfish type of man and any comfort he provides will be short-lived. Imagine, getting her to lie to the police when her only daughter was missing in order to protect himself!"

They separated inside the school with Judith going into Principal Johnson's office to, reluctantly, phone Dana Lezinsky. She did feel sorry about the woman's loss but knew that putting those feelings into words and listening to Dana's emotionalism would be an ordeal. She wasn't good at this sort of thing and she resented being pushed into the role. However, Pat didn't ask to get sick and Judith felt she was obligated to step up.

When the phone rang and rang she had a hopeful moment thinking she was off the hook then chided herself for being such a coward. When Dana did finally answer she sounded like she'd been sleeping.

"Dana, it's Judith Taylor from the school, I'm so sorry did I wake you?"

"No... I haven't really slept but when I sit on the couch I can doze off or zone out... something like that."

"You can't be well if you're not sleeping, are you eating? do you have any appetite?"

"I try to eat. Neighbours and friends from work – and customers even – have all been round with casseroles and easy microwave meals. I don't want to sound sorry for myself–"

"Don't worry about that, you've got a horrible tragedy to deal with and you can feel as sorry as you like. I'm afraid I'm not very good at offering comfort but if there's anything practical I can do, like phoning people on your behalf or taking you to the funeral home, anything like that you mustn't hesitate to call on me. I'm not just saying that," Judith was surprised to discover that she did mean what she said.

Dana replied: "Thank you, that helps. I'm just... I don't know, so unfocused. Nothing seems important. I just... I just miss her so much."

Judith felt at a loss and was disappointed with herself. She wanted to say the right thing but didn't know what that was. Then she realized there is no right thing to say.

"I know you do. We miss her here as well."

"Yes, she wasn't a straight-A student or anything but she had friends and she sure loved being chosen for that play. *The play this* and *the play that* is all we heard around here for weeks! Oh, I never thought... I guess it's cancelled."

"Yes, it has been. Well, Holly was the star."

More sobbing on the other end of the phone. Judith continued with a brisk tone of voice saying:

"Meanwhile I did call for a reason. First though, have you been seen by a doctor? you might be able to get something to help you sleep?"

"Huh! I had Billy round here offering me pills to *take the edge off* – that's his kind of sympathy I guess – but I told him to get out and stay the hell away from me."

"Oh! So he's no longer living there with you."

"No, and good riddance. I mean look what he did, bringing the cops round when I was worried sick about Holly. What if they didn't look as hard as they should have once they knew he was in the picture?"

"Oh I'm sure that's not the case. The two police I met, well one of them is very nice and both of them are professional."

"Well, I still figure I'm better off on my own then having him here. He's a scrounger and a drunk and a waste of space!"

"You are definitely the best judge of what's right for you so *go with your gut* as they say. And that's related to something I wanted to discuss with you. Billy showed up at the school drunk and yelling curse words, not in front of the students, they'd all gone home by then but it was... disturbing. I mentioned it to the police and they asked me to press charges. I wondered what you would think if that happened? I don't want to add to your problems."

"Go ahead! They can pile it on with his other charges. God, he's such a fool and I was too to be taken in by him. The only good thing I can say is my anger at him distracts me from this hole that Holly left behind."

Again, Judith heard sobbing and waited in uncomfortable silence. Finally, Dana gave a loud sniff and Judith said:

"I also wanted to let you know that we're having an informal parents' meeting at the school tonight and people will ask about Holly's death–"

"Her murder!"

"Yes, yes that's right. We'll share that news. We won't mention the pregnancy but if anyone does ask, we'll confirm it in case someone knows something. Someone could have seen or heard something that could lead to the father's identity and who knows what else?"

"All those parents... they're so lucky and they don't even know it! I mean I'm sure they do but not deep down where it gets you. They have no idea. I can't be around parents right now. I'm sorry but I'm not up to coming tonight." said Dana.

Judith hastened to reassure her that she wouldn't dream of asking, "I only mentioned it because I was wondering if there's anything you'd like me to say on your behalf?"

"Oh, well... people have been very kind so could you thank them for me? and tell them when they get home to give their daughters an extra-hard hug because... you just never know."

Chapter 30

After her meeting with the Larkin family Judith realized she's been told next-to-nothing about the investigations into Holly's death and Beth's disappearance. As Acting Head she needed to be kept up-to-date. People were expecting her to know what's going on. Especially with tonight's meeting with the parents.

"It's already been two days since Beth went missing," she reminded herself. "The police need to keep me informed."

She dialled Grant's number but once again had to leave a message. She spoke quite brusquely:

"It's Judith Taylor and I'm waiting for an update on both the Holly Lezinsky and Beth Penner cases. Please get back to me as soon as possible. Thank you."

She hadn't wanted to become involved in the investigation but the parents who phoned and came by the school, and the students, teachers, and benefactors all dragged her into it. "Forcing me into the acting administrator position has pushed my boundaries to the limit. I'm at the edge of my 'comfort zone' and itching to crawl back to the safety of anonymity so the least the police can do is help me out with this new role," she complained to herself.

"Instead, I'm stymied in every conversation. The only responses I can give are *let me find out about that* and *I'll have to get back to you* and that's the problem: I can't deal with these enquiries with a quick and easy answer. Each question always ends with me having to go chasing down an answer and then making another phone-call. It's ridiculous."

She sat there fuming over her thoughts. It was so unfair.

"And the situation with Beth is getting dire. Holly was missing for a week before her body was found, is Beth in danger, too? Does she know something that makes her a risk to someone? or is there a maniac preying on schoolgirls? What about the rest of the students? Or even the teachers – even me – if it's not some guy with a fetish about underage females. What if Beth is already dead?"

She spent a moment considering Brian Penner, Beth's father. He'd already lost his wife – how would he handle it if he lost his only child as well? Judith thought about him working two jobs to provide Beth with a good home and a good school but what did that matter if he wasn't there when she needed him? That's the sort of guilt that could – would – eat away at the survivor, especially a parent. She gave her head a quick shake to clear her thoughts. *No point imagining the worst.*

At that moment her phone rang and she saw from the display that it was Grant calling. Except it wasn't, it was Suzanne using Grant's phone. She sounded amused that Judith could even imagine the police would share information with her but was quick to change her tone when Judith fought back demanding to know why Suzanne had lied to Beth's father.

"I didn't lie--," she began.

"You made up a story about me and the result was you delayed an investigation into a missing child. YOU did that, no one else, and we lost a whole night of searching because of your nonsense."

"I did nothing of the sort, I can't help if people misunderstand–"

"Why are you calling me back? I left a message for Grant, why are you using his phone?"

"I'm returning his calls while he's in a meeting with our boss, that's what partners do. At least, I thought I was returning business calls but maybe you have something else in mind?"

"What are you talking about?"

"Grant's an attractive man but don't imagine he's available because he's not."

"Well I wish he was available to answer his own damn phone," retorted Judith. "Have HIM call me when he can spare the time." And she pressed *end call.* Slamming down the handset of a phone would have been much more satisfying. She wished now she'd called from one of the school's old-style phones.

Chapter 31

As of 5:30 pm Judith, Lila, and Marta were waiting in the lobby to welcome parents. No other teachers were attending. After ten minutes of very stilted small talk they were relieved to spot the headlights of a car turning into the school's driveway, then another, and then several cars in a cluster. It looked like they were going to get a good turnout after all.

Andrea Sealy was first through the door, "no surprise about that," thought Judith. Andrea was followed by the Rasmussens, an older couple; Brian Penner; the Grewals who brought their baby as well; another mother on her own, Debra Andrews; and a slender Chinese woman Judith didn't know. She left Lila and Marta to escort the parents to their seats while she approached the newcomer.

The woman was very chic and surprisingly tall until Judith noticed the thick platform soles on her boots. She was overdressed for a parents' meeting at the school but Judith wondered if she was going on somewhere else or had come from a formal event. Extending her hand Judith said:

"Hi, I'm Judith Taylor, School Bursar and temporary Acting Head."

The woman's small hand was cold but her smile was bright as she introduced herself saying:

"I'm Wendy Zhang, liaison for the Police Information Services."

Judith paused for a moment to consider what an unfortunate acronym that name made.

"I understand you're having a meeting with parents who are concerned and want information about the investigation into the death of your student Holly Lezinsky." She pronounced Holly's surname with some difficulty, and spoke all her words with a slight accent.

"Oh I'm very pleased to meet you! We weren't too hopeful that the police would be able to send someone, and after-hours too. Thank you so much for coming."

Judith was guiding the woman towards the auditorium as she spoke. It wasn't 6:00 pm yet and she wanted to stay by the door. When they arrived in the room she waved Lila over and introduced her to Ms. Zhang.

"I'm going to wait a bit to see if anyone else is coming," she said, then in an aside to Lila added: "Watch Marta and don't let her take charge with the parents."

By time Judith got back to the entrance two more couples had arrived and another mother on her own. She ushered everyone in noticing the slushy trail across the floor despite the visitors stamping snow off their boots. Deciding *any latecomers can locate the meeting by following the wet, messy tracks*, she headed into the auditorium herself.

Judith planned on standing throughout the meeting in the hopes of keeping it short but saw that Marta had placed three chairs facing the audience and she was already seated alongside Wendy Zhang.

Lila rolled her eyes at Judith when she joined them and moved to sit at the back of the room beside Brian Penner. It seemed he wanted to distance himself from the other parents and Judith sympathized, the man looked awful.

Judith welcomed the group and thanked them for coming on such short notice and at such a busy time.

"I'm very pleased to introduce you to Ms. Zhang from the Police Information Services," she said, gesturing to Wendy who immediately stood up to address the parents.

"Hello! you can call me Wendy. Thank you for giving me this opportunity to speak with you–"

Brian Penner interrupted by calling out:

"Where are the real police? Why aren't they here?"

"Why aren't they here? Well, that's because the police investigating this case are out there right now investigating."

"They better be," replied Brian but he didn't add anything further. Judith saw Lila give his hand a couple of light pats.

"Before coming here tonight to meet with you I spoke with the Senior Investigating Officer, Detective George Grant, who has given me a statement to pass on to you. He did ask that I mention to you that this information is only being given out because you are parents. He doesn't want you speaking of it to other people or the press or–"

"Does he seriously think we're going to gossip?" demanded Andrea Sealy.

"Going to gossip? no, I'm sure not, but what I'm going to tell you is sensitive to the family."

Andrea looked ready to speak again but Judith stopped her by saying:

"Please let's let Ms. Zhang, Wendy, give us the statement and then we can ask questions and have our discussion."

She sat back down with a nod to Wendy who continued:

"Thank you, Ms. Taylor. I have the statement of facts to read out." She opened a leather file folder and glanced down at the page. Speaking with care she read out the statement:

"Holly Lezinsky was aged thirteen at the time of her death. The cause of death appears to be murder, but it could possibly be an accident that was then, criminally, covered up by not notifying the authorities of the death and also by moving the body.

Her body was found by a dog-walker at approximately 11:00 in the morning. The same dog-walker, a Mrs. Kellogg, had been walking in that area several hours before and was positive the body was not there then. Mrs. Kellogg frequents that area of School Woods on a regular basis and is considered a trustworthy person and a reliable witness."

The parents were nodding at each other, complacent to be receiving these insider facts. Wendy's next comment had them exchanging shocked looks.

"At the autopsy Holly Lezinsky was found to be pregnant. The Medical Examiner advises it's too early in the pregnancy, believed to be about eleven weeks along, to determine the sex of the baby."

Brian Penner was on his feet with his fists clenched and his pale face now red.

"Holly was PREGNANT?" he bellowed.

Wendy's face was a picture of confused surprise and Judith hurried to explain to her, and any of the parents who didn't already know, that:

"Mr. Penner's daughter Beth, who is missing, was Holly's best friend."

"She can't be pregnant, she's a child. I can't believe this. Did Beth know? she must have if it's true."

"Could Beth be hiding to protect Holly's secret?" asked Debra Andrews. She was a pretty woman but her looks faded beneath a distracted air. She always acted as though her mind was somewhere else and she was worrying that she was supposed to be at some other place. It made conversation with her distracting and difficult.

"Or because she knows who the father is!" cried Brian.

The Grewals looked down at their baby peacefully sleeping in its carry cot. Mrs. Grewal straightened the blanket which was blue so Judith assumed the child was a boy then wondered if the Grewals subscribed to more modern parenting ideas.

"Did she have a boyfriend?" demanded Andrea.

Judith ignored that question. She was surprised Holly's pregnancy had even been mentioned. Turning to Wendy Zhang Judith asked if there was anything else she wanted to add.

"No there is nothing else that I want to add, but I will take questions now and hope I am able to give you some answers."

"I asked, did she have a boyfriend?" repeated Andrea.

Judith answered that question stating:

"To the best of our knowledge, no. I have spoken with Dana Lezinsky, Holly's mother, and she was quite certain about that."

"Of course, parents don't always know, do they?" Judith wondered when Marta was going to jump into the conversation. She decided to let the parents themselves argue with her over that remark, and they did.

"I know about my daughter..."

"You can't just make a blanket statement like that..."

"I know Dana Lezinsky and she's a good mother. It's wrong to imply..."

"Did Holly know she was pregnant? At that age a girl isn't necessarily regular."

Lila stood up from her seat in the back and the parents turned to her when she said:

"Holly did know, she mentioned it to me."

"Did you tell her mother?"

"I'm sorry but Holly's death doesn't release me from my legal responsibilities under the Privacy Act. Medical conversations between me and the patient and the patient's family are confidential. So I'm afraid I can't answer that. Anyhow, it isn't germane to the issue."

"Parents should be told! they have the right to know what's going on with their daughters."

Brian stood up and headed for the door adding:

"Everybody's hiding behind the red tape of can't or won't say. I've had enough of this."

He stormed out and the other parents murmured to each other. Judith believed they sympathized with the man but had been uncomfortable in his presence. She felt the same way.

Marta took the opportunity to slip out of the room as well. Judith wondered if the teacher was following Brian Penner for a private word.

Wendy Zhang also stood up to explain that it was true that the Privacy Act did tie their hands. It was something that she, as a liaison to media, dealt with every day.

"We have to be very careful protecting the rights of our citizens. The press talks about the 'right to know' but we have to do our duty, as well."

"Yes, but we're talking about minors now. As parents we truly do have the right to know what's happening with our girls. I'm sure you can understand our frustration?"

"Yes, I do understand your frustration. It's very difficult at times."

Judith listened to Wendy continually repeating phrases back and wondered if this was a technique of active listening that she'd be trained in or if she was stalling while translating in her mind. Regardless, Judith found it an annoying mannerism.

"Do you have problems with boys hanging around here at the school?" asked Mr. Rasmussen, speaking for the first time.

"I can answer that with a confident 'no,'" said Judith. "The office windows of both Principal Johnson and myself look out over the parking lot and the entrance to the school. If we ever see anyone outside one or the other of us goes and inquires about their business. It doesn't happen often but it has occurred.

In fact, back in November there was a boy who, when questioned, said he was waiting for his sister. Principal Johnson immediately called the student's mother who confirmed that yes, she'd asked her son to pick up her daughter. So we are careful. We understand that you've entrusted your children to our care and we are honour-bound to protect them."

"Of course there are males in the school itself," said Marta. Returning with a tray of Christmas goodies while Xiao followed pushing a trolley-cart loaded with cups and two large jugs of what appeared to be punch with dried bits of cinnamon and lemon peel floating in it.

Ignoring the black look Judith shot her Marta paused her statement to say: "Here's a little seasonal baking of mine. You can't visit Edgemont School at this time of year and not enjoy a nibble or a sip of something festive!"

Xiao pulled two chairs together beside the trolley and Marta set the huge tray down. The guests dutifully got up and sampled the offering. Judith and Lila abstained.

"As I was saying, we can't pretend the girls never meet men at the school because we do have male teachers." Judith kept a blank look on her face but inside she was fuming. How dare Marta start spreading malicious gossip amongst the families?

"But as you all know our teachers are vetted carefully and everyone working or volunteering in this building, male or female, has provided a Police Clearance report. Including our part-time Tae Kwan Do instructor, and the IT people at the computer lab where the older girls go for training. As I said before, we are extremely careful."

Lila chimed in to support Judith stating:

"And we are confident the police will get a result. Detective Grant has visited the school several times over the past couple of days and we've found him very helpful."

Nothing new came up in the ensuing conversation and when one couple made a move to leave the rest hurried to join them, with the exception of Andrea Sealy. She stayed behind after everyone else had said *thank you, good night,* and *Happy Holidays* when they left.

Andrea wanted to speculate about Holly's pregnancy, she wanted to know where the girl had been for the week or so before her body was found, she wanted to know exactly how much Beth Penner knew and how involved she was, but of course no one could answer any of those questions. With a dissatisfied expression on her face she left, complaining that she was running late for a very important function.

Judith and Beth made no move to help Marta and Xiao clean up the mostly untouched goodies. Instead, they walked Wendy Zhang to the door thanking her for her presence.

"It made a difference and we do very much appreciate you coming to help us out."

The young woman beamed at them and they watched her until she was safely inside her car. They stayed in the foyer until Marta and Xiao appeared with their coats on. Neither carried any goodies so Judith expected the leftovers would be produced for the staff next day.

She mentally decided to bring in a couple of dozen fancy doughnuts from that new bakery near her apartment. They were sure to put Marta's treats to shame.

Chapter 32

Judith decided that sitting in Principal Johnson's office meant she was too accessible for interruptions so she moved her laptop back to her own desk in the Library. She got herself nicely settled into the Accounts Receivable when she noticed a student wandering around the main room.

"There are only a handful of students at the school today so why can't the teachers look after them?" she grumbled, angry at herself because she forgot to put up the *Library Closed* sign.

She decided to ignore the girl. Judith kept her head down and focused on her work but she could sense the girl moving closer. It was Margaret Sealy and she meandered over in a curious side-stepping way. Finally arriving in the doorway and hovering there, waiting to be acknowledged.

The nine-year-old daughter and only child of a neurotic and demanding mother. Judith realized she might as well get it over with saying:

"Yes, Margaret? What do you want?"

"You're not the Librarian," replied the girl.

"No, you'll have to come back later or else wait until the new year if you want to see Ms. Callahan."

"You could probably help."

"Mm, doubtful but what is it? I'll try to get you sorted and on your way. Are you looking for a particular book?"

"Actually I don't need that kind of help, I need someone to listen to my project and tell me if it's good enough or if I need to choose something else to work on over the holidays."

"Margaret, the whole point of holidays is to take a break from your chores, tasks, whatever." replied Judith.

"Don't you want to know what our project is about?"

"Not particularly," but seeing Margaret undaunted by her response she relented in order to speed things up: "Okay, tell me about it."

"Well. It's for our Natural Sciences class and we have to find an uncommon fact about an animal that is odd or something and share it with the class. The example the teacher gave us is that sharks are always swimming, even when they're sleeping, because they have to keep moving or they'll die.

So my fact is about ostriches. Now, what's the first thing you think of when you think about ostriches?"

"Hmm, I don't spend much time thinking about ostriches but let's see..." Judith was impressed by Margaret's enthusiasm and decided to play along. "When I do think of ostriches I remember that when they're scared or trying to hide they bury their heads in the sand and think nobody can see them! They're silly."

"HA!" shouted Margaret. "You're wrong! That's what everybody thinks about them, even I did before I read up on them. Ostriches don't do that."

"Oh? You mean them burying their heads in the sand is a myth?"

"No, they do bury their heads but only to protect their eggs because the nests are under the sand. It's not a scared or silly thing to do at all."

"Oh, so that's your little-known fact. I see."

"No, you don't, I haven't even told you what it is yet."

"Ah. Well please hurry along with the story."

"It's not a story. But anyhow, ostriches aren't easy to scare, in fact they're real fighters. They have two toes on each foot (most birds have three, you know) with long, sharp talons. Also, they run really fast so if an ostrich is fighting with you the only thing you can do is climb up a tree. And you have to climb high because they're also very tall and big. But they can't fly so if you can get beyond their reach, you'll be okay."

"Good to know."

"Yes, I think so too. Nobody thinks much about ostriches because they aren't pretty to look at, and because of the burying their heads in the sand thing that makes people think they're stupid or shy or cowards – but they're not. Ostriches fight back."

"Well that's a very good, unusual fact for your project, Margaret. You can go ahead and enjoy the holidays once school lets out."

"Oh I'll be here again tomorrow. My mother has an important engagement. Actually it's the Christmas get-together of her Bridge Group and she's been looking forward to it for weeks. She can't possibly cancel now. She hasn't seen any of the group for the longest time because she's been busy with her Christmas crafts and shopping and decorating. So I'll be in class tomorrow. My mother said the school is still open."

"Yes, we'll be here and it sounds like you will be as well. Why don't you go find a book with photos of ostriches and draw a nice picture of one?"

"Why don't I photocopy it?"

"Because a hand drawing takes more time which shows you've made more of an effort."

"But a photo is way more professional looking."

"True, but does a Grade Two project need to look professional?"

"I'm not in Grade Two," Margaret indignantly replied, "I'm in Grade Three!"

"Even so..."

"I've already read all of the books on ostriches but there might be something in the National Geographic magazines. I suppose I could take a look."

Without a word of thanks for the help or an apology for the interruption the girl turned away and headed to the Periodicals section.

Still," thought Judith to herself, "It is true that I never knew ostriches could fight."

Chapter 33

Judith heard the library door open and sighed deeply. She'd put up the *Library Closed* sign after Margaret Sealy had finally left but now someone else had entered. She sat waiting for the intruder to come and pester her. It seemed no matter where she went she couldn't escape the interruptions. She was starting to feel frustrated.

After a minute or so, when no one appeared she wondered if it was a library patron – and nothing to do with her. Lovely thought but unfortunately it didn't seem likely since she'd also turned out the lights when she'd hung up the sign. Anyone browsing for a book would switch the lights on right away. The library only had windows on one wall and the wintry December sky didn't shed much light anyhow.

Annoyed, Judith threw down her pen and marched into the main room calling: "Who's here? what do you want?" into the darkened room but no one answered. "WHO IS THERE?" she hollered, angry now. Still, no one stepped forward.

Judith became very aware of how isolated she was in this room that anyone on the outside would think was empty. She tamped down feelings of fear because this was her realm, and she wasn't going to be chased out of it.

As she drew a deep breath to bellow her demand that the intruder reveal themself, she heard a light tap-tap and realized someone was knocking on the door. She marched over and yanked it open to see a surprised-looking Grant standing there.

"I thought that was your voice I heard," he commented. "Is everything okay?"

"No, it's not. I can't seem to get a moment's peace. I came here to get away from everyone and yet I've had non-stop visitors! Well, the last one hasn't even visited – it's somebody playing a joke, hiding out in here."

"What do you mean? There's someone else in here? In the dark? Well let's put on the lights--" but he didn't get the chance to complete his sentence before a figure came hurtling from behind the stacks and knocked Grant to the ground before fleeing out the open door.

Judith was startled and bent to help Grant up, she never even thought of pursuing the person. Grant struggled to his feet and hurried into the hall but there was no sign of anyone in either direction.

"Who was that?" he demanded.

"I have no idea. I heard someone come in but when I called out to them they didn't answer. I thought it must be one of the girls playing games."

"That was no girl, that was a man. What did he want in here? with you?"

The stared at each other for a moment and Judith felt fearful. Grant's look was full of concern yet she hadn't even considered that she might have been in any kind of danger. But why would a man skulk around in the dark library, drawing her out of her room with his silence? Was he waiting to catch her unawares? waiting to pounce?

"Was it that Billy MacNeill again?"

"No, definitely not. He's in jail."

"You've caught him! Where's Beth?"

"No, sorry, we arrested Billy MacNeill on other charges. He has an alibi for when Holly went missing and for the time when her body got dumped outside your woods.

He did want an alibi from Dana Lezinsky but only to prevent us discovering his other crime. He's involved in what's called a *chop shop*: stolen cars dismantled – chopped up – for parts that are sold out of the country. The garage is in Calgary, and he was there for several days over the time period in question."

"So he didn't kill Holly and he doesn't have Beth."

"We don't know that anyone actually has Beth. She might be hiding for reasons of her own."

"For this long? No, I can't believe that. Beth is a quiet girl – Holly was the leader in that friendship, she had all the initiative. I can't see Beth staying away on purpose. She'd have to realize her father is worried sick."

"But maybe worrying him – punishing him – is the point? I seem to remember that the girls I knew as a teenager all hated their parents."

"Hmm, Beth does have a lot of autonomy for a girl her age and it could be that she's a bit resentful and is trying to get her father's attention. I suppose that's possible, it's not something I would have imagined though."

"You've always had a good relationship with your father, then?"

"Oh no. Well yes, Dad was great, but he died when I was quite young so I really can't say."

"I'm sorry to hear that. It must have been hard growing up without him."

"Yes actually, it was..." Judith paused for a moment remembering and Grant gave her space. "But getting back to the intruder – if it wasn't Billy MacNeill, and it wasn't a student, who could it be?"

"Judith, I mean Ms. Taylor—"

"Judith is fine."

"Thank you. Judith, is anyone angry with you for some reason?"

"Other than Suzanne Mireau?"

"I'm being serious. Could anyone have any reason to harm you?"

"No! Why would they?"

"Could they think you know something that could shed light on Holly's murder?"

"It is murder for sure, is it?"

"Yes, I'm afraid so. Well, moving the body made murder seem probable although someone could do that trying to cover up a drug overdose or something. However, the coroner has now confirmed that evidence of perimortem bruising and injury has shown that the blow to the head wasn't accidentally inflicted."

"Poor girl."

"Especially since she didn't die immediately. There's no way to know for sure but it's possible that if whoever hit her had called 9-1-1 something could have been done to save her."

"So, the poor girl lay there dying alone until that person came and moved her."

"We don't know that she was alone, and it was only a matter of an hour or two – not days."

"But she was either killed and her body stored somewhere, or kept alive for days and then killed. Either scenario is awful to contemplate. All the while we were thinking she'd run off with some boy she was dead or being held prisoner. So what about Beth? We can't be sure she's playing up to get back at her father, what if she's been imprisoned too?"

"Could someone think Beth has been in touch with you? Could that be the reason this person broke in?"

"But I wasn't able to get hold of Beth! I went to her house, I've phoned repeatedly, her father came to the school to talk to me. By the way I let your Suzanne know what I thought about her for that."

"She's not 'my' Suzanne. So, you called her to talk?"

"We talked but I didn't call her I called you. Look, I've been pretty frustrated with everyone asking me questions and me not knowing anything despite having to be in charge here at school so I phoned you to get some answers. I left a message. Since you were in a meeting with your boss Suzanne returned the call."

"Wait a sec, I want to be absolutely clear about this: Suzanne answered a message you'd left for me on my phone?"

"Yes, but I didn't mind. It was a business call after all, no matter what she said."

"What did she say?"

"I forget the exact words – something about you not being available. As if I care whether or not you're married or her boyfriend or anything."

"I'm not married, and I don't have a girlfriend. And I would never choose Suzanne to be my girlfriend."

"Grant you don't need to explain your personal life to me. It's none of my business," said Judith, feeling a little puzzled by the look Grant was giving her.

She felt her head spin with thoughts of the intruder, of Beth, of Holly, and Billy MacNeill having an alibi. Unaccustomed tears threatened to spill and she turned away from Grant and headed back into her office. He followed but she told him her head was pounding and all she wanted was to be alone.

"I'm sorry Judith but I don't think you should be. At least, not here in the library. Go to the staff-room or get someone to stay in the principal's office with you. We can't be sure that the man who sneaked in here isn't hiding somewhere else in the building."

"Oh great, that's helped my headache enormously. Thank you so much."

"I'm sorry, but I want to keep you safe."

"No Grant, I'm the one who should apologize. I realize you're a policeman who is only doing his job. If it wasn't so early in the day I would go home."

Grant's manner was diffident as he asked, "Would there be anyone at home to keep you company?"

"No, I live alone but I have been thinking of getting a cat."

Chapter 34

Judith walked through the school hallways opening each classroom door and checking to see if there was a teacher or any students inside. Grant trailed along behind, keeping her company until she paired up with someone else. Safety in numbers. Judith still believed the incident in the library must have been a prank of some sort, she couldn't think of any reason why anyone would want to harm her.

"Oh and I'm sorry but I forgot – I should have thanked you for sending Ms. Wendy Zhang along to our Parents' Meeting. She was very nice and, surprisingly considering our parents, we only had one brief issue when she caused offence by warning them off talking to the press. You know," she stopped and gave him a searching look,

"It really is something that the media hasn't been camped out on our front lawn. I mean the murder of a young student, who was pregnant, at an All-Girls School – those are all the ingredients for over-the-top sensationalism and lurid headlines. Honestly, it's a wonder they've left us alone."

"I suspect you can thank Eleanor Frampton for that. She's got *friends in high places* and with her nephew working here well... money talks."

"Well, I can only say that I hope it keeps talking until we shut down for the year."

"It is a nice break not to have my footsteps dogged by shouting reporters pushing their microphones and cameras in my face. It's so difficult to shake the press once a story hits the headlines."

"Oh of course, the party! That will explain it."

They'd resumed walking but this time it was Grant who stopped and turned to Judith saying that didn't explain anything to him.

"There's a big party scheduled for the 24th to celebrate Noel Larkin's birthday and Christmas. It's an annual event and sounds like quite the gala. All kinds of bigwigs and assorted influential people will be attending and they certainly won't want to fight their way through a crowd of reporters going in and coming out again. It's probably some high-profile invitee who has brought pressure on the media."

"I didn't know anything about this party, I wasn't invited," said Grant.

"No? I'm not going either," Judith replied, ending that conversation.

Continuing down the corridor she discovered two teachers with only a handful of students in two classrooms and suggested they might like to join up in one room and have a singsong or play a game. The teachers were happy to comply.

With renewed determination Judith headed for the staff room. She stifled a giggle at the image of herself elbowing open the bat-wing doors of the saloon in an old-fashioned Western looking for a showdown but that's how it felt.

Over these past few days Judith had come to realize how much animosity there was between the teaching and the administrative staff. She felt it was one-sided, on the teachers' part, but was honest enough to admit that she'd never made any friendly overtures herself.

Perhaps Lila, with her fun and friendly attitude, would be the one to bridge the gap.

Grant left her outside the staff room door saying he'd check in again later. When Judith stepped out of the alcove silence descended on the room but she didn't get the impression they'd been talking about her. Which made a nice change.

"Where's Cindy Callahan?" she asked.

"The Librarian went home because there are no Library Classes today," said Xiao in a sulky, challenging manner. Marta was quick to jump in and add:

"And Cindy wasn't feeling too well. She worried that she might be coming down with the flu bug and didn't want to pass it around."

Xiao caught on and hurried to add,

"Yes, that's right. Cindy said she was ill so it was lucky she didn't have Library Classes."

"I hope she doesn't have the flu, that would ruin her holidays," replied Judith mildly. Marta and Xiao looked at her warily but the other teachers in the room regarded her with interest.

"A student came into the library while I was in my office and I don't want the girls wandering around the school unsupervised."

"Well, you can't expect us to babysit!" exclaimed Xiao.

"If that's what you call looking after your young charges then yes, that's exactly what I expect."

"We don't work for you." Marta chimed in.

"No, but you do work for the parents of the girls who are in this school today. I saw that Jennifer and Joanna each only had a few students so they've combined into one classroom. What I want to know is does anyone have any ideas about entertaining the students along with keeping an eye on them?"

Tanya, who taught History and Science, spoke up:

"What about watching a movie? Eddie, I've got the DVDs I borrowed from you in my bag because I wanted to return them before the holidays. It's *The Bill Murray Collection* and it includes the movie *Scrooged*."

"There's a DVD player in the Library," said Judith. "That sounds like a very good idea that should see us through pretty much to the end of the day. In fact, we could do this again tomorrow if any students show up."

"Is *Scrooged* age-appropriate?" asked Marta.

"Let's see what it says on the box," answered Tanya. She went to her locker and took out a bag with a set of DVDs inside and read the cover.

"It says PG-13 but I watched the movie a couple of nights ago and honestly there's nothing to worry about for the younger students. Just like with Bugs Bunny cartoons – the adult allusions will go over their heads."

"I've got other Christmas movies I can bring in for tomorrow," said Eddie. "I've got *Elf* and *The Santa Claus* and, well I guess *Bad Santa* isn't a good idea..." The teachers who knew that movie laughed along with him.

"That's great, thanks, all of you, for helping out. I'll go see if I can find some snacks in the kitchen."

"I'll get this movie set up," said Eddie with Tanya adding that she'd round up the kids and bring everyone to the Library.

"I guess I'll stay here and listen for important phone messages – like from the police or even another one from Beth Penner." Marta's comment had a chilling effect but Judith chose to let it pass and simply said:

"Thank you, Marta. That will be a great help."

Tanya and Eddie left the staff-room with her. In the corridor Tanya stopped Judith saying:

"We've been discussing something and want you to know that there's been some talk, and I know it's second-hand gossip but anyways, some of the students have told teachers that they saw Noel Larkin kissing Holly Lezinsky."

"What! Noel? No, that.. well, what do you think? Are they making it up?"

"No," said Eddie explaining: "It not only the students who have seen things. I've witnessed stuff myself but what I saw seemed innocent. I don't want to imply that there's been any kind of wrongdoing, but I do think you should know that things are being said."

"To give you a heads-up, like," added Tanya.

"I appreciate that. Stepping into the principal's shoes, even just for a few days, is burden enough without being blindsided if I'm questioned by a parent about this. So, what exactly have you heard, and seen?"

The two teachers signalled to each other with their eyes and then spoke quickly as though relieved to get it out.

"This usually just happens at rehearsals, but they do stuff like hold hands and exchange notes and laugh together over private jokes."

"They whisper and giggle a lot."

"The other girls in the play became quite jealous of all the attention Noel was giving to Holly but that could be explained by the role she was playing. They've written their own play so I don't know details but Holly was the lead and Noel said it was all part of the coaching. That could be true."

"Has anything like this happened with other students, in leading roles in the plays from other years?"

"I never heard any rumours until Holly got cast as the star."

"Ah, it sounds like you think it might be what, sour grapes or something?"

"Or it could be because Holly is now a tragic-romantic figure, at least to adolescent girls. Kind of a Juliet Capulet."

"Yes, I see. Do you think I should say anything to the police about the tales?" Judith was actually wondering if the two teachers were telling her this hoping for that exact result but instead they said:

"Oh, I don't know if I'd go that far."

"It could cause problems – unfairly, like."

"You're right. They don't know Noel like we do and anything like this well, I wouldn't want to give them ideas. The lead detective seems very level-headed, but his partner is definitely given to flights of fancy. It's enough that we know about the rumours and can quash any speculation or exaggerations."

"That's right. We felt you should know, but a teacher's reputation is easy to tarnish with innuendo."

"Especially a male teacher in an all-girls school!"

"Thank you very much for passing this on." After they separated Judith found herself speculating about Noel and Holly. She couldn't believe he could be so foolish but if Annalise was anything like Cindy Callahan then all of her conversation would revolve around the wedding with questions like what colour for this? who should sit where? what kind of music? Holly, on the other hand, could provide Noel with the true *girlfriend experience*. Starry-eyed admiration, a young girl's innocent delight, sweet stolen kisses... enough to turn any man's head.

She was glad the teachers hadn't urged her to pass their information on to the police.

Chapter 35

A search of the kitchen cupboards unearthed an unopened box of microwave popcorn. Judith zapped several bags which made a horrible stink but were welcomed with enthusiasm by the moviegoers.

She saw them all settled then went into her office to finish her Accounts Receivable work. She wanted to come back after the holidays to a fresh start.

She thought it likely that most people felt this way in January. Of course, academics and other school workers also felt this in September. Judith started at Edgemont School for Girls almost ten years ago so her life followed the rhythm of the school year although she didn't get to stop work for ten weeks each summer.

While at University she'd applied for entry-level positions at several accounting firms who offered placements to graduates. She'd been accepted by a few of them since her grades were very good. She chose the largest company but found it to be a soulless environment. Sitting in a cubicle working her way through that day's assignments wasn't particularly fulfilling but that wasn't the problem. It was overhearing a comment her boss made to his boss that disillusioned Judith.

The man was boasting that he only hired what he called *the perfect accounting personality type* and went on to disparage all of his employees for being timid and easy to burden with extra work. Some of them could be attractive – if they'd made an effort – but with no social graces. Easy to intimidate, subordinate, fearful little people. Judith had burned with shame hearing his contemptuous words spoken so condescendingly.

That's when she resolved to find a job where she could be in charge of her own domain and Edgemont School was the answer. She was over-qualified for the work, and it meant a drop in pay, but Judith settled well into the school environment. It was Principal Johnson who hired her and Judith was grateful that the woman was willing to take a chance on her. Both of them were satisfied with the result.

She looked out of her office window to her view of the parking lot and a bit of the front driveway. The sky was full of snow and a sleety mix was falling. Not a pleasant day.

Judith thought about the scheduled vacation she'd been forced to forego and decided she wasn't missing out on anything. Her plan had been to drive to various hiking trails in Kananaskis Country and enjoy bracing fresh air and the quietude of a snowy mountain landscape. Winter in southern Alberta meant cold temperatures with sunny skies of bright blue but so far this year the weather was milder and wetter.

Even if the weather had co-operated the shortened days would have meant long nights indoors on her own. She had books to read, streaming TV to watch, and an Internet connection but the restlessness she'd been feeling the last few days made her dissatisfied with her own company.

It was odd, she'd never acknowledged being lonely before, but she suspected that's what she was feeling now. The thought of a cute kitty was even more appealing.

She shut down her laptop and turned out the office light before joining the others to watch the rest of the movie.

Chapter 36

After the movie was over Judith was tidying up the library when Lila walked in saying:

"Aha! so this is where you've been. I thought the handsome detective might have whisked you away for a *tete-a-tete*."

"Don't be silly." Judith was embarrassed to feel her cheeks get warm. "Where have you been?"

"Tending to the sick. We've got one teacher and a couple more students down with the flu. I've been nursing them until someone could come pick them up. The flu is an awful illness and people don't give it the respect it deserves. I can't understand why people don't get the flu vaccination: it's free and it's easy to get. I hope you take the shot."

"Every year. I had flu once and let me tell you, when you're single and you've got the flu it's the worst. I was only bad for about three days but those three days were utterly miserable. I piled every blanket I owned – plus my winter coats – on top of me and I was still shivering. In fact, I thought I had bugs crawling on me and when there was nothing to see I was afraid I was hallucinating. Turned out that sweat was pouring out of my skin so fast it felt like insects running up and down my sides!

I lay there sweating and shivering and wishing someone would run me a bath and then wash my sheets while I was in it but of course there was no one to do that so I suffered and felt sorry for myself. I've gotten the flu shot every year since!"

"The flu is a killer, especially of the elderly, and people end up in hospital because of dehydration. It's a shame you had to learn the hard way but at least you did learn something. What about other vaccines?"

"I've had the one for shingles and when I reach age 65 I'll get the pneumonia shot as well. Our benefit plan paid for most of my shingles vaccine and the pneumonia one is free for seniors."

"Hmm, might not be by time you're a senior."

"Oh great, thanks for that..."

"I only meant it's because you're too young to be talking about what you'll be doing as a senior."

"I know how old you are, Lila, and I'm the same age. Anyhow, if I have to buy that shot I will do so."

"Yeah, it was the shingles vaccine I was wondering about and I'm glad to hear you got it. That is a nasty infection and it's extremely painful, too."

"I heard that if you get shingles around your waist and the circle of rash joins up you'll die but that's just an old wives' tale, right?"

"Right, but you'd be in such agony you might wish you were dead!"

"I knew someone who had it when she was younger than me and she recommended I get the vaccine so I did."

"Good for you. That's being sensible. Now, let's move away from sensible and into the realm of speculation..."

"What do you mean?"

"Welllll, let's be BFFs and you tell me your deepest, darkest secrets. What's been on your mind lately?"

"As a matter of fact, I've been thinking about buying a mobile home."

"What?"

"Yeah, I rent right now, and it will take forever for me to afford to buy but when I visited Dana Lezinsky at the Trailer Park I was impressed. It wasn't at all like what I thought it would be. The whole complex is very well-kept and the actual trailers are quite roomy and—"

"Stop! that's not what I'm talking about! I want to hear what's happening with you and Grant."

"Me and Grant? Nothing. There's nothing happening, why would there be?"

"Well he likes you and don't you think he's good-looking? His colouring is unusual and he's very attractive."

"Mmm, yeah. I suppose he is."

"You suppose?"

"I've never been attracted to blond men. Except for Peter O'Toole in *Lawrence of Arabia*, that is."

"Oh God yeah, when the camera does that close-up of his blue eyes in his sunburnt face... to die for!"

"True! but Grant doesn't have that colour of hair or eyes: he's white-blond with pale blue compared to Peter O'Toole's yellow-blond with bright blue."

"But he's got a look that's so, I don't know, aloof or something? Totally hot, eh?"

"That reminds me – if we're going to tell-all what's the scoop about you being married? Where's your husband?"

"Oh, that's a story for another day. I'll require a whole bottle of wine all to myself before I can get into that tale. Hey, I would actually be drinking the whole bottle since you are my non-drinking companion. But anyways I asked first. So, tell me the truth: you aren't interested in Grant?"

"As anything other than the detective who I hope is going to solve this case? no, I'm not. I'm not looking to meet anyone. Do you remember that old Simon and Garfunkle song 'I Am A Rock?' well, that's me. I'm a rock that feels no pain."

"Nobody can love a rock, Judith."

"Love? I will fall in love when... hmm, I can't say when hell freezes over because climate change, eh?"

"Omigod you made a joke! Now stop avoiding the question and tell me what you think of Grant?"

"Okay, he's personable and yes, he is good-looking, seems intelligent and common-sensical and I expect he'd make a great friend but that's it, that's all I feel."

"Really?"

Judith laughed saying: "You sound disappointed."

"I am! First of all because he's I can see that he's interested in you, and secondly it would put that Suzanne in her place, and thirdly I'm a born matchmaker. So if not Grant what about Brian Penner?"

"Brian Penner! are you serious? the man's told us repeatedly that he's frantic over his daughter. Finding Beth is the only thing on his mind, why would you even think about him in those terms?"

"Because he's drop-dead gorgeous, that's why!"

"He's... yeah, I guess but sorry, I can't get past his red-rimmed eyes from tears or lack of sleep or both."

"Well I didn't put your phone number in his phone for nothing you know."

"Lila!"

"Oh don't Lila me, he's extremely handsome and so macho too."

"I don't believe you," said Judith, shaking her head. She wasn't sure how serious Lila was being, this kind of bantering back and forth was a new experience for her.

"And I don't think I believe you about Grant being only a friend. You told me that you've called him a couple of times..."

"As part of his job, and my job. That's it."

"Mmm, so you say.."

"It's true. Grant is nothing more than like a work colleague and even that's only going to be temporary. Until the cases are solved."

"'Methinks the lady doth protest too much.'"

"I'm not! Believe me the last thing I'm looking for is a date. And by the way I'm not Lady MacBeth."

"Oh, is that where that's from? I thought it was Hamlet."

"You're right it is."

"Good way to change the subject, Judith. Anyhow I heard some of the girls singing in the hallway *Cop and Bursar sitting in a tree, k-i-s-s-i-n-g, first comes love—*"

"No students were singing that! although I wouldn't put it past the teachers!"

"They left the library laughing and there was Grant waiting in the hall.

"What are you doing here again?" asked Judith.

"I wanted to discuss something with you. About the case."

Lila smiled and gave them a little wave as she walked on. They could hear her singing softly:

"...then comes marriage, then comes baby in a baby carriage."

Grant raised an eyebrow at Judith who felt her cheeks blush as she hurried to explain:

"That was something from the movie we watched. Anyhow, you said you had something to discuss?"

"I'd rather not have the conversation here, if you don't mind, could we go get a Tim Horton's or something?"

"Oh, sure. Before we go let me check for messages on the answering machine and I'll grab my coat and meet you out front."

"I'll walk with you, and you can tell me more about this movie you saw."

Judith gave him a sharp glance, but his expression was bland.

Chapter 37

None of the messages on the school's answering machine required a call back so Judith grabbed her coat and she and Grant headed out of the building. Unfortunately, they were forced to stay by the presence of Margaret Sealy in the foyer.

"Why are you still here, Margaret?"

"No one came to pick me up."

"Alright, who can we call to come and get you?"

"There's only my mother and I've called and called. There's no answer. I left a message on the home phone, and I even called her cellphone – although I'm not supposed to – and left a message there. Why do people carry phones around with them if they're not going to answer them?"

"It looks like something's come up. Whereabouts do you live?"

"At the Executive Estate."

"Oh, that's where Mr. Larkin lives, right?"

"Yeah, his home is a couple of houses down. Sometimes Mr. Larkin takes me home but I haven't seen him today."

"No, I haven't seen Noel either. He should have been in school today. If he called in someone else took the message. Well, that's okay I will drive you home. Phone back your mother at both numbers and leave a message to let her know."

She turned to Grant saying:

"We'll have to have that discussion another time. I'll be here again tomorrow."

"Actually, it would be much better to do it tonight. You'll understand when I explain everything. Look, why don't I come with you two and after we drop off Margaret," he looked at the girl and smiled a hello, "we can grab a coffee then. Or we can talk in the car on the return trip."

"I can't get into a car with a stranger," announced Margaret.

"But I'm not a stranger and it's my car so that should be okay."

"I don't think so. He's still a stranger."

"He's a policeman."

"Are you? Can I hold your gun? Do you have a badge?"

"Yes. No. Yes, again – would you like to see it?"

Margaret giggled at his answer and Judith was surprised because Margaret was definitely not a giggly type of girl. She decided Grant's looks must be more appealing than she thought.

"Yes, I need to know what it says. What's your name? and don't look at the badge before you tell me."

"My name is George Grant and I'm a detective." He handed over the slim wallet that housed his badge and Margaret inspected it carefully – even running her finger over the embossed lettering.

"Okay Detective George Grant, you can accompany us in Ms. Taylor's car," she decided.

Judith locked the front door and they hurried to the car park. The air was cold with a chilly dampness but at least the drizzle of sleet had stopped. The parking lot was slippery underfoot but once they got on the main road the salt and gravel laid down by the maintenance crews had done its job and the tires got traction.

Margaret chattered away. She discussed the plot of *Scrooged* and explained which parts of the movie she loved and which she hated. Margaret Sealy didn't like or dislike, she lived her emotions to the extreme.

"It sure wasn't like the real movie."

"It was a real movie, Margaret."

"You know what I mean. The one where Alistair Sims plays Scrooge, and he wears a funny nightgown and a hat with a tassel. That was way better."

"The actor's name is Sim, not Sims. But I agree with you, I preferred the original."

"I don't think that is the original, there was one made in the thirties," commented Grant.

"Really? who was in that version?"

"Oh, I've no idea, I never saw it. In fact I haven't seen *Scrooged*, I've only seen the Alistair Sim one. I liked it."

"I loved it," replied Margaret. "But you know, the character of Scrooge might only pretend to change because he got scared by the ghosts. After awhile he might not change at all."

"Hmm, that's quite insightful for someone in Grade Three, Margaret. What do you think, Grant?"

"Yes, but there's another layer of truth that you haven't reached yet."

"What do you mean?"

"Well, there's the top layer – the surface – where Scrooge has his eyes and his purse opened. And then there's the second layer – his subconscious – where he's been frightened by the ghosts and thoughts of his own mortality into behaving properly. Are you with me so far?"

"Yes, of course, what's the next layer?"

"Ah, that's his heart and soul. In his heart of hearts, he always knew his greed was wrong. Greed is one of the Seven Deadly Sins, but he conveniently forgot that. But the soul wants to be good and to do the right thing so when the opportunity arose his heart and soul conquered his miserliness, chased away his fears, and opened him up to love."

Nine-year-old Margaret Sealy only understood half of what Grant said but from the look on her face and in her shining eyes he'd won her over completely. She loved him with the sudden devotion of an awestruck child. Judith found herself feeling a bit sentimental as well.

Then Margaret broke the spell by saying: "So it's like the World Wide Web, the Deep Web, and the Dark Web, right?"

"What on earth do you mean? What are all these 'webs', Margaret?"

"Oh, you know, Ms. Taylor. The World Wide Web is what everybody goes on when they're surfing the Internet. The Deep Web is where the banks and you know, hospitals, put their secret stuff. Everybody can go into the Deep Web but only if they have the right log-in passwords. Then there's the Dark Web where all the criminals hang out and do crime. I don't know much about it because every computer I get to use has parental controls on it. Even the floor models at Best Buy!"

Judith looked helplessly at Grant who turned to look at Margaret who hung over the back of his seat.

"Are you wearing your seat-belt?"

"Is that all you've got to say?"

"I know you heard me, but I'll repeat myself: are you wearing your seat-belt?"

Margaret flung herself back and they heard a click as she buckled up.

"There are you happy now?"

"Ecstatic."

"So, are the Scrooge layers like the web layers? You didn't answer."

"I'm afraid to answer a child as precocious as you."

Margaret thought that reply was hilarious. Looking out the car window she hollered:

"You passed it. Back up, back up!"

Judith complied and pulled into the driveway of a house with an ultra-modern design. The facing wall was blank but huge slanted windows ran up both sides. Andrea Sealy stood in the entrance holding the door open. She was wearing her coat, hat, and boots evidently having just arrived home herself. Margaret hopped out of the car saying:

"Thank you for the ride, Ms. Taylor. Bye," and ran halfway up the brick walkway before spinning round to yell:

"Goodbye to you too, Detective George Grant."

As Judith reversed out of the driveway back onto the road Grant commented:

"Are they all like that?"

Chapter 38

Judith continued driving away from the village centre towards the highway. That's where the Tim Horton's and other fast-food franchises were located.

As Grant made easy conversation, she realized that he was the first man to ever sit in her car. Judith was aware of the intimacy of the two of them travelling in a darkened car but felt completely comfortable. She was starting to see Grant as the man who could possibly be a friend instead of just Grant the policeman.

When they arrived at the coffee shop and saw the harsh indoor lighting Judith suggested they use the drive-thru and have their coffee and discussion in the parking lot. Grant readily agreed saying:

"You're not going to like what I have to say so it's best to have the conversation in private."

"That sounds ominous. Although if you're willing to be out in public having coffee with me, I guess I'm not on the verge of arrest!"

"Not you, but... let's get settled first."

They were served with coffees – his a double-double, hers milk only – and doughnuts – his a Boston Cream, hers a plain old-fashioned – with quick efficiency and were soon parked in a far corner of the lot. Each half-turned in their seat to face the other and use the cup holders for their hot drinks.

"What I'm about to tell you is in confidence. The decision stems from a meeting I had yesterday with my boss. I don't agree with the action we're about to take but I gave my opinion and that's that. I have to do what I'm told which is bring in Annalise Sutherland for questioning in the death of Holly Lezinsky."

"WHAT? Annalise? No way."

"Well, there's evidence of trouble between her and Holly. We have witnesses to an argument Annalise had with Noel about Holly, also another person witnessed Annalise having a very heated discussion with Holly herself."

"How did you find these witnesses? There were no interviews with students in the school because I would have had to be present if that was the case."

"You're right, I would have called on you to be the *appropriate adult* but these witnesses, and yes, they were students, came to us at the police station."

"But they're teenagers!"

"They came with an adult, that teacher I met at the school, Marta Smith."

"Oh, Good Lord. She's such an interfering, nasty... ugh! Please tell me what happened, what was said, and when."

"They came in yesterday. Remember she was out front along with Suzanne and me when you arrived?"

"Yes, I was a bit late. Despite driving slowly, I was still clipped in a fender bender."

"Why didn't I know about that?"

"Because I never had a chance to say anything before Suzanne attacked me about playing Nancy Drew, remember?"

"Right. Well, your car seems to be running fine, is your bumper damaged?"

"I have no idea, I forgot to look. If there's anything it won't be much and, after all, that's what bumpers are for."

"You didn't look? What about the other car, did you look at that?"

"Oh, sorry I didn't explain. The other car didn't even stop. He, or she, was driving right behind me – and following too close – the whole way to school but when I arrived all of a sudden the car sped past me dinging my rear bumper in the process."

"A hit-and-run. Doesn't sound like you got a licence plate, or did you?"

"No, I was too busy trying to control my car from skidding straight into one of those big old trees that line the road just there. I was lucky that I didn't hit anything and was able to get into the driveway."

"I'm sorry to hear about this and sorry too that you never got a chance to mention it. You must have been pretty shaken up."

"I was, but the argument with Suzanne did a great job of putting it out of my mind!" she said with a laugh. "Anyhow, go on with what you were saying about Marta."

"Oh yes. Well, while we were waiting for you Marta said she had someone who wanted to talk to me about Holly's case but not at the school so could she bring them to the police station? I said *of course* and we arranged a time.

When she arrived, she actually had three teenagers with her. Two of them didn't do much more than nod but the third girl made a clear statement and answered all the questions we put to her.

She's stated that Annalise often dropped by during rehearsals and on one occasion, shortly before Holly disappeared, when Annalise arrived she caught Noel with his arm around Holly's shoulders. The two of them were reading her part in the script but Annalise started yelling that she was *fed up with his behaviour with this girl.* Everyone at the rehearsal heard it and Noel grabbed Annalise by the arm and drew her away from the stage where everyone was watching. It seems Annalise didn't lower her voice and didn't care who heard her.

They couldn't hear Noel's side of the conversation because he kept his voice low, but it was obvious he was trying to calm her down. The girl—"

Judith interrupted asking: "Which girl?" but Noel shook his head and said they were minors, and he wasn't naming any names. Then he continued with the statement:

"So, the girl reported that Annalise said things like *he needed to get his head straight* and *why was he jeopardizing everything?* and *why this girl? what's so special about her?*. I gather the whole cast was eagerly listening to every word. Afterwards they talked about nothing else and when Holly went missing, they discussed telling someone and finally chose Ms. Smith as their confidante. *Because she heard us talking about it anyhow and asked for an explanation* the girl told me.

I asked Ms. Smith why she hadn't passed the information on to the police, but it seems she thought the girls had 'blown the whole thing out of proportion in order to dramatize themselves'. Once

Holly's body was discovered the girls were afraid to say anything because they didn't want to get Mr. Larkin in trouble. None of them seem to care too much for or about Annalise Sutherland."

"No, I expect they're jealous of her engagement to Noel."

"Sounds to me like there's plenty of jealousy going around."

"Ha! you haven't met Mrs. Larkin, Noel's mother, yet. She's the most possessive of them all! But you can't seriously think Annalise kidnapped this girl, killed her, held her body for days – God knows where because she's staying at Noel's place for the holidays – then put her in a car and dumped her in the woods. I don't even know if Annalise can drive, she's always got a chauffeur when she comes to the school."

"I pointed out the unlikelihood of Ms. Sutherland being able to do any of those things and my superior said it was up to me to figure out how it was done because, obviously, it was done."

"That's helpful. So tonight you're going to go to the Larkin's home to arrest Annalise?"

"Not arrest and not tonight. No, I'll be picking her up tomorrow morning and taking her into the police station for questioning. I'm sure they'll call a lawyer for her and we're hoping we'll get a statement. I have to act on the evidence and if the Sutherlands and Larkins weren't such influential people I bet I would have been given a warrant for her arrest but for now I only get to ask questions."

"That's all to the good actually because I'm sure she didn't do it and this way you won't get sued for wrongful arrest."

"If she's got an alibi the whole thing won't take long at all."

"But an alibi for when, exactly?"

"Exact is the one thing we can't be. However, we know Holly left the school about 17:30 on December 12th but she never arrived home. She was by herself having told Beth Penner that she didn't want company, she 'had some thinking to do' on her own."

"Wait a minute, that reminds me: is there any news about Beth?"

"No, nothing yet. We've talked to classmates and neighbours, took her photo round the malls and the video arcade at the movie theatre but no luck so far. We believe she's hiding out with a friend who is keeping it quiet at Beth's request."

"Oh. That's disappointing of Beth. Anyhow, sorry to interrupt – go on."

"So, the time period needing to be alibied is the evening and night of December 12th for sure. Then, in general, what the person was doing over the next few days, and finally a witness to their activities early on the morning of the 19th, since Holly's body was discovered mid-morning and she hadn't been lying there all night."

"What about this other accusation about Annalise and Holly quarrelling?"

"That came from Marta Smith herself. She says she saw Holly go chasing down the hallway after Annalise and then, when she caught up with her, having an intense conversation that turned into a real argument and ended with Annalise shoving Holly away and marching off. We don't know if it was the same day as the Annalise and Noel argument, but it doesn't seem likely. I can't see Noel letting Annalise leave by herself, not when she was so upset with him."

"I see that you need to speak to Annalise based on all this but I'm certain, absolutely certain, that there's no way she killed Holly."

"I agree with you but it's the facts that need to be in agreement. I'll know more tomorrow after the interview."

"Will you let me know?"

"I'll call you for sure." Judith felt Grant's gaze intensify. She caught her breath and let her eyes stare into his. It felt like a long moment before she was forced to exhale. Without a word she started the car and drove them back to the school.

Chapter 39

Normally the Senior Investigating Officer and his partner wouldn't pick up a suspect to bring in for questioning, that was a job for patrolmen. But since Annalise Sutherland came from such a high-profile family, and since she was currently staying with her *fiancé* at the Larkin-Frampton residence, another powerhouse family, Grant and Suzanne were in attendance.

Judith heard both Grant's and Noel's version of the incident.

All members of the household gathered in the front hall while Annalise was asked to accompany the two detectives to the police station for further questioning, and to make a statement. This action was met with outrage, disbelief, tears, and temper.

"Noel, do something!" cried Annalise.

"What can Noel do?" answered his mother.

"Call our lawyer. Get someone here right now to clear this up," said Aunt Eleanor.

"Definitely call your lawyer and ask him or her to meet us at the station," Grant replied.

"No, you'll have to wait here for him. No one will be going to any police station."

"I'm sorry but Ms. Sutherland is required to comply with our request."

"Is she under arrest?" Grant turned to Noel, the man was distraught and aggressive with his concern.

"She can be, but we'd prefer not to take that step right now. It's better for everyone if Ms. Sutherland comes with us and your attorney meets her at the station. Since we've been notified that an attorney is requested, we cannot legally question her until that attorney is present."

"But what questions can you possibly have for Annalise?"

"I'm sorry but I can't give specifics."

"I'm coming too!" declared Noel and Annalise clutched at his arm.

"You have every right to do so but you won't be able to join Ms. Sutherland and her lawyer in the interview."

"Why not? I'm her *fiancé*!"

"And she's an adult. Sorry, but we're leaving now. Do you want to get your purse and a coat Ms. Sutherland?"

Eventually Annalise, tearful and trembling, was put in the car along with the two police, followed by Noel and reassurances from the older women.

When Noel told Judith about it afterwards she could see that he was still upset.

"It's just so wrong that anyone could even imagine that my sweet Annalise would ever harm anyone," he'd said.

It wasn't the type of neighbourhood where lace curtains would be twitching but everyone in the family knew that word would get around soon enough.

Chapter 40

News that Annalise Sutherland was at the police station rapidly spread through the school. There weren't very many in attendance, but word got out and the answering machine kept filling up with messages from parents – and other people – wanting to know what was going on. Judith erased the lot and headed back to the principal's office to phone Pat Johnson. She wanted to keep the principal up-to-date.

Mark Johnson answered Judith's call and agreed that he was screening his wife's calls but knew she'd want to take this one.

"Oh Judith. I couldn't have chosen a worse time to get sick," complained Pat.

"I'm quite sure you didn't choose it at all!" laughed Judith. "Listen, don't worry about it. We're good at this end. None of us believe this about Annalise, well except for Marta Smith and her crowd, so–"

"What's this about Marta Smith?" interrupted Pat sharply.

"Well, I was told that she's the one who pushed the three students into reporting a scene they witnessed and overheard between Annalise and Noel about Holly, plus Marta also witnessed an incident between Holly and Annalise. It's because of those statements that the police feel Annalise needs to provide some answers."

"I've just about had it up to here with Marta Smith. What is the matter with the woman? She used to be nice – a good teacher and a good person, too – but she's changed."

"Well despite the witness statements the lead detective told me he doesn't believe Annalise had the opportunity or the means to commit the crime."

"So why was she taken in?"

"The higher-ups insisted and he couldn't continue arguing with his boss. I guess they want to show that the wealthy aren't being treated differently. Except that of course they are."

"Oh Lord. That family are our greatest benefactors and Noel is one of our favourite teachers. This is a sorry mess."

"It is, but it will be cleared up. I'm quite sure Annalise has been provided with a top-notch legal team and her interview will be short and professional."

"There is that to be thankful for. Other than this how is everything else going?"

Judith has no intention of burdening the sick woman with Beth's disappearance, so she breezily replied: "Some gripes and grumbles – only to be expected – but otherwise surprisingly smooth. You've got some good teachers who are happy to pitch in and Lila Morelli is a big help as well. We're all managing fine."

"I'm so glad you're there, Judith, although I am sorry about you missing out on your time off."

"Not to worry, I mean look at the weather! I'll take my vacation later on. Meanwhile, I've kept you on the phone long enough. I don't want Mark mad at me! So don't fret, we need you rested and well for start-up in January. Take care, Pat!"

"Bye, and thanks again!"

Lila had come into the office partway through the conversation. When Judith ended the call Lila said:

"So how is Principal Johnson doing?"

"Her voice sounded weak, not like her usual self at all, but flu does hit hard."

"That's for sure, and she's getting on in years, too. Meanwhile, good news: Annalise has been released by the police."

"Already? That's wonderful! how did you hear?"

"Marta is telling everyone. I guess she's been subject to some backlash about how the school folk should be sticking together and not being police informants.

Well, that had to hurt her ego. I've only known the woman for what, three months? but I know that type and being popular and one-of-the-crowd is very important. So, she's been calling the police station all morning demanding news. Finally someone told her about Annalise and she's passing it on as quickly as she can."

"I doubt if she's feeling remorse, but maybe guilty. What do you think?"

"In my professional opinion Marta Smith is a woman who has gone as far as she ever will go in her chosen profession and she resents that fact.

Since there's no longer any chance that she can move up she will cement her existing position by criticizing and stirring up trouble for anyone who has surpassed her. Her habitual nastiness and spite will poison a few of her younger coworkers but because they're young they'll move on and soon she'll have no one left willing to listen to her vitriol. She'll be shunned and lonely, and she should be.

At the moment I suspect she's revelling in all the attention and being 'in the know' so she'll milk her news for all it's worth. Ignore her."

"Great diagnosis. I can tell you've had some experience in the mental health field as well as treating schoolgirls for sniffles."

Lila stuck her tongue out and Judith laughed saying:

"Oh very mature."

"I'm literally back in Middle School so what do you expect?"

"Anyhow, I deleted a bunch of 'what's going on?' messages left on the machine but I'll ask Marta to answer the calls. You and I can send out an email and text update about Annalise. Also, we need to remind everyone that the school is closed tomorrow."

"Are you going to be here?"

"Yes, for the morning. I want to make sure no students get dropped off and are locked out. It's too cold for the girls to be left outside."

"Well then we'll have plenty of time to get ready for Noel's party."

"I forgot about the party. Do you think it's still on?"

"For sure! They'll want to parade Annalise to show she's a free woman."

"That sounds a bit tacky."

"It will also be a great opportunity to get their complaints about the police publicly aired."

"As to that, well I think the police did jump the gun. So to speak! I mean, they did have to question Annalise after Marta pulled her little stunt but I'm sure it could have been done in her home, or rather the Frampton home, instead of at the police station."

"They were making a public show. God knows why. Did I ever mention that I come from a family of cops?"

"No, you didn't. Your dad's a policeman?"

"Actually he's the only one who isn't! well, and Mama of course. No, it's all of his brothers and even his sister, plus his dad – my grandfather – was, and his brothers too. And now my brother, who is twelve years younger than me, is joining the Academy. Real family affair."

"So what does your father do for a living?"

"He's a carpenter. He discovered in high-school Shop class that he loves working with wood so after school he trained as an apprentice and eventually became self-employed. He has a real knack for it and really enjoys his job. It was a good choice for him but it caused a rift for a time in the family."

"I guess in a big family that would be a problem."

"Family support really does matter. In fact, that's why we should go to Noel's party so we can show our support of Annalise."

"You're right YOU should go but I have no interest."

"Oh, come on, let's hobnob with the great and good of Edgemont."

"Why on earth would we want to do that?"

"To poke fun and feel superior!" replied Lila with a smile. "In fact, the stores are open late tonight so let's go buy new outfits to wear!"

"I'm not going anywhere near a store or a mall on December 23rd, thank you very much! and I wouldn't buy a new dress for this anyhow."

"Do you have a party dress?" Seeing the look on Judith's face Lila was quick to say: "Because I've got lots and you can borrow something."

Judith felt a twinge of something emotional, she couldn't identify the feeling, but it made her smile back at Lila.

"That's very kind of you but I won't be attending, I don't want to go. But you go and be sure to tell me all about it."

"I wouldn't miss this party for anything! Now, let's get to work on the next round of updates for the parents."

"You get started, I'm going to organize everyone into the library for another Christmas movie."

Chapter 41

As Judith left the office she saw Brian Penner, Beth's father, coming in the front door. The man looked like he had aged twenty years in the past couple of days. His face was white, his eyes were red, and his gaze was unfocused. It looked like he hadn't slept since discovering his daughter had disappeared.

He was clearly suffering a terrible ordeal and Judith's heart went out to him. She took his arm and drew him back into the principal's office. Lila jumped into professional mode and got him seated, felt his forehead, and listened to his pulse.

"I'll be right back with a hot drink," she said.

Judith sat down on the love-seat and taking Brian's hand asked:

"What have the police told you? and what are they doing to find Beth?"

Brian sounded completely dispirited as he replied:

"Nothing. They don't have any news and I don't believe they're taking this seriously. They refuse to admit she's been kidnapped. Instead, they talk about runaways and hiding out to get my attention, teach me a lesson, something stupid. They don't know Bethany! She would never, ever do something like that."

He turned a pleading face to Judith as though willing her to understand and agree.

"When I heard they arrested somebody I thought we'd find out where Bethany was but the police said this person has been released! I don't know why they let him go. I don't know if they even bothered to ask about Bethany."

"I'm going to call George Grant, he's the lead detective on Holly's case—"

"That's the problem," interrupted Brian. "They're only working on Holly's case and they don't give a damn about Bethany. They refuse to put two and two together to figure it out. They act like there is no 'Bethany case' but there should be."

His voice rose on a shout and Judith was relieved to see Lila hurry back in the room bearing a steaming mug.

"Drink this – don't argue, just drink," she insisted, helping the man hold the drink to his lips. He made a face exclaiming:

"Ugh, I never take sugar!"

But Lila pushed the mug back to his mouth saying: "You need it, you're in shock. When's the last time you ate? or slept? Don't bother answering it's easy enough to see by your face. Finish this up first."

"I was just telling Mr. Penner that I'm going to call Detective Grant to find out what's being done about Beth."

"Call me Brian."

"Thank you. I'm Judith, and this is Lila our school nurse. Now, give me a minute and I'll make that call."

Judith was glad to get through to Grant right away. Brian Penner was barely keeping it together and she was very worried about him. It was obvious he'd forgotten having met with her and Lila before.

"Grant, hello it's Judith Taylor with Brian Penner, Beth's father. We're wondering how the search for her is coming along?"

Judith schooled her face into showing no expression which was good because Grant told her there was no search. They'd been told Beth had turned up at a friend's house claiming she and her Dad had had a fight and she didn't want to go home yet, she was still upset about it.

"That's a lot to take in. Who told you this?"

"Told them what? What's happening?" cried Brian.

Judith lifted her hand to stop Brian for a moment while she listened to Grant's answer. She asked a couple more questions then said a quick 'thank you' and hung up. Turning to Brian she again took hold of his hand and said:

"Someone phoned into the station saying Beth has been staying with their daughter at their home. She's fine but upset with you because of some fight the two of you had?"

"Wh-what? That's not true! This isn't right. Who was it who phoned saying this?"

"They think it was a man and he wouldn't give his name–"

"They THINK it was a man?" His ashen face quickly turned red as anger took hold.

"The voice sounded like it might be disguised. This voice claimed to be the father of a girl who is also a student here. He said both his daughter and Beth pleaded with him to let her stay another day or so to get over things. He was also adamant that he didn't want to be identified. So they weren't suspicious about his trying to disguise his voice."

"They should have been!"

"I couldn't agree more. The efforts of the police in this enquiry have been distinctly underwhelming."

"It's not right, you know. There was no fight, no argument. I'd hardly seen Bethany in the days before she vanished. This man has got her! how stupid are the police? Why did they believe him?"

"Because he knew about Beth having Holly's diary and being upset over something she read in it. Now, none of us knew about the diary until Beth left a phone message here. That's when we went to your house looking for her. The police had no reason to doubt him. They believed Beth was upset and hiding out and this father didn't want you finding out who or where he is."

"Judith that doesn't sound right to me," put in Lila.

"No, it isn't right. From an outsider's viewpoint the police have been very lax to accept this phone call as a solution. Mr. Penner, Brian, I strongly suggest you go back to the police station and convince them to take your concerns seriously. I can't leave the school—"

"I can," said Lila. "And it's best if I drive, Brian. We won't leave until we've lit a fire under somebody's butt."

The distraught man straightened up and grasped Lila's hand in thanks. He was almost out the door before he turned around to say *thank you* to Judith as well.

Once he and Lila were gone, she phoned Grant back to give him a heads-up about the forthcoming visit. She didn't mince her words when giving her opinion.

Chapter 42

Judith decided the Beth situation qualified for a telephone tree. Pat Johnson had given her the password to Samira's computer, and she found the file right on the desktop.

Before clicking the phone links of the six parents who would start the rounds of calling their six who would then call their six, etc... she composed what she was going to say writing:

"Hi, it's Judith Taylor for Edgemont School. I have a few important items so please spread the word.

One, Beth Penner has been missing for a couple of days. We urgently need to find her so anyone who knows anything must get in touch with the police. Beth was Holly Lezinsky's best friend and is very upset about Holly's death. She's only fourteen.

Second item, the school is closed tomorrow December 24th and won't re-open until January 2nd. No students should come here tomorrow, we're not open.

Final item, rumours have been circulating about Annalise Sutherland, the fiancé of our teacher Noel Larkin, being questioned by the police but she is back at home now. It was a misunderstanding and there are no charges. Can you repeat that back to me? and do you think it's clear enough to easily understand?"

She made her six calls and waited for the telephone tree to do its job. If it's true that Beth was staying at the house of a school parent she would be flushed out. Everyone would know the seriousness of the situation now.

Judith was ready for a coffee and a ten-minute break. She went to the staff room but on entering heard Xiao speaking in his quick, high voice, arguing with someone. His back was to the door, and Judith spotted Tanya trying to shush him when she saw Judith. She gave a shoulder shrug of apology.

Xiao whirled round and paused for a moment before confronting Judith about an anonymous letter left in the staff room.

"So, I'm embarrassed that you walked in on that but I'm not sorry about what I said, what I am saying. This anonymous letter makes accusations and we're entitled to an answer." He was belligerent and blushing but unapologetic.

"What anonymous letter? I can't answer you without knowing what's going on."

"This!" he thrust a sheet at her. She'd expected to see words cut-out from a newspaper but the missive was printed by a computer, an easier way to disguise the sender. It was a short message and she read it out loud:

"Judith Taylor and Holly were lovers. Holly wanted out but Taylor wouldn't let her go. Beth knew."

The words didn't register for a moment and when they did sink in Judith couldn't prevent a bark of laughter escaping her lips.

"This is the most ridiculous, utterly ridiculous thing I've ever seen!" she exclaimed.

"That's what you say," jeered Xiao. "But you just denying it isn't good enough."

"It's good enough for me," asserted Eddie.

"Me too," chimed in Tanya.

"Well, I say there's no smoke without fire," announced Marta, her voice carrying over the others' conversations. "You owe us an explanation."

"I owe you nothing," hissed Judith, whirling round to confront her. Marta pulled back in the face of the younger woman's anger but Judith wasn't finished:

"You keep your nasty suspicions to yourself or I will prosecute you for defamation of character. You've been poking your nose into everyone else's business but I will not tolerate you interfering in mine. Do you understand?"

Marta turned to Xiao, expecting him to defend her but before he could utter a word Judith shouted:

"I SAID DO YOU UNDERSTAND? ANSWER ME!"

"Yes, I'm not deaf. You don't have to shout. Xiao was only saying—"

"I'm not talking about Xiao, I'm talking about you spreading gossip and innuendo, egging on the younger teachers, and even involving the students. I demand to know what everyone knows or has heard about this accusation and this filthy poison pen letter."

Everyone denied knowledge of the rumour or the letter.

"Is the accusation true?" questioned Xiao.

Judith was taken aback that he – or anyone – could even think that of her, but her voice was calm and quiet as she replied:

"I'm sorry you feel the need to even ask."

The other teachers looked at Xiao and shook their heads but he lifted his chin and wouldn't meet anyone's eyes. Judith looked down at the piece of paper in her hands, pleased to see they weren't shaking as sometimes happened when she got angry.

"What does he mean when he says 'Beth knew'? Shouldn't it be 'Beth knows'? Does it mean..."

"I don't think you should read too much into that phrasing," said Tanya. "If the accusation in the letter isn't true and of course it isn't! then it follows that no part of the letter is true. See what I mean?"

"I definitely don't believe the accusation," Eddie declared, and there were some murmurs of agreement.

"I'd better keep this," Judith said.

"Don't think you can destroy it, we've all seen it and read it. We all know about it," cried Marta shrilly.

"Why don't I take a photocopy of it for you, Marta? In fact, come with me now, I want to make a copy for the police anyhow."

Judith acknowledged Tanya and Eddie with a nod then left the room without a word, not caring if Marta followed her or not.

Chapter 43

Judith's mouth trembled and she felt her throat closing but she pressed her lips tight and held her head high. She would not give in to the unaccustomed and unwelcome tears that threatened.

She was shocked by the poison pen letter and devastated when Xiao asked if there as any truth to the accusation. Did he really think she was capable of that and was he the only one? or would many people have no trouble believing the ugly rumour?

First of all, it was inconceivable that she would have an affair with a young student and secondly there was the awful implication that she'd harmed – in fact killed – the girl rather than let her go.

Absolutely ridiculous! but would people, some people, find it plausible? Would the police? Look what happened to Annalise Sutherland because of malicious gossip and all the talk that resulted.

How could she continue to work at the school, a place she loved and where she felt completely comfortable, if she had to live under the weight of her coworkers' condemnation? She couldn't bear to walk into a room where everyone went silent and turned their backs to her.

And what of the parents? would they exert pressure on Pat Johnson to get rid of Judith? She couldn't stand the thought of people whispering about her while exchanging knowing glances with each other.

"Oh, what do I care what they think?" she told herself. "I don't actually like any of these people. If I never saw any of them again it wouldn't matter to me in the least. But it isn't the idea of their poor and misinformed opinion of me that's the problem – it's the utter unfairness of it all. That's what's so frustrating. I've done nothing wrong."

Judith wasn't used to feeling helpless. She regulated and planned all the aspects of her life in order to be in control because being in control had always been very important to her. She'd long ago figured out that was because she'd been forced to take on a custodial role while still very young.

Those times when her mother couldn't take care of her Judith had managed to get by. Her hands and face weren't clean and her clothes weren't washed often enough but she'd gotten herself to school every day. The mess left in the house was always waiting for her and she always came back. Although she'd only been a child somehow she'd coped.

Now, she was struggling with despondency – even despair. At the moment there didn't seem to be a way forward.

She'd been too distant, too unrelatable and cold-hearted. She could identify her failings as a human being but realized she'd never thought they were faults. These traits kept her safe from the hurt the world could – and did – inflict on the unwary and the unknowing. She had learned that lesson at the age of six.

Since then, she'd seen strength in her lack of emotion. No feelings equalled no drama and that meant she could feel superior, except she wasn't feeling very superior now.

"Judith!" she told herself sternly, "Nobody's going to fix this for you so you better hurry up and figure things out for yourself. First of all, what exactly is the problem? Huh! where to begin... someone's made a nasty accusation against me. It's not true but how do you prove a negative? Okay so problem number one is who wrote the letter?

Next problem is why would anyone say something like that about me? am I supposed to be some kind of a threat or something? Is that possible? But why would anyone feel... oh, Holly's killer might think Beth has told me something incriminating.

Or could it have something to do with what's written in the diary or what the killer is afraid might be written there? But I haven't been able to connect with Beth, she's hiding or... or worse.

That other day when I was leaving school I noticed Beth's backpack looked full yet it shouldn't have been since there wouldn't be any homework so close to the holidays. She must have had the diary and some other things of Holly's.

Why didn't I pick her up and drive her home? I might have been able to help her, and there's a chance that together we could have discovered the solution to Holly's murder. Why was I in such a rush? it's not like I have any reason to hurry home."

Yet Judith knew that wasn't the answer. The truth was she hadn't wanted to get involved with a mess of emotions, she wanted to remain at a safe distance.

"And look where that's gotten you," she thought sourly.

"Am I responsible for what's happened to Beth? If she's killed will that be my fault?" Judith was sick at the thought. The guilt was overwhelming and for several long moments she was paralyzed by it. Finally she straightened her shoulders and said:

"Well, enough of that. I need to keep trying to figure out what's going on. So far I need to solve the puzzle of why the letter was written and who wrote it. I can't control whether or not someone thinks I have inside knowledge about Holly that threatens them. No... but I can be alert to that idea and keep my eyes and ears open.

And finally what has this letter accomplished? Can I figure out its purpose? Oh, if only there was someone to confront but who? That's why anonymous letters are so poisonous!"

Chapter 44

Snow had started falling when Lila arrived back at the school. Judith could see her in the vestibule wiping her feet on the mat, shaking out her hair, and brushing flakes off her jacket. Brian Penner wasn't with her. As she came forward Lila explained:

"Brian is still at the police station. He's determined to see action taken in the hunt for Beth and won't leave until the cops start looking for her. He's very convincing, I totally believe Beth is missing and not hiding. Let's hope he can convince the police, too. Anyhow, that's sorted for... hey, what's up? you look like you've seen a ghost!"

In reply Judith handed over the anonymous letter. Lila read it, looked up in wide-eyed surprise, read it again and made to crumple up the paper but Judith stopped her saying:

"No, I need to give this to the police."

"This is awful, disgusting, despicable, and when we find out who wrote this... this THING well, just let me get my hands on them!" threatened Lila. "But honey, listen, you can't let this get to you. No one could believe this and–"

"As a matter of fact there are teachers in the staff-room right now who asked me if it's true, and Marta's saying, 'no smoke without fire' so it seems that some people do believe it."

"They don't count. They're nothing people, you can't give them serious consideration."

"But I have to!" cried Judith. "Those are exactly the people who will spread it around. Sure, they don't matter to me but this... this garbage does because it can hurt my reputation!"

"Not with anyone who knows you – it's laughable. But–" she put her hand up to stop Judith's protest, "I can see how it's affecting you so we'll figure this out together and fix it. Okay?"

"Well, I have to do something. I plan to give this to Grant and let him investigate because it's obvious this has got something to do with Holly and her murder."

"Before you call him let's get the facts straight. First off, where did you get this?"

Judith told Lila about going into the staff-room and being confronted with the letter but didn't know who found it or at what time. Lila said:

"Let's go find out."

The two women were walking down the hallway when the staff-room door opened on Marta and Xiao. She turned her head away, snubbing Judith, and Xiao followed suit. Lila gave an unladylike snort and said:

"I'll be sure to let Principal Johnson know how well you two protect the good name of the school."

The teachers refused to rise to the bait, which disappointed Lila since she was spoiling for a fight.

Inside the staff-room they found Eddie and Tanya, joined by Jennifer, discussing the letter.

"We're trying to figure out when it was left here. We all agree it wasn't here when we put away our outdoor things and that was by 9:00 am."

"Actually, I was late getting in this morning so I can say for sure it wasn't here at 9:22 by that clock, and it's right," added Tanya.

"Did you have trouble starting your car again?" asked Eddie. Tanya shook her head and smiled saying:

"No, I had trouble starting me! I didn't want to get out of bed this morning."

"So the letter," began Lila, bringing the conversation back on topic. "Can you be sure you would have noticed it?"

"Oh yes!" they all agreed. Jennifer explained that the teachers had all brought in some Christmas goodies to share: home-baked cookies, candies, chips and roasted nuts. Everyone's offering was added to the table and free for anyone to nibble on during the day. When they came in at the lunch-hour all the plates had been pushed to one side and the letter laid out in the cleared space.

"So, the letter was placed on the table at some time between, roughly, nine-thirty to noon?"

"Yes, thereabouts."

"Uh, no actually," disagreed Eddie. "I came in for a snack and a coffee about quarter to eleven. I didn't sleep so well last night either," he added, smiling at Tanya. The women all exchanged a look, for a moment enjoying the budding romance that was going on. It was a pleasant respite from the poison pen letter.

"Actually, that's great, Eddie. It means we can really narrow down the time frame. You were in here for how long?"

"No more than fifteen minutes," he answered.

"Okay so we're talking about roughly a one-hour window for someone to set out the letter and leave."

"If they left," said Lila.

"Oh! who did discover the letter?"

"Several of us came in together. Joanna agreed to take the kids outside for a bit of fresh air before herding them to the lunchroom for hot chocolate. That left the rest of us free to come as a group. We met Marta and Xiao in the corridor."

"They were coming to the staff-room and not from it, right?" clarified Lila.

"Yes, definitely."

"Right, so the actual discovery of the letter hasn't provided any clues but who could have had the opportunity to deliver it?" questioned Judith. "You three were together, with Joanna, this morning."

"Except for the time I was here."

"Oh Eddie, no one suspects you of writing a poison pen!" chided Tanya.

"But we need to look at all absences, even bathroom breaks, because it wouldn't take long for someone to nip in here and set it out."

"But the risk of being seen!"

"Oh that's a good point. The letter writer, we'll assume the writer is also the person who left it here, has to be someone no one would query if they were found in the school."

"And in the staff-room."

"So a teacher, admin, or the janitor. I'm quite sure we can rule out the students," said Judith.

"But a parent could explain their presence saying they were looking for a teacher, right?"

"True. Still, it does narrow it down because the most likely person is a teacher."

"And the most likely teacher is..." Lila didn't get to finish her comment because at that moment a student burst through the door with tears and a bloody chin after taking a fall outside.

Joanna came hurrying in after her and spotting Lila was relieved to hand the crying child over to her care.

Judith thanked the teachers then turned to leave but they pressed her to join them in a snack.

"But I didn't contribute anything," she protested but her objection was waved away by Tanya saying:

"We've got plenty already. Sit down and try a couple of things. I made this, it's a mini-marshmallow chocolate-coated yule log that's sweet and quite tasty despite the irregular shape!"

Judith suddenly felt emotional and had to look away when her eyes brightened with tears. The others pretended not to notice while she regained her composure.

Chapter 45

After enjoying a relaxing chat with the teachers, everyone careful to avoid the topic of the letter, Judith excused herself with thanks for the Christmas treats.

She planned to go back to the principal's office to make copies of the letter and phone Grant. Instead, she found herself grabbing her coat and heading outside thinking a bit of fresh air would help clear her thoughts.

"I can't explain why anyone would do this to me with one exception... but that's something that makes no sense whatsoever." She strode to the edge of the woods and began walking the perimeter of the lawn. Absentmindedly she pulled up her hood to cover her hair from the falling snow. The flakes were fluffy and soft and the temperature was mild even without sunshine.

"What is the purpose of the letter?" she asked herself and answered: "To throw suspicion on me. But why? any investigation will prove it's all a fabrication. Ah, but what is the immediate result of this letter? Well, it focuses attention on me and away from Annalise. Who would want to do that – besides Annalise herself? The answer to that is Noel but Noel is my friend, or at least a friendly acquaintance, and has been for several years.

Why would he want to do this to me? Oh. What if he doesn't want to but might find it expedient in the short run. After all, the big party is tomorrow night. Him wanting to divert suspicion from Annalise makes sense. He could even mention the letter about me being something laughable – as laughable as imagining the possibility that Annalise could be involved. Sounds pretty convoluted but who knows? It's an idea."

As Judith continued her walk her path was marked by her footprints in the snow but they wouldn't last as the flakes were falling steadily. Her thoughts turned to Noel, and to Noel and Holly, and she wondered.

The two of them had spent a lot of time together working on the play. It was possible – even likely – that Holly had developed a crush on the handsome young teacher. She was pretty girl with a flirtatious manner which would please and flatter Noel. She'd already considered him a likely candidate for the *girlfriend experience*. Could things have gone too far?

Despite being the victim of a false accusation herself, Judith had no trouble believing the gossip about Noel and Holly.

"And that's odd," she thought, "Since I never linked Noel and Holly in my mind before."

She strode along, unconsciously hurrying as her thoughts quickened.

"Did Noel accuse me of the very thing that he's guilty of committing? He would have no trouble printing out the letter on his computer at home and bringing it to the staff room. No one would think twice if they met him there, he'd simply say *Merry Christmas* or confirm the person was coming to his party. So, Noel could have reason to write it, plus he does have the means to write it, and to deliver it."

She just couldn't imagine her friend doing such a thing.

"Again, I can't figure out *why me?* Xiao or Eddie would be far more likely. Eddie himself recently said something about the importance of a teacher's reputation, especially a male teacher in an all-girls school. Yes, that's very apropos. Choosing a man to accuse makes more sense so there must be a specific reason why I was named."

The rhythm and pace of her walk stimulated Judith's thought processes and she was able to put everything else out of her mind to concentrate.

"The reason I have to be discredited is because of the phone message Beth left on the answering machine. I commented to myself at the time what bad luck it was that so many people heard it. Noel was one of them. And Noel could have been the intruder in the library. He knows his way around that room and also the hallway for a quick escape.

In fact, the night I left the school and was accosted by Billy MacNeill I felt like I was being watched. At first I put it down to imagination and then to Billy but what it someone else was lurking in the shadows? Lurking! listen to me, so melodramatic! But it is a possibility.

And then there was the guy who dinged my car on the icy road. I put that incident down to bad driving but that car did follow me, mimicking my movements, for quite a ways before hitting me. I was lucky that there must have been a dry patch on that bit of road by the school's driveway, otherwise I could have crashed into one of these big old trees."

As Judith reasoned out her thoughts it did seem possible that Noel was behind the attacks against her.

"But I can't see him as a killer!" she exclaimed. "Although Annalise is biased she was right when she called him a gentle and sensitive man. I can believe him falling into an affair but I can't believe in him committing murder. However, what would happen to Noel if the truth about his affair with Holly came out? I'll think of the worst-case scenario for each consequence:

Number one is that Annalise would break off her engagement so he'd lose a very pretty fiancée and her wealthy, powerful family would make him persona non grata in Edgemont.

Two, would be that Eleanor might cut him out of her will and ostracize him from her social circle. It's only natural that Audrey would stand by her son but their lavish lifestyle is entirely dependent on Eleanor who owns the estate and has all the money. I remember Pat Johnson telling me years ago that Audrey Larkin lived off her sister's goodwill.

Then three would be Noel losing his part-time teaching job. He doesn't need the job which sure doesn't pay enough to support him, but he loves teaching. This job is something he really enjoys doing. But he wouldn't get hired on anywhere else. No school wants a teacher who can't keep his hands off the students.

The final point is the most important because losing his fiancée, home, and job means nothing compared to being jailed for statutory rape.

So, wow, he sure does have a strong motive for silencing Holly and Beth, too, if she knows about their liaison. Especially if she has written proof in Holly's diary.

Where is Beth? I hope the police listen to Brian Penner and pull out all the stops to find her.

She thought about Noel so insistent on driving her and Lila to Beth's home. No wonder he wanted to find her before Judith had a chance to notify the police about the tearful and worried message Beth had left behind.

"And giving in to Noel's urgency got me in trouble with Grant. Suzanne tried to make out that I was playing Nancy Drew or some such thing. She made sure she got her digs in."

Thinking of Suzanne – and Grant – was a distraction. Judith felt she was close to figuring out something important about the case. She now believed she'd let Beth down and felt terrible about that.

"Why didn't I talk to her, or let her talk to me? How hard would it have been to listen to a girl who was so unhappy? Even if it was, as I suspected, just a need to express her grief – why was I so selfish?"

Judith felt that, to an extent, she could excuse herself because of her own upbringing. No one had been willing to help her out – but maybe she'd never asked? and just because she'd developed a thick skin didn't mean every young girl could.

Thinking those thoughts wasn't pleasant but Judith forced herself to face up to her responsibility for what happened and for what she could do going forward.

"I need to stop pretending I can keep everybody at arms-length when the truth is I've been involved all along. It doesn't matter if that's not my choice, not when it is the reality. I can't sidestep the burden, I need to fix this, and I can!"

Chapter 46

Lila had finished bandaging the injured child and was on the phone asking the girl's mother if someone could come by and pick her up early. Judith only heard one side of the conversation and was impressed by the nurse's crisp, yet reassuring, manner.

"No, as I said no stitches are required and there won't be a scar," she winked at the girl who gave a tremulous smile back. "Yes but she's a very healthy and active girl so these scrapes and bruises are only to be expected. However, she does need some of the TLC that only Mom can provide." The girl nodded.

"I'm glad to hear that and we'll be waiting at the front door. How long do you think? That soon? Wonderful, see you then."

She took the girl's hand saying:

"Lucky you! Mom is going to drop everything and hurry right over. She'll be here inside of ten minutes so let's go get all your gear – remember the school is closing until January so you don't want to leave anything behind.

You will have worn a coat today, what about a hat? boots? mittens in the pocket of your coat? There's no homework – phew – but are you taking any books home to read over the holidays?"

As the girl answered each of Lila's questions Judith noticed that her colour improved. She looked less weepy and more alert.

The three of them headed out of the nurse's office and Lila made the girl laugh when she asked about 'any muddy, stinky gym clothes that need to go home for a wash?' They gathered up the girl's belongings and had her buttoned into her coat and wearing her mittens just as her mother's car pulled up to the school's front door. Lila went out for a quick word then came back in shivering.

"You look the picture of health with your bright eyes and rosy cheeks," she told Judith. "A big improvement since I last saw you, what have you been doing?"

"I've been tramping around the yard getting my thoughts in order and I've come to a decision."

"Do tell."

"I want us to go to Noel's birthday-Christmas party. If, no when, the story of this poison pen letter makes the rounds I don't want it to look like I'm hiding. The party is the perfect opportunity to show that I've got nothing to hide."

Lila clapped her hands in delight, teasing Judith by saying:

"Oh if only Grant could see you now with your high colour and your challenging words. He'd be smitten!"

"First of all that's a silly thing to say and secondly I wouldn't want him to feel that way. I like him but I don't know if we could ever be friends. Friendly, yes, but that's it."

"Suzanne will be relieved, but I'd like to shake you! Not that I believe a word you're saying."

'Oh Lila, you're such a kidder. I do have to phone Grant to tell him about the letter, I meant to do it earlier. I expect Marta has beaten me to it!"

Lila went back to tidy up her office while Judith went to the secretary's office to make her photocopies and then into Pat Johnson's office for some privacy to phone.

She hadn't shared her real reason for attending the party and that was to search for Beth. Judith was certain that Noel had the girl hidden somewhere on the estate. Judith resolved to find her.

Chapter 47

Judith got Grant's voicemail, as usual, and left a message saying she had something to show him. He called back right away to say he would stop by in an hour or so.

Judith used that time to get the few remaining students and teachers settled in the library with today's movie. In fact, they would be watching two animations, 'Charlie Brown's Christmas' and 'How the Grinch Stole Christmas'. Judith remembered seeing – and very much enjoying – both of them on TV when she was a kid. She decided to join the audience until Grant got there and sent a text telling him to come to the library.

In the following hour they saw all of the Charlie Brown and half of the Grinch. Judith found that time to be a much-needed break from the emotional upheavals of the day. She was able to relax, chuckle, and hum along to the familiar tunes.

When she saw Grant in the doorway she almost regretted calling him but knew it was best to get this over with. For an hour she'd managed to put the poison pen letter and all of the nasty, suspicious thoughts that stemmed from it right out of her mind.

"It feels like I'm intruding," said Grant by way of greeting. Judith smiled and said 'not at all'. She led the way to the principal's office where the original letter and a couple of copies were on the desk.

Grant read the short letter silently but when he looked up she saw anger in his narrowed eyes and tightened mouth.

"What's the meaning of this?"

"We've all been puzzling over that question. It was left in the staff room between 11:00 and 12:00, all of the teachers who are in today arrived and discovered it together, and it's been handled by everyone. We were thinking it's likely the author is a teacher or a parent. Not a student."

"What is it with you?" he demanded.

"What do you mean?"

"What are you doing to draw attention to yourself? You've become the focus of this investigation." Judith, stung by Grant's comment, gaped at him.

"That's not fair! I'm not doing anything."

"Well it's obvious you've done something! Something has gotten this letter-writer worked up. Something you've said or done has made you a target of his and this is the result," he argued.

"Oh really? That's how you see this? I get criticized if I don't pass on information and then I get criticized when I do. *Memo to self: don't bother Grant anymore, he'll only get mad at you.*"

"Judith I'm not mad."

"No? well I am. I'm giving you this letter and if you don't think it's important feel free to throw it out. I don't care. Investigate or not, I don't care."

"Oh all of a sudden you don't care. You've stirred things up plenty with Brian Penner, we're gonna end up arresting the guy if he doesn't stop harassing us."

"He should harass you. His young daughter has been missing for days and first your sidekick Suzanne cancels the search because it involved me and then all of you have covered up her mistake by pretending to believe Beth is hiding. No girl hides away from her home and family days before Christmas. She shops and socializes and spends hours on the phone. Your actions, or rather lack of, are a disgrace!"

Lila chose that moment to walk into the office to see the two of them squared off against each other with angry expressions, their harsh words vibrating in the air.

"Uh-oh, I'll come back."

Judith said: "Don't bother, we're done!" At the same time Grant said:

"Never mind, I'm leaving," and went with the anonymous letter crumpled in his hand.

"That was some quarrel, I could hear you right down the hall," commented Lila. Judith was drumming her fingers on the desk and counting under her breath:

"One, two, three, four. One, two, three, four." As a calming technique it seemed to work. She finally looked Lila in the eye and said:

"He's insufferably arrogant and I hate him."

Lila smiled.

Chapter 48

"Never mind smirking at me," said Judith. "I'm desperate for a distraction and you've got beans to spill so come on, tell me what's going on with your marriage."

"Sure, I see. You want to feel better by making me feel worse, is that it?"

"Oh no, I don't want to pry if it's painful."

Lila laughed and said: "I'm teasing you. Actually, talking it out with someone impartial might be a good idea. With Christmas so close I've been feeling a bit maudlin and second-guessing my choices so... let's move to the comfy seating and you can tell me what you think. Okay, here goes:

I've been married to Arnie for a long time. We were high-school sweethearts who married after graduation. He got a job with the City of Toronto and supported me while I studied Nursing. I got a good job in a big hospital and our lives were progressing according to plan except we both wanted children and I wasn't getting pregnant. Neither of us had physical problems but there was an issue and that was Arnie's marijuana consumption. It wasn't legal then so he couldn't tell the doctor. I looked into it and although there's been some controversy the majority of studies show repeated use causes a decrease in sperm count and a less motility meaning less capable of fertilizing the egg. But simple solution, right? Arnie just needed to stop toking. Except he wouldn't.

He complained that when I worked nights he got bored on his own. Shift-work is normal for nursing, plus I was doing a lot of overtime due to shortages and, of course, for the money in order to build up a nest-egg. I meant to cut back to part-time once we started our family so a rainy-day fund was a good idea. It seemed to me that this was Arnie's fault for being selfish.

However, I had a good friend who was raising two girls on her own and one time she told me that she didn't blame her husband for leaving. They were very young when they'd married and he wasn't ready to have kids right away. But she pushed it because she was ready and wanted her own home and family. It was her forcing a family on him that ended the marriage.

She was a hard worker, a good saver, and she went on to buy a townhouse and raise those girls by herself because that's what she wanted out of life. Some years later, once he'd matured, he tried to come back because by then he did want to settle down and have a relationship with his daughters, but it was too late. There was no place for him in their lives and no desire to create one.

So, I thought okay I'll back off for now. We're both young and healthy and we've got time. I'm Italian so I had to fend off the constant nagging from my Nonna, wait I've got to do the accents here, okay *drink some wine and get sexy with him*, and enquiries from my Dad asking *is he shooting blanks, or what?* Mama always said: *relax and it will happen when it happens.* Family dinners, weddings, and especially christenings were a nightmare. I got to the point whenever someone asked, I'd say, *don't ask me ask God* and that always shut them up for a bit.

One good thing was that Arnie's family didn't put any pressure on us at all. They're a brainy, academic bunch and he doesn't fit in with the rest of them. Their expectations were low, they'd kind of written him off, and were satisfied he had a steady job with a good income. I get along fine with them but we've never been close.

Life went on with me working plenty – which I loved, I'm not complaining – and Arnie acting like he was still eighteen: getting high, watching tv and playing video games into the wee hours, and talking sports with his buds. My time off was spent cooking, cleaning, doing laundry, and grocery shopping while Arnie looked after the yard, the cars, minor household repairs and maintenance. We always kept busy and we were happy, but we could have been happier.

I know people say it's a mistake to think a baby will solve a couple's marital problems but I really believe having a family of our own would draw us closer together. Not having a family was our only problem. At least it was in the beginning.

Eventually I felt a rift between us. At first I thought he'd met somebody else. God knows he had enough free time on his own and could have fallen into a relationship. I thought that's why I felt him drawing away.

As I mentioned before I'm Italian so I wasn't going to let something like that slide. I confronted him and he was shocked. He said he hadn't even looked at another woman since we got together in ninth grade. I totally believed his denials. But he wouldn't tell me what was wrong. I quizzed him about work and about his health and even about his family. 'Nothing's the matter' he'd keep telling me.

But things got worse. He began having bad dreams and started drinking heavily in addition to smoking a lot of pot."

"Sorry to interrupt but what about his job if he was doing drugs so much?"

"Yeah, about that. Ha. Once marijuana became legal his union managed to stop the City from drug testing. Said it wasn't fair because weed can stay in your system for like a month or something and what people legally did on their off time was their business."

"Oh that's too bad because if it had meant losing his job he might have stopped."

"I think he definitely would have stopped. He likes his job a lot which, believe it or not, is driving a garbage truck!"

"He's a garbage collector? and he likes doing that?"

"Loves it. Ever since they added those mechanical arms to the trucks to pick up the blue and black and green bins he doesn't need a helper and gets to work by himself, He only sees his boss at the start and end of day – if then! He's on his own, out early in the morning, listening to his tunes and, no doubt, smoking all day, enjoying his job.

Anyhow, things between us got even worse. I couldn't stop probing and he just kept shutting me out and finally shutting me up.

I know something is wrong but I can't help him if he won't open up. He says I can't help anyways because nothing's the matter. So we lived in this stalemate situation for awhile longer and then I told him I was leaving. I thought the threat of separation would force him into confiding but it didn't and I can't live with a man who doesn't trust me."

"Oh surely it's not that he doesn't trust you–"

"What else can it be? Unless his secret is something so terrible that he refuses to acknowledge it. Has he done something that he's buried deep down? hoping it will go away? What is he – an ostrich?"

"Ostriches can fight."

"What?"

"Oh that Margaret Sealy, she's doing a report for her Natural Sciences class about ostriches and told me all about them. Far more than I ever wanted to know actually but that's Margaret. Anyhow, go on."

"Not much more to tell. When I decided we should separate I realized I couldn't be accessible. If Arnie really wants me he's going to have to make an effort to come and get me.

And I knew I couldn't stay separated if I didn't get away from all the familiar places and faces. I checked out a bunch of jobs in the National Nursing Registry and saw this advertised. It's completely different from what I'm used to and the money is the pits but it does offer small-town living and a fresh start so here I am."

"What did your parents say?"

"They told me I'm crazy and to hurry back home when I come to my senses. They're okay so long as I'm not talking divorce. But, it's been a few months already – actually since August so like four months – and Arnie hasn't come knocking.

When Principal Johnson hired me I told her I would commit to one year and we could discuss renewing or terminating in the summer. I'm starting to think that it's possible I won't be a married lady by this time next year and I'm not sure how that makes me feel. You see, Arnie and I have been together forever. I have to admit that he's the only man I've ever been with.

So, that's my story. I hope it's been sufficiently distracting?"

"Yes, very much so. You've given me lots to think about," said Judith, obviously going over in her mind everything she'd just heard.

"Good, now let's go check the answering machine one last time and then clear everybody out of here. I'm going to sort through my closet and choose outfits for each of us to wear tomorrow. Since you don't drink you can be the designated driver and pick me up. The thing starts at 4:00 in the afternoon, right? We don't want to be the first people there do we?"

"No, we want to show up when the party's in full swing with a good crowd."

"Okay, so come by my place whenever and we'll get dressed up and go in your car. Does that sound okay?"

"Sounds great. Yesterday wasn't a great day and today has been worse so you're right, it's time to finish up and get out of here."

Chapter 49

It was snowing on the morning of December 24th and the air was crisp and cold. Once again Judith appreciated the underground parking in her building. It was comfortable and time-saving to get into a warm car that didn't need to have snow brushed away or ice scraped off.

Of course you never felt the weather was really like until you got outdoors and there had been times when she'd been unpleasantly surprised by the depth of snow on the roads, or the bitter cold of a windy, winter day.

She only saw two or three cars on her way to the school. Most businesses were closed, or closing at noon, today. She was glad today's drive was uneventful.

Judith parked in the no-idling zone to block any cars coming in. Half-an-hour should be enough time to make sure no students got dropped off for a school day. She thought about running inside to check the answering machine but decided no, the school was closed and she would keep it that way. She'd brought her Kindle so was happily occupied reading her book, *Finders Keepers* by Stephen King. She was really enjoying this series.

When the car cooled off enough for Judith to notice the cold she felt she'd waited long enough. Thankfully, No one had come by. Starting the car and setting the heater on high she headed to the grocery store to restock her perishables. She figured the store would be packed and it was.

Despite the crowds and the sense of urgency she felt in the shoppers around her Judith found herself enjoying the bustle as she hummed along to the piped-in Christmas music and wished the cashier a *Merry Christmas*.

By the time she got her groceries home and put away, had lunch, and put some make-up on it would be time to head over to Lila's. Judith wondered what outfits her friend would choose for them to wear to Noel's party and was ready to argue if the choice was *too Lila* and *not enough Judith*. She realized she'd have time for a nap and set her alarm accordingly.

Lila was living in the basement suite of an older bungalow and Judith had no trouble finding the place when she arrived a few hours later. She parked out front at the curb and Lila met her there before leading the way to her entrance at the back.

"I have a a great arrangement here," she said as she took Judith down a flight of stairs to an open plan living space. "My landlady, she's an old dear, lives on the main floor. She can't manage the stairs which means no one ever comes down here. She has an apartment-sized washer and dryer unit upstairs and I have use of the full-size appliances, including a freezer, downstairs. And plenty of space and privacy. I also get the whole garage since she no longer runs a car. The rent is laughable after Toronto prices, and when I shovel the paths and sidewalk she cooks for me."

Looking around Judith commented on it being cozy and colourful and not what she imagined a basement apartment to look like.

"Oh I'm sure there are plenty of damp, dark, and dingy places but not in Mrs Piernitsky's home. She's Polish or Ukrainian or something and has very definite 'Old Country' values. She keeps the place spick-and-span.

Mrs. P. is a widow who never had kids but there are nieces and nephews and their children who've visited several times since I've been here. She cooks huge meals for them and always passes on platefuls of leftovers to me.

Now, I think I've made a good choice for you to wear but come and try it on to be sure. Judith followed Lila into her bedroom where a dress was laid out on the bed.

"Here's what I'm wearing," said Lila, pointing to a party dress on a hanger with a pair of matching strappy shoes placed beneath it. The outfit looked pretty but Judith was pleased to see a more modest dress waiting for her.

"I'll slip into this and check that it fits me okay, but it looks great." She got into the dress and when Lila spun her fingers, motioning for Judith to turn around, the hem of the dress twirled. It flattered Judith's figure without being the least bit provocative and she was delighted.

The process of dressing up and styling each other's hair was a new and fun experience for her, and she was excited to be going to the party.

Chapter 50

The invitation to Noel's combined birthday and Christmas party is always styled as an *Open House* with people coming in and out all afternoon, evening, and night. Since it's Christmas Eve no one stays too long or too late.

It's a huge social event in the community and is attended by oilmen, ranchers, philanthropists, University presidents, and corporate bigwigs. All the school staff are invited.

Buffet tables laden with festive foods are replenished frequently, and mulled wine, hot toddies, and spiked eggnog flow freely. It's always well-attended and highly anticipated.

Judith and Lila arrived to see the older crowd leaving as the noise levels rose with the vocal enjoyment of happy party-goers.

Judith was going to drop Lila off at the front door since she wasn't wearing boots but they discovered a valet service ready to park the car. They hurried inside and offloaded their coats in the front entrance. They'd timed if right for the party was in full swing, just as Judith had hoped.

Lila had streaked her blonde hair with pink to match the rose-pink spaghetti-strapped dress she wore. She'd found a more conservative style for Judith, rightly guessing that her friend wouldn't wear anything too low-cut or too short. The dress was sleeveless but had a fitted bodice and full skirt that was feminine and flirty. The deep gold fabric flattered her dark colouring. They blended well with the celebratory crowd.

Lila immediately began introducing herself to strangers and was soon surrounded by a laughing group of men and women. Judith envied her ease of manner and knew it wasn't something she could imitate. She turned when a voice called her name. It was Suzanne Mirteau. Judith looked past her to see if Grant was there as well.

"He's not here," said Suzanne still snide even at a party.

"I guess you mean Grant? I'm surprised that the police would be invited considering what happened with you and Annalise."

"Ha! the police weren't invited or if they were the invitation was rescinded," smiled Suzanne with a toothy grin. "No, I'm here as a plus-one." At Judith's curious look she explained: "I'm somebody's date. What about you? where's your date?"

"Oh I didn't need one, I got my own invitation." Judith was dismayed at sounding like she was playing Suzanne's game of one-up-manship so she added that all the school staff, teachers and admin, were invited every year.

At that moment a big, jovial man shouldered his way through the crowd towards them carrying two mugs of rum-and-eggnog. He didn't wait for Suzanne to introduce him saying:

"Hi ya, I'm Raj, sounds like Taj as in Taj Mahal."

"Raj Mahal?" as soon as she said it Judith realized he'd set her up for a favourite tag-line.

"Not Taj Mahal but I do sell palaces! I'm with ReMax." He gave Suzanne her drink and offered his to Judith but she politely declined.

Suzanne's presence was unexpected and unwelcome and Judith could feel the woman's eyes on her as she slipped away through the crowd. Judith most definitely did not want a witness or a watcher. She could imagine Suzanne's jeering voice calling her *Nancy Drew*.

Judith attached herself to a crowd of women who were going upstairs to *powder their noses*. She knew they'd all snoop a bit into the other rooms. Judith planned to stay behind when they came back downstairs and do a bit of snooping on her own. Upstairs there was a wait for the bathroom and women were milling about in the hallway or waiting their turn in the chairs set out for that purpose.

A young woman was offering soft drinks, coffee or tea and Judith gratefully accept a cup. She wandered away with her cup and saucer in hand, sipping tea and admiring the artwork on the walls. She moved further and further from the crowd but discovered that every closed door she tried to open was locked. Reaching the end of the hallway she returned and tried the doors on the other side but with the same result. Then she spotted Lila eyeing her.

"What are you up to?" her friend enquired.

"Oh I'm looking around and being nosy. I saw you made some new friends and it looks like you're having a good time."

"I did, and I am, and I still want to know what you're doing."

"I told you."

"You're snooping, aren't you?"

"Yes, that's what I said. It's a gorgeous house and I want to see it all."

"You're not snooping, you're investigating!"

"Don't be silly."

"You never had any intention of attending this party and then, all of a sudden, you wanted to come. Why?" demanded Lila.

Judith decided to come clean. "I'm trying to find Beth. I'm sure Noel has got her."

"Noel?! You think it's Noel?"

"No! Yes, yes... well I'm not sure. Listen, Noel is a great guy and a kindhearted man, but the consequences of Holly's pregnancy are huge and scary and life-altering for him."

"But murder? I can't believe he would kill anybody."

"Okay not murder but what about an accident? He's been spoiled all his life and that's made him weak and when weak people are trapped they lash out. What if he killed Holly by accident and everything that's happened since has been to cover that up?"

"But why cover it up? He's an upstanding citizen with a good reputation and from a good family. I'm sure the police would believe him if he told them it was an accident."

"Right, but then everything he wanted to keep hidden would have to come out. He might be charged with accidental death instead of murder but he'd still be charged. He'd still lose Annalise and his job and his reputation and his freedom."

"Oh yes, of course. Whether or not he meant to kill her only lessens his culpability by courtroom standards – not public opinion."

"That's for sure. So, if Noel has been involved since Holly's death do you think he's responsible for Beth's disappearance?"

"I'm certain of it and that's why I, we, are here. We've got to find her, we've got to!"

"Jeez, keep your voice down! You're convince that she's here, in the house?"

"If she is she's well-hidden. What about in the attic? or the cellar?"

"Cellar? That sounds like something out of a Gothic novel. I don't see how she could be hidden here, there are too many people around. Not just the guests but the employees too and the caterers as well."

"I know, and this place is so big it does seem hopeless."

"Well I'm helping you, no argument. And since it is such a big job why don't we call Grant? Not now, we can keep scouting around now, but you need to call him tomorrow and he can see about getting a warrant to search the place."

"I hardly think my suspicions are solid enough for a judge to issue a warrant on the Frampton estate – especially on Christmas Day!"

"That's not your concern. Go ahead and tell Grant everything you know and suspect. You convinced me about Noel and both you and Brian convinced me about Beth. Let Grant figure out what he can do."

"Grant won't do anything because he thinks I'm a nosy meddler playing detective. We don't need him. He's already told me to butt out and stop interfering so that's fine, I won't pester him anymore."

"He meant that he doesn't want you to get hurt, he's concerned for your safety."

"And I'm concerned for Beth's safety. Tomorrow is Christmas Day, nothing's going to happen, and then it's Boxing Day so again he won't be able to do anything even if he is willing to try."

Another group of ladies arrived at the landing so Judith and Lila excused themselves and got through them. As they made their way downstairs they could see more hallways branching off each leading to many more rooms. Lila spied an open French door leading outside and suggested they leave the hot, noisy room for some air. Judith followed keeping an eye on the pink dress as Lila manoeuvred her way through the crowd.

They stepped outside into a snow-covered world of silence and immediately relaxed. Snow was still falling and the scene, with lighted windows behind and snow-draped trees in front, was picturesque. Looking down to ground-level they saw several smokers standing around indulging in cigarettes and cigars. A pathway led away from the house past garages and other outbuildings.

Judith made up her mind that after they left the party and she dropped Lila off at her home she would come back on her own and explore that pathway from the other end. She was afraid that Beth couldn't wait much longer.

Chapter 51

Lila was having such a good time Judith suggested she should stay at the party and get a lift home from one of the teachers or call a cab. Lila said no, she'd stick to their original plan. If she stayed any longer she'd end up drinking too much and she certainly didn't want to do that.

"Besides, these sexy-as-hell shoes are absolutely killing me."

"They do look fantastic."

"I know, and they make my legs look great too, but there's always a price to pay and in my case it's pinched toes!"

They laughed together then made their way through the crowd, which had thinned considerably, to find their host and hostesses to say goodbye. They spotted Noel first, with Annalise close by his side, and wishing him a *Happy Birthday* thanked him for a great party.

"You can't go yet!" cried Noel.

"It's been a blast, truly," answered Lila, "but we're a couple of Cinderellas and it's time we left."

"Thank you so much for coming," chimed in Annalise.

"No, thank you for inviting us. Happy Birthday! Merry Christmas! and thanks again," replied Judith moving away. In the front hall a few Queen Anne chairs were grouped on a colourful Persian carpet with hand-painted Chinese screens providing shelter from the drafts whenever the door opened. Audrey Larkin and Eleanor Frampton were seated here, accepting the congratulations, thanks, and goodbyes of their guests.

"It's so nice to see you two again," said Eleanor.

"You too! and thank you so much for a lovely Christmas party – so festive with wonderful food, a great crowd, and lots of fun."

"We do try," preened Audrey, "So glad you enjoyed it."

"We did, very much! Thanks again and Merry Christmas to you both."

They were led away to find their coats and then out the door to describe Judith's car to the valet. They only waited a couple of minutes and then were on their way back to Lila's, admiring the many houses with Christmas lights and lawn displays that they passed.

"I can't even think about food but I can offer you a cup of coffee," said Lila.

Judith yawned in response and Lila laughed saying,

"You need a coffee to manage the drive home! and then it's definitely an early night for both of us. But I did enjoy myself."

"So did I!" said Judith, surprising both of them.

"You're a fun date, Judith Taylor!"

"Ha! You're not so bad yourself, Lila Morelli."

"I know. You've already got your own clothes in the car, right?"

"Yes, I put them in the trunk when we left your place."

"The richest neighbourhood for miles around and you were afraid of having the car broken into over a bag of used clothes?"

"Hey, fancy neighbourhoods have the richest pickings. Nobody's going to rob a slum."

"You're definitely belt-and-braces, aren't you Judith?"

"I don't see anything wrong with that."

"Not wrong exactly but... does anybody ever call you Judy?"

"Only once."

Chapter 52

When they reached Lila's place she directed Judith to a garage in the lane-way that ran behind the property. She had a fob to open the garage door on her key-chain and Judith parked in the empty space beside Lila's car. To get in the house they only had a short walk along a bricked path across the backyard to Lila's private entrance.

"Feel free to have wander around or if you're tired just take a seat. Coffee will take two minutes. I've got Vanilla Hazelnut if you like flavoured coffee, or else regular medium roast coffee, your choice."

"I wouldn't mind trying that flavoured coffee if it's not too much trouble."

"It's no trouble at all, I just pop in a pod." When Judith looked quizzical Lila showed her the single-serve coffee maker. It sat beside a huge stainless-steel machine which Lila explained made wonderful espresso and cappuccino with frothed milk but she wasn't firing up the contraption tonight. "It takes so long to get it going that I feel obligated to have several cups and I'm just too tired. I don't know if it was the drinks or the cold air when we came out but I'm ready to crash."

"Oh don't bother with the coffee then–" began Judith but Lila interrupted saying:

"Too late! it's already made, see?"

They took their mugs over to the couch and Lila flipped a switch on her stereo system and Christmas music began to play.

"Won't your Mrs. P. object to the noise?"

"No, the old sweetheart is deaf as a post once she takes her hearing aids out which happens about 8:30 each night."

Judith sipped at her hot drink and felt comfortable and relaxed. She needed to kill some time before sneaking back to the Frampton home and the coffee would help her stay awake.

Lila, having kicked off her high-heels when they walked in the door, now massaged her feet and sighed with pleasure.

"Despite everything else that's been going on this evening I've found myself thinking about your marriage, well, your separation. It's surprising. You seem very upbeat but it can't be an easy situation for you. If I'm being intrusive just say so, I'm not trying to poke my nose in."

"You're funny, Judith. To answer your second question no, I don't mind you asking. As for the first question well, yes and no. Being so far away from everyone I can forget about my 'Toronto problems', for awhile anyhow. Tomorrow is going to be tricky. Arnie and I have celebrated every Christmas together for almost twenty years, I mentioned we started dating in high-school, right?"

"Yes, that's a long time."

"I'm kinda thinking this holiday will be the catalyst, I guess, for what comes next in our married life."

"You don't strike me as the kind of person who just sits back and takes what life throws at you. I mean, you've mentioned your Italian temperament and Arnie, well with a name like Morelli he must be Italian too so—"

"No, Arnie's not Italian, he's a Canadian with British ancestry. Morelli is my maiden name. I figured if I'm making a new start I don't want to be making explanations over name changes or stuff like that. If I stay here I'm Lila Morelli, if I end up going back to my married life no one here will realize I was using my maiden name all along.

I don't know if I'm being practical or practising for life on my own. I've never been on my own, actually. I went from my parent's home to my home with Arnie. This is the very first time and I have to admit I quite like it."

"I've pretty much always been on my own. I'm an orphan. Dad died when I was a little kid and my mother passed a few months before I finished high-school."

"Oh that must have been devastating!" exclaimed Lila.

"Well, no," after a brief pause she continued saying: "The Vice-Principal at the school had me stay with her and her family till the end of the semester. They were very kind. I lived in the dorm at University and that was almost like living alone because I rarely saw my roommate. She was the 'party hearty' type. Her expression, not mine."

"And she didn't manage to convert you?"

"Ha-ha. I know you're kidding but funny enough we stayed roommates all the way through because our differences meant we suited each other. Since we had minimal contact we didn't have the falling out issues or raiding each other's wardrobes or stealing boyfriends problems that I would hear other roommates fight about.

Halfway through my last year she dropped out to get married and they didn't assign me another roommate so it all worked out great for me."

Lila was giving her a funny look but when Judith said: "What?" Lila just shook her head saying,

"Well I'm one to talk, I've only ever had the one boyfriend. Only one man has ever seen me naked and that's hard to believe at my age and especially in this day and age. I've seen more nudity on TV then I have in real life and I'm a nurse!

Arnie and I have been best friends since we were young and we never really formed other close relationships. He has buddies from work, as did I, plus I've got a ton of cousins and plenty of young aunts, too. I've always had female companionship to go out for a meal or to gossip with but not a close girlfriend. Oh boy..." she interrupted herself with a jaw-cracking yawn. Judith laughed and gathered up her things saying,

"I can see you do need your bed so I'll be on my way."

"I'm being a crappy hostess but I'm not going to argue. I really am beat. Just leave that mug. I'll zap the garage door and after you back out jut give a quick honk so I can zap it shut again."

They walked up the stairs and Lila opened the door and pointed her fob. Judith heard the garage door open and said goodnight. Lila thanked her for the ride and she thanked Lila for accompanying her to her first-ever Noel Larkin birthday-Christmas party.

"Maybe the first of many, who knows?" replied Lila before closing the door against the cold night air.

She stayed there looking out through the small window. Judith backed out and gave her horn a beep then waited while the garage door closed before entering the back lane and heading home.

Chapter 53

Judith studied the map on her computer, zooming in to the Executive Estate subdivision. She was pleased to see that, as she suspected, there was a service road leading around the back of the big properties.

It was a proper-sized road, big enough for garbage and recycling pick-up as well as delivery vans.

Judith followed the line to the boundary of the Frampton home. She planned to pull her car over under a cover of trees and then slip down the lane entering the property from the rear, as unobtrusively as possible. She already felt self-conscious, silly even, in her all-black outfit and switched her phone to airplane mode now before she forgot.

Leaving one lamp on in her living-room and careful to be quiet Judith left her apartment. There was some sort of get-together going on downstairs and guests had blocked the driveway, forcing her to leave her car on the street. She'd been annoyed about that when she got home but now realized this was a good thing. She was able to leave as anonymously as any visitor.

Driving back the same route she'd taken hours earlier Judith felt a thrill of excitement. For such a non-adventurous person she sure was having her share of intrigue tonight.

There was very little traffic. The still-falling snow was melting when it reached the road but piling up to transform the shape of hedges and gates and even parked cars. As she neared the Estate she again admired its Christmas card type of scenery.

Finding the service road, she slowed down since it was unlit although the driveways into the properties had lights or fancy lanterns to outline the way. She found the Frampton place and driving her car a little further along the road she pulled over onto the verge and parked.

It was pitch dark and utterly silent. Walking back Judith felt the first frisson of fear. She couldn't distinguish the ground from the driveway, the snow lay thick everywhere, but she kept moving in the direction of the house even though she couldn't see it yet.

It was so quiet. She strained her ears to pick up any noise but couldn't hear a thing, the falling snow deadened all sound. If she'd been walking here with a friend it would have been pretty, but on her own it felt a little creepy.

Judith had an aha! moment when she spotted a small building, like a cottage. She'd remembered Noel once talking about their guest house and how it was great in the summer but not much good in the winter since it wasn't heated.

"There is a wood-burning fireplace," he'd said, "but that only lasts for an hour or so, it won't keep you warm all night." He'd gone on to describe what a cozy little place it was hidden away in the woods and Judith had thought it sounded like a rich man's love-nest.

She recalled that conversation now as she crept closer. "The guest house looks deserted," she thought. "It's dark and there's no smoke coming from the chimney."

Cautiously looking around Judith noticed her footprints following behind her. Looking ahead she saw a fainter, smaller set – almost filled up with flakes – leading into the woods. "Beth!" she thought and followed the trail.

Tree roots snagged underfoot and thorny branches stabbed at her. Despite moving with as little noise as possible Judith knew she'd been heard when a gasp and a tearful hiccup sounded about a yard or so in front. The woods were too dense to let in much light from the moon, so Judith was relying on her other senses to direct her.

"Beth it's me, Ms. Taylor, Judith Taylor. I've come to take you home," she called in a loud whisper.

"Ms. T-Taylor?" quavered a young voice.

"Yes, yes! I'm so glad you're okay. You are okay, aren't you?"

"I will be now that you're here. I've been so scared. I don't know how long I've been in that cabin but I finally got up the nerve to break a window and climb out. I'm sorry about breaking the window, though. I feel really cold but I was cold inside there too."

"Well, I'll crank up the heat to high once we get in my car and you'll soon warm up. Oh, I'm so happy to find you! your father's been half-crazy with worry."

"Dad! Oh, I've missed him so much. I want to go home! Let's go right away."

The girl stepped out from behind the tree where she'd been hiding. She wasn't dressed for a December night outdoors and was visibly shivering. Judith hurried forwards and put her arm around Beth's shoulders. She immediately turned it into a hug and Judith could feel the cold of the girl's thin body right through her own outdoor clothing. She slipped her coat off and wrapped Beth in it. Then locking their arms together the two of them started back.

As they reached the edge of the clearing and got closer to the house Judith could see larger footprints coming towards the guest house and overlaying Judith's as the larger prints went around to the back of the small building.

The size of the print and length of the stride indicated a man made them – and he was running. The sight was terrifying.

Judith hesitated, feeling unsure which way to go. She could barely see the lights of the main house which mean it was quite far. The follower might still be at the guest house itself and going deeper into the woods to head for the back road was scary.

What if they got lost? Beth couldn't take too much more exposure. The girl was weak and frightened and bitterly cold. But Judith, indecisive in such an unfamiliar situation, had to make a choice. She felt safer hidden in the confines of the woods although she knew it could be a dangerous route.

"It's time to get rid of *sensible Judith*," she told herself, "But taking risks sure is scary so I hope my sensible self will return as soon as we're safe and sound."

As quietly as possible they waded through the snow and around the trees. Every now and then Judith's head would brush against a branch releasing a shower of snow. It was dark, it was cold, and they were frightened.

They heard the occasional skitter of some small creature but had no fear left over to worry about it. They knew there was a man nearby and he was tracking them.

Chapter 54

The silence and blackness of the woods was unnerving. Judith was glad to have Beth to hang on to but she could feel the young girl's strength running out. She dragged her feet, sometimes threatening to pull them both to the ground as she stumbled and almost fell.

They weren't moving very fast and Judith feared it wouldn't be difficult for their pursuer to catch up. Their only hope was to remain hidden by the trees while he stayed on the path.

Beth cried out when the man suddenly jumped in front of them. Judith's heart started pounding when she saw he was Noel.

"Finally!" he exclaimed. "I've been up and down around here. I was following your footprints but couldn't believe you'd stay in the woods. I don't know if you're brave, crazy, or stupid but I've got you now."

"Let us go!" screamed Judith but Noel grabbed her and covered her mouth.

"Shut up!" he demanded. "There's nobody around to hear you but I don't want to listen to that noise."

He snagged Beth's arm with his other hand and started pulling the two of them back where they'd come from, towards the guest home. Judith kicked her feet then let her body sag inert weighing him down, slowing him down. Noel struggled with her for a bit then flung her away. She fell in the snow in a half-sitting position, the wet seeping into her thigh and hip and side. Her black track suit was no protection and she'd given her coat to Beth.

"You don't want to come with us that's fine," shouted Noel. "You're not the one I want anyhow, she is." And with that he started dragging Beth away.

Judith saw that the girl was too weak and too tired to put up a fight. She let him lead her away.

"Stop Noel! stop right now," Judith hollered but he ignored her and kept going.

She thought of running back to her car to turn on her phone, get help... she wanted to do all that – so much! – and it would be the smart thing to do, but she fought the temptation because she couldn't abandon the girl. Noel had Beth so Judith had no choice but to follow.

Chapter 55

Judith reached the guest house shortly after Noel and Beth. She raced inside expecting to find him holding Beth with a knife to her throat or a gun to her head. Instead, she saw Noel striking a match to the logs laid in the fireplace and Beth huddled on the couch with a blanket. Before she could speak, she heard the front door open and a voice complaining:

"Oh Noel, we only lost one, but you've brought back two! Who is this? a teacher? no it's the accountant woman. What is she doing here?"

Audrey Larkin, well-bundled against the cold in a smart coat, fur hat and warm boots, whining about Judith should have been farcical. Instead, Judith was terrified.

Noel's mother had a strong sense of privilege but surely, she understood she couldn't sweep away Noel's crimes of kidnapping, false imprisonment, and murder? Motherly love taken to the nth degree. Unless she was raving mad.

"Mother stop, please. This has gone too far."

"Darling boy, so sweet and sensitive. You've always needed me to take care of you and you always will. And I will always do so. The solution to this problem of yours has been very tricky but I'll figure it out, don't worry.

I thought I'd given this little Miss a strong enough dose. She's very thin so what she drank should have done the job. I can't understand what went wrong."

Judith gasped at the realization that Audrey Larkin wasn't covering up for Noel's criminal acts but for her own.

Beth stared wide-eyed at Audrey, too petrified to move. Both Noel and Judith stepped between the woman and the girl.

As Audrey reached into her purse Judith had to suppress an hysterical laugh at this crazy lady primly carrying her handbag over her arm. The laughter was choked off at the sight of the gun Audrey now held in her hand.

"Step aside, Noel. I need to take care of the girl and do a proper job of it this time."

Shaking his head and giving a deep sigh Noel said: "Oh, Mother you aren't going to shoot Beth, I won't allow it."

He stepped forward to take away the gun, but right then the door banged opened startling Audrey who fired the weapon. The noise was immense. Noel fell to his knees and someone screamed, it sounded like they all screamed.

Eleanor Frampton stood framed in the doorway.

Chapter 56

"Audrey! what have you done now?" Eleanor exclaimed, but her sister didn't answer. She had rushed to Noel and was crying over him.

"Mother I'm fine, well it hurts but the bullet only grazed me."

"You're bleeding!" she screeched in horror.

"It's only my ear, you know ears bleed a lot. Honest, it's okay, I'm okay."

Keeping her eyes on Noel and the women Judith edged towards the couch unnoticed. She sat down and pulled Beth tight against her. The girl buried her face in Judith's shoulder and her whole body heaved with sobs. She was terrified.

The other three forgot about them as they squabbled about why Audrey had a gun and where she's gotten it:

"I took it from Bas's office right after he died. You never missed it."

"I never knew he had it."

"Well, I knew. I saw it lots of time when I was in there just... looking around."

"Snooping, stealing, prying – up to no good as usual," Eleanor retorted.

"Well never mind that now. Noel needs to go to the hospital and I have to get rid of this girl. Oh, and I guess this woman too."

"What are you talking about? Noel, what is your mother going on about now?"

"God knows, Auntie. I don't. At the party I saw Judith poking around like she was looking for something then I realized it was someone that she was looking for. It had to be Beth. But I knew Beth wasn't in our house because she'd gone into hiding or something and then, I don't know why, but I thought of the guest house. It's a perfect hideaway–"

"That's what I thought too!" said Audrey brightly. Her son and sister stared at her in consternation then Noel continued saying:

"I came out and spotted traces of footprints which shouldn't have been there so I followed them. The door was locked but, as usual, the key was on the door-sill.

When I came in I felt a strong draft and discovered the window was broken. Looking out I could see signs that someone had left here by breaking the glass and falling onto the snow. Other things in this room had been moved about, and a knapsack with Beth's name on it was left behind.

It was unimaginable that Beth was hiding out here by choice, and the broken window told its own story so–"

"She shouldn't have broken anything!" said Audrey with annoyance.

"I went out looking for Beth and followed a trail of two sets of footprints into the woods. I wasted time heading back home, thinking that's where Beth and whoever had gone, but ended up having to double-back. I found them – still in the woods – on their way to the road. I didn't even think about what Judith was planning to do, all I could think was that I wanted to bring Beth back here to get her warm. If she's been locked in here, in the cold, for a few days she must be suffering from exposure. How far were you planning to go?" he asked, turning to Judith.

"My car is on the service road."

"Oh, I should have asked instead of just acting but I wasn't thinking straight. It's a shame though because we three would have been away by now and I wouldn't be bleeding like a stuck pig... Mother you could have killed me!"

"It's obvious that the girl is fine," said Audrey. "I guess she was out cold for most of the time. I thought she'd be dead. It never occurred to me that she'd wake up and escape." She shot Beth an evil look but the girl's face was still hidden and she didn't see it.

"But why? Why did you want to kill this girl? Noel couldn't have gotten her pregnant as well."

"WHAT!" shouted Noel. "I've never gotten anyone pregnant, what are you talking about?"

"Well dear we know about the condition Holly was in when she died–"

"And you thought it was mine? That I got her pregnant? She's a child! And she's a student. I would never have relations with student. How could you ever think something like that of me?" Noel was flabbergasted – and hurt.

A feeling of shame swept over Judith as she realized that because of gossip and innuendo she'd also believed the worst about Noel. She was no better than Xiao and Marta for so readily believing the accusation made about herself in the poison pen letter.

She owed Noel an apology but if he even imagined she had accepted that rumour as true then their friendship would never be the same. She decided not to admit to her thoughts.

"When I see the doctor to get my ear stitched up I'll arrange to give a DNA sample as well. I – God, I can't believe you could possibly think..." he shook his head and a few drops of blood out flew striking his mother in the face.

"She told me so, that's why!" Audrey answered. She looked around at all of them saying:

"You all know she'd been phoning the house for Noel. Well I demanded, as his mother, to know what business she had with him. She said it was a matter best discussed in private. That set off warning bells in my head and I was angry too. This nothing of a girl insinuating something underhand.

So, we arranged a time, and I told her to meet me here in the guest house and when she hung up she said, laughing, 'bye-bye Granny'. I slammed the phone down. Right away I realized her plan was to ruin my son. Well, I knew I could deal with that by buying her off since it was obvious from the type she was that it was money she was after."

"Mother you have no idea what Holly was like. Sure she could be flippant but she was funny and clever and had a future."

"Noel you are so naive! and don't interrupt me. Anyhow, this Holly did turn up but was very late with some excuse about her planned ride not being available, so she'd had to hitchhike and walk a long way. She was very cranky and sassy, and I was annoyed too because of the long wait – it's so cold in here – and next thing I knew she was saying something smart-alecky and I hit her. She fell right there." Audrey pointed to the floor to the side of the fireplace. "I waited for her to get up and when she didn't, I went over and pushed her with my foot. Her body lifted a bit and I saw a big pool of blood. That's when I realized she was dead."

"How could you be sure?" cried Eleanor. "Did you check for a pulse? what if she could have been saved? you should have called 9-1-1!"

"No, no I knew she was dead, and I was glad. I didn't want her resuscitated. It actually worked out well because even though I'd come prepared to pay her I expect she would have kept coming back for more. This way the problem was taken care of once and for all."

"There was no problem!" thundered Noel. "If she was pregnant it certainly wasn't by me!"

"But how could I know that, son? She was very convincing and I'd heard Annalise complain about this girl who was cozying up to you at rehearsals, holding your hand, whispering in your ear, and after all you are a man."

"That's right, Mother. I'm a man, not some predator or child-molester. You killed her for nothing."

"Noel no, don't say that! I killed her for you!"

Audrey's dramatic cry brought Grant, Annalise, and Lila came through the door. They'd been standing outside with Grant holding the women back so he could listen to the conversation, which turned out to be a confession.

Annalise rushed over to Noel and hugged him tight, exclaiming over his injury. Lila ran to Beth and began checking her over, saying:

"I need to get this girl to the hospital right now, she's severely hydrated and running a fever."

She glanced at Noel and frowned at the blood, but he smiled at her over Annalise's shoulder and gave a thumbs up sign.

Eleanor Frampton sat down on a kitchen chair and started to cry. Audrey looked around in surprise saying:

"Don't you want to know how I go the body to the school?"

Chapter 57

Judith might have been very angry with Lila if she had known what her friend was up to but she didn't find out until much later.

Then she learned that Lila's worries stemmed from not being able to reach Judith on the phone. Lila said she'd woken after napping for a few hours feeling refreshed but regretting her poor hostessing. She wanted to make up for it by inviting Judith to have Christmas dinner with her next day.

It wasn't like she'd had a premonition of danger or anything, only a sudden thought that neither of them should spend Christmas alone. She got worried when she couldn't reach Judith even though it was after 11:00 at night. It didn't make sense that Judith wasn't answering.

"I had a very good reason for not answering!" laughed Judith when they did sit down and talk through the events that led up to the confrontation in the cabin.

Lila wanted to go over to Judith's apartment to make sure she was okay but knew she had drunk too much at the party to drive. Although she felt fine and alert her nurse's training taught her that she must still have alcohol in her system. Too much to be out driving.

Thinking about all those peculiar incidents that had befallen Judith over the last few days made up Lila's mind. She called the police station and asked for George Grant, claiming it was an emergency. Lila couldn't care less if she caused trouble – she was deeply worried about her friend.

Again, Judith laughed. It was easy to forgive after the fact.

Lila insisted Grant come get her to accompany him to find Judith. He tried to get her to divulge Judith's suspected whereabouts but Lila was adamant that she wanted to tag along.

They all met up again at Judith's apartment. It was late, the wee hours of the morning in fact, but all three wanted to talk about the night's events and each had a story to tell.

Chapter 58

Grant took a sip of his coffee before starting. He noted that Judith used a French Press and the coffee tasted great. Since his presence wasn't required at the police station and as it was now actually Christmas Day he was on his own time which he mentioned:

"I can now say *Merry Christmas, Judith and Lila* because it's officially the 25th. Since I don't have a family I usually offer to work over the holidays but this year I think I'll enjoy the break."

"I've worked my share of Christmas and New Year's shifts too. Judith, you're lucky you're in a nine-to-five job."

"You wouldn't know if from this past week – that's for sure! Anyhow, Grant, tell us what happened with Audrey Larkin."

Grant told the two women how Eleanor Frampton had called in some favours and Audrey had been whisked away to a psychiatric facility masquerading as a *rest home*. Grant's boss had assured him that the woman was under police guard and would be arrested, but Grant suspected the doctors would pronounce Audrey Larkin unfit to plead so the case would be resolved without going to court.

"So they're saying that she's some kind of psycho?"

"Yes, they are. According to Eleanor Audrey suffers from *one of those pathys* but she couldn't remember if it was psychopathy or sociopathy. She claims Audrey was diagnosed many years ago and the family has always had to keep an eye on her. So long as the afflicted person is never thwarted they never need to act on their latent tendencies."

"I can believe that," put in Lila.

"Well, it all sounds a bit gobbledy-gook to me but I'm only a dumb copper," replied Grant with a smile.

He turned serious and said to Judith:

"Speaking of dumb, I want to apologize for snapping at you yesterday. It happened because of my concern for your welfare, but that's no excuse. The truth is both Lila and I took those near-misses far more seriously than you did. I believed that someone was after you, and I thought it had something to do with Holly's diary."

"Which I never did have."

"But the person chasing after you didn't know that."

"That was Noel," said Judith. "While Lila went to the hospital with Beth, and you were busy with handing over Audrey, Noel and Annalise and I had a good talk. He felt guilty that Holly died because of him and said he couldn't believe what his mother had done.

Annalise and I reassured him that he wasn't to blame for that but then I said, *your mother didn't come into the school and leave an anonymous letter in the staff room,* and he said he was really, really sorry about doing that. Annalise didn't know what we were talking about and when I explained she burst out laughing. Well, it was ridiculous.

Anyhow, her laughter broke the tension and Noel confessed that he was desperate to deflect suspicion from Annalise, her being questioned really upset him. It was touching to witness because he really does care for her. Also, he'd heard some of the whispers about him and Holly, and I think that was an eye-opener for him.

He told me *I was going to name Marta, because no one likes her very much so it would be believable, but you're the one Beth left the message for on the answering machine* and he apologized again." Judith didn't add that Noel had also said *besides, you're tough* because she wasn't sure how she felt about him saying that.

"But what about the intruder in the library and your car getting rammed?"

"The intruder was Noel. He was trying to scare me away from my desk so he could search it for Holly's diary. He was worried that Beth had somehow gotten it to me or hidden it for me to find. Noel went too far in his flirtation with Holly but it never went beyond kisses and compliments. He was afraid she might have written a glamourized version of their friendship making out it was something much more. Sounds to me like he's learned his lesson and won't be so susceptible to adolescent hero-worship in future!

You know, I do feel badly for believing the rumours about him. Since Noel is so good-looking and the heir to a huge fortune I guess I assumed he'd be spoilt and have a weak character. I was wrong. He's a nice guy and a good guy and I should have been a better friend. Especially since I know how it feels when people are ready to think the worst of you."

"Nobody believed that letter, Judith. But you're right about Noel, we all made assumptions. Just like people do with blondes, right Grant?"

"Don't go there Lila," he growled.

"Getting back to the incidents, the bad driver following me might simply have been a bad driver but I think it was Audrey. We know she has her own car and could come and go with no one the wiser from the estate."

"Yes, she explained that when she told me how she'd moved Holly's body."

"Tell us about that part. She's a small woman, did she have help?"

"No, she bragged about how clever she'd been. Do you remember seeing a bearskin rug – a real black bearskin – at the side of the fireplace?"

"No," said Lila, while Judith answered:

"Yes, I noticed because it should have been in front of the fireplace and I was admiring the skin. Usually people have a small white rug in fake fur."

"Well, Audrey told me she rolled Holly onto the rug and dragged her to the door. Then she brought her car around and drove it right up the guest house. It has its own gravelled driveway which we couldn't see because of the snow. It must have been a struggle, but she managed to get Holly, still wrapped in the bearskin, into her car.

Then, she said she was exhausted from the effort and took the car back to her own driveway where she left it with a body wrapped in a bearskin rug for several days because she forgot!

She's lucky it was cold but not cold enough to freeze the body once rigor mortis ended otherwise she wouldn't have been able to get it out of the car.

It wasn't until the chauffeur finally asked if she'd like him to move her car into the garage that she remembered Holly's body was still inside. She drove to the woods behind the school, unrolled the body and returned the rug back where is belonged but moved to a different position to cover up the blood stain."

"That wouldn't have worked for long though. The guest house must get cleaned?"

"Not thoroughly, not until the summer when it might be used by visitors."

"But wouldn't the blood stain still be there?"

"Yes, but faded and why would anyone think the stain was blood? And if they did the family would simply have called the police to report a break-in and some sort of incident of which they'd claim they were unaware of.

Without a body we wouldn't take a sample and even if by some chance we did it wouldn't be tested, lab fees are expensive and we have to justify the costs."

"Wait a bit," said Lila. "I know crazy people can sometimes find incredible strength but how did that old lady manage to do everything?"

Grant laughed replying: "You made the same mistake I did, Lila. What makes you think Audrey Larkin is old? She isn't fifty yet!"

"Wow, really? Oh my. I guess it's just her being Noel's mother and not working, sitting around a cozy fire all day with servants taking care of everything while she griped and complained, with her cameo brooch pinned to her cashmere dress... hmm. You're right, I assumed she was much older."

"Well Eleanor Frampton is considerably older and they're sisters so that adds to the assumption, I guess."

"Do you realize," said Judith with a surprised look on her face, "She could very well have gotten away with it!"

"The perfect crime."

Chapter 59

Lila swallowed the bite of shortbread cookie she was eating to say:

"She might have gotten away with killing Holly but then Beth got involved. She told me about that while we waited for her Dad to get to the hospital," Lila turned to Judith saying: "You should have seen his face! he was so happy he cried, and he even gave me a kiss. You should have been there."

"Why? Does Judith want to be kissed by Brian Penner?" asked Grant with a wry smile that didn't quite reach his eyes.

"He is very good-looking, if you like that type…" Judith let the sentence trail away. "I'm sure he considers Beth's return to be the best Christmas present ever."

"Is Beth going to be okay?"

"She'll be fine, Grant. She's a healthy girl and at that age they're able to bounce back. Still, she was at risk and not only from Audrey Larkin! exposure to cold temperatures for a long period of time has adverse effects on the body's organs.

Fortunately there is no frostbite so now we just have to hope she can get out of the hospital without picking up the flu bug. They've got a lot of people there who are sick with it."

"That's another reason why nobody likes hospitals!"

"Anyhow, when Beth couldn't get hold of you, Judith, she tried to reach Noel. See, she'd read Holly's diary. She had no reason to be afraid of Noel because she knew he wasn't the father of Holly's baby."

"Who was?"

"According to the diary Billy MacNeill was the father," said Grant. "Beth turned it over to us and it seems Holly had enjoyed stealing her mother's boyfriend and the two of them acting like they were barely friendly under Dana's watchful eye. Holly had complained a lot about Dana being too strict with her.

I bet Billy MacNeill was the ride who never turned up to drive Holly when she met Audrey at the guest house. Remember? he was in Calgary that day."

"Does that mean he cooked up this scheme to extort money by claiming the baby was Noel's? and Holly was going along with it? I guess she must have been, she's the one who made the phone call."

"They must have figured Noel's mother would pay to hush up a scandal without investigating the matter."

"And they figured correctly. Audrey Larkin just went off on her own to take care of things. I wonder what would have happened if she had asked Noel about it?"

"Holly was pretty brazen. She'd probably have laughed it off telling him that because he was so rich it was worth a try."

"Poor Dana. I know she kicked Billy out after discovering the whole car theft thing but to find out this as well... does she have to find out?"

"Yes, she has the right to know. It will be painful but it's always better to know."

"So, before you hijacked my story I was saying..."

"Sorry, go on Lila."

"Beth called up Noel but, like Holly, got his mother instead. I guess Audrey was feeling invincible after killing Holly and the subsequent disposal of her body, so she arranged to pick up Beth outside the school.

Instead of taking her to the house she told her that the servants were terrible gossips and she'd prefer to have a private chat. When they got to the guest house she poured out hot chocolate from a thermos for both of them. That's the last thing Beth remembers until she woke up feeling sick to her stomach, stiff, and very, very cold."

"The hospital will look for traces of a drug or poison in Beth's bloodstream but it's unlikely that Audrey Larkin will ever be charged with attempted murder," put in Grant.

"So that's it? No one is held to account and we're all supposed to go ahead and get on with our lives like none of this ever happened?" Judith looked intently at Grant and he returned her stare. Lila, feeling out of place, stood up saying:

"I've got to get going, my family will all be calling at the crack of dawn because they always pretend to get the time difference backwards. They'll start off nicey-nice, wishing me a Merry Christmas, and then complain that I'm not there to help cook the big dinner.

Speaking of which Judith just come over whenever you feel like it. I don't have a turkey but I'll make you a nice dinner." She gathered up her coat and purse then remembered she didn't have her car since Grant had picked her up.

"Oh, I'd better call a cab."

"You won't get one on Christmas Eve, actually it's Christmas Day now, isn't it?"

Grant paused a moment then got up as well casually remarking:

"Yes, it's been a long day for all of is, hasn't it? Maybe we can meet up for a drink or a meal or something over the holidays?"

"Maybe," answered Judith.

Chapter 60

"Happy New Year, Samira," said Judith, happy to see the secretary over her flu bug and back at her desk.

"Same to you, Judith. I'm sorry we left you in the lurch," she dropped her voice to whisper, "I think Pat's going to tack on another couple of days when you do take your vacation, but don't let on I said so," she added.

Judith winked at her to the amazement of both of them.

Knocking on the partly opened door Judith still wore a smile as she entered the principal's office. She plopped down in the visitor chair announcing:

"I am so glad to be sitting on this side of that desk again. Imagine, it's only been two weeks! Holly's body was found on December 19th and here we are on January 6th, two-and-a-half weeks later, and it's all 'done and dusted' as I've heard people say."

"Judith, I can't thank you enough for everything you've done. I know I said some of this when we talked on the phone but you were wonderful. From having to cancel your vacation, to dealing with school issues and parents and teachers, then the murder and the police, and Beth Penner going missing and then finding Beth!

You know Eleanor Frampton can't say enough about you. I gather you were in the nick of time to prevent a bad situation from becoming very much worse."

"Oh everyone helped in that regard: Noel, Lila, Grant, and Eleanor herself. But to be honest I did get more involved, in fact way more involved, then I thought possible. There's something about these girls that... I don't know – grows on you? There's a strong feeling of responsibility but it's good, it feels right. I'm not making any sense, am I?"

"On the contrary, you are crystal clear. Judith, I can see that this experience has changed you, and for the better. I mean, there was nothing wrong with you before but now you seem happier, more relaxed, or something."

"You're right. I felt okay about myself and my life before but now I feel... great!"

"It shows. I'm so very glad that things turned out the way they did."

Judith left Pat's office deciding to grab a coffee before starting her day's work. As she passed Samira the younger woman looked up and asked:

"Judith have you met someone?"

"Don't you start, I hear enough of that from Lila!"

A few teachers were still in the staff room when Judith walked in and they all exchanged friendly greetings. Even the people she suspected had doubted her before now made friendly overtures, including Xiao. Judith answered questions about the Christmas Eve incident to the satisfaction of everyone except Marta who glowered from the corner.

In the corridor on the way to her own office she called out "Love the new glasses, Margaret!" and "Happy New Year" greetings to the other students she passed. The spirit of community wrapped its warmth around her.

In the privacy of her office Judith opened her purse and once again read the *Happy 2020* New Year's card she'd received from Grant. It made her smile and it felt right, but for now it was her secret so she didn't display it on her desk.

Second book in the Village of Edgemont Cozy Mysteries series

A Fatal February
in Edgemont

Della North

A Fatal February
in Edgemont

Della North

copyright 2023

publisher Lynda French

cover design by Dezynetek

Chapter 1

Saturday, February 8, 2020

Robert Wilcox knows this meeting isn't going to be pleasant, but he never imagined it will be fatal.

The retired Reverend, fondly known as Rev Robbie, arrives at the Edgemont Activity Centre with apprehension. As usual on a weekend, the parking lot is full but he has a reserved space in Staff Parking.

The weather is surprisingly mild for February in Alberta. Normally, a day like today with the clear blue sky, crisp air, and bright sunshine would have lifted the elderly man's spirits. But now, as the early winter darkness rolls in, he can't escape a strong feeling of foreboding.

He is facing up to a difficult task, an onerous duty, and the lighthearted greeting he receives from his visitor is disconcerting. It catches him off guard. Otherwise he might have survived because underneath his benign appearance Robert is an astute observer with no illusions about the darker side of human nature.

Lila Morelli checks her medical bag to ensure the first aid kit is fully stocked. Her movements are mechanical and her mind is miles away. She's been wrapped up in her own unhappy thoughts for weeks now, and the misery she feels leaves her numb.

She has a problem but it isn't actually *her* problem, just as she has a secret that isn't *her* secret to keep or to tell. In every action she is simply going through the motions, her usual ebullience missing. She is in limbo.

However, she has schedules, deadlines, and obligations to meet. Like now, heading out to The Centre for a mixed league volleyball game. Lila isn't playing, she'll be on the bench in her capacity as volunteer nurse in case there is an injury on the court.

She's been attending the games for a few months and enjoys being involved except... well.. now she doesn't enjoy much of anything anymore. Drowning in unhappiness Lila carries her gloomy mood everywhere she goes.

Last night had been special and so much fun. Judith Taylor and George Grant had driven out to the Banff townsite for what he'd called a *non-Valentine's February date.*

Both had enjoyed mingling with the upbeat crowd of tourists and skiers, everyone celebrating the season. The chill mountain air was fresh and clean.

After a dinner of back-ribs at Tony Roma's the two had wandered in and out of shops on the main drag. Stopping at a boutique confectioners Grant got chewy maple fudge and Judith had a gooey caramel chocolate for dessert. Then they drove to the Falls – which were half-frozen over – and followed the road to Surprise Corner where they admired the view of the Banff Springs Hotel all lit up like the castle it was styled after.

They were far enough away from Calgary's light pollution to witness what seemed to be a million stars in the sky. Looking up, trying to find and identify constellations, Grant had slipped his arm around Judith's shoulders and they both enjoyed the warmth that they felt inside and out.

Today, Judith is savouring the memory of a lovely night. Her friendship with Grant, which began so unexpectedly, is deepening in importance as well as intimacy.

They met when they'd been forced to work together because a flu bug decimated the administrative staff last year at Edgemont School for Girls while Grant was investigating the death of Holly Lezinsky, and the disappearance of Beth Penner, both students.

His unusual looks of very pale blond hair and ice-blue eyes made him a handsome man, but it was his gentle nature – despite his profession – that had attracted Judith the most. She feels scared, delighted, and intoxicated in anticipation of what the future will bring.

This evening she is joining Lila at The Centre to watch the volleyball tournament and have a final meeting with Rev Robbie. She's decided to take on the volunteer job of bookkeeper to free up more of his time. As a CPA Judith knows she'll have no difficulties with The Centre's books. It is a good cause with a friendly group of people, and Judith is experiencing the pleasure of helping out.

Chapter 2

Eleanor and Basil Frampton were the driving force behind The Edgemont Activity Centre. They both spent a lot of time fundraising among their wealthy friends, and Basil served on the Board. When he passed away Eleanor took over his position.

Quite a large number of people call Edgemont Village home. Located in the foothills of the Canadian Rockies many types of people are attracted by its natural beauty.

The outer circle reside in a wide surrounding area on acreages, ranches, and hobby farms. The inner circle range from *comfortably off* in the Executive Estates enclave to the folks *getting by okay* in the trailer park. In between are bungalows and semi-detacheds, apartments and basement suites, townhouses and penthouses, with residents in all the tax brackets but mostly the top tier. Edgemont Village is home to wealth.

The land acquisition and building of The Centre, as it is known locally, was 100% donation-funded. At lot of money had poured in and what wasn't used in the building and hiring has been wisely invested.

Now that the Board includes an experienced grant-writer some government funding is coming in to promote specialty programmes. Originally geared towards sports The Centre now boasts Arts, Crafts, and Music classes.

A group of string musicians teach the Suzuki Method in bi-weekly lessons; there are drawing and painting classes for all ages; and visiting instructors give one-day demonstrations in activities such as painting on silk, researching your family tree, and photorealistic illustrating. There's a Bridge Club; a Karate Club; several types of Yoga, Conversational French, Italian, German, and Chinese language classes; and lessons for all kinds of dance styles from tap to rap.

Patronage by the area's elite has made The Centre a worthy cause for its rich donors, and the volunteers enjoy a certain cachet from the association.

The Reverend Robert Wilcox's support increased after his retirement and when Peg, his beloved wife of almost fifty years died, his work at The Centre became the main focal point of his life. The short, and short-sighted, man with his fluff of white hair and cheerful smile is a familiar fixture.

As the little jobs he has taken on become big jobs he happily hands control over to younger volunteers, but he still oversees management of The Centre, and takes charge of the monies received each day.

Fees for the classes are usually processed online – which saves everyone a lot of time and bother – but earnings from the snack bar and donation boxes help build up the kitty.

The refreshment area sells canned soft drinks, coffees, and snacks – donated by local stores – and most of the visiting patrons will stuff a twenty or even a fifty into the cash-box by the front door. Edgemont Village is a retreat for the well-heeled and they are a generous bunch.

Patricia and Mark Johnson are at The Centre attending an early Valentine's get-together of the Horticultural Society. They are both friendly, sociable people. Overweight – but not in a worrying way – with Pat's figure best described as *stately*. She's slightly taller than Mark but only because she always wears heels.

Other than an evening walk they don't exercise, but spend plenty of time outdoors happily working in their garden in the warm weather, and coaxing along their houseplants during the wintertime.

Pat is especially devoted to her African Violet collection, while Mark's interest lies mainly in the preservation of native plants. He is able to spend more time working with the Society now that he's retired.

The Society occasionally hosts guest speakers who bring slides to illustrate their talks, often accompanied by samples and cuttings. Most of their meetings are luncheons, but today is an evening event. Now, the members gather to enjoy decaf coffee and sweet nibbles catered from a local doughnut shop.

Pat plans to drop in on the volleyball tournament to lend support to the players from her school. She is the principal of Edgemont School for Girls and knows that several of her students will be playing, while some of her staff will be cheering them on. As usual, Mark is quite happy to socialize with their friends for the short time she'll be making an appearance in the auditorium.

Detective George Grant and his partner, Suzanne Mirteau, are also at The Centre on this Saturday night checking the safety of the location before the visit of a couple of VIPs.

Some local bigwigs have fundraised enough to build an indoor skating rink. The ribbon-cutting ceremony is being performed by two holidaying minor Royals travelling the Trans-Canada Highway to ski at all the resorts from Banff National Park to Whistler, BC.

Their visit isn't happening until next month, in time for the Spring ski season, but protocol demands that all the arrangements be made, and the venues vetted by security professionals, well in advance of the event.

The two detectives make an eye-catching couple with her dark beauty offsetting his pale Nordic colouring. And as usual, they are arguing because they aren't a couple in the romantic sense and Suzanne is unable to accept that fact.

"Suzanne please, let's just finish off our checklist so we can leave. This day has already gone on forever and it's Saturday, I just want to go home and relax."

"Oh right, like I'm supposed to believe you don't have a hot date with your teacher or whatever she is."

"If you mean Judith Taylor she's the school bursar and, not that it's any of your business, we don't have a date tonight – hot or otherwise."

"Then you and I can go for a couple of drinks and discuss what we're going to have for breakfast," she says, flashing him a wicked grin that lights up her lovely face. Sparkling dark eyes, a cascade of wavy hair, and an athletic build always attracts the attention of all the men in her vicinity... except Grant.

When Suzanne flicks her tongue over her lips he doesn't see a sultry seductress but a narcissistic ego-driven control-freak. They've worked together for too long for Grant not to have encountered every aspect of Suzanne's nature. He's learned that beneath the beautiful looks she is bad-tempered, possessive, spiteful, and jealous.

With two divorces and quite a few bitterly ended romances all before the age of twenty-eight, Suzanne has grown more and more dissatisfied with her personal life. Grant, who had decided at the very start of his career not to get involved with coworkers, remains steadfastly immune to her charms – to her great annoyance.

Chapter 3

Saturday, February 8, 2020

Judith's pleasant thoughts of Grant end, and now her mind is dismayed over the troubles her co-worker Lila is enduring. Unfortunately there is very little Judith can do because Lila has thrown up barricades and refuses to explain.

Judith knows her friend's unhappiness has something – everything – to do with Arnie Chalmers, Lila's estranged husband. He'd flown out from Toronto at the New Year and Lila had been so excited that he was, finally, coming to see her, but whatever happened between the two of them wasn't good.

That's as much information as Lila is willing to give and Judith, afraid of damaging their new and valued friendship, doesn't push too hard. She will wait for Lila to confide and hopes it will happen soon.

The change in Lila is heartbreaking. Nothing seems to bring her out of her depression although Judith and Grant have tried, as have Beth Penner and her father Brian. Those two feel they owe a debt of gratitude to Lila for her support during Beth's ordeal in December.

Not too long ago Judith and Lila would have travelled to The Centre together, either from the school where they both work, or meeting at one or the other's home. After the game they'd have had a coffee and a gossip before returning to pick up whoever's car had been left behind.

When Judith suggests she drive them both tonight Lila has hurriedly said:

"No, I'll see you there," with no explanation.

Judith thinks back to her last visit to The Centre when she met with Rev Robbie to discuss her taking on the bookkeeping duties that he was finding too time-consuming.

"It's not that I mind the time I spend doing the work," he's told her, "but I sure resent the time I spend trying to find and fix my mistakes!"

He's a quiet-spoken jolly old man and Judith is very fond of him. Everyone thinks the world of Rev Robbie.

He isn't shy about asking when he wants something as Judith discovers at their recent meeting. He's come right out and asked her why she hasn't made Lila confide, and relieve some of her burden by sharing it.

"Lila will tell me what's going on when she's ready, Rev Robbie," admonishes Judith. "She knows I'm a willing listener, I've told her repeatedly, but she needs to come to me in her own time."

"No, I think you're wrong there, Judith," he replies. "How long have you been waiting for Lila to come to you?"

Judith experiences a moment's discomfort when she realizes it has been weeks. "Um, I guess it's been about a month. A bit more than that actually," she admits.

"Well then. It's obvious that Lila has been deeply hurt and she needs some help, a push, to see her way clear."

"Hey confession is your line, not mine, so why don't you coax the truth out of her?"

"Oh I've tried. Unfortunately I don't have the authority of a priest. Lila's Catholic, or I might have been able to browbeat her into telling me."

"That sounds a bit heavy-handed!" laughs Judith seeing the twinkle in the elderly man's eyes.

"I do admit that back in the day I sometimes envied my Catholic counterparts for the rigid control they had over their parishioners."

"I think Lila is what they call a *lapsed Catholic*."

"I'm pretty sure the Catholic Church doesn't even acknowledge such a state! But no, I tried several times and got no where. I think it would do her a world of good to share her secret with you and with God."

"Doesn't God already know?" teases Judith.

"Of course He does! but it's still important that Lila tells Him herself."

Judith retreats from a theological discussion about her friend, it makes her feel she is prying, and their talk returns to accountancy.

Lila spots Judith's car pulling into The Centre's parking lot just as she reaches the front doors. She doesn't wait for her friend but enters the building on her own. The volleyball players are milling around the foyer, dressed to play and ready to get started, but complaining that the auditorium doors are locked.

The Centre itself is always open during the day and evening, but not the gym unless a game is scheduled. The hardwood floors need plenty of the TLC provided by Mr. Miller and his son, the custodians, to keep them in good shape. Outdoor shoes can only be worn for the walk from the door to the bleachers.

"Kyle's got keys, is he here somewhere?" asks Lila.

"If he is he's hiding—" says one of the players.

"Yeah, and we know why!" interrupts her team-mate. A few sniggers are heard followed by some loud whispering and giggles.

Lila announces she'll go get Rev Robbie who must have lost track of the time. She heads to his office down the hall, her nurses' shoes making no sound.

The team-mates wait until the silence is broken by a cry from Lila. They surge forward in a group, including Judith who has arrived at one end of the hall and Patricia who appears at the other end. With tears streaming down her face Lila waves everyone back and chokes out that someone needs to call 9-1-1 for an ambulance and the police.

"The police!" everyone starts questioning at once except Judith who makes the emergency call and then phones Grant as well. She has no idea he is already at work in the building.

Pat switches into her Principal Johnson role and instructs the young people to go to the change-rooms and get back into their regular clothes. They won't be able to play tonight. They'll have to wait until the police arrive but there is no point getting chilled in their uniforms of shorts and t-shirts.

Judith moves forward purposefully against the tide of teenagers. She joins Pat and Lila in the doorway of Rev Robbie's office to see the man lying on the floor with his frail limbs contorted. They don't go further inside the small, sparsely furnished room. Lila says she'd already checked him for vital signs and found none.

A whitish substance, like foam, dribbles over his lower lip and chin, and his teeth are bared in a grimace. It is the most horrible sight any of the women has ever seen.

"He's had some sort of fit," says Pat in a shocked whisper.

"No, he's been poisoned," replies Lila flatly.

Judith gasps and is about to ask if Lila is sure, but stops herself knowing that of course her friend, the nurse, is certain. She has to strain to hear Lila's anguished muttering:

"What am I going to do now? I was counting on him to help me."

Chapter 4

"Hey Judith," says Lila answering her cellphone.

"Hi, it's... oh, you know it's me. Okay listen, Grant came by and gave me some tickets, it's the strangest offer, but I said I'd ask you anyhow."

"Oooh, that sounds intriguing! What's it all about?"

"He was *gifted*, he said, dinner for two at that Indian casino on the edge of town – a buffet apparently – but he can't go so he suggested you and I use the tickets. What do you think? would you want to do that?"

"Are you kidding? of course! The food there is really good. I don't know about being gifted, though. Was it a comp? is Grant a player?"

"At the casino? I don't think so. Why would you think that?"

"Well if you're a regular and you spend enough money you get complimentary – comp – stuff."

"Oh, I see what you mean. No, he got the tickets as his gift from the Secret Santa draw they had at their Christmas party at the police station. So, you do want to go?"

"For sure! it will be a blast. I'll drive because I've been there before and getting onto the grounds is a bit tricky because of construction."

"Oh you've been before? Good, because I haven't. What should I wear?"

"Casual clothes, something comfortable. Last time I was at a casino I saw a guy wearing a pyjama top tucked into his jeans. He obviously thought it was a regular shirt and no doubt figured he got a great price on it! You'll see people in work coveralls, hooker gear, wedding parties, you name it.

Casinos are great equalizers. You get people of every colour and creed sitting at a table united against the dealer, or rather *the House*' It's all about playing together to beat the House."

"I don't want to gamble, I just want to have dinner and definitely take the opportunity to look around a little - if they allow that?"

"Sure. You don't have to gamble, and there's no cover charge or anything. It'll be fun, you'll see. Let me just finish up what I'm doing here and I can get you in about 45 minutes, is that okay?"

"Um, yeah sure. What time does the casino open?"

Lila laughs as she answers: "You're better off asking what time does it close? which is only for about five or six hours out of every twenty-four, seven days a week, unless you play poker and that's continuous. We aren't Vegas yet, but we're getting there."

"I can see I'm in for an education going to a casino with you," replies Judith.

"You can be sure of that and, seriously, the food will be fantastic so I hope you're hungry. See you soon."

Judith has driven by the big new hotel on the outskirts of Calgary but didn't realize it houses a casino. There are a couple of buildings and a huge parking lot that is packed.

Judith is surprised, she didn't realize a night out at the casino would be so popular. She wonders if it is only busy at weekends. Lila has explained that there are five casinos in the city and another Indian casino halfway to Banff.

"What's the difference?"

"Difference between...?"

"All the casinos. You said there's five but then you specifically mention Indian casinos. Are they different?"

"Oh probably, but I couldn't tell you why. It will have something to do with being on reservation land. Maybe the rules are different? I do know that the Province has authority over gambling but the reservation is Federal jurisdiction so that might have something to do with it."

"Are there really enough gamblers in this city to support that many casinos?"

"Oh yeah. Of course some are busier than others – location does matter – and what kind of parking is available, stuff like that. Anyhow, we're here so let's have some fun."

Lila spots a car pulling out and drives over to wait for the space. It is close to the main doors. The unseasonably warm temperatures have turned the lot slushy but neither woman complains. Wearing boots is a small price to pay to avoid the bitterly cold windy weather more common at this time of year.

They enter the warm lobby and, smelling cigarette smoke, Lila says:

"I remember now, one of the differences is that customers can smoke in the Indian casinos."

"I can smell it, remember when everywhere smelled like this?"

"Yeah, I have to confess that I never noticed the smell when I smoked. It's embarrassing to say now but back then I even smoked between courses at meals. And in restaurants, too!"

"You were a smoker? but you're a nurse!"

"Well I wasn't always a nurse, I used to be a kid! I started smoking in Grade Nine so at thirteen or fourteen years old 'cause all the cool kids smoked so naturally... but you'd be surprised how many nurses and doctors do smoke – even nowadays. Those minutes of camaraderie while you're huddled outside to feed your addiction can be a great stress reliever from a demanding job."

"I've never smoked."

"I can't say that surprises me, Judith. Do you want to check your jacket? I don't think I'll bother."

"No, but do you want to eat first and then look around? I'm kinda hungry."

"That's a good idea, otherwise if we get stuck at a blackjack table or on a machine we might end up missing dinner!"

"Lila, that's not going to happen. Believe me."

Lila laughs with her friend and they head towards the restaurant with Judith's head swivelling left to right taking in all the sights. She is surprised at the number of customers there, and notices the varying ages and races.

A slot machine blares triumphant music and she stops to watch the flashing lights and colourful, swirling graphics.

"It's a penny slot and all that hoo-hah is for about $50.00," comments Lila.

"$50.00 is an excellent return for a penny!" exclaims Judith.

"True, but you probably have to bet about 25 pennies per spin to hit bonus payouts, and you can spin three or four times a minute - maybe more - I'll show you later."

"This is the ugliest carpet I've ever seen," comments Judith looking down at the garishly coloured haphazard patterns of the floor covering.

"It's supposed to be. The decor of a casino is very carefully thought-out and planned. They don't want you looking down, you should be looking up at the slot machines, attracted by the bells and whistles and flashing lights. The loudest, and supposedly more frequently paying, machines are at the end of the rows to grab your attention as you walk by. The mirrored walls reflect back the lights and simultaneously make the rooms look larger and more crowded. Gamblers are turned on by the buzz, the noise, and the action.

An Indian casino probably doesn't go in for Feng Shui but some casinos in town have hired professionals to do their cosmic energy thing, it's something to do with harmonizing individuals with their surroundings. Obviously, I don't know much about it but I did spot a golden dragon statue way up high on top of the door-sill at another casino and that would have been put there for good luck."

"Good luck for the players or the House?" asks Judith.

"I guess for whoever believes in it."

There is a fairly long line-up when they arrive at the restaurant but a sign directs Buffet Patrons to go down a short corridor. Judith hands over the tickets to the hostess waiting there and is told to hang on to them until it is time to pay their bill.

The woman adds that the tickets don't include alcoholic beverages but soft drinks, coffee, or tea are no charge. She leads them to a table for four so they have room to pile their coats on a spare chair. As soon as the hostess steps away a server comes forward with a water jug and a menu of drink specials.

"Since I'm driving I can only have one drink so I'll make it a glass of the house red. Why don't you try a mocktail? That's a cocktail with no booze in it."

"I'll pass on that, thanks," answered Judith, "but I will have a ginger-ale, please."

After the server leaves Judith turns to Lila saying:

"It's not very busy, is it?"

"No, but it's still early for the Saturday night crowd. Also, it's very expensive. That long line we sashayed past was for the main restaurant which is menu service and cheaper."

"I don't *sashay*," laughs Judith.

"Well you should!" retorts Lila explaining: "You've certainly got the booty for it."

They don't have much opportunity to look around before their server is back with the drinks and telling them to go up to the buffet whenever they are ready.

"Please take your purses with you, but your coats will be fine where they are."

Judith and Lila stand up with Judith whispering, "Of course I'm taking my purse."

Lila didn't exaggerate when she spoke of a great meal. There is seafood, beef, ham, chicken, Italian dishes, Chinese dishes, Ukrainian food, and even a vegetarian casserole in addition to salads of all kinds, raw veggies with dip, a variety of fresh fruit, potatoes cooked three different ways, two kinds of rice, dumplings, and several vegetables.

"Just take a small bit of each thing and then you can come back for a second serving of whatever you liked best. Remember to leave room for dessert as well."

"I took lots of fruit. It's so expensive to buy at this time of year but look, I got pineapple and strawberries and raspberries."

"There was mango and kiwi fruit too, didn't you see it?"

"I did, but I don't know if I like those fruits."

"Well that's the whole point of buffet – you get to have a taste of new stuff. Judith, you really need to get out more!"

Judith waves off Lila's teasing knowing it is good-natured. Besides, it's true. She does need to spread her wings a little. Imagine if she came here with Grant and made a fool of herself? But no, he wouldn't embarrass her or anything, he is a good friend.

They both eat with enjoyment and take another trip to the hot dishes, but make sure to visit the dessert tables as well. Neither woman can resist heaping a plate from the temptingly presented chocolate-dipped fruit, cakes, pies, squares, cookies, and ice-cream with do-it-yourself topping selections.

"I'm stuffed," announces Lila with a satisfied smile.

"Me too! You're right about the food here, everything is delicious."

"I'll phone Grant to thank him but you'll have to find a better way to show your appreciation of the wonderful feast we just had."

Lila wiggles her eyebrows suggestively and Judith smiles saying:

"Hmmm, I won't ask you for advice in that department."

Lila's face falls as she says: "No, I'm obviously not an expert in relationships these days," with a big sigh.

Judith chastises herself for saying something that reminds her friend of her failing marriage.

"Oh, I didn't mean—"

"I know you didn't, and I'm resolved to having a good time tonight, no moping over Arnie. I did enough of that over my first Christmas without him. So, let's settle the bill and then we'll try our luck on the gaming floor."

They both contribute a good tip to the delight of their waitress who tells them most people don't tip at a buffet since they have to serve themselves.

"But you brought us drinks and cleared away our used plates."

"Several times!" adds Lila. "We did get table service and it was great, thank you."

"Good luck to you both, I really hope you win," says the girl.

An hour later both women are ready to head home after walking all around the casino. They have looked in the poker room, where the players seemed to hunch over their cards; and in the high-limit room where the amount of the high-value chips being wagered shocks Judith; and then they checked out all the different table games and money wheels and slots machines.

Lila said she isn't in the mood to sit down at a table and play cards but she would like to try her luck with a few spins at roulette. She leads them over to the table she wants to play.

Lila buys playing chips and places her bets. Soon the layout is full of coloured chips and the little white ball is whizzing round the wheel. As it clatters to a halt everyone, including Judith, leans forward to see where it landed after bouncing twice. The dealer announces the winning number and its colour and, somehow, marks its location despite stacks of playing chips covering all the squares. Judith is fascinated.

The croupier, as Lila explains he's called, is very skilled. He moves smoothly and maintains his smile even while some customers are grumbling at him.

Lila wins on some spins and loses on the others explaining to Judith that although she lost her column bets she won on the inside which pays more so she is up a bit. Judith isn't sure what Lila means, but is happy for her friend.

She changes the roulette chips for money chips and gives the dealer a tip, he thanks her nicely.

Judith notices that almost all of the casino workers are members of *visible minorities* and she wonders if these are government-subsidized positions? Strong English-language skills – particularly written – wouldn't be essential in a job dealing cards. In fact, there is very little conversation going on, mostly the only voices heard are from the dealers counting the hands out loud.

It would be good work experience for newcomers to the country. Many immigrants, as well as Canadians from other provinces, gravitate to Calgary. Its young population, high-paying jobs in the energy sector, and proximity to half-a-dozen provincial and federal parks makes it popular.

Everyone wears a uniform of black pants and long-sleeved, high-necked shirts in solid colours of teal-blue or maroon at the tables, and forest-green at the slot machines. The security guards wear all-black and the supervisors dress in black blazers over white shirts.

Lila shows Judith the chips she's received from the roulette table when she cashed out.

"See these are money chips which I can play at any table, but I'll have to go to the banker's cage to cash them out."

Judith studies the chips with interest but doesn't want to touch them saying they are probably very germy.

"Uh yeah, thanks for that. Now what about you, you've had a look around at the different games so do you want to try something?"

"Yes, I'm going to invest twenty dollars in one of those million-dollar slot machines over there."

"It would be so cool if you won with beginner's luck!"

Heading towards that particular bank of slot machines Judith comes face-to-face with Andrea Seely, a demanding and overbearing school parent she would have avoided if she'd seen her coming.

Both ladies exclaim at the same time: "What are you doing here?"

"I'm part of a bachelorette party, we figured with our social standing visiting a male strip club was out of the question but these casinos give half their profits to charities – by law – so it seemed like a good idea, and fun too."

"Lila and I got free tickets to the dinner buffet and we recommend it. We both ate a wonderful meal with a huge variety of well-prepared foods."

"Lucky you! I heard that the buffet here is a bit on the pricey side but it's because of all the seafood."

"Yes, well I'm hoping I'm also lucky on that slot machine over there."

Andrea Seely's participation in the conversation has been mechanical but now she looks at Judith with interest.

"You like playing the slots, do you?"

"I don't know, I've never tried before. Do you play them?"

"Not really, I'm looking around enjoying the atmosphere. It's real 'slice of life' stuff, isn't it?"

"Where is your party?"

"Scattered about. It turns out a couple of them are Vegas regulars so they're whooping it up at the Craps table and I think a few more are cheering them on. In fact, I'm heading that way myself."

The women move in opposite directions. As they reach the *Million Dollar Jackpot* machine Judith chose she looks at Lila asking:

"She seemed awfully interested in me playing the slot machines – do you think she's worried that I'm gambling away the School's tuition fees?"

"I think she's just a nosy snob."

"Ahhh, so does a million-dollar slot machine fit with my social standing?"

Lila laughingly replies:

"If you win a million bucks you can have whatever standing you like! Just don't spend it all on perfume!"

"Omigod yes! the woman just reeks of scent. Some places, like dental offices, won't even let people wear it any more because of allergies. Especially when it's put on so strongly that it's overpowering like that! By the way, when we're back in the car remind me to tell you a story Pat Johnson passed on about Mrs. Seeley."

"Oooh, juicy gossip?"

"I thought so!"

Judith feeds the money into the bill slot, reads the 'how to play' instructions and chooses a maximum bet for $3 then she pushes the Spin button. She is disappointed at not getting to pull on a handle but Lila explains the 'one-armed bandits' are a thing of the past. The first spin produces nothing but the second spin pays out seventy dollars which Judith promptly cashes out.

"You don't want to play anymore?"

"No, of course not. I've got my original twenty back *and* I'm up fifty bucks!"

"But I thought you were going to spend twenty to invest on a million-dollar chance?"

"Oh Lila, it's that kind of thinking that got the jackpot up to a million in the first place."

Chapter 5

Saturday, December 28, 2019

After dropping Judith off in the half-circle drive of her apartment building Lila waits to see her friend safely unlock the front door. Instead, Judith turns suddenly and hurries back to the car saying:

"I just remembered, I was going to share some hot gossip about Andrea Seely."

"That's right! get in again, it's too chilly to stand outside."

Lila puts the car in park while Judith climbs back in the front-seat, pausing to recollect exactly the conversation she'd recently had with Pat which she then passes on.

"Pat started with this long speech saying since I've never been chummy with my coworkers I'm not part of the gossip grapevine. She knows I hear things in passing, but usually don't know any details so I don't have a bias or false information. *Fake news,* as they call it nowadays.

It wouldn't be appropriate for Pat, as School Principal, to hang out in the staffroom sharing tidbits but she said I'm always discreet. But what makes me so valuable to her as a listener is that I'm a fresh audience. Also she complimented me by saying I have good insights into *why* so-and-so *did* do such-and-such, and I'm always willing to speculate as to motive. From all of that flattery I figure her husband, Mark, isn't the least bit interested in discussing this stuff. So, anyways, that's the background. Here's what she said:

Judith replayed the entire scene in her mind and relayed it from memory.

"Mark and I belong to the Horticultural Society, as I think I've mentioned before," said Pat and Judith nodded, not commenting that Pat had actually mentioned it many, many times before. "And we've been at The Centre quite a bit lately because during the winter we have the time to listen to speakers and presentations, work on Society bylaws, memberships, newsletters – things we're too busy to deal with once the gardening year is in full swing."

"I've heard from more than one person that no matter how nice the Spring weather might be there's no point planting until after the May long weekend, is that when your season starts?"

"Pretty much. I mean, what you heard is true but goodness knows how often we've forgotten and been misled by false Spring into hurrying into the season before the snow has finished with us!" laughed Pat. "It's also the first big camping weekend of the year and it invariably turns cold, rainy and – very often – snowy!"

"Ugh, I have absolutely no interest in camping and, since I live in an apartment building, no need to garden."

"Oh! but there's quite a bit you could do with indoor plants, and you have a balcony, and what about east-facing windows? my plants just thrive in that location."

"Hmm, maybe I could go with you on one of your trips to the garden centre and you can advise me on some selections. Every now and then I pick up something at the grocery store but they never last."

"Oh, you don't want to buy from there! Those plants are no good," exclaimed Pat.

"Well, I still have a poinsettia I got from Costco a few Christmases ago."

"Yes, well Costco is different. I'd be delighted to take you, and actually there's a new plant nursery I'm looking forward to visiting so we'll go there. Although I have to admit I can get a bit carried away, Judith, so we each better take our own vehicle or you'll end up stuck there much longer than you'd like!" Pat laughed again. She has such a deep chuckle that it's impossible to resist joining in.

"Okay, it's a date," declared Judith. "But that's not why you came to visit me at my desk so what's on your mind?"

"Oh, I just had to talk to someone about that Andrea Seely. You'll never believe what she's been up to... and that poor young man, he doesn't know which way to turn. She's always there in hot pursuit and she must have twenty years on him – at least!"

"What young man and what won't I believe? Frankly, I think I can believe anything about Andrea Seely. I really dislike that woman. Oh I know I shouldn't say that about a parent but honestly..."

"Well she's out-done herself this time. She's set her sights on Kyle Danby, the Sports Director?"

"The name doesn't ring a bell, I don't know him."

"Oh, he's a lovely young man, so polite and friendly, smart, very diplomatic, he'll definitely get on in life. And he's such a handsome guy as well, mixed blood often produces outstanding features. His mother is Asian, from Indonesia I think? and his father is Black. I know Kenneth Danby from our Church but not Mrs. Danby, she doesn't attend. I believe she's Muslim but non-practising or something.

Anyhow, I've known Kyle since he was just a little fellow and now he's in his early twenties and extremely tall. You know he wanted to be a pilot but there's a height restriction and he outgrew the limits. Isn't that interesting? normally when there are height issues it's because someone isn't tall enough but apparently, with the air force, there's a standard size to cockpits so they have a maximum height."

"Oh that is interesting, that would never have crossed my mind. But we're getting sidetracked. What does Andrea Seely have to do with Kyle... Danby, you said?"

"Yes, Kyle Danby. Well she's making such an obvious play for him that it's embarrassing for everyone around them! He tries to avoid her but she's shameless, doesn't care who she involves in her attempts to form an intrigue or whatever with this poor guy. She's constantly poking her nose into one room after the next asking 'is Kyle in here?' or 'I'm trying to find Kyle, have you seen him?' She's making a laughingstock out of herself."

"Oh, ewww," Lila interrupts, screwing up her face in disgust.

"I know, eh?" I said to her: "Oh, don't make me feel sorry for Andrea Seely, I quite *like* disliking her."

"Ha-ha, I know what you mean. Sorry for butting in, go on with what Pat said."

"She said: Yes, she does have that effect on people, doesn't she? Awful woman."

"Isn't this Kyle very young to be a Sports Director?"

"Well it's a case of big title in lieu of decent pay. He probably doesn't get much more than minimum wage but he's taking classes at the University so this is a part-time job for him. He's a godsend during the summer, though. The Centre is busy year-round, particularly on weekends, but summertime it's full all week with day-camp programmes for the school-age children on vacation. Some of our teachers volunteer their time which I think is so good of them."

"It is, we've got some great people on staff."

"And then there's Marta..." Pat stage-whispered.

"I'll bet she can tell you all the ins and outs of the Andrea Seely/ Kyle Danby affair, or wanna-be affair, plus plenty of salacious details true or otherwise."

"Oh no doubt she could but listening to her would make me feel dirty."

"Pat really said that?!" exclaims Lila with delight.

"Yes, and when she did I was the one who gave a loud laugh!"

"That Pat is so funny, eh? But jeez, Andrea Seely is a married woman and a mother. What the heck is she doing chasing around after some young guy? and so publicly, too!"

"Well Lila, even I've heard of *cougars*. Andrea's not old and she's well... a bit chunky but you could call that voluptuous..."

"Only if you're very kind – or blind!"

"Stop, she's not that bad."

"Judith she's certainly not a MILF! oh I feel for that poor fellow being pursued by an overpowering harpy like her!"

"Do I want to know what a MILF is?"

"Ask Grant," Lila replies with a devilish smile.

Chapter 6

Lila and Judith plan to bring in the new year together. They choose to celebrate at Lila's place so she can have a drink, and Judith can drive home sober as ever. Lila enjoys cooking and has promised a feast of tasty nibbles, sweet treats, and fattening junk food.

Judith has seen Grant a few times over the holiday week, with and without Lila in attendance, but he hasn't mentioned doing anything on New Year's Eve. It's likely he has to work. and Judith doesn't mind because she wants to spend some one-on-one time with Lila.

Her friend has put a good face on things at Christmas and the days following, but Judith can see she is sad. Lila has had a couple of outings with Beth Penner and her father Brian, a combined trip of lunch and shopping the Boxing Day sales, and a day out ice-skating.

Judith knows Lila finds the widower very attractive – well he is a handsome, well-built man. Has she told him she's married? It's the state of that marriage that is causing Lila her unhappiness. Judith is pretty sure the marriage is over.

"What time do you want me tonight? and can I bring anything?" Judith asks when she calls Lila in the afternoon.

"Come whenever you like, the only schedule we have is midnight countdown and singing 'Auld Lang Syne'. Oh you could bring a bottle of champagne, I thought I had one but I don't."

"Oh! I could, I guess... is there a liquor store on the way to you? I've never been to one. Do they take credit cards? I do have some cash on me... what kind should I buy?"

"Ha-ha," laughed Lila, "I got you good. I'm just joking, I've got two bottles of champagne chilling in case you change your mind about joining me. You can always crash on the couch. You really don't have a clue about booze, do you?"

"You did have me going! And I'll have you know I know plenty about booze just not from personally indulging – thank God. I might as well explain because you won't let up, will you?

My mother was an alcoholic who drank herself to death. There was only me to deal with her so my hands-on experience was cleaning up stinking messes and listening to a constant litany of self-pity and recriminations from when I was in primary school. As a result, to this day, I can't stand the smell of wine, beer, or liquor."

"Oh Judith, I am so sorry. I promise to never pester you about it again." Lila does sound contrite and Judith, surprised that the admission had been relatively painless says:

"You know it's probably a good thing for me to get it out in the open. You see no one ever knew, it was Mum's secret, but it became mine as well. I guess I could have told someone – a teacher, or neighbour – but somehow I knew it wasn't something to share, it was something to hide."

"Oh you poor thing. You were forced to grow up when you should have been a carefree kid."

"I don't think I'd ever have been that carefree..."

"No, maybe not," agrees Lila. "Anyhow, come over when you like, I'm just wearing a fleece track suit, and just come as you are because I've got everything we need."

Judith has already bought a box of Lila's favourite treats: *Hedgehogs* from Purdy's Chocolates, so she certainly won't be arriving empty-handed.

The two women enjoy their feast of snack foods while watching some TV but mostly talking. They talk and talk about themselves, their work, their relationships.

Although Judith has had a wonderful night she detects the underlying sadness when Lila talks about herself. It looks like her marriage, after all these years, has now failed and that's weighing her down. She was so disappointed that Arnie still refused to open up to her despite saying he wanted their marriage to continue. And, of course, not coming to see her for Christmas.

Once Lila has talked her feelings out Judith lets the subject drop. She doesn't feel qualified to give relationship advice, and having never met Arnie she can't even take on the role of knowledgeable bystander.

They count down the New Year and toast it with a glass of champagne clinking against a glass of ginger-ale. Lila points out that Judith's glass has more bubbles than hers does.

"Serves me right for choosing the stuff that was on sale but I'm actually not a big fan of champagne so I figured it wouldn't really matter."

"You've heard the advice that *you should always buy the best you can afford?* well the corollary to that is *and you should also be satisfied with it.* So you might as well enjoy what's you've got."

It's cold and frosty at two in the morning when Judith drives home. It's easy to find your way around Edgemont Village with numbered streets, few traffic lights, and no one-ways. The planners deliberately made the roads curvy to keep traffic moving at slower speeds, but the many bends and turns can be challenging in winter weather.

Judith is alert to her surroundings and keeps an eye on the few cars she sees, being especially careful at intersections in case some drunk driver is going to barrel through against the light.

She sees a red row of tail-lights ahead and figures it's a CheckStop by the police looking for impaired drivers, but once she gets closer she realizes the cars have stopped to let a few dogs ... no, they are coyotes ... cross the road. She watches the animals bound into the wooded area on the far side of the road and wonders for a moment if it's coyotes or wolves that have such bushy tails.

Seeing the animals trotting along so unconcerned, so confident, so carefree, seems like a good omen for the new year.

Chapter 7

Wednesday, January 1, 2020

On Wednesday, the first day of the *twenties*, Judith wakes up to a text from Grant wishing her all the best for the new year. She texts back good wishes and, smiling at her own daring, adds that the school is closed until the following Monday. He replies that he is off Friday night and would she like to get together for a meal?

JUDITH: sounds gr8 thx

GRANT: + movie 2

JUDITH: whats on

GRANT: no clue what do u like

JUDITH: comedy, mystery

GRANT: terminator sequel #1 doctor sleep #2

JUDITH: scary s king novel what else

GRANT: ford v ferrari

JUDITH: whos in it

GRANT: matt damon

JUDITH: sounds ok

GRANT: fri matinee dinner

JUDITH: perfect

GRANT: tty fri am

JUDITH: k bye

Judith spends the rest of her day doing laundry, taking down the few Christmas decorations she'd put up, and cleaning the apartment. She likes to have the place fresh and tidy for the new year.

Then she tackles a personal tidy-up with a manicure, pedicure, leg shaving, and eyebrow tweezering. Having accomplished a lot on this, the first day of the new year, she relaxes with a long soak in a bubble-bath before donning her flannelette pyjamas.

Scrubbed pink and feeling warm and cozy she settles on the couch with hot chocolate and her laptop to watch a show on Netflix. Grant has recommended a TV series that started a few years ago called "The Blacklist" and so far she is really enjoying it.

"Who is calling me so early in the morning!" complains Judith when her cellphone rings loudly. Each night she plugs it into the charger in the outlet behind the dresser, the phone propped up to serve as her clock. Squinting she can see that it reads 09:09 – angel numbers – and it's really not early at all.

I probably shouldn't have stayed up watching those last two episodes," she thinks, *"but they end on such cliffhangers! I couldn't resist."*

The caller ID shows that it is Lila calling so Judith tries to sound bright and awake when she answers.

"Oh no, I woke you up!"

"No, well yes but I should be up anyhow. It's after nine."

"Good well, I'm bursting and had to tell someone. Arnie phoned, and he's coming to see me! He's off until Monday as well so he's flying in, he'll arrive this evening, and we'll finally get to sit down face-to-face and hash things out. I am so relieved. I have to admit that Christmas was really hard without him."

"Oh I'm really happy for you, Lila. When did he call?"

"Just now. Well, I guess it was actually about an hour ago, he's two hours ahead of us. We talked a lot, I mean we both miss each other so much, and well... I'm so happy. I can't wait to see him!"

"I hope I get a chance to meet him too although I don't want to intrude, you only have a few days together."

"You're definitely going to meet him. How about you and Grant double-dating with us? We can go out for a nice steak dinner at The Keg on Saturday, oh wait it will be packed and they don't take reservations. We'll figure out a place."

"Maybe Arnie would like to see Banff?"

"That's a terrific idea! There's a Keg there, or Tony Roma's, or wow there are quite a few places to eat so we'll find something for sure."

"I'll ask Grant but I'm actually seeing him on Friday night for a movie–"

"So you see him two nights in a row, that's okay."

"Well, I'll ask him but I want you to clear it with Arnie first, he might just want you all to himself."

"Judith you do know how many years we've been married, right?"

"Yeah so? You haven't seen each other for months."

"Oh, I'd better let Mrs. Piernitsky know that he's coming tonight and who he is. She'll probably cook something. I'll do that right now before I forget. Then I've got to go get some groceries, stop at the liquor store, clean up the place.. Okay bye, Judith!"

She disconnects before Judith realizes her *good luck* comment has gone unheard. Judith can picture Lila bouncing from room to room tidying, checking cupboards and fridge to make a shopping list in her head, a whirlwind of blonde curls as she prepares for the husband she hasn't seen in months.

Judith finds she is smiling at the good news although she realizes it will probably mean that Lila will move back to Toronto. It isn't a happy thought to lose her friend, but she does have Grant in her life now.

Chapter 8

Judith isn't sure what to do. She doesn't want to intrude on Lila and Arnie's time together but she hasn't heard anything since Thursday's phone call. Until this morning's text arrived.

A text from Lila usually involved lots of exclamation points or question marks, uppercase words, and emojis of hearts and smileys, frownies, or WTF graphics. Today's text was simple:

LILA: cancel sat dinner sorry ttyl

Judith had immediately replied:

JUDITH: no prob is ev ok

That was hours ago and she hasn't heard a thing. So she'd phoned but her call went to voicemail. She hung up and tried again but same result. Unsure what to say in a message Judith chose to say nothing. Lila would see from the call history who had phoned. Now Judith was undecided, wondering if she should call again.

Instead, she chose to finish getting ready since Grant would be arriving soon to take her to the afternoon show.

Judith has deliberately dressed down to go to the theatre. She puts on older clothes that she will immediately toss in the wash when she gets back home. Sometimes she'd see moviegoers wearing shorts and she'll shudder to think of their bare legs rubbing against the seats. She always wears socks and running shoes as well, nothing is going to crawl up her leg!

Looking in the mirror she acknowledges to herself that even in this old sweatshirt Lila's comments about her figure being shapely are accurate. She wants to look nice for Grant, he has good dress-sense and always looks just right for the occasion, but the movie theatre is well... not clean by Judith's standards.

She decides she won't say anything about Lila and tomorrow's cancellation until after the show when they stop for a bite to eat.

Judith had called Grant after talking to Lila to mention the Saturday night dinner invitation. When he said Sure, that sounds interesting she'd given him an out for Friday but he'd insisted on keeping their Friday date as well.

Judith toys with the idea that maybe things are becoming serious, but realizes it's only the rare circumstance of Lila's estranged husband's visit that means having two dates in two days.

Grant spends more money at the concession stand than he's paid for their tickets to the show. But the snacks are filling because after a large popcorn, large drink, and a chocolate bar each neither feels like dinner.

Judith is annoyed that she's worn a dark sweatshirt since it shows up every tiny bit of popcorn that she's managed to spill over herself.

"How about coffee and a doughnut at Tim Horton's? My treat," she suggests.

"Actually, I'm in the mood for ice-cream."

"It's still winter!"

"Dairy Queen is open, do you like soft-serve?"

"I love Dairy Queen. My favourite is a chocolate-dipped cone but I usually get a sundae because when it's hot outside the cones melt and drip so fast."

"Well, it's not hot now so you can have your first choice. I like butterscotch sundaes so long as it's butterscotch and not caramel."

"Chocolate is my favourite flavour, but caramel is okay. I don't care for butterscotch. Lots of people can't tell the difference. You really prefer butterscotch?"

"Definitely, I have a refined palate."

Judith laughs answering: "Well you can't prove it by what you've eaten today."

Grant has to agree. He drives them to a Dairy Queen restaurant and she's surprised to see several people inside, after all it is January. She mentions this to Grant who tells her that the burgers are pretty good as well as the ice cream.

He asks the server if the sundaes are butterscotch or caramel and she gives him a confused look before saying they're the same flavour. When he says no, they aren't, she goes to ask someone in the kitchen area.

"If she has to ask," he explains to Judith, "That means it's not butterscotch."

Sure enough when the girl returns she says they have caramel, adding it's practically the same thing. Grant doesn't want to argue so he orders two large chocolate-dipped cones instead then steps aside to let Judith pay.

"Thank you," she says once they choose a table and sit down with their desserts.

"Why thank me? you paid!"

"And you let me do so without an argument. Also, I'm glad you didn't argue with the girl about butterscotch versus caramel."

"Well she's a teenager so nothing I say would penetrate anyhow."

"Teenagers aren't stupid, they're just young."

"No, I didn't say stupid, I just mean that there's nothing I can ever say that will be more important to her than the thoughts currently occupying her mind. Her clothes, her make-up, her girlfriends, her boyfriends, her plans for the weekend... all those things are swirling around in her head. I'm just a brief interruption who is then quickly forgotten. Believe me I am infinitely patient with young people, I have five nephews and four nieces."

"Oh my! big family."

"It is now. There were just the three of us growing up but both of my sisters love being Moms."

"Christmas must be a blast!"

Grant thinks he hears a faintly wistful tone in Judith's voice. He answers briskly:

"Christmas is damn expensive!" and they both laugh.

"On a more serious topic I have to let you know tomorrow's dinner is cancelled, and I need your advice."

"What's up?"

Judith explains about Lila's uncharacteristically brief text message and subsequent lack of response to text and phone calls.

"I don't know if I should leave a message. I don't want to interrupt them but all of this is so unlike Lila that I'm a bit concerned. What do you think?"

Grant considers for a few moments before saying:

"I'm not sure, Judith. I mean I don't know her well and I don't know him at all. I really can't say."

"Well, what would do if you were me?"

"Hmm. I guess leaving a message wouldn't hurt but personally I wouldn't bother. She knows you've called and they're either in the middle of a massive fight or well... the opposite. Either way, they're busy."

"Or maybe they finished the fight and now they're enjoying *the opposite*," says Judith with a smile.

"Make-up sex, yes, lucky them!" Grant smiles as well, admiring the way Judith's surprisingly shabby top hints at her curves, but she gives all her attention to her cone. Watching her lick the ice cream drips Grant is momentarily distracted.

"There's no reason why you and I can't have dinner just ourselves tomorrow night, is there?"

"We've both got to eat so sure, let's eat together."

Grant gives her a sharp look but Judith's artless expression leaves him wondering.

Chapter 9

Grant pours the last of the red wine from the carafe into his glass. Judith has graciously offered to be the designated driver so he can enjoy some drinks with his meal.

As a treat, Grant has brought her to The Black Angus, Edgemont's oldest and fanciest steakhouse. Built from riverstone the decor is subdued lighting over wood panelling, and snowy linen cloths on tables with plenty of elbow-room.

The menu offers hearty servings of red meat: tomahawks, t-bones, rib steaks, *filet mignon*, with Alaskan King Crab legs as its surf and turf option. Both Judith and Grant dine well on expertly prepared steaks cooked rare.

The restaurant caters to an older, monied crowd but the bar is a popular weekend drinking spot for singles.

Judith enjoys the opportunity to get all dolled up. Last December Lila had loaned her a dress for Noel Larkin's birthday/Christmas party and afterwards insisted Judith keep it saying:

"It looks so much better on you! You fill it out properly, and have the long legs to set that skirt swirling."

When Judith protests Lila tells her to consider it a re-gifted Christmas present. Grant wasn't invited to that party so he is seeing Judith in the dress for the first time, and is generous with his compliments.

"This is the second Saturday in a row I've eaten an excellent and expensive restaurant meal, thanks to you. And thank you again, Grant, for the casino buffet tickets. Lila and I had a great time.

Did I tell you we ran into Andrea Seely there? she's Margaret's mother and such a pushy, bossy woman."

"So Margaret *comes by it honestly* as they say..."

"That's true! It seems whenever I'm out I always run into somebody associated with the school: a parent, teachers, student–"

"Have you spotted someone here?"

"Yes, a couple of teachers and you know, it looks like they've just gotten engaged! So nice, we've all been waiting for news of this sort. Lila will be pleased for them."

"Where are they?"

"Cozied up nicely over at that banquette, Eddie and Tanya."

"Do you want to go have a word?"

"Oh no, I'd rather let them enjoy their moment. Speaking of enjoying... when I eat in fancy restaurants I usually order two or three appetizers instead of an entree," Judith explains: "That way I get to indulge in a good variety of gourmet cooking. Tonight, though, I felt a craving for red meat and this has been absolutely wonderful. I'm stuffed!"

"It's even tastier when accompanied by this wine–" the rest of Grant's sentence is cut-off by a loud blast of music from the bar. They've both noticed that the crowd gathering there is growing noisier and with the music playing they have to shout to be heard.

Glancing in that direction again Judith notices lots of people laughing with some trying to dance despite the crush.

"Why don't we finish up here then go back to my place for coffee?"

"Good idea! I remember that you serve great coffee," says Grant, agreeing with her suggestion.

"It is good stuff, the brand is called *Kicking Horse*," Judith replies.

"I've heard of that I think," Grant tilts his head while chasing a memory. ·

"The name comes from the Kicking Horse Pass but the company is actually in Invermere."

"That's it! I've driven through there on the way to Fairmont Hot Springs and must have seen signs or something."

"I haven't been there but a couple of the teachers went in the Fall and had a great time."

"It's a beautiful spot and there's lots to do, lots of different outdoor activities. Definitely worth seeing."

"Good to know. Well, that's the story behind the coffee. I can't stand bitter coffee so I tried a few of their styles and finally settled on *Hola* because I prefer a lighter, milder blend. They have some medium and dark roasts with cute names like *Smart Ass* and *Half Ass* and *Grizzly Claw*."

"I drink all kinds in my job from convenience store to k-cups to the station house sludge... I can't stand an aftertaste."

"I agree, and that's why I like using a French Press."

A popular song comes on and the bar crowd starts clapping and singing along. It is after 10:00 on a Saturday night. Grant settles the bill while Judith wraps a wool scarf around her throat and puts on her coat. She knows they'll feel the cold once they step out of the warm restaurant.

Sipping coffee, while sitting side-by-side on the couch in Judith's living-room, Grant looks around and says:

"This place does need a cat. I remembered you saying you were thinking of a cat and I thought about getting one for you, you know. But that very day I read a guest column in the newspaper by someone from the Alberta SPCA saying how pets should never be given as surprise Christmas gifts. Or any kind of present if it's a surprise. They said the recipient should always be the one to choose which makes sense. Growing up we always had pets in the house and the animals responded differently to each of us."

"I've never had a pet but I think a cat would be ideal for an apartment. Although a dog would be good for taking on walks."

"True except dog-walking isn't an option it's a twice-daily chore no matter what the weather is like. Even when it's -30 below they still have to go out. And unless you've got a Newfoundlander or some other big hairy creature your dog might hate being out in the bitter cold too! Cats take care of their business indoors."

"Oh, I never thought of that aspect. Does it smell bad?"

"No, not if you keep the litter box clean. And you know you can talk a cat on a walk, just make sure you have a good harness so he or she doesn't escape. We have a leash by-law for pets and that includes cats. It's a good thing because they're too vulnerable to cars and kids and other animals."

"And they kill a lot of birds, too."

"Birds, squirrels, mice... cats are predators. The leash by-law also means we can have a *No-Kill policy* because if the cats aren't out roaming all night they're not dropping litters three or four times a year."

"Hmm, I can see I'm going to have to do a bit of research before I commit to a pet."

"Well they say the Internet was created to share cute cat videos so you'll find plenty of stuff to choose from."

"I guess I better be careful not to put 'pussy videos' in the search engine," she quips and Grant laughs out loud in surprise.

They finish their coffee and putting the mugs back on the table relax back comfortably. Grant slips an arm over Judith's shoulder and says:

"Judith, can I ask why you don't drink?"

"Now you sound like Lila!" she replies.

"Well, it's not totally unheard-of but it's not all that common. The usual reasons for someone being a non-drinker are it's a religious stipulation, or concerns about a family history of alcoholism, or sometimes it's because of a bad experience with alcohol, or the person is on medication."

"In my case it's none of the above. I did talk about this a few weeks ago with Lila and having said it out loud once now it feels easier to say it again:

I don't drink because my mother was a drunk and just the smell of alcohol repulses me. I'm not worried about inheriting alcoholic tendencies because I know I'll never touch the stuff. In fact, I'm not even sure I believe in alcoholism being a disease. Anyhow, drinking just involves too many messy, smelly memories, ugh."

"Oh that's too bad. I'm not going to say *you don't know what you're missing* because you sound pretty definite and I would never try to persuade someone to drink."

"Thanks for that but it doesn't matter, I couldn't possibly be persuaded. The thing is I began helping my mom cover up her problem at a very young age. My father died when I was just starting school and that was devastating to both Mom and me. Anyhow, so far as I recall Mom held it together for about a year or so and then she started bringing a bottle or two when she came home from work, along with her married boss.

I have no brothers or sisters so there was no one to turn to and no help dealing with my grief. Instead I had to take care of my mother, and to keep our home life a secret. And that's how things were until she died."

"Poor thing. I can imagine you as a little girl struggling and worrying."

"Yes, I did worry all the time. Looking back I don't know what I was so worried about, I mean in retrospect if someone had found out about my mother's problem it would probably have been good for me. But maybe not and there's no pointing thinking *what if?* is there?"

"Poor little Judith, or were you a Judy back then?"

"My father called me Judy. I wouldn't let anyone else."

"Not even your Mom?"

"Huh, she called me *Jude* because she could only manage to slur the first syllable. I wouldn't answer to Judy and insisted on being called Judith because I thought it sounded more grown-up."

She rests her head against Grant's chest and his arm tightens around her shoulders. They sit like that in companionable silence for an enjoyable interval before he finally says he'd better get going. Judith walks him to the door saying thank you for the delicious meal. Grant kisses her goodnight and they both pause waiting for the other to deepen that kiss but instead each pulls back with a smile.

Judith goes to bed shortly afterwards and falls asleep quickly and deeply.

Chapter 10

Monday, January 6, 2020

Judith's first task when she finally gets to her office on January 6th is to create a text graphic for her screensaver. She's chosen a quote from George Bernard Shaw that resonates with her, and she decides it will be her new year's inspiration:

"The possibilities are numerous once we decide to act and not react"

Judith has already put this into practice while walking through the halls of the school by greeting people instead of just replying to their remarks. Everyone notices her new cheerful attitude and responds with smiles except Marta Smith. She completely snubs Judith.

Last year Judith would have loudly sniped back with a comment like *Marta must be getting old since her hearing's going!* but this year she just shrugs her shoulders. She is spotted by a couple of schoolgirls who giggle and Judith knows the story of the encounter will soon spread.

She has visited with Pat Johnson, the principal, chatted with Samira, the school secretary, drunk a coffee in the staff-room, created her motivational screensaver, and is now ready to tackle setting up the books for the new fiscal year.

Judith loves the look of a brand-new, pale-green ledger sheet. She uses an accounting programme as a back-up to her handwritten entries. That wouldn't have been allowed at the major accounting firm where she'd once worked but here Judith is the boss. She settles into her work and is surprised when Cindy Callahan, the part-time librarian who shares Judith's office space, comes in for her afternoon shift.

"Is that the time already?" exclaims Judith. "I've missed lunch and now that I'm thinking about it, I'm starving!"

"Don't you usually have lunch with Lila Morelli?" asks Cindy.

"Yes, you're right. I wonder why she didn't call? Must be busy, like I was, so I'll pop down to her office to see if she wants to head out for a bite." Judith gathers up her purse but before heading out the door she pauses to remark:

"I like your haircut, Cindy. That style really suits you."

The younger woman stares after Judith with her mouth fallen open in surprise.

Frustrated by no phone calls from Lila over the weekend Judith is anxious to get together with her friend to find out about Arnie's visit. She'd been expecting Lila to drop into the library office sometime during the morning, but now it's already the afternoon and no Lila.

Judith marches down to the Nurse's office ready for a long overdue gossip. When she arrives it's to discover Lila pushing aside a half-eaten sandwich.

"Oh, hi Judith. What can I do for you?" she asks, blatantly disinterested.

Judith is taken aback and stumbles over her reply:

"I wanted us to go have lunch," she says.

"I've already eaten," Lila gestures to her sparse meal. She wraps the remains of the sandwich adding: "Turns out I wasn't hungry anyhow."

Judith stands there nonplussed while Lila sits silently. Finally Judith bursts out with:

"What happened with Arnie?"

"He's gone home. We talked a lot and now I have plenty to think over. When I make some decisions, and am ready to talk about it, I'll let you know."

Lila isn't forthcoming and Judith is left wondering if she's done something wrong. Her home-life growing up had precluded friendships and Judith's relationship with Lila is still very new. New, but very important to her.

She senses Lila is hurting beneath the cold exterior but obviously doesn't want to share. Judith is completely at a loss and doesn't know how to react.

Deciding that she has no choice but to accept Lila's dismissal she leaves the office and heads out of the school to get a quick lunch. She takes comfort thinking of Grant's New Year's card in her purse.

Judith is watching another episode of 'The Black List' when her phone rings indicating Grant is calling.

"Hi Judith, how was your first day back after the holidays?" he asks.

"Work was great – I love getting set up for a new year – but on a personal level not so great: Lila skipped our lunch date and when I saw her she snubbed me!"

"Why? I thought she was going to catch you up on the news about her husband's visit. You were looking forward to the two of you getting together."

"That's what I thought too! but it's not what happened. Remember how she's been avoiding my calls and we thought she and Arnie must be busy figuring things out between them? well, now I'm wondering if it's something more than that."

"Like what?"

"Like... well, I don't know."

"What exactly did she say to you?"

"Very little, actually. I asked what happened with them and she said they talked a lot and she had to think things over and she'd tell me about it when she was ready."

"Oh."

"What does *oh* mean?"

"Well, it sounds like things aren't good between them, but hey, I really don't like speculating."

"No, I need you to speculate. You know more about this kind of thing than I do."

"Yeah, but I don't want to say the wrong thing and... look, maybe I shouldn't get involved. Lila's asked you to give her some time and I think you should respect that."

"I see. Well you're right, you shouldn't get involved. Oh look at the time I've got to go now."

"Judith, wait–"

"Bye. Grant." She disconnects the call and when he rings again she lets it go to voicemail. Tossing the phone aside she returns to her TV show but finds her concentration has broken. A few moments later her phone dings to signal an incoming text message. Judith reads:

GRANT: dont be mad pls

She realizes she *is* mad at Grant and doesn't care whether or not she is being unreasonable about it. She switches her phone off and goes to bed early.

Chapter 11

Sometime overnight, while tossing and turning in her bed, Judith decides she has to confront Lila. For Lila's sake and for Grant's. It isn't fair to vent her frustrations on him.

Tuesday morning she is waiting in the school parking lot early, waiting for Lila to arrive. Her car is easy to spot, a white 2-seater convertible that Lila says is a Miata but Grant calls it an MX-5. Judith couldn't care less, she has absolutely no interest in cars other than as a convenience.

Spotting the sportscar as it wheels in Judith hurries over and knocks on the passenger door. Lila reluctantly opens it and Judith climbs in.

"Lila, something is going on and I want to know what it is."

"I told you I'd tell you when I'm ready," snaps Lila.

"Why are you being so... so hostile?" asks Judith. "Our friendship means a lot to me and I thought it did to you as well."

For a moment so brief Judith has to wonder if she's imagined it, Lila's face softens but then her eyes narrow to a glare and she answers:

"Of course it matters but right now you need to back off. I've asked for some space and you need to give it to me."

"That's what Grant says," complains Judith, "But it's obvious that something's wrong. If I'm truly your friend you should turn to me for help and I should be able to give it, or at least give comfort, and be a sounding board or something."

Again, Lila seems to waver but then she says in a sharp, dismissive tone:

"I can't be plainer, Judith. For now just back off."

Lila gets out of her car and without looking back strides toward the school. Judith, forlorn, has no choice but to follow.

Once she gets into her own office Judith turns on her computer and studies the message that's popped up on her screen:

"The possibilities are numerous once we decide to act and not react"

She thinks about that message and decides this can't be about her and her own hurt feelings. Instead, as a good friend, she has to give Lila the distance she wants. Lila knows she will be here for her when needed.

Besides, the two of them have some matching interests and duties that will keep them in contact, for instance they each hold volunteer positions at The Centre. Although Lila is the newcomer to Edgemont Village she is the one who brought Judith in to meet the Rev Robbie with the idea of taking over some, or all, of the bookkeeping in the first place.

Lila is a friendly, outgoing joiner-type and Judith hates to see her friend in this state but she will go along with Lila's request for now. Grant doesn't seem keen to give advice and he is probably wise not to do so. Judith will figure it out on her own.

Judith has already gotten into bed but finds she can't sleep so she texts Grant:

im sorry i overreacted

and he answers right away:

its ok good to hear from u call me

When he answers the phone Judith begins in a rush, trying to get all her thoughts out at once:

"I'm not going to talk for long because I'm already in bed. But I had to apologise. I tried sleeping but my conscience kept me awake, and I had enough tossing and turning last night. I don't like it when we're on the outs and I sure don't want to go through another sleepless night again. Anyhow, I was wrong, and I am really sorry about yesterday."

"Honey, it's okay. Now that you've called everything is good. I didn't get much sleep either."

Judith absorbs the 'honey', spoken so casually, with pleasure.

"Well I won't keep you. I just felt badly because I'd been unfair to you."

"No, it's not all on you, I'm guilty, too because you asked my opinion and I sidestepped," he pauses a moment before asking: "Do you still want to know what I think?"

"Yes, of course I do."

"Okay here goes: I think Arnie told Lila something bad... serious... you know – like maybe he'd had an affair – and she has to decide whether or not she can get past whatever it is to keep the marriage going. And I'm only guessing at infidelity, but whatever it is she needs time and space to think it through. I'm sure once she does she'll tell you all about it.

Lila has a strong personality. She doesn't really seem to be the type who asks everybody else what she should do so, as she said, she'll let you know when she's made up her mind."

Judith is quiet for so long that Grant wonders if he's offended her or something. He's about to speak when she says:

"I understand what you're saying and yes, that does sound like the kind of thing Lila would do but... if I'm really her friend shouldn't she confide in me? I mean, I'm not *everybody* I'm... well, I guess I'm not – or rather we're – not the friends I thought we were."

She sounds so sad and forlorn that Grant is wishing he's waited until they are face-to face before voicing his thoughts. It isn't possible to give a hug of comfort in a phone conversation. He doesn't like feeling inadequate.

"Or it could be that Lila is embarrassed or ashamed about whatever it is. She might be *licking her wounds,* so to speak, before sharing the news. It might have been a real shock that's left her not knowing how to react."

"Maybe... I guess I really do just have to be patient and wait."

"Now I want to know the answer too. You'll have to keep my in the loop and in the meantime we'll be curious together."

She chuckles at that and says now she feels sure she can sleep and wishes him goodnight.

"You're in my thoughts, Judith. Sleep well," Grant replies.

Chapter 12

Saturday, February 8, 2020

"Lila, what are you saying? What was Rev Robbie going to do for you?" demands Judith, gripping her friend's arm. Lila turns away saying in a dead and despairing voice:

"It's nothing. Nothing to do with you, and there's nothing you can do. Nobody can do anything. Forget about it."

"But Lila, I want–"

"Look at that," interrupts Lila pointing to the old-style computer set-up on the desk. The monitor and speakers and printer are there, but the CPU is missing. Looking around they discover open desk drawers have been rifled with papers scattered over the chair and floor. The door to the safe is wide open showing an empty interior. The body lies on top of an old-fashioned ledger, as if Rev Robbie has died clutching it to his chest.

Judith notices that one of the man's loafers has been kicked off in his struggles and the sight of that brings her to tears. She is sobbing when Grant arrives. He notices that Lila stands frozen and dry-eyed.

The police get hold of Mr. Miller to open the auditorium. His precious hardwood is going to get scuffed and marked with everyone traipsing through to be interviewed, but he and his son will deal with that tomorrow. Right now they need to do whatever they can to help the police find Rev Robbie's killer.

Grant appreciates that Patricia Johnson has corralled the volleyball players and their entourage together but wished she'd thought to do the same with the Horticultural Society and the rest of the people in the building. They will eventually figure out who is supposed to be there - and where, who is actually there, and who is missing, but the person with the answers is currently on his way to the morgue.

Grant knew the Reverend Wilcox, although only very casually, and is saddened by his death.

He calls for more personnel to attend the location. They need to gather everyone's name and contact information before releasing anyone. Soon parents are arriving to pick up their teenagers and that adds to the general confusion. Everyone knew Rev Robbie, and everyone is shocked and mournful at his passing.

Inevitably the media pick up some of the tweets and send out reporters and TV crews. The wealthy of Edgemont Village are always news.

At some point someone mentions the opioid Fentanyl. Soon a story of poisoning by drug overdose is circulating. No one believes Rev Robbie was taking recreational drugs but a painkiller? that rumour gets traction. A whole new avenue of investigation opens up.

Calls are placed to Board Members and several descend on the scene brimming with questions and demands. Rich, influential people who are used to getting immediate answers. Grant is relieved when both his boss and his boss's boss present themselves to deal with the upper echelon, and that Suzanne has gone to attach herself to the big brass.

Andrea Seely joined The Centre's Board as a *Member at Large* waiting until a Director's spot came open. When the position of Treasurer became available she offered to take on that role.

Initially, it seems a much bigger job then she's imagined. The Centre collects membership dues and hosts a lot of activities which require user-fees, wages, services, utilities... until she learns that Rev Robbie takes care of the day-to-day business.

He balances the petty cash, handles the bank deposits, and makes the ledger entries. They also have an accounting firm, working on a pro bono basis, to process payroll, remit taxes, and produce a quarterly financial statement plus file an annual return.

Andrea's job is simply to oversee operations, although she does have to register with the bank for signing authority in case she ever has to deal with one of Rev Robbie's duties.

She enjoys the Board Meetings and likes to use her title when discussing The Centre, hinting at her friendship with Eleanor Frampton and other wealthy townspeople. It also gives her the excuse to spend plenty of time at The Centre, allowing her the pretense of Treasurer business to cover meeting up with Kyle and trying to further their relationship. She only makes a halfhearted effort at secrecy.

Andrea Seely is a flamboyant presence with her brightly coloured clothes cut to flow over her heavy build, and a loud voice matched to a loud laugh. She sees herself as someone to be reckoned with, a very self-satisfied woman.

Now she tries to thrust herself into the police investigation. She announces that as Treasurer it is imperative that she investigate the contents of the safe immediately. Everything is of *the utmost urgency and importance.*

The scene-of-crime staff aren't impressed and refuse to allow the woman into the Reverend's office until they've completed their evidence-gathering. Besides, they already know the safe is empty.

Andrea huffs but her demands are ignored. Finally, she stomps off to vent her complaints to the other board members who are present.

Once the all-clear is given for the ambulance attendants to remove the body Grant goes to find Andrea Seely. She sticks her nose in the air while leading the way back to the office.

First she looks for the petty cash box that resides in the top drawer of the desk during office hours. The box is there, but when she opens it there is nothing inside. No cash, and no vouchers to account for the missing money.

The safe isn't hidden, it sits in a corner of the room and serves as a coffee stand. It doesn't matter if the coffee-maker gets hot, the safe is fireproof, and its surface is resistant to drips and wet spots. The safe sits on a solid base so that anyone opening it won't have to stoop too low to reach inside.

With the door swung open wide it only takes a quick glance to see there are no ledgers or receipt books, and definitely no money inside. The two donation boxes, when opened, prove equally empty of cash although there are several cheques folded inside. There is a sprinkling of some white substance that looks like dust or powder on the floor of the safe, but otherwise it's bare.

Andrea's great show of consulting a note on her phone to get the combination has fallen flat. Now she demands:

"Where are the missing funds?"

Grant schools his face to avoid showing exasperation and begins the painstaking task of asking Andrea Seely question after question trying to get answers.

"How much money was there?"

"Well I don't know, do I?"

"How much do you think should be there?"

"I just said, I don't know."

"Then, how do you know that funds are missing?"

"Of course they're missing, they're not here in the safe where they should be."

"Yes, but how do you know that if you don't know what should be there?"

"Because there has to be something."

"If you don't know how much money should have been in the safe, then you don't know if *any* money *was* in the safe."

"Well of course there was. It's Saturday night, there should be a whole week's worth of collections. The banking is done every Monday morning."

"And how much would a week's worth of collections come to?"

"I don't know. A lot of the money comes in on the weekends... but there's stuff on every night of the week as well. I'm fairly new to the position of Treasurer so I don't have it all at my fingertips just yet."

"Fair enough. We haven't found any ledgers–"

"They would have been kept in the safe," Andrea interrupts.

"Okay, and we can't check the computer–"

Again she interrupts demanding to know why not, pointing to the monitor on the desk. Grant explains that the CPU, the computer's processing unit, is missing. It seems she is about to complain about that as well but settles for pursing her lips and giving him an annoyed look. He feels ready to return it too because sitting in this room absorbing the strong smell of the cloying perfume she wears is making him headachey.

"So we've been robbed, is what you're saying."

"No, I'm not saying that. I have a dead man and indications show he was likely murdered. I have an empty safe and a missing computer but there might be reasonable explanations."

"I doubt that! Like what? No, don't bother to answer, it's obvious to me what's happened: thieves falling out."

"You're accusing Rev Robbie of theft?"

"Who else could it be?

Exasperated Grant retorted: "One possibility is the killer."

"Killer? oh no, he must have committed suicide."

Grant bites back the urge to snap *oh is that likely?* and instead settles for raising an eyebrow. Andrea Seely hurries to add:

"He probably figured he was about to get caught for the stealing and took this way out."

"So then where is the money?"

"Well I don't know. Stashed away somewhere."

Grant appears to consider this then replies mildly:

"So your theory is that Rev Robbie stole the money from the safe, took it somewhere for safekeeping, then returned to this very room to kill himself. Have I got that right, Ms. Seely?"

"Oh honestly, you can't expect me to do your job for you," she huffs before flouncing out of the room. Grant watches with interest having never known exactly what flouncing meant before.

Chapter 13

Sunday, February 9, 2020

Judith doesn't get out of bed until late but she hasn't enjoyed a refreshing sleep. Not surprising with the shock of Rev Robbie's death and afterwards having to hang around waiting around to be interviewed.

Then, once she does get home, it's difficult to fall asleep. Plenty of thoughts about the killing, the method, Lila's concern – to name a few – chase round her head as she lies in bed. And of course Grant's involvement. In the few moments they spent together she can tell he is preoccupied and eager to get started.

Grant hurriedly explains that it appears to be a poisoning death but they don't know yet how it the poison was taken. Accidentally? or deliberately, and if so, by whose hand? Even once the method is confirmed they still won't know those answers. He has a difficult task ahead of him, especially since the victim is so well-loved. No one has a motive.

She gets dressed, eventually, and makes herself look presentable on the off-chance that Grant might stop by. She isn't surprised when he doesn't, certain he will be extremely busy.

After a couple of attempts to reach Lila by phone and by text Judith gives up. Time weighs heavily on her and although Sundays have always been a stress-free, relaxing day in the past today feels like it's dragging on and on.

When Pat Johnson finishes loading up the dishwasher she's tempted to switch it on but knows she'll hear about that from her husband. Ever since Mark retired he's taken a critical interest in how the household is run, and complains if any of the appliances are used unless they're as full as possible.

He checks over the utility bills to make sure they are consistent with the previous month. If the electric bill is really high he'll dig out his copies from the year before and compare. He is always on the look-out for a power drain or, in the case of the water bill, a leak that is running up costs.

Both he and Pat are shocked and upset about Rev Robbie's death, especially since both of them were there at the time. They figure out when they had last seen and last spoken to Rev Robbie then each sits quietly for a moment remembering the man.

"I wonder who will take his funeral service?" muses Pat. "It won't be the reverend who replaced him, surely it will be someone higher up."

"I really don't know. Haven't given it any thought. Actually, sad as I am about Rev Robbie, I have to confess I was really interested in what Jim Henley was telling me about his collection of cacti. Someone gave him a Christmas cactus for a gift and did you know that these plants are completely different from most cacti?

Also there are Easter and Thanksgiving versions, too All flowering. Anyhow, he's giving me a cutting and tells me I'll have no trouble growing my own cactus that can easily last for decades! I was reading about it online just before we had lunch and I'm looking forward to giving it a try."

Pat agrees that flowering cacti will be very nice during the winter months but inside she longs to gossip about Rev Robbie's death.

Mark never has any interest in speculation, he's all about facts and truths, but she likes to ponder the how, why and, who behind the mystery. And she really likes to have a good chat with a like-minded friend.

She has no idea what Judith Taylor does on her days off but decides that under this circumstance, and their mutual feeling for Rev Robbie, that she is justified in phoning for a gossip. Judith answers her phone on the first ring and is delighted that Pat has called.

They discuss their suspicions and theories about Rev Robbie's death then Judith says:

"I'm concerned about Lila. As you know she discovered Rev Robbie's body first when we went into his office at The Centre–"

"I was glad to see the two of you together last night because I know there'd been some sort of falling out or whatever..." Pat's words trail away but the interest in her voice encourages Judith to elaborate.

"Oh Pat, it's been awful. Lila and I weren't at The Centre together, we met up after having both travelled there separately although I'd offered to bring her.

She and I have barely spoken in the past five weeks. Ever since her estranged husband came to town for a weekend. We were all supposed to get together while he was here but then but she cancelled. She refuses to discuss Arnie's visit at all. Whatever happened has upset her deeply and then there was last night's gruesome discovery. And she was so close to him, too."

"Oh I am disappointed to hear that, Judith. It's been a real pleasure for me to see you two getting on so well. I mean, and I know you won't mind me saying this, you aren't the easiest person to get along with. I like you just as you are and have no problem, neither does

Mark, neither does Eleanor Frampton! but I know some of the teaching staff gets on your nerves and, well, they aren't happy when you won't join in on their various functions. At least they weren't, I thought I'd seen a lot more friendliness from the teachers lately."

"That's true, and you've got some good teachers who are dedicated to their jobs. The one or two bad apples can only exert so much influence. The rest are now standing up for themselves."

"So you've been a good influence on them and Lila's been a good influence on you."

"She really has. I just wish I could be as good a friend to her as she's been to me."

"Oh, I'm sure you are–"

"But Pat, even Rev Robbie spoke to me about Lila and how I should be pushing her to talk. I told him I'd tried but he just said *'try harder'* and I didn't."

"Oh Judith, I'm sure things will work out. We just have to be patient and give it time."

Lila's phone is blowing up with texts and phone-calls. She doesn't answer any of them. People are morbidly curious about the finding of the body, wanting to know what she saw, and how it made her feel. At moment's like this Lila feels like shunning the entire human race.

When she hears the thump-thump of her landlady's cane on the floor above Lila hurries upstairs. She isn't in the mood for company, but there is always the chance that her elderly neighbour is in difficulty and needs Lila's help as a neighbour or even as a professional nurse.

Still wearing her pyjamas she comes through the door inside Mrs. P's kitchen and inhales deeply, enjoying the sugar and vanilla smells of home baking. Fortunately the spry old lady is fine, just concerned about her tenant, and has wrapped up a dozen cookies as comfort food for her. Hiding her reluctance Lila agrees to stay for the kindly offered cup of tea.

Mrs. Piernitsky isn't fooled but she pretends not to notice Lila's lack of enthusiasm, knowing that half-an-hour spent consuming a hot drink and a slice of freshly baked cake will do the younger woman a world of good. She is very fond of Lila and had been prepared to like her husband too, but she saw very little of him and can't form an opinion. The landlady is very deaf and totally unaware of the yelling that has gone on in the basement of her home during Arnie's weekend visit the month before.

Chapter 14

Valentine's Day is coming up and Grant's partner, Suzanne Mirteau, has been making snide remarks all day. Suzanne, despite all she has in good looks, brains, and skills, lacks self-confidence. It seems she measures her worth by the degree of interest shown by the men around her.

Grant thinks highly of Suzanne as a co-worker – and his safety depends on her as his partner in law enforcement – but he isn't attracted, and she won't or can't accept that.

She was flirtatious and possessive before he met Judith Taylor, but now her jealousy is almost out-of-control. Grant is seriously considering requesting a change of partner and only hesitates because as the senior officer it won't reflect well on Suzanne who he knows is ambitious.

He's spent the day ignoring the nasty comments which he's sure will be even worse tomorrow. He's even thought of sending Suzanne an anonymous bouquet from *A Secret Admirer* just to keep her happy but decided against shelling out for the inflated cost of Valentine's Day flowers. He isn't planning to send flowers to Judith so why would he spend money on Suzanne?

He lets his mind drift to thoughts of Judith. She'd looked very pretty and he was flattered she'd dressed up for her dinner date with him on Saturday night. Quite a contrast to the well-worn clothes she had on when they went to the show. The small smile that plays around his lips while he reminisces serves to infuriate his angry partner even more.

He is surprised – and secretly pleased – when Suzanne suddenly blurts out that she's being reassigned, at her request, to the opioid task force.

"I won't bother asking if you'd like to go out for a farewell drink in case your girlfriend gets jealous," she says with a sneer that turns her beautiful face ugly.

Grant recoils slightly from the anger in her eyes before calmly replying:

"I'm sure it won't be goodbye, Suzanne. In fact, I expect your investigation will overlap with the Rev Robbie murder now that the lab has confirmed the cause of death iss, as suspected, an overdose of Fentanyl."

In a phone-call later that afternoon he passes on the news about Suzanne's departmental change to Judith.

"I have to admit that I'm glad I won't be seeing or talking to Suzanne anymore. She's never hid her dislike or contempt for me, and I still don't know what I did to rub her the wrong way," confides Judith in reply. Grant is quite sure the problem has nothing to do with Judith herself, but with Grant's attraction to her.

"Suzanne is a very good police officer except she's got a blind spot when it comes to self-appraisal. She's narcissistic and vain, and quick to take offence at any perceived slight. It took me a long time to see this. I used to ignore her come-ons but finally had to out-and-out reject her when her antics interfered with our work. She seemed to accept that until I met you. Once she realized I wasn't going to *come to my senses* as she put it – she turned nasty. So long as she gets her own way everything is rosy but boy she sure is a trial to work with when she's been thwarted."

"So her transfer is a relief to you as well?"

"It is. I don't care if my next partner is male or female but I sure do hope they're happily married!"

"It must be difficult being married to a police officer... I mean, the hours and worrying about their safety."

"It's one of many jobs where there is risk involved: firefighters, military personnel, EMTs, construction workers... even someone doing a routine job like meter-reading could be in danger from a gas leak explosion. Tragically, schools have been venues for deadly violence, too."

"Every time we hear about a school shooting it just terrifies all of us."

"Unfortunately it's the very strong taboo of harming defenceless innocents that attracts the biggest headlines. From what I've learned the shooter is often an ex-student exacting revenge – of real or just perceived threats or attacks – but schools have become the target of thrill killers as well. It is a very scary situation."

"So you're saying any marriage could face career issues – even dangers?"

"Hmm, yes, but for example I've been a cop for seventeen, no it's eighteen years now, and I've never been shot at.

Anyhow, with Suzanne gone and no new partner assigned yet I was hoping you could be my sounding-board since I trust your discretion and judgement."

"I'm flattered," Judith replies, and he smiles at hearing the seriousness of her tone.

Chapter 15

It is unseasonably mild and sunny when Grant drops in at the school just as Judith is finishing up.

"This is a nice surprise!" she exclaims. Grant gives a crooked smile and tells her she is to be his antidote to a rotten turn of events.

"I thought we could go for a walk. It won't be dark for another 45 minutes or so and it's so nice to see the sun."

"That's a great idea. In fact, I walked to school today because it was 7 C when I was ready to come to work so at the last moment I decided to leave the car behind."

"Perfect, that means you'll have walking shoes. In fact that sweater and pants outfit looks perfect for a brisk outing, it uh, fits you very well."

Judith is wearing a Nordic-patterned sweater in white/green/blue with matching navy slacks. She usually wears pants to work in the winter time.

"Thank you! I don't wear the sweater often because it's quite warm but it will be perfect for a hike."

"How about this then: we'll drive to Picnic Hill but we'll avoid the off-leash dog park and wander along one of the trails until the sun starts to set. By then we'll probably feel a bit chilly so I'll take you back to my place for a hot chocolate in front of the fireplace. Sound good?"

"You've got a fireplace? Lucky you!" Judith says with enthusiasm adding, "Let's go, you can tell me about your rotten day and get it off your chest."

"I'll wait till we're out walking," replies Grant, opening the front door to lead her out to the parking lot. They both spot Lila at the same time and Grant waves while Judith calls out to her but Lila just gives a quick wave back and hurries into her car.

"Still no word from her, eh?"

"Nothing. She's always just like that – polite-friendly rather than friend-friendly. It's been going on like this for weeks." Judith is unhappy, but also resigned to the new reality of her relationship with Lila.

"She's on my list to be re-interviewed. I'm not looking forward to it but I should get it taken care of sooner rather than later, I guess."

Neither one says much on the drive to Picnic Hill, so called because it's a local beauty spot that serves families, lovers, and pet owners. Edgemont School for Girls frequently organizes science class trips to study nature during the different seasons there so Judith knows her way around the area quite well.

After he parks the car Judith leads Grant to the far left pathway which she says is an easy 25- to 30-minute walk that circles back to their starting point.

The walking paths have been cleared of snow by the volunteers from various service clubs who take turns looking after Picnic Hill. That usually means cleaning up the messes left by human visitors, but also keeping the pathways free.

"So what happened to ruin your day?" asks Judith once they get walking at a good pace.

"I had a likely lead to pursue, I'll tell you the backstory in a minute, and it took ages to track down the person in question only to have him alibi up right away. I didn't realize how much I was counting on this being the solution and now I've been let down hard. Serves me right because I have to admit this never felt right in my gut but I ignored that. Anyhow, the story is..."

Judith draws closer so she won't miss a thing. Grant has a knack with words that make his interviews come alive. They slow down a bit and he tucks her arm into his, holding her close to his side.

"Rev Robbie's wife Peg – Margaret, actually – died a year ago September. They'd been married for a very long time and everyone felt so sorry for him having to live on his own without her. Everyone, that is, except for her brother Matthew.

Matthew is still working, he's about 12 years younger than Peg was, and he's in sales and boy, so difficult to pin down for a meeting. Just to talk first of all, because my lead was based on hearsay, not actual evidence, but he just wouldn't make himself available. So of course I started wondering if he was avoiding me and if he had a good reason to do so. A good, guilty reason. However that's not how things turned out.

I got onto Matthew from a neighbour of Peg and Rev Robbie's, another one called Margaret, who was the oldest of them all. She's frail, but her mind is still sharp and she said Matthew had accused Rev Robbie of killing Peg and then proceeded to threaten he'd *get him.*

Apparently Peg had been in charge of Matthew's raising for much of his life so he'd gotten used to being spoiled by her. But once she got married to Rev Robbie Matthew lost all that special attention and, according to this Margaret, was bitterly jealous for the entire fifty-year's of his sister's marriage! Can you imagine?"

"I can't imagine being married for fifty years?"

"No?"

"Well, that's the Golden Wedding Anniversary, right? You don't hear about very many of those."

Grant's voice lowers to a murmur when he says: "I could imagine fifty years – with the right woman, that is."

At his words, said in such a confiding tone, Judith feels a little shiver of pleasure ripple through her body but hopes her down-filled jacket hides it. Grant correctly interprets the movement he feels coming from her, but gives no indication.

"Anyhow, the brother never specified exactly how Rev Robbie was supposed to have killed Peg, I think she died of a stroke, but he kicked off at the funeral, at the burial site, and again in the Church's social room where they served refreshments afterwards.

Margaret said he made an awful fool out of himself and that Rev Robbie, his brother-in-law, tried to calm Matthew down but it was no use. He just shouted out his threats of vengeance, warning Rev Robbie that he'd *get him* no matter how long it took.

So, he sounds like a pretty good suspect, right? certainly worth a chat. Then, when I realized he was dodging my calls I really thought I was on to something. When I finally got hold of him at his work and managed to pin him down to a time and place he was a no-show.

So, now I was really thinking this guy was trying to hide something. And he was but, talk about ridiculous: he was avoiding me because he thought I was after him for driving with an expired driver's licence. I mean, how would I even know that? how would anyone know something like that? but it was his guilty conscience.

I'm investigating a suspicious death that's probably a homicide and this guy is dodging me because of traffic tickets? What a waste of time.

Turns out he has several speeding tickets, a couple of red-light camera tickets, and *a shitload of parking tickets* as he put it. Well you might not know this but here in Alberta you can't renew your driver's licence or your provincial plates if you've got outstanding fines. So he's been driving without a valid licence, but to make matters worse because he knew that his insurance would go up because of demerits for tickets and fines he let that lapse as well.

So here's this guy in his late fifties or early sixties driving around with no licence and no insurance. His $1,000 worth of fines has just jumped up an additional $4,000 or so.

Anyhow, I was so angry at him wasting my time with his foolishness I reported his licence plate to Traffic and he'll get stopped unless he's smart enough to have cabbed it straight to a Registry office today to get paid up."

Grant shakes his head in disgust but Judith can't help letting a giggle escape, explaining:

"It's so anti-climactic."

Grant chuckles and quipped: "And that's always frustrating."

"Oh good one!" laughs Judith.

Grant's apartment is brand-new and built over the homeowner's garage. It's done up in shades of gray accented with black. Even the bathroom fixtures are black. All the appliances are brushed stainless steel, and the counters are marble. It's very modern, very masculine-looking, and stops just short of being cold and sterile.

Both Judith and Grant agree that a wood-burning fireplace would be cozier but the gas fire lights up instantly at the flick of a switch. Having no wood to bring in, or ashes to take out, is a convenient bonus.

Grant's living-room furniture consists of oxblood leather seating, Mission-style tables, and he has a few big Hudson's Bay signature striped cushions adding colour. Judith pushes a couple of them onto the floor and sits on one with her back resting against the couch and her feet warming by the fire.

When Grant comes in with their drinks on a tray he pauses to admire how relaxed she looks, and how pretty in the glow of firelight. He sets the tray on the coffee-table then slides down onto the other cushion. Taking her in his arms he gives her a tight squeeze and covers her face with kisses.

"That tickles!" she cries pulling back with a smile. They stare into each other's eyes for a long moment before meeting in a deep, satisfying kiss.

The marshmallows have melted into the hot chocolate - that is no longer hot but still chocolatey and delicious - when they finally came up for air.

Chapter 16

Thursday, February 13, 2020

As things turn out Grant is able to interview Lila the next day. They meet in her nurse's office at the school and he is shocked at how she has changed from a happy, vibrant woman to someone who is despairing and despondent. Her hair needs washing and the shadows under her eyes speak of too many sleepless nights in a row.

She sits slumped in her chair while he starts off with a few work-related questions to put her at her ease:

"I understand that your job at The Centre is a volunteer position to deal with potential injuries during sporting events?"

Lila nods.

"Anything else?"

"I've given first aid a few times."

"Can you give me some examples?"

She sighs deeply then slowly answers:

"Once when an art instructor cut her fingers quite badly with an X-Acto blade, and another time a girl fainted... but I don't remember why."

"And how well did you know Rev Robbie?"

"Really well, and I just loved him and I miss him so much! For the first time Lila's voice became animated. "When I'm at The Centre it's always with the hope that my professional skills won't be needed so I spent a lot of time talking with him. He was a wonderfully kind and caring man. He had a great sense of humour, too."

"Did you work alongside him at all, by that I mean in his bookkeeping work for The Centre?"

"Well, we spent time in his office and he'd be working then. Is that what you mean?"

"Actually, Lila, I'm trying to get a clearer picture of Rev Robbie's day-to-day activities. I know he handled the bank deposits for The Centre's donations, and monies collected from refreshment sales, and collection boxes. All the funds that were paid the week prior to his death are missing, and there were only a few cheques in the safe. Someone said he always did the banking on Monday mornings, would you say he was regular in his habits?"

Lila take so long in answering that Grant wonders if she is going to do so. He's just about to prompt her when she finally says:

"Is someone accusing him of something? How could they? that's just... oh, what does it matter now, anyway? He's gone, and... sure he was a stickler for routine but so what?"

"Lila, I have a very unprofessional urge to offer you a shoulder to cry on! I'm very sorry you've lost your friend and I know, when you feel a bit better, it will be important to you that I find out what happened.

Meanwhile, I'll reschedule this re-interview for another time. Let me know if there's anything I can do. And you must know the same goes for Judith, too. Please, take care of yourself, okay?"

"I'm sorry, Grant. I'm in a bit of a fog and I can't seem to get my head clear. Yes, please, let's finish this another time."

He gives her a small smile and leaves.

Driving away from the school Grant can't stop thinking about the dramatic change in Lila. He knows she's struggling with a problem in her personal life, as well as losing Rev Robbie, so she's had to deal with a lot of sad, pressured, and stressful situations in a short time.

"I hope she and Judith can repair their friendship because if anyone needs a friend right now that person is Lila Morelli," he thinks sadly. "Especially since she's the one who discovered his body."

That makes him consider the logistics more closely:

"Why *did* the murder happen when it was likely to be discovered right away? there was a huge risk of being caught so what forced the killer to act so precipitously?"

Chapter 17

The student's are excited to exchange St Valentine's Day cards at the school. Edgemont's policy is that anyone who wants to give out valentines has to give to everyone in their home-room class. The local card shops don't have a lot of variety to choose from in their card packs so each student seems to be carrying several identical cards.

There are about three dozen of them on Judith's desk. Last year – and every year before that – she'd received none. This year every card she opens gives her a pleasant-feeling pang in her heart.

She's been hoping she'll be able to see Grant for awhile this evening. They aren't going to go out, they've just planned on spending some time at her place.

Judith understands that making plans during an investigation is tricky so she is baking a dessert for him as a Valentine treat. It's especially sad that it is Rev Robbie's murder that might prevent him from getting away.

Judith had spent almost an hour reading the verse inside every single valentine card in the store before finally settling on something that fell far short of what she wanted to say, but at least didn't make any assumptions – or promises.

Some of the cards had sentimental wording that was way over the top, some so-called funny cards were downright insulting, and it seemed like 90% were addressed to "My Adorable Husband" or "My Darling Wife".

Judith sighed over her choice of a friendship card but really, that was the most suitable option.

She's forgotten to pack a lunch today so she decides to go check up on Lila. Maybe she'd like to go out for lunch or would appreciate having something brought in? Judith takes her purse out of the desk drawer and heads to the Nurse's Office only to discover Lila has phoned in sick today. Judith puzzles over that since Lila hadn't been sick yesterday.

Grant had told her about his failed interview though, so maybe Lila has taken his advice and is catching up on sleep and getting a good rest.

Judith tells herself: "I'll go over to her place now and see if she needs anything."

Always happiest when she has a firm plan in mind she fetches her outdoor things from the staff-room and heads out to her car in the parking-lot. Unfortunately her plan gets derailed when she sees the shattered glass from one of the back-seat windows of her sedan. The window has been smashed and the pile of ledgers and manilla folders that she'd gotten earlier from Rev Robbie are missing.

Judith is glad, for the millionth time it seems, that Suzanne Mirteau is no longer working alongside Grant. She could just imagine that bad-tempered police officer's sneer at the idea of Judith calling Grant because her car got vandalized.

Except this isn't so much about the damage to her car as the content of the stolen articles. Judith is quite sure Grant will be interested in the theft of the murder victim's files.

Grant has dispatched a patrol car to come by the school. The two officers have taken photos of the broken window and written down Judith's statement. They give her a copy of the report explaining she'll need it for her insurance company.

"Oh, it's just a side window. I expect it will cost way less than my deductible to replace."

The officers exchange a look and one answers Judith saying:

"That window will probably cost about $650 to replace, maybe more, depends on the hourly rate for labour."

Judith is shocked at the estimate and says so but the officers just shrug it off, telling her she's lucky the thief didn't damage the car door or she'd be replacing much more and at a higher cost.

She just shakes her head at that. Confirming that it's okay for her to drive her car, she then thanks the two officers for coming out so promptly.

"Oh a friend of the boss will always get prompt service," says one of the young men with a cheeky grin. He winks at his partner but Judith's expressionless face makes him think twice about adding any further remarks.

When Judith had first phoned Grant he'd told her that he definitely planned to keep their coffee date tonight although he might be late arriving and unable to stay for very long. When she sees him she'll ask about how the officers know she is his friend. She doesn't want to get anyone in trouble, but she does want an answer.

She sorts through her feelings for a moment trying to make up her mind whether or not she is flattered or offended that people are linking her and Grant as *friends*.

Then she gives a little smile and decides she likes the idea, hoping the young police officers aren't this very minute wondering what it is that Grant sees in her. She would blush if she could hear what they are saying.

Chapter 18

Judith turns back into the school searching for Mr. Glover, the school's caretaker and custodian of all the keys. He is an older man, probably past the usual retirement age, who is always on hand to help out.

After wandering from one end of the building to the other Judith finally finds him in her own office, cleaning the inside of the windows.

The most striking thing about Mr. Glover is his extremely bushy eyebrows with bristly hairs jutting straight out. His eyeglasses always sit low on his nose as if the frames have been pushed down.

"Oh Mr. Glover, hello! I have another job for you that might not wait until you're done here, and I'm afraid this one's outdoors. Someone's smashed my car window and there's shattered glass in the parking-lot, it's quite dangerous."

The old man stows his window-cleaning supplies neatly until he can return and quizzes Judith about the damage, tut-tutting over such vandalism.

"If you can wait a moment I'll just get my broom and a bin for that glass then you can point me in the right direction. No point you coming outside in this chill wind."

"Oh, I've got to find some cardboard or something I can put over the open window because, as you say, it is windy and cold."

"I'll take care of that for you, don't you worry about it."

"Oh no, Mr. Glover, fixing up my car's broken window isn't part of your duties for the school, I'll take care..."

"Never you mind, Miss Judith. Miss Patricia will read me the riot act and take a strip off my hide if I don't help out a damsel in distress. Especially when the trouble occurred on school property."

When Judith felt he'd run through his repertoire of applicable cliches she gave him sincere thanks and pointed through her office window to her car, the wine-colored Subaru.

"Ah, that foreign car. Bigger than most of them are. And it's supposed to be good for winter driving too, eh?"

"Yes, all Subarus come with four-wheel drive. Of course I still put on winter snow tires because well... no one wants to get stuck waiting on a tow-truck in miserable weather."

"Yup, you need snow tires or chains for Alberta winters. Well, you just sit tight and I'll let you know when you're good to go."

"Actually, I'll be in the principal's office, I need to get some cheques signed. Thank you very much for your help, Mr. Glover."

He tips his hat and heads off to work on this new task, which is much more interesting than window-cleaning.

Judith gathers up a couple of file folders and heads out of the Library to see Principal Johnson.

An hour later Judith is in her car heading to Lila's. Wind protection in the form of cardboard securely taped has been applied by the janitor and Judith tipped him with a book of Tim Horton's coupons. Mr. Glover is delighted. She knows cash wouldn't have been accepted, but honestly can't see the difference.

After getting Pat's signature alongside her own on a number of cheques from the school's two accounts Judith tucks her reading glasses back into their case and asks for permission to leave early.

"Oh by all means, that's rotten luck about the vandalism to your car. Unless it was kids throwing rocks or something?"

"No, this wasn't vandalism, I was robbed."

"What?!"

"Well, not me personally. I had a couple of ledgers and files from Rev Robbie's office at The Centre. He'd given them to me a couple of days ago, did you know I was helping him balance the books? anyhow, I hadn't carried them up to my apartment yet. Entirely my fault and I feel badly about it but yeah, that's what was stolen from the backseat of my car."

"Files and ledgers don't sound valuable, certainly not to a casual thief."

"No, you're right. That's why I put a call into Detective Grant. I think it must be connected to Rev Robbie's murder."

"They're certain it was murder? or can't you say?"

"No, I misspoke. The police are certain it was poison but they can't tell, or at least won't tell me, how it was administered. Right now it's still a suspicious death but that just means it could be an accident, a suicide, or murder."

"I don't see how it could be an accident except that it must be. Suicide is out of the question, and Rev Robbie was a lovely man, no one could possibly want to do him harm."

"I agree except... he was tough. If he was on the track of some wrongdoing I'm sure he would pursue it and maybe that frightened someone."

"Oh Judith. What a sorry mess. Anyhow, by all means you can leave now, see to your car or just go home and relax with your feet up and a cup of tea."

"That sounds wonderful but actually, I'm really getting concerned about Lila. So, although she's been giving me the cold-shoulder if she's home sick I think I should check in, see if she needs anything."

"By all means, go to her place and tell her I've officially sanctioned the visit and want to see things resolved between the two of you."

"Hmm, not sure how well Lila Morelli will bow to authority–"

"Oh goodness, nobody's scared of me except the parents and that's only because they don't want their little darlings sent home to be in their care all day!"

The two women share a chuckle and Judith packs up her files. She returns her work to her own office, locks up her desk, and grabs her winter coat from the chair where she'd dropped it an hour before, then heads out to her car. All the glass has been swept away, and the parking-lot is now safe for drivers and the tires of their cars.

Lila isn't pleased when she answers the door but she doesn't want Mrs. Piernitsky, her elderly landlady, to hear an argument so she invites Judith in.

Lila is wearing a track suit, her hair is a tousled mess, and her eyes red-rimmed. Judith can't tell if the marks indicate lack of sleep or a bout of crying. The whole dishevelled look – so unlike her friend – makes Judith blink back tears herself. When Lila sees and feels Judith's true caring emotion her face crumples and she bends her head sobbing. Judith gathers her into an embrace and hugs tight.

Moments later they are on the couch, holding each other's hands, and both talking, explaining, apologizing, and finally laughing together. Judith is so relieved.

"I guess we, or rather I, do need to talk. I owe you the truth, Judith. It just isn't easy."

"Well, let's talk over food. I haven't eaten since breakfast and I'm starved. We'll get a delivery of what? chicken or Chinese or pizza or? What do you feel like?"

Before Lila can answer there is a thump-thump noise on the ceiling.

"That's Mrs. P banging on her floor. Give me a second to just check on her." Lila hurries upstairs from her basement suite and Judith is just beginning to worry when she hears her friend clattering back down the stairs calling:

"Thanks again, it smells divine!"

Lila comes into the room bearing a large pot of fragrant homemade chicken noodle soup. She explains that Mrs. P made it because she thought Lila was sick. Lila has told her that she's just unhappy about the death of her friend, Rev Robbie, but the old lady presses it on her saying she needs building up.

"It's making my mouth water!" exclaims Judith breathing in the aroma and checking out the flat noodles and juicy chunks of chicken. She helps by setting out bowls and cutlery while Lila fetches some crusty rolls.

"Butter?" asks Judith.

"Oh right, I always forget you don't eat your bread like an Italian."

"This is delicious soup!"

"She's a wonderful cook and I'm so lucky to live here," Lila lifts a brimming spoon and says: "Cheers!"

"Happy St. Valentine's Day," returns Judith.

"Don't remind me about that, I'll start bawling again. Oh wait, don't you have plans with Grant?"

"I texted and cancelled when you were upstairs. It's more important that I spend time with you right now."

"Oh shut-up or I will lose it."

"That's okay, that's what friends are for."

The two exchange happy smiles then delay their conversation until after finishing their meal.

Chapter 19

After tidying up from their meal the two women go into the living-room area. Judith sits down on the sofa but instead of joining her Lila moves to the armchair.

"This is going to be a difficult conversation," she begins. Reaching for the box of tissues she holds it in her lap. "I don't think I have any tears left but I say that every day and then surprise myself."

Judith leans forward, her face full of sympathy, waiting for Lila to find the words.

"I expect you've been thinking up all kinds of things, maybe speculating with Grant–"

"I tried to because, well as you know I'm pretty new to this friendship thing, but he wouldn't play along. Stubborn man. But Lila, just come right out and tell me what happened. Just say whatever it is fast, like ripping off a bandage."

"You're right. There's no point beating around the bush. You wouldn't be able to guess, not in a million years, so dragging this out is just stupid. Okay, here goes:

Arnie has committed a very serious crime and he's gotten away with it. But, it nagged at him until he was no longer himself which is what caused the rift between us. Now that he's told me he wants me to help him cover it up. I don't *think* I can do that, but I *know* I can't betray him. But I also know I should."

Judith's mouth drops open. Lila is right, she would never have guessed at something like this. This is so much worse than an affair.

"He's making you an accessory."

"And now that you've dragged it out of me you are, too. Unless we stop right here. If you can forget what I just said then I can as well. There's no need to involve you further, Judith. You know what kind of a problem I'm dealing with, and you know that I have to resolve it on my own. It would be great to have you play Devil's Advocate but I love you my friend, and that means I love you too much to put you in this position."

"Oh Lila, I don't know what to say. Of course I'm here to listen to you. Accessory? I'm not even sure if that applies. This is Alberta and the incident occurred in Ontario, right?"

"It's not an incident, it's a crime. It's the crime of... manslaughter, I think. It was an accident but it wasn't reported so I think that escalates it from unlawful killing, or something like that, to manslaughter. Probably involuntary manslaughter? Oh, I don't know, it's a goddamn mess!"

Judith is sitting stunned, her face white as she asks:

"Somebody died?"

Lila hurries over to sit on the couch and takes Judith's hand.

"I'm sorry, I've lived with this for weeks and forgot how deeply shocked I was when I first heard about it. Oh Judith, it's awful, I know."

"What exactly happened?"

"Are you sure you want me to tell you?"

"Oh, we're well past that point now, Lila. I mean, somebody *died*."

"An old lady, although that doesn't make it any better of course. Here's the story that Arnie told me:

It was in the morning and he was out working his usual route. The garbage trucks drive one way down the street picking up the bins, and then they turn around and come back up the same street doing the other side of the road.

Here in Edgemont this all happens in the back alleys but in Toronto the bins are mostly put out at the end of people's driveways on the road. But there are some alleys too, and it was in one of them that this happened.

The alleys are usually behind commercial or multi-residential, like apartment buildings, and most businesses pay for private garbage collection so the alley runs are pretty quick.

Well, he has no idea how it happened but I'm sure he was wearing his headphones and unable to hear a cry or anything like that, and, of course, slightly high so not as alert as he should have been."

"Slightly high?" interrupts Judith.

"Actually yeah, because Arnie is a habitual user and I don't mean daily I mean several times a day. He's in a constant state of high and has developed a tolerance. If it wasn't for the stinkweed smell you probably wouldn't be able to tell. He takes a few tokes, gets a buzz, goes about his merry way. Functioning. Some alcoholics are like that too, and often no one knows until they sober up and then you see the difference.

So, he's driving along one side of the alley and from the corner of his eye he sees a person, no idea if it's a man or a woman, approaching the truck. They aren't trying to get his attention, not waving their arms or anything so he doesn't think anything of it. He stops to grab a bin, I think the mechanical arms only take about 30 seconds to hook up, lift, dump, then replace the emptied bin back down, so he's only been stopped for about half a minute and no one has crossed in front of him. He thinks he might have possibly felt the tires bump over something maybe – that's how he described the event – but he isn't sure, and he doesn't stop. Instead, he continues to the end of the alley, crosses a road, picks up at the next alley, crosses another road then picks up at the last alley, before turning around to repeat the process in reverse.

By time he gets back to do the other side of the first alley he sees it's now blocked by a police car, and an ambulance, but its lights aren't flashing.

A couple of people are standing watching the paramedics picking up a person huddled on the ground. There's no urgency in their movements so he knows right away the victim is dead. At least, that's what Arnie said.

He isn't too worried about the cops smelling weed on him because people expect the garbage truck and its driver to smell, plus he keeps a tin of coffee grounds in the cab which work well to absorb the odor. So he gets out of the truck but the police just shoo him away saying they need to preserve the scene in the hopes of finding evidence of the hit-and-run vehicle.

So he backs out of the alley, reports back at the depot why he couldn't finish his collection and like Chesterton's postman no one notices him so he got away with it."

"That's just an incredible story," says Judith quietly.

"I know, eh? So anyhow, turns out the victim is a elderly woman but they don't know exactly how old she was, in fact they don't know much about her at all. She's homeless and, according to the newspaper, she's known at a local shelter as Betty.

She's been in the area for years, people know her by sight, and give her change, but she doesn't go around begging, she scavenges for recyclables and turns them in at the bottle depot. The folks at the homeless shelter say she never causes any trouble, obeys all their rules, and doesn't seem to have any particular friends."

"Sad life, sad death."

"Oh, don't..."

"Sorry."

They both sit there with sad faces thinking about the victim and about themselves. Then Judith sits up straight saying:

"So, now... what happens now? Do you move back to Toronto? back to your old job? back to your marriage?"

"No, none of those things. Arnie says he wants to keep our marriage, that he still loves me and I'm the only woman for him, but I told him flat out we're done. That can't – won't – change. I no longer love him and it's because of him, it's his actions that destroyed the feelings I once had.

I realize that seems to have happened really quickly, but you know, we'd been together for so long that our love has probably been more from habit than from being *in love*. But it was always enough for me.

I mean, having children would have made it better, but the kids would have come along in time. There's an old song by Alice Cooper, believe it or not, about a couple living a life *of bed and TV being enough for a working man*, and that's always felt right to me, too.

I'm never going to attend a Gala Movie Premiere or some swanky Art Gallery's Grand Opening, I won't ever be filthy rich or famous, and that's okay. I'm okay with just enjoying a comfortable and hmm, unexciting life. Not boring, because I'm almost never bored, but happy.

Not the 'happily ever after' of a fairy tale but, well, when we did make love it was pretty damn hot and fun, too. I'm gonna miss that. I do miss that, when he was here we did it right away, but after what he told me? no way."

"It's so unfair, Lila. You did nothing wrong but you're sharing the punishment."

"Yeah, well punishment is the issue, actually. What am I going to do about Arnie?"

"I don't think you have a choice, really. You have to get him to turn himself in, otherwise it will eat away at you, the way it's haunted Arnie."

"Believe me I tried! He wouldn't come to dinner on a double-date with you and Grant when he found out Grant was a cop. He couldn't keep the secret any longer but begged me not to tell anyone. I told him I needed to think about that and that's what I was still doing when you ambushed me today."

"Then you'll have to be the one to tell his secret."

"Huh! To my family? They're cops. That's why he wouldn't spend Christmas with them, he's got a guilty conscience."

"Does he? because wouldn't he turn himself in if he did? I mean, wouldn't he have it pretty easy – easier than most, anyways – if he confessed to his in-laws and had their help to guide him through the system?"

"I think that ship has sailed, months ago. He had a chance to do the right thing but he deliberately chose not to. And of course it hasn't helped that the victim is a lonely bag lady with no one to push the cops for a solution. I'm sure they'd like to nab her killer, but time and resources being what they are well..."

"So he's feeling secure, wants to sweep it all under the rug – in fact he tried to do so, tried to pretend that nothing happened and nothing was wrong. You leaving him forced him to address the problem. Then he eased his burden by dumping half of it on your shoulders."

"Just like I've done to you. And just like I pushed him to confide, you forced me. Now we're all miserable!"

"Hopefully we can find a way to fix this. I'll ask Grant about jurisdiction–"

"Oh God Judith, no! You can't tell Grant about this! Just like I can't say anything to my family. You and I can get in trouble for knowing but cops? they'd be forced to act or else be complicit. No, no, no! You can not breathe a word of this."

Lila has gotten quite agitated so Judith calms her friend by agreeing to keep the secret between the two of them.

"But what am I going to tell him? He likes you, Lila, he's definitely going to ask."

"What does he think is the reason? Oh no, you said he wouldn't gossip about–"

"I kind of pushed it, well actually I shut him out so he did finally give me his opinion which is that he suspected Arnie had confessed to an affair and wanted forgiveness and reconciliation."

"Then let's go with that. Arnie broke my heart – that much is true – and I don't think I can go back to him. The last bit's a fib, because I already know I can't, but we could say I'll still undecided. I truly am undecided about what I should do."

"You know what you should do, Lila."

"Knowing and being able to act on that knowledge well... be glad you're not in my shoes."

"Those high-heels you wear? I'm *always* glad not to be in them!"

It isn't much of a joke but it helps a little and Lila smiles.

"You know, I do have the option of doing nothing at all. Other than file for divorce, that is. I could just pretend Arnie never told me the truth. It happened 2,000 miles away and I don't ever have to see him again. I can just forget all about it."

Judith studies her friend's face for a long moment before replying:

"No, I really don't think you can."

"I can try."

"You have been trying. Ever since Rev Robbie was killed and you realized he wouldn't be able to counsel you."

"What?"

"Oh Lila, your face when you discovered his body. I've never seen such a look of bleak anguish."

"You're smart, Judith. And you're right, I knew he would steer me in the right direction and insist I follow through. And I'd have to pay attention to him because he is, was, a man of God. He could be very forthright and forceful too when dealing with people being wishy-washy about sin."

"Sin? You didn't commit the crime."

"No, but I'm sure Rev Robbie would tell me that my inaction, my silence, is putting Arnie's immortal soul in jeopardy."

"Oh. Do you believe in that?"

"I'm trying very hard not to."

Chapter 20

"I'm glad we've got a chance to get together. I missed you yesterday," says Grant.

"I missed you, too. This is the first Valentine's Day when I've actually been seeing someone and... well, I guess, after all, it really is just another day."

"No, it isn't. It's a day when the someone who's being seen gets to do this..." and with that Grant pulls Judith close and gives her a long, expressive kiss. The fingers of one hand tangle themselves in her hair and he holds the other hand flat along her jaw, keeping her mouth in place. When he pulls back her eyes are still closed and she opens them to see his happy smile. Time suspends for a moment and then Judith gives a little laugh saying:

"Definitely *not* just another day then," and shifts back in her seat widening the space between them. Grant takes the hint.

"So, I've been wanting to hear all about your session with Lila yesterday. What happened with Arnie, and what's going to happen with the two of them?"

"Oh. Oh, it's a bit of a mess actually... nothing's been decided one way or the other. Lila is still trying to sort out her thoughts about it all. Grant, she did ask me not to talk to you about this. I'm sorry, I'm really caught in the middle between you and her."

Judith looks so uncomfortable Grant quickly assures her that he doesn't mean to put her on the spot.

"Don't worry about me, I don't need to know. I'm a nosy guy, probably why I became a detective! but not everything is my business and I'm absolutely fine with that. You can tell Lila with a clear conscience that you didn't tell me a thing, and that I didn't press you."

"Thank you, thank you so much," replies Judith with relief.

"Don't thank me yet because there is a corollary: if I see you looking utterly miserable and burdened by a secret then I will start asking questions and probing but I won't pester you, I'll go straight to Lila."

"That's okay then because I won't let Lila's problems drag me down. I will do my best to help her however I can, but ultimately she'll make her own decision because she's the one who has to live with it."

"Good girl," Grant smiles, and looks ready to draw Judith close again but he sits back instead.

"I spoke with one of the Constables who attended to the crime scene at the school," he began but Judith interrupted to ask,

"The cheeky one?"

"Umm, what do you mean?"

"One of them made it clear that they were dispatched pronto because of my *friendship* with you."

"Oh, he did, did he? Which one?"

"I didn't get a name, but Grant I wouldn't want to get anyone in trouble. I wasn't offended and I was pleased that they showed up so quickly to look after the paperwork so I can send it off to the insurance company."

"The body shop should be able to do that for you, where are you taking the car?"

"Oh my agent emailed me the names of three places in Calgary and suggested I pick one of those. Hang on, let me bring up the email so you can have a look and see if you recognize any names."

"It's probably not a good thing if I recognize the names," he chuckles. Taking her phone he reads the short list and says: "This first place is good. I had work done there a few years back and they've been around a long time. Good reputation."

"Thanks, I'll get in touch with them."

"So anyhow, it looks like there was some degree of planning in this robbery because number one: the thief picked a time when there was nobody outside. A school often has people, students, out and about. And two: there was no rock or anything left at the scene so the perp brought a tool or picked up something to use and then took it away with them. Finally, number three: they didn't rifle through the front-seat console or your glove-box. By the way the Constable told me you don't keep that locked?"

"My glove-box? No, of course not. There's nothing of value."

"Some people keep their GPS device or a battery pack or even cash in their glove-box."

"But I don't so if anyone ever broke in to steal I'd rather they popped it open and saw there was nothing then broke it to bits just to make the same discovery."

Grant thinks about that for a moment before saying,

"Okay, fair point."

"So my car was smashed for the sole purpose of getting at Rev Robbie's books from The Centre."

"Yeah, and since they took his computer too we have no way of–"

"Really? The Centre doesn't have everything backed up to the Cloud? Wow, I would never have guessed they'd be so lax... good thing I have a copy of his computer files."

"What?"

"On my last, no second-last, meeting with him I copied everything over onto a thumb drive. I told him I'd take the physical copies as well in case I needed to find an actual receipt but it wasn't likely. The ledgers and boxes weren't important at all – well, they were but they aren't essential."

"So whatever the thief stole thinking they were covering up... you already have it."

"Yes, I've copied the files onto my laptop so you can take the original thumb drive."

"Judith! this is wonderful news, you're a marvel!"

"Well thank you, but hold the compliments because I've had a quick look over the files and I can't see anything incriminating."

"Ahhh, but you're not a forensic auditor. If there are any secrets they'll be revealed and at least now, thanks to you, we've got some material to work with."

Judith flushes becomingly at Grant's praise and on impulse he leans over and kisses her lips. Startled, but pleased, she looks up with a smile and when their eyes met they each feel the thrill of a momentary connection. This time she doesn't move away but he does, he stands holding up the thumb drive and explains he wants to hand in the evidence right away.

"Can I take you out for dinner this evening?" he asks.

"Oh I think everywhere will be booked, don't you? All the people who didn't manage something yesterday will be celebrating today."

"Well I could get take-out and bring dinner over if..." he leaves the decision with her. Judith holds his gaze while answering:

"That would be lovely, Grant."

He grins happily adding:

"Are we going to keep kissing? because if so, I'd better choose something with no garlic."

"I'll leave that choice up to you," she replies enigmatically.

Chapter 21

Sunday, February 16, 2020

Judith was enjoying a leisurely, but solitary, breakfast thinking happy thoughts about the night before.

Grant had returned with two dinners from Swiss Chalet that they followed up with the upside-down cake Judith made that afternoon.

"I meant to serve it with whipped cream but I forgot to buy some, sorry!"

"Don't be, this is perfect as is. Such a moist, flavourful cake."

"That's the peaches. I love gingerbread either way: plain or with the added fruit."

"Me too, it's delicious. Thank you for making it for me."

"You're very welcome."

"Do I get to take the rest home?"

"Of course, I'll put it in a tupperware for you."

"Well, not yet, we might eat some more after..." When she lifted an eyebrow he amended that to: "I mean, later. Later with coffee or tea."

Judith hid a smile and handed him the Valentine's Day card she'd bought. He opened it and chuckled at the joke.

"I actually wanted something that said more but the cards at the store all said too much! so in this case I had to settle for *less is more*."

Judith hides a smile and hands him the Valentine's Day card she'd bought. He open it and chuckles at the joke.

"I actually wanted something that said more but the cards at the store all said too much! so in this case I had to settle for less is more."

"It's perfect, thank you again." Grant leans in for a kiss and Judith doesn't pull away so he kisses her again, more deeply. Then he gets up and going to his coat takes out a little wrapped package from the pocket. It is a small box and he hands it to her saying:

"Don't worry, it's not a ring even if the box is that kind of shape!"

Judith makes a production of wiping her forehead with a loud *phew*!

Then she unwraps her gift and finds herself looking at a beautiful pair of emerald stud earrings. They are in a yellow-gold setting with a surround of tiny diamond chips. They are breathtaking, and Judith gives him a wide-eyed, dazzled look.

"They're beautiful, so utterly beautiful!" she exclaims.

"I hoped you'd like them."

"Like them? I LOVE them!" Judith flings her arms around Grant's neck and meets his lips in a warm, passionate kiss. When they break apart she studies the earrings again, saying:

"These are gorgeous. Absolutely perfect! Thank you so so so much! Oh, but they must have cost an awful lot of money?"

"I delighted to spend my money on you, Judith. I noticed that you wear a lot of green so I thought these would match."

"That's so thoughtful! Oh Grant..."

This time when they kiss they don't break apart but lie back against the couch cushions with their arms around each other. Kissing, staring into each other's eyes, then kissing some more. Judith has never been with a man but she trusts Grant and follows his lead.

They end up lying together on the couch and after they've been kissing and exploring with roving hands for some time Grant sits up saying:

"Enough of that missy, you're getting me all worked up. We have a murder to solve so why don't you make me some of your delicious coffee and we'll get cracking. Right after you direct me to your bathroom," he says, standing up.

"Grant there are only four rooms here, how hard can it be to find the toilet? especially for a detective?"

He turns back to look at her saying:

"I don't want to take a wrong turn and end up in your bedroom, Judith."

Part of her wants to ask if it really would be a wrong turn but since that is way too forward she ignores his remark altogether and tells him the bathroom is on the left side.

She makes coffee, cuts Grant another slice of cake, then wraps up the rest for him to take home. She's put in her new earrings and is admiring herself in the mirror at the front door when he comes up behind her. He slides his arms around her waist and she leans against him while they both study the effect. Judith tilt her head and the earrings sparkle in the reflected light.

"I just love them," she says.

With a squeeze he replies: "I'm so glad."

Judith has laid out the coffee and cake in the kitchen's dining area so they sit down there and discuss the murder case.

"Another avenue of investigation led me to the trailer park."

"Ooh, talking like this makes me feel like I'm in an episode of PBS 'Mystery' or something. So exciting!"

"Well, as I mentioned before I need a sounding-board and you're a very good listener, Judith. And you don't interrupt *too* often," replies Grant with a smile.

Judith makes a gesture of zipping her lips shut. Once again she realizes that Grant is a natural-born storyteller, relating the details of his interviews so clearly she feels like she is actually there. She doesn't want to miss a word. He leans forward and using his hands to draw pictures in the air he is able to make his characters live.

"Edgemont Trailer Park has been around for years. These parks get a bad reputation – sometimes deserved – but the Edgemont park is well-run and the residents are law-abiding householders who maintain their properties. However, there are one or two troublemakers.

In this instance the homeowner, a Mr. Jonathan Pederson, an elderly man who lived in the park for many years, was sent to hospital by his home help and subsequently transferred to the hospice. He isn't going to be coming home.

His granddaughter has moved into the trailer and because Mr. Pederson isn't dead there's no will or probate or anything else to stop her from doing so. She is, frankly, an *unsavoury character* and her boyfriend is worse. They're both known to police, and he has a lengthy record.

So Belle Pederson and Antwon Pruitt, which he spells *w-o-n* instead of *o-i-n-e,* are shacked up in the trailer park and causing trouble.

Now the trailer park manager... uh, I should explain. The Edgemont Trailer Park is co-operative housing meaning the land is owned by Edgemont which also pays for a full-time resident manager but the residents own their own trailers and also shares in the co-op itself. They pay a monthly maintenance fee and have a say in how the place is run.

Jerry Bennett, the manager, is really on the ball. He keeps a close eye on the comings and goings of the residents. Quite a few are elderly now and they like having Jerry drop by to check up on them. Belle and Antwon don't like Jerry coming around at all. They had a few run-ins and finally he came to the police station to make a complaint because he said the problem – drugs – was more than he could handle on his own.

We were all a bit surprised about that because the police don't have trouble at the trailer park and that's all down to Jerry. He's always managed to keep things under control without involving us. But drugs... well, that's a different story.

In fact, your old friend Billy MacNeill was mentioned as one of the *bad influences*, as Jerry calls them, hanging around.

Well, as you'll recall we arrested Billy awhile back but I guess he's out on bail.

Anyhow Jerry – he's a big guy, by the way: stands about 6 foot 3 or 4, just over 200 pounds, huge walrus moustache that's still mostly black although his hair has gone gray. Jerry looks to be a match for anyone even though he's gotta be getting up there in years.

So, he comes to the police station to make a report claiming the trouble is coming from the Jonathan Pederson trailer. He explains that the old man is in hospital, well in the Sally Ann, you know, the Salvation Army hospice? and is there anything the police can do to protect his property for him? saying the granddaughter has moved in and brought a noisy, disreputable crowd who, he suspects, are dealing drugs from that location.

It's a tricky situation though, because the girl claims she has permission from her grandpa to live there but he's not well enough to tell us if that's true. If she's lying we could charge her with trespassing but we can't prove she's lying.

So all they do at the station is tell Jerry Bennett to get the trailer park co-op to find out who Mr. Pederson's lawyer is, and see if they have a will or any written instructions from him. The girl definitely is his granddaughter, but if she isn't his heir then whoever is supposed to inherit can hire a lawyer and issue an eviction notice. But none of that addresses the immediate issue of Jerry's suspicions that drugs are being dealt out of that trailer.

As you know, though, someone's suspicions aren't enough for us to act on. A patrolman went by to knock on the door but Belle Pederson wouldn't let him in and it's her right not to do so. The officer had nothing to report that we could use. For example, if he believed someone was in imminent danger – like a screaming child – then he could have entered the premises without a warrant but that wasn't the case.

So, Jerry came away frustrated with us and our inability to do anything. Since then he's taken to sitting in the common area with a few like-minded residents who are taking photos of everyone coming and going along with pictures of the licence plates on their cars. I don't know if that's going to rattle anybody enough to slow down business but it might, however it's a bit of a risky manoeuvre, from our point of view.

So that's the unsatisfactory situation at the trailer park. Now, *the plot thickens* because we learned that Rev Robbie was out there at the trailer park a couple of days before he was killed. Trouble is, we don't know if he went there to remonstrate with the alleged dealers – apparently there have been stories of drugs coming into The Centre – or if he went there as a customer to buy."

"Surely not," interrupts Judith.

"That's my thinking too but then how did Rev Robbie die from an overdose of the latest popular drug: Fentanyl?"

Grant left shortly after their conversation taking the other half of his cake with him.

Judith has a busy Sunday, much better than the previous week, taking care of household chores like grocery shopping, housework, and laundry, but all the while last night's conversation is playing in her mind.

After dinner she calls Grant and is pleased to get hold of him on the first try. She's been giving their discussion about the drugs a lot of thought and a nagging idea just won't leave her.

After the preliminary greetings and the endearments that naturally come about after their closeness last night Judith tells him she's had a thought she needs to share.

"First off, did you ever meet Rev Robbie?"

"I did, but we were in a crowd, I never got a chance to speak to the man one-to-one. But from everything I've heard about him I'm sure I would have liked and respected him."

"Oh, for sure you would have. He always spoke quietly, like never raising his voice or shouting, but he was forceful in making his point. There was no pretending innocence or lack of understanding with Rev Robbie! Even Lila mentioned he could zero in on sin and be relentless in pushing you do the right thing. And that's the point:

I think Rev Robbie caught someone with drugs at The Centre and–"

"But surely he would have turned them in," interrupts Grant.

"No, hear me out. I think he caught someone with just enough for their own use, not dealing, and he confiscated the drugs. That means he had to take them from someone who couldn't intimidate him. So not a drug dealer, not a gang member, not one of the guys you described from the trailer park. No, I think it was a young person. So say Rev Robbie takes away the drugs well he wouldn't just stick them in his pocket or toss them in a drawer, he'd lock them away to keep everyone safe."

"He'd put them in the safe."

"Yes! and, if he believed it was a first-time offence and that the young person, 'cause it could be a boy or a girl, if he thought that putting them through the justice system really wouldn't be justice – and you can be sure he had his own high standards there – then I don't think he'd call the police. I think he'd try to handle the situation himself."

Slowly Grant completes the thought: "And that decision forced the killer's hand."

"Exactly. The killer – or killers, I guess I should say – didn't exactly panic because there was some planning involved but they must have acted quickly. So, what young people were around that day or at the most the day before? and who else might have known about the drugs in the safe? Who was around who knew the combination to the safe? or which of Rev Robbie's visitors that day was comfortable enough with for him to open the safe himself while they were there? There might be other questions but those ones have been nagging at me. So far, the only answer I can come up with is the volleyball team."

"The whole team?"

"No, don't joke it isn't funny."

"I know, I'm sorry. It's just I started this phone-call with no suspects and all of a sudden I have six – it is six players on a volleyball team, right?"

"Maybe seven or eight with substitutes. No actually there would be more because it's a tournament so more than one team would have been in The Centre practising."

"Oh cool even more suspects! Well thanks for that, Judith!"

"So do you think the killer intended to kill? Maybe they just wanted to incapacitate Rev Robbie long enough for them to get their drugs back?"

"Or maybe they wanted to get him high and incoherent so he'd lose credibility. Any accusations he might make wouldn't carry much weight if he himself was a suspected drug user. There were only very faint traces of Fentanyl left behind in the safe but enough to identify the drug."

"Lots to think about."

"I do thank you for your help, it really is a help you know."

"Good night, Grant."

"What do you think about me coming over so we can brainstorm some more?" he asks hopefully.

"Good night, Grant," Judith repeats, but with a smile sounding in her voice.

"You don't have to work tomorrow, right? It's Family Day—"

"Good night, Grant," she interrupts, adding: "I'll dream about you." Then disconnects while chuckling at his groan.

Chapter 22

Monday, February 17, 2020

Judith waits until 10:00 before phoning Lila but even so her friend's voice sounds sleepy.

"Sorry, did I wake you?"

"I was dozing, I haven't been sleeping too well."

"I'm not surprised but listen – today's a holiday so what do you think about spending the day together, just the two of us, and I promise not to say a word about the Arnie thing although of course I'm willing to listen if you want to talk. But if not we'll have a holiday from our problems, okay?"

"Oh that sounds very okay. What do you feel like doing? Have you been bitten by the gambling bug and want to go back to the casino?"

"No way, I want to do something outdoors. Would you be interested in going to the Zoo? Even at this time of year there's plenty to see."

"I'd love to! I love zoos and I haven't been to the Calgary Zoo yet."

"Oh you're in for a treat. I go there so often I've got a pass for admission and parking! and I get a discounted friend rate so today will be my treat and it will cost me practically nothing."

"You accountant-types... I need a coffee and a shower but I can be ready right after. Do you want me to pick you up?"

"No, I'll have to drive because my free parking is based on my licence plate. How about if I'm at your door in say... 45 minutes?"

"Perfect, and Judith? thanks for this. I really appreciate it."

"That's what friends are for!"

Warmly dressed with scarves, mitts, and hats the two women have a great day out. Lila says the Calgary Zoo compares very favourably to the Toronto Zoo, adding that it's so well laid out. She likes the fact that they see plenty of animals who have room to roam without lots and lots of walking from one exhibit to the next.

Despite it being February they each have an ice-cream and decide they don't want a big dinner, settling on a fish and chip supper that Lila pays for. Since they can see the coffee looking black sitting in its half-full pot they decide to wait until they can stop at a Tim Horton's. They find one on the way back to Lila's and have their hot drinks in the car in the parking lot. That's when Judith speaks seriously about her relationship with Grant and the next step.

"I know he wants to make love to me but I also know that he isn't in love with me."

"Okay, how do you know that?"

"Well, he wanted to come over quite late last night so—"

"That's not what I meant," laughs Lila. "He's probably wanted to have sex with you since the first time you two met. That's how guys are, they look at every woman with sex on their brain."

"Ewww, no way."

"Yeah, Arnie told me that years ago. We were arguing about some guy and I was saying *he's just a friend* and Arnie's like *there's no such thing* and he's wrong about that, but he might be right about what the guys are thinking even if they really do just want to be friends. Arnie said guys think that way even about women they don't want to screw. I have no reason to doubt him, I mean it's not the kind thing you'd brag about is it?"

"You know you're guilty of that yourself, aren't you?"

"What?!"

"For awhile there it seemed like you were trying to match me with every guy we met, remember?"

"Well, we were suddenly seeing a lot of three really handsome men: Brian Penner, Noel Larkin, and George Grant – your Grant. All are total hunks."

"Besides being engaged already Noel is too young for us, and I see you put Brian at the top of the list..."

"Yeah well I wasn't thinking marriage. Judith! are you still a virgin waiting for your wedding night?"

"Yes, and no–"

Lila laughs again saying: "Sorry, but that actually is a *yes or no* question!"

"Yes, I'm a virgin but no, I'm not particularly waiting for marriage... I've just never had a boyfriend."

"Are you serious? Judith, you don't have a pretty face exactly but you're still really good looking, and as I've mentioned before, you've got a great body. I can't believe guys haven't chased after you."

"Oh, I've had offers – propositions, actually – but from married men. Even when I was in school the guys who came on to me were already living with, or married to, someone else. It really turned me off. I mean, why bother to get involved with someone if you're only going to cheat on them? That makes no sense. So no, no boyfriends."

"So then how can you know that Grant isn't *in* love with you?"

"Well, why would he be? I mean, he's really only known me for a few months and we didn't start dating right away. No, we'll have to get to know each other a lot better before we can fall in love."

"You don't believe in love at first sight?"

"Oh! well, attraction and, um, lust at first sight, sure. But no, not real love."

"Real love as opposed to lust love?"

"Ummm, something like that."

"So you're not in love with Grant because you haven't known him long enough *to* fall in love, is that right?"

"Uhhh, yeah... yeah, that's right."

"So you don't love Grant."

"Oh, no."

"But you're thinking of sleeping with him? Judith, you slut!"

"LILA! stop laughing at me!"

"I can't! you're too funny, Judith. Listen, it sounds like you're ready, so I guess just let Nature take its course. It'll happen when it happens... but make sure you shave your legs and pits every day and wear matching bra and panties."

"I always do."

"Yeah, that figures. And hey, you have to promise that after it happens you'll tell me right away!"

"God, we sound like teenagers."

"Oh Judith, most teenage girls have already done it!"

Judith doesn't speak to Grant that day. She'd sent him a text in the morning explaining she and Lila were spending the holiday at the Zoo and he'd answered *have fun*. Just before she gets into her bed that night a second text arrives saying he hopes she and Lila had a good day, and he's looking forward to seeing her soon.

She replies "me 2 xxx".

Chapter 23

Tuesday, February 18, 2020

A light tap-tap on the door frame signals Beth Penner's arrival at Judith's office in the school library. The girl's looks and manner have changed over the last while. Beth is still a quiet, unassuming girl but she is far less hesitant and shy. The events of the last couple of months brought added maturity to the girl who was already quite self-contained, and of course, she's at the age of physical growth spurts, too.

Judith closes the file on her laptop and clicks off the screen while motioning the girl to come in and sit down.

"Hello Beth, you're looking well. That's a great colour on you – it really brings out your eyes."

The girl gives a close-mouthed smile that dimples her blushing cheeks. Beth is turning into a very pretty teenager, especially since she hasn't coated her eyelashes in thick black mascara or chosen unsuitable lipstick.

Edgemont School for Girls is strict about not allowing excessive make-up on the students, with Principal Johnson as the sole arbiter of what constitutes *excessive*. Some of the girls try to get around the stricture by having their make-up tattooed on, or semi-permanently applied, but in those instances the Principal calls the parent for a chat and when the time comes for a touch-up that work isn't performed.

However the school has no rules regarding the students' hair styles or lengths or colours – only that it has to be clean. Pat confided to Judith that she has to let the girls enjoy some freedom of expression and whereas skillfully applied make-up could add years to a teenager's face, a messy punky hairdo won't do so.

"Sorry to bother you when you're busy Ms. Taylor but I'm a bit concerned, mostly about Margaret Seely, but also about Ms. Morelli, and I hoped I could have a word." Beth's anxiety shows up in the way she is rubbing her fingers tightly together.

At least she's not biting her nails or cuticles, thinks Judith before saying: "Absolutely, what's on your mind?"

Beth inhales a deep breath and explains: "I've been seeing quite a bit of Margaret lately because her mother is never home so she's been coming over to our house a lot. Lila – she said it's okay to call her Lila when we're not at school – would stop by quite often too, and we'd play board games or cards or watch a movie on TV. Sometimes Dad orders in a pizza or chicken and he always takes us out for Taco Tuesdays. If something comes up and he has to work then Lila treats us. We've all gotten used to it but Ms. Morelli doesn't come by any more, not even on Tuesdays, and Margaret is... well, she's angry all the time."

Judith considers about how much she can say and decides to be as upfront as possible with Beth. She knows Beth's attachment to Lila runs deep so the girl must be hurting at being shut out. *I know that feeling!* thinks Judith.

"Beth, this is confidential but of course you can share it with your father, just like you can always repeat to him anything an adult tells you, even if they say it's a secret, right?" The girl nods in agreement. "Okay then, I'm relying on your discretion and your friendship with Lila.

I don't know if you realize that Lila is actually a married woman? She is estranged from her husband who lives in Toronto."

The girl nods more vigorously so Judith pauses to let her explain.

"Lila told us. I think Dad was going to ask her out on a date – you know, just the two of them – but maybe she thought so too because right out of the blue she told us she was married but she and her husband were living apart. Far apart, he lives in Ontario!

She's booked a flight back to Toronto on April 9th in order to spend Easter with her parents and, she said, *to come to terms with her marriage.* She also said she's pretty sure it's over but she wants to be certain. Because the next day is Good Friday she'll get an extra-long weekend and she said that will be enough time for her trip."

"Oh, I didn't realize she as going away for Easter. You see Lila and I had grown quite close but something happened at the beginning of January and since then Lila has been withdrawn. It sounds like she's been distancing herself from you and your father as well.

What happened is that her husband flew out here to visit. Lila was looking forward to seeing him but I'm pretty sure things didn't go well. I don't know why, because she won't say, however she will talk things over with me, and with you two as well, I'm sure, once she gets it all sorted out in her own mind first."

Beth sighs deeply saying: "I... I guess I should be sorry if her marriage is in trouble but I'm not. I don't want her to move back to Toronto, I want her to stay here and go on dates with my Dad. But, that's being selfish."

"Then that makes me selfish too because it's what I'd like as well." Judith replies with a smile. They sit silently for a moment sharing their mutual interest. Finally Judith says:

"Now, what's all this about Margaret Seely? What is she so angry about?"

"Her mother, I guess. Mrs. Seely is hardly ever home and even when she is she doesn't seem to have any time for Margaret. Instead she's on her computer all the time and then, when Margaret's in bed, she sometimes hears her mother taking the car out. Late at night."

"And leaving Margaret alone in the house?"

"Yes but... I'm pretty sure Margaret wouldn't want me to tell anyone about that, she's only ten or soon to be ten and afraid of being taken away–"

"She doesn't have to worry about that, it's not illegal to leave a child that age alone here in Alberta. It's up to the parent's to decide what's best, but if there are issues Child Protective Services can step in. Like, if she was being left for long periods of time or if there was something harmful in the house like a handgun."

"Oh no, I don't think there's anything like that. My Dad has some hunting rifles but he keeps them in a gun safe and has his certificate and licence and everything. No, Margaret is just worried about whatever it is her mother is doing because it seems like it's a big secret."

"Where is Margaret's father? Do you know?"

"Oh yeah, she talks about him a lot. Her mother kicked him out, but he was always away a lot anyways because he travels so much for his business. That's what Margaret told us. Now when he comes to Calgary he stays at the Palliser which is really nice, and Margaret gets to stay overnight with him. It has a swimming pool plus sometimes they go to the zoo and have brunch there. She really misses her Dad."

"That's a shame. Maybe Mr. and Mrs. Seely will be able to work things out?"

"From what people are saying it doesn't sound like she wants Mr. Seely back."

"What do you mean?"

"Well…" the girl is obviously embarrassed so Judith figured she'd heard some of the stories circulating about Andrea Seely and that young man, Kyle Danby.

"Never mind, Beth. We can't solve the Seely's problems, but I hope I've given you some insight into what's going on with Lila right now. She needs us to give her space and time and that's what we have to do."

"Yes, I'll tell Dad what you told me because he was wondering if he'd scared her away but he didn't, did he?"

"No, you can reassure your father on that point."

The girl bounces out of her chair like she didn't have a care in the world. The *resiliency of youth*, Judith thinks to herself.

She wonders if she should have a word with Pat Johnson about Margaret Seely's home situation? but decides not to. While Judith can hear a rumour and call it hearsay the school principal has to act on any supposition if one of her student's is possibly in harm's way.

She decides she'll give the situation some more thought, but unfortunately circumstances dictate otherwise.

Chapter 24

The sight of Margaret Seely slumped on the bench outside Principal Johnson's office with her arms tightly crossed, her heels drumming, and her face red with fury is almost enough to make Judith turn around. But when Pat called her she agreed to help so she can't turn back now. She sits down beside the girl and asks:

"What's going on, Margaret?"

The girl tucks her chin into her chest and commences rocking back and forth but doesn't say a word.

"You're obviously angry about something, so please tell me what it is."

Still no eye contact or verbal response from Margaret. Changing tactics – and resisting a strong urge to shake the girl – Judith deliberately softens her tone and asks in a syrupy voice:

"Do you need to have a good cry? Hmm? Is that it?"

And a small tornado erupts with Margaret on her feet stomping up and down while loudly shouting that she never never never ever cries. Principal Johnson opens her office door and commands silence:

"Stop that racket right now, Margaret Seely. You're already in more than enough trouble, you don't need to be adding to it. Get in here and sit down quietly."

Judith finds herself actually feeling a bit sorry for Margaret when she sees how the girl deflates under the voice of authority. With her head bowed and shoulders drooping Margaret slowly shuffles into the office and sits in the furthest chair.

"Since we're unable to reach either of your parents, Margaret, I've asked Ms. Taylor to sit in as your Appropriate Adult. Due to the seriousness of the situation, and the school's policy of zero tolerance for fighting, we need to deal with this right away.

Let's begin."

Pat thanks Judith for taking on the supportive *in loco parentis* role. She introduces the other woman in the room, a Mrs. Vivian Sanderson, who Judith has previously met in her job as the school's bursar.

Vivian, a good-looking woman dressed in soccer mom gear, is accompanied by her daughter April who has obviously been crying and now sports a bruised and swollen lip.

Margaret Seely sits quietly but directs a poisonous glare at the older girl.

"April, please tell us what happened outside at lunchtime."

The girl sniffs loudly before turning to meet Margaret's eyes and pointing at her says:

"SHE punched me. She busted my lip and made it bleed. She's violent and mean."

Before Margaret can respond Principal Johnson holds up her hand palm out saying:

"You will get your chance, Margaret. For now it's April's turn to speak." Then turning to April and her mother she asks: "Why did Margaret punch you?"

"Because she's crazy," spit April, just as her mother is saying:

"Surely the 'why' doesn't matter when the result is a physical injury like this. Look at my daughter's mouth! There's no disputing what happened."

"And I'm not disputing it, Ms. Sanderson. I've already spoken to other witnesses who confirm that Margaret Seely knocked April to the ground and punched her, hard, in the mouth. It's a very serious offence with consequences which is why it's vital to get all the facts on the record."

"Now, April. Please answer the question properly. What did you do, or say, to provoke Margaret's actions?"

Again Vivian Sanderson expostulates angrily claiming Principal Johnson is blaming the victim.

"It doesn't matter what happened before the physical assault because there is no justification for it, none, no matter what was said."

Pat Johnson waits a moment in silence, allowing the upset mother to regain her composure.

"I agree, Ms. Sanderson. There is no justification for violence however, something provoked nine-year-old Margaret into launching an attack against thirteen-year-old April. I want to know what that something was."

"I'm almost ten," states Margaret. We all look at her and notice she is a rather puny-sized girl compared to the tall and stoutly built April.

"Did you push Margaret or hit her first?"

"No! of course not. Nobody can say I did 'cause I didn't touch her."

"Then what was it you said to upset her so much?"

Caught out April folds her lips together as well as she can with the swelling, and wears a stubborn expression on her face.

"I can't make you give your side of the story if you don't want to, April, but a victim's statement does impact the offender's punishment."

"Oh just spit it out April, I don't want to spend all day here."

"Welllll, I might have said some something about how everybody's laughing about her mother being a real cougar always chasing after that Kyle Danby."

Vivian Sanderson briefly closes her eyes but my gaze turns to Margaret to see hers filling up with tears.

"It's not true, take it back! my mother isn't doing anything like that. You're calling her names, calling her catty and she's not!"

I look at Pat and see she realizes, as I do, that Margaret doesn't understand the insulting 'cougar' reference. Glancing over at Vivian her exasperated expression tells me she's picked up on that as well.

"April, why are you repeating gossip? You don't even know what you're saying."

"Mom, it's not me it's everybody. They're all saying it."

"Well, I'm ashamed of you for joining in. Of course that's still no excuse for the fight," she finishes, turning back to Pat.

"No, you're right. There is no excuse."

"So what happens now?"

"I will consider everything I've heard and determine Margaret's punishment."

"The school's policy on fighting is suspension—" Vivian begins but Pat interrupts her saying coolly:

"I'm well aware of the policy, after all I'm the one who wrote it, so yes, Margaret will definitely be suspended. The question I have to consider is – for how long?"

"Well, what's the normal time?"

"Actually fighting isn't normal at Edgemont School for Girls so there's no precedent for me to follow," Pat pauses again, quite effectively, to let that statement sink in.

"I do feel that Margaret coming to the defence of her mother's reputation deserves more leniency then if she'd struck out because of name-calling against herself. And, of course, April should definitely have know better than to hurt the feelings of a much younger girl by spreading a rumour."

Everyone sits in silent expectation but Pat merely reverts to formal Principal mode and thanks Vivian Sanders for coming in before escorting her to the door suggesting April might like to leave school early today.

"But I've got Art Class this afternoon," whines the girl and her mother says she can stay if she likes. The two of them leave and Judith signals to Pat with her eyes asking whether or not she should follow. She indicates yes, but not until instructing Margaret to thank Ms. Taylor for interrupting her work on Margaret's behalf.

Margaret, still determined not to make eye contact with adults, mumbles a 'thank you and sorry, Ms. Taylor' which Judith graciously accepts while winking at Pat.

As she leaves the room she can hear the girl telling the principal she'd much rather have had Ms. Lila because she, at least, would have stuck up for her.

Chapter 25

Wednesday, February 19, 2020

"Judith? It's Samira. Can you come down to the principal's office? the sooner the better."

"Sure, but why didn't Pat call me directly? is she okay?"

"Yes, but she's on a conference call with some trustees, I'm afraid Andrea Seely is stirring up trouble. I think Pat needs your moral support."

"I'm on my way,"

Judith hangs up and thinks for a moment. Pat in a tizzy is not a pretty sight but Pat in a white-hot rage well, that most certainly is something best avoided. She'll have to do her best to calm her boss down.

After yesterday's lunchtime meeting about the schoolgirls fighting Judith has typed up notes of the conversation on her computer. She prints the sheet off now and takes it with her. Arriving at the principal's office she waits outside with Samira until Pat's call ends.

Both women enter the inner office. Pat waves them to chairs then dry-washes her face with her strong, capable hands. Judith is just thinking *it's a good thing Pat doesn't wear make-up* when Samira suggests:

"Pat, put on some lipstick, it will make you feel better."

"You mean like war paint?"

Samira shrugs, "Call it what you like, to me it's like armour so yeah, I guess war paint is appropriate."

"I've got Andrea Seely coming in and she's bringing Margaret because she thinks Margaret is starting back in class today. She isn't. I gave her a three-day suspension and she won't be welcome back until Monday."

"So am I here to referee or what?"

"Ha, maybe! No, you are my witness. I told Ms. Seely she's welcome to bring along her own."

"Hmm, frankly I'd be surprised if she has a lot of friends."

Just then we hear Andrea Seely arrive with Margaret in tow.

"Run along to your class now, Margaret," she commands but Principal Johnson overrules her telling Margaret to sit quietly in the secretary's office with Samira. As Ms. Seely opens her mouth to protest Pat gestures her into the big office. The strong smell of her too-liberally applied perfume quickly fills the room.

"You know Judith Taylor, our bursar. Ms. Taylor is here as witness in case a third party account of our interaction is required. Please be seated."

Pat takes her chair and switches on the tape recorder she keeps on her desk announcing into it the date, the names of those present, and a statement that this meeting has been requested by Ms. Andrea Seely, parent to student Margaret Seely.

"Go ahead, Ms. Seely."

"Fine. My name is Andrea Seely, I am Margaret's mother therefore a school parent, parent of a paying student, and also a Board Member and Treasurer of The Centre.

My daughter has been suspended from school on the ridiculous charge of fighting with another student. That's simply not possible. Also, it's inconvenient. I have many committments on my time and I can't have my child sent home on a whim. She needs the structure and supervision of school. Margaret must be accepted back into her classes immediately."

"Ms. Seely, Edgemont School for Girls has a strict code of conduct. That's one of the reasons why you have put your daughter in our care. I'm sure you will agree that it would be remiss of me not to impose the standard punishments when required.

Our disciplinary policy for fist-fighting is mandatory suspension. The number of days are at my discretion, probably one to two weeks would be usual, but there is no precedent because in all the years that I have been principal here I have never had to deal with this offence. However, Margaret is an exceptional student with an excellent record for good conduct so I'm being lenient on her. I sent her home for these three days: Wednesday, Thursday, and Friday and I do not expect to see her back here until Monday."

"But you can't suspend Margaret!" cries Andrea Seely.

"I assure I can, and I have done so." Principal Johnson is implacable.

"I can't stay home with her until Monday morning! I have things to do."

"Well, Margaret is not under house arrest, you'll just have to take her with you. You mentioned that you're busy with work for The Centre and I know she'll be welcome there."

"No, I don't want to take her!" Andrea Seely is practically shouting.

There is really nothing to say to an outburst like that. Pat and I simply sit there watching the warring emotions cross the distraught mother's face. She chooses anger, and casting a scathing look at Judith declares:

"I'll be complaining to my School Trustee!" before hurrying out of the room and slamming the door behind her. We could hear her call sharply to Margaret to *come along, NOW!!*

"I don't know why she threatened me, I never said a word," complains Judith.

"That's probably why... she saw you as the weak link."

"Oh thanks Pat. You keep dragging me in here for one Seely thing after another and all I get are insults!"

"You're welcome, Judith," said Pat with a chuckle. "I know you can take it."

Chapter 26

Judith is outside the nurse's office next morning, waiting for Lila. The meeting with Andrea Seely has nagged at her all evening. She's kicking herself for not speaking up. She should have pointed out that Margaret is being left on her own far too much, and the fist-fight is a sign of a deeper problem. The girl is filled with anger and acting out, reacting to her parent's separation, and resenting her mother.

She wants to rant and rave a bit but changes her mind when sees how tired and haggard her friend looks.

"My heart is breaking for you, Lila. You're exhausted. You're under enormous strain and something's got to give. It'll be your sanity if this keeps up."

"Well good morning to you too, Judith."

"Oh stop. You're killing yourself bit by bit, Arnie's secret is eating you up."

"Arnie's secret is off-limits. Talk to me about something else."

"Okay, how about when's the last time you saw Beth Penner or her Dad, or Margaret Seely? They all miss spending time with you. And Margaret – of all people – has taken to fighting in the schoolyard."

"No way!"

"She's currently under suspension."

"Margaret Seely?! she's like what, nine years old?"

"*Almost ten* is how she puts it, and yes, she was fighting. I got called in as the appropriate adult although she made it clear she'd much rather have had you."

"Oh jeez, what's been going on?"

"Just life, Lila. Everybody else is living it but Arnie has taken yours away. You've been in limbo or something for the last six weeks."

"Oh I know, I know. I just can't make up my mind, I can't. I don't know what to do. I'm not a ditherer but all of a sudden I am because it's not my secret. That's the real problem. I can handle my own messes but I don't know what to do with Arnie's."

"Yes you do, Lila. You have to tell Arnie that if he doesn't turn himself in you will. He dumped this on you because he wants *you* to make the decision—"

"No! he swore me to secrecy."

"And he had no right to do so! If he wanted to keep it a secret he should have kept his mouth shut."

"But I pushed and pushed him to tell me what was wrong. I can't complain now that he's done so."

"Of course you can. Look, you pushed because you wanted to help—"

"Yeah well, the road to hell really is paved with good intentions."

"Lila, listen. He needed a push, you gave it, he confessed to you and eased his burden but that's not helping, not in the long run, he needs to face up to what he's done. His delay has already cost him his marriage – what else is going to lose?"

"Rev Robbie would say *his soul.*"

"Rev Robbie would say *Lila I'm going to kick your butt if you don't drag that husband of yours to the police station pronto!*"

"Oh Judith, you're right. He would say that," she gave a sad chuckle, "But I'm not ready yet."

"Yes, you are. You don't need any more time to think about it. You know the difference between right and wrong, you have to help him acknowledge it, too. Please, Lila. If you can't convince Arnie to tell your family then you'll have to do it yourself. And ask them to help him navigate the legal system. Lila, he could have just stayed in Toronto and kept his mouth shut while waiting for you to file divorce papers. He told you for a reason. You have to help him."

"Oh dammit, Judith. Now you've given me even more stuff to think about and my head's already pounding. Look, Arnie's been calling and I told him I'd let him know what I decided before the weekend. Just give me another 24 hours."

"Lila, I wish I could say I'll give you all the time in the world but I know I wouldn't be doing you any favours if I said that. This is just such a horrible, horrible situation and I'm so sorry you're in it."

"Thank you for that, my friend."

"You know, speaking of Rev Robbie just now reminded me that he admonished me in his gentle but persistent way for not having pushed you into confiding your secret. I told him at the time that I respected your privacy but... well, he made me feel like I'd failed you and wasn't a good friend."

"You are, Judith, never doubt it."

Feeling ready to tackle any chore Judith carries on to her office resolved to get in touch with Andrea Seely and speak her mind. Her feistiness has to be contained though because she gets the Seely's answering machine and, worried that Margaret might hear the message, has to be very guarded in what she says.

Chapter 27

The end of the school day can't come soon enough for Judith. She is eager to find out what Lila is going to tell Arnie. Not least because Judith is feeling a bit anxious about keeping the secret from Grant any longer.

Just as Judith is packing up her desk for the weekend Lila appears in her doorway.

"Come on in, I've been wondering what your plans are."

"Well, I'm not giving Arnie an answer right now–"

"But you said you would!" interrupts Judith. "I can't keep this from Grant any longer. He's got to be told."

"Judith! It's really not Grant's business – or yours, for that matter."

"Yes, it is. It became my business when you told me the truth. I know I pestered you to tell me so I've only got myself to blame but there it is. I can't unhear the words. You know what I mean, you probably feel exactly the same way."

"I do, except I needed to know. In the wee hours of the morning, when I was tossing and turning, I had the most awful thought: what if instead of telling me the truth Arnie had made up some plausible story that I believed and we got back together? It would never have felt right because he'd always know he was living with a horrible secret and a lie like that it always going to come out eventually. Thank God he was only evasive and didn't actually lie to me."

"Oh Lila, you really are *between a rock and a hard place*. As for Grant, well I've already held back for a week and he's curious. I feel that if I keep this from him any longer then I will be wronging him."

"I see that, I do, but... here's what I've decided: I had planned on flying to Toronto for Easter with my parents but instead I've bumped up the trip so I can take Arnie to the police. I've let him know I'm coming home tomorrow but I haven't told him my decision yet. I have to do that face-to-face.

I already told him our marriage is over but he probably figures he can change my mind. He can't, and he'll realize that because I'm staying with my parents, not in my own home.

I hate burdening my parents but they hate being left out of the loop even more, so... I will tell them first and then we'll enlist whichever of my relatives will be able to help out the best. I still have no guarantee that Arnie will co-operate, but he'll know that I've revealed his secret and there's no turning back from that."

"Oh Lila. It's hard but, it's the right thing to do and you know that, right?"

Lila studies her friend for a moment before answering in a quiet voice:

"I do, but I also know that I feel betrayed by you, Judith. I feel you've pushed me into this position which, I believe I would have come to eventually because it is the right thing to do, but, as I say I feel you've forced my hand. I'm afraid I find that unforgivable, at least for now, but I hope I'll change my mind."

With that she gets up and leaves. Judith stays behind her desk, stunned and tearful. Lila's calm rejection is devastating.

Judith thinks about how she and Grant had originally been so sure Arnie had confessed to an affair and wanted a second chance and that Lila was dealing with betrayal when in fact the truth is so much worse. Arnie committed a crime. An accident, yes, but his failing to report it was deliberate act, a criminal act.

It occurs to Judith that the idea of Arnie-the-Adulterer serves as a very effective distraction. It's such a *cliche,* making it easy to look down on him. It certainly is a million miles away from Arnie-the-Killer. The killer has been effectively disguised by the sleazy, repentant husband.

What if someone else is playing that same game of misdirection?

She immediately thinks of how everyone is sniggering over Andrea-Seely-the-Cougar, but what if that's merely a cover-up? No one is looking past the shameless behaviour that discredits the woman and makes her ridiculous. No one considers that maybe there is a calculating mind plotting the camouflage to hide Andrea-the-Killer?

Have we all been tricked by the stereotype of a sex-starved woman grasping for a last chance at fulfillment? she wonders.

A sudden cacophony of emergency vehicle sirens: fire, police, ambulance shatters the air. Looking out the window Judith can see a line of flashing red lights heading east where black smoke is just visible as it rapidly billows upwards.

At least four people died in the fire at the trailer park and two fire-fighters were sent to hospital with serious injuries.

Jerry Bennett, the trailer park manager, has suffered second-degree burns to his face and hands. Half his moustache is burned off. When Grant speaks to the man the skin of his face has already turned red and glossy-looking. He is probably in severe pain but reaction hasn't set in yet. He is still distraught over the lives lost.

The fire's point-of-origin is the Pederson trailer, taken over by the granddaughter and her squatter friends, so that is no surprise. Both the girl and her boyfriend are believed to be among the victims but it is too soon for official identifications. Everyone deplores the loss of young life but no one actually liked Belle Pederson or Antwon Pruitt so their passing isn't mourned.

The group of residents who volunteer to keep an eye on that trailer were quick to call in the emergency response teams but the explosion generated extremely high heat and shooting flames so it was impossible to do more than contain it, and try to protect the trailer homes nearby. During all the excitement, fear, and noise an older resident suffers a heart attack but is expected to recover fully.

Fire trucks respond from all the surrounding communities and the investigating team has come from Calgary. The older fire-fighters recognize the sweet smell and quickly surmise that someone free-basing cocaine is the culprit.

"I haven't heard of that in a long time," comments Grant.

The crew members who are gathered around nod in agreement.

"That's because crack's become so popular. It gives pretty much the same punch as free-base but it's a lot safer. Easier to get hold of, too."

"Yeah, and you don't need ether to make it."

Grant turns to the Fire Chief asking: "Ether? that's used in free-basing?"

"It's the most, or was the most, commonly used solvent to *free* the cocaine from its *base*. Unfortunately for everyone involved it's also highly flammable. Crack just needs baking soda and boiling water."

"And smoking crack is the most addictive form of cocaine use, so that's another reason the dealers prefer it."

The horrible smell from the burning hangs in the air, and the stomach-churning sight of melted household goods haunts the witnesses.

Chapter 28

Saturday, February 22, 2020

Although he'd showered when he got home last night and then again this morning Grant thinks he can still smell the fire like it's embedded in his skin. *Maybe it is in my nostrils, throat, lungs?* he wonders.

When Judith opens the door to Grant she notices he looks sad and exhausted, but he brightens considerably on seeing her welcoming face, saying:

"You are a sight for sore eyes, sweetheart."

Judith bows her head, shy at the compliment but pleased. She has taken extra care getting ready using a new shampoo and conditioner, putting on mascara, and adding a dab of perfume to each of her pulse points. She wants to look and feel her very best since she is hoping for a special night.

He reaches out and lifting her chin meets her lips with a soft kiss, then he pulls her close and just stands there for a long moment hugging her to him.

Judith is happy to provide comfort. She's seen the news coverage of the fire and of course the phone lines have been humming as people pass on what they've heard and guessed at, and wondering if she has anything new to add.

"So, what's happening with Lila? You mentioned she was sorting things out by today – or yesterday, rather."

"Oh I let's not talk about that. Lila doesn't want me to say anything to you anyhow."

Grant found that suspicious and asks: "Why not?"

"Just because... it's a sad and sordid story and with the fire last night you've had your fill of death and destruction–"

"Death? What do you mean?"

"Grant, really, let's just leave it for now. Let's forget about other people's problems and just concentrate on each other, here, together..."

"Judith I would love to, truly truly truly, but I can't ignore it when you mention a death. Who died?"

"A homeless person, a bag-lady, Arnie ran her down–"

"WHAT?" Grant yelps but when Judith tries to continue he holds up his hand to stop her insisting:

"No! Don't tell me another word. Omigod, Judith! You've known about this for like a week?"

She isn't sure if she could speak yet so she just nods.

"How could you do that to me? Do you have any idea how much trouble I would be in for even hearing the little bit you've just said? My whole career – poof, gone – in one minute. Jesus Christ, Judith. I can't believe you'd do that to me–"

"Grant, I haven't done anything to you," Judith cries. "This has nothing to do with you, it all happened back in Toronto so–"

"Nothing to do with me? You're making me an accessory to a felony."

"I'm not! You don't know the story yet–"

He interrupts again: "And we'll keep it that way, right? Don't make things worse, don't say another word about it. Judith, shit, I can't believe you put me in this position."

"But I didn't know, I mean this is Alberta so you can't be responsible for what happens in Ontario!"

"No, but I am guilty if I keep silent. You should know that law enforcement personnel are held to a higher standard of conduct than civilians! I *have* to report the possibility that Arnie Morelli has committed–"

"His name isn't Morelli, that's Lila's maiden name," she puts in.

"Well goddamn it don't tell me his real name. In fact, don't tell me anything. I'm just... wow, I have no words. I thought you and I had something... I at least thought I had your respect, your consideration..." Grant stands up abruptly and heads back to the front door. He grabs his jacket off the coat-rack and with a sober "Goodnight, Judith" is out the door. Gone.

Judith bursts into tears. She'd hoped their night would end quite differently but it wouldn't matter if it didn't, not so long as she and Grant are still together. This stiff, angry, and hurt man is a stranger to her and she has no one to blame but herself. She cries bitterly.

Grant has walked several steps down the hall before he realizes he hasn't heard the sound he's been subconsciously listening for: the snap of the deadbolt locking into place. He turns back but then he hears Judith sobbing. Part of him wants to soothe away her tears but another part feels badly used, his trust shattered.

How can she care so little? Why has he let himself be fooled into thinking that... Grant isn't used to feeling indecisive. He stands in the hallway trying to piece together what he wants and what he should do.

He's exhausted from the late night and heartsick at the destruction he witnessed, and he knows he's not in the best place right now. He can't think clearly, he's too upset.

In the end he turns away from her door and continues to the stairs. Once he's hurried down to the ground floor he sends her a text saying:

'lock yr door'

Judith sees the text and runs out to the hallway but Grant is long gone. *He does care, he still cares!* is her wild thought until she realizes he was just reacting the way any cop would with any... civilian.

Chapter 29

Judith is feeling listless, dull, and depressed. She's stayed in bed much later than usual and her muscles ache from lying down too long. Dragging herself into the kitchen she makes a cup of coffee she doesn't even feel like drinking. Food is out of the question.

Looking up at the clock she groans over how many stultifying hours she has to get through until she can reasonably go back to bed. Sundays are settling into a dreary pattern.

Grant doesn't want to speak to her, and neither does Lila who is in Toronto, anyhow. Now nobody is friendly, and everyone is unhappy.

Judith wonders if the onus is on her to apologize – but to whom and for what? Grant shouldn't expect her to reveal Lila's secret – she isn't a tattletale! and Lila shouldn't have demanded she keep a secret from Grant in the first place. It isn't a big stretch of the imagination to figure out it will come between them.

Judith feels sorry for herself, deciding it isn't fair for her two friends to put her in the middle with their demands and priorities. But it is hard to feel both justified and miserable at the same time.

She's heard the church bells and finds herself wishing she is one of the faithful but she hasn't grown up with religion. When she did learn about God she figured He'd forsaken her a long time ago. It's hard to overcome the absolutes of childhood – especially the self-taught truths.

Still, it would be nice to have somewhere to go today. She could have sang the hymns and listened to the sermon from the Reverend. Thinking of the Reverend makes her think of Rev Robbie... of course! she can go to The Centre and make herself useful. She has her copy of the thumb-drive and from it she can reconstruct the finances up until Rev Robbie's death, and then work on getting it all straightened out. And arranging an off-site back-up, too. It feels good to have a plan, and good to have something useful to do.

Now Judith feels energized as she gets herself ready to go out. She has just hopped in the shower when someone knocks at her door but too quietly for her to hear over the spray of the water.

About twenty minutes later, dressed comfortably in jeans and a hoodie, Judith is locking her door when she is hit hard from behind. The force of that blow knocks her forehead into her own apartment door and Judith collapses, senseless, in her hallway. She has no idea who attacked her.

Brian Penner is worried about Lila Morelli. He thinks he's done a good job of keeping his feelings for her hidden, but his daughter Bethany sees right through him. Beth has turned into a conscientious and empathetic girl. Brian is proud of the way she'd taken that Margaret Seely under her wing even though the girl is quite a bit younger. Smart though, and with a smart mouth, too, but Brian keeps that opinion to himself.

Beth has told her Dad that she's spoken to Ms. Taylor, the school bursar, about Margaret's mother leaving her alone so much.

"I don't like to be a rat or anything but Dad, Margaret's only nine. She's too young to be left alone overnight. The Seely's have money and if somebody noticed that only a child was in the house well, they might decide to rob the place."

"Yeah, well Miss Margaret Seely could give that *Home Alone* kid a run for his money if crooks tried to invade her place, don't you think?"

This makes Beth laugh. She and her father had watched that movie, again, this past Christmas. He is right about Margaret being clever and ingenious but nevertheless she is just a kid.

This morning, however, it's her Dad she is concerned about. When she asks him what's up and he tries hedging she steers him straight to the point:

"You're worried about Lila, aren't you?"

"No, not really. Well, maybe a little.. just a little bit anxious. She's been so bothered lately and just not herself."

"Well you know what Ms. Taylor said about Lila's husband coming out here and getting her upset."

"Yeah, she still hasn't talked to me about that but at least she did call to tell me she was going to Toronto sooner than planned and expected to get everything finally sorted out. I just wish I could help her somehow. You know, Beth, I'm very, uh fond of Lila. Even as more than a friend."

"I know, Dad, and I'm so happy about it. I think she's great."

That makes Brian grin as he agrees.

"I am worried about her though but I don't think it would be right for me to phone her. Not when she's in Toronto and not when she's working out whatever it is," he says.

"Well then, why don't you go talk to Ms. Taylor? Remember how she helped when I went missing?"

"Oh God, I'll never forget that time Bethie."

Hearing her childhood name makes Beth smile. She gives her father a hug and says she has Ms. Taylor's address from sending her a thank you card back in January so why doesn't he drop round to see if she can give him some news? or at least some reassurance?

Brian had cut back on his work hours after Beth was safely returned home but at times like this he wishes he had something to do and somewhere to go. He realizes sitting around moping and fretting isn't doing him any good so he agrees with his daughter's suggestion.

"Guess I better change out of these grubby old sweats, eh?"

"Uh, yeah, unless you want Ms. Taylor to tell Lila to run the other way!"

Taking Beth's advice is the reason that Brian Penner arrives to find Judith Taylor lying on the floor in front of her apartment with a woman rifling through her victim's purse.

Brian Penner is a big man, strong with a construction worker's muscles, and the sight of Judith lying unresponsive is all he needs to grab and subdue the attacker, Andrea Seely.

"Let me go," she shrieks, "She knows! she knows! and she must have some proof, I've *gotta* find the proof!"

Brian has seen Andrea Seely before but he doesn't recognize this maddened creature with her wild eyes and fingers curled into claws. He doesn't care how roughly he handles her as he pulls her arms behind her back and pushes her down to the floor. She twists and turns and yells but is no match for him. He half-kneels on her back to restrain her wildly struggling form. Holding her wrists together he uses his other hand to dial 9-1-1 on his cell-phone, requesting an ambulance and the police.

Judith recovers consciousness during the ambulance ride but is admitted to the hospital for tests, then kept in overnight for observation. The medical staff are concerned about the severe blow she's taken to the back of her head.

She is bruised and shaky and has no memory of what happened since the moment she locked her door – in the middle of a Sunday afternoon.

Grant feels sick when he learns about the attack on Judith, and deeply dismayed that he wasn't the one to rescue her. He remembers Brian Penner from that case last December. He is a devoted dad and a well-built, good-looking, single man who had garnered the sympathy of both Lila and Judith.

Grant knows he should be glad that Penner was on the spot at the right time, but he isn't feeling grateful.

Chapter 30

Judith learns that when an ambulance brings you to the hospital it's up to you to find your own transportation when the time comes to return home. That's fine, except they won't let you go home in a taxi or an Uber, it has to be with someone who will see you safely indoors and stay with you.

Judith has patiently explained that no, there is no one at home because she lives alone. When the nurse repeats the regulation yet again Judith's patience runs out.

"For the umpteenth time I am a single woman who lives alone, no room-mate, no family, an orphan, no relatives. There is no one at home and there probably never will be!"

"Well, we need the bed and since you don't need it anymore you have to leave," replies the nurse.

Judith gives her a puzzled look saying "I don't want the bed, I *want* to leave. I want to go home."

"But as I've already explained," the nurse continues in an exaggeratedly patient voice, "You can't go home if there's no one there to look after you."

"Don't be ridiculous," snaps Judith. "I'm going home and I'll make my own travel arrangements since you won't help."

"I'm going to get my supervisor," threatens the nurse.

Exasperated Judith retorts: "Yes, you do that, just go."

"Well there's no need to be rude—" the nurse begins when Judith interrupts to say that apparently, there is.

While the nurse hurries away Judith retrieves her belongings from the bedside locker and checking that her cell-phone still has a charge calls Pat Johnson.

"Judith!" exclaims Pat, "Samira has just this minute been telling me about what happened to you. Beth Penner came in and told her. How are you? What happened? Where are you? Goodness I'm babbling, aren't I? Can I come see you?"

"Actually Pat I'm calling to see if Mark still does his volunteer driving for people needing to go to and from the hospital? They don't want to let me go home in a taxi. Some bloody stupid regulation they have."

"Oh poor Judith! I'll call Mark right away and he'll be waiting for you out front. I'll head over to your place now so you can tell the staff that someone is at your home."

"You don't have to do that, Pat, it's a school day and you're busy—"

"Never mind about that. I will see you shortly and you can tell me everything, or if you're exhausted I'll tuck you into your bed and leave you in peace."

"Thank you so much, Pat. I look forward to seeing you and finding out what actually happened to me."

Judith ends the call just as the nurse returns with her supervisor.

"I've arranged to be picked up and delivered into the care of Patricia Johnson, Principal of Edgemont School for Girls. I'm sure you'll agree she's capable enough of keeping an eye on me."

The supervisor, busy with more pressing issues, is thankful that everything is sorted and approves this plan. The nurse gives an almighty sniff of displeasure which Judith happily ignores.

She completes her paperwork and makes her way to the front door, relieved to escape the odor and atmosphere of the hospital. She only has to wait two minutes before spotting Principal Johnson's husband pull up in front in his blue sedan.

Pat Johnson arrives at Judith's apartment and recognizing her husband's car she parks behind him. Mark and Judith have just reached the lobby so Pat takes over from there.

Once they are settled upstairs in Judith's apartment Pat makes a pot of tea and passes on all the information she has learned.

"You were attacked by Andrea Seely who, apparently, poisoned Rev Robbie with the drug Fentanyl. I have no idea how Andrea got hold of it–"

"She knew the combination to the safe," replied Judith and at Pat's quizzical look she explained: "This is only supposition but Grant.." she paused a moment remembering the look on Grant's face last night during the brief visit the nursing staff had allowed him, but she preferred to reminisce about that on her own so she continued: "Grant and I discussed this and we think Rev Robbie caught somebody with the drugs which he confiscated and locked in the safe out of harm's way."

"But surely he would notify the police?"

"Would he? if it was a young person who Rev Robbie felt could be turned around without getting a criminal record?"

"Ahhh, you're right. That scenario does sound likely."

"And anyone who knew the combination to the safe could get hold of the drugs themselves. Andrea Seely, as Treasurer, knew the combination."

"Well she's got a lawyer and isn't uttering a word now but Brian Penner got quite an earful from her, he rescued you, you know."

"I heard that, but I don't actually remember anything."

"No, well you were unconscious so not surprising!" laughs Pat. "Oh, I shouldn't laugh because she really did do some damage – have you seen your face?"

"I don't want to. I can feel a goose egg on the back of my skull and I've got what feels like a huge bandage on my forehead."

"Be glad it's not the other way around or they'd have had to shave off a patch of your hair."

"Oh, ewww!"

"I know, eh? Actually the bandage isn't too big but you do have a black eye and you're very pale so bit of a mess, I'm afraid, but you'll heal and that's the main thing."

"Okay so why did Andrea Seely do all this?"

"Well we don't know! In fact we're all hoping your policeman will tell you so you can tell us. Will he be coming by?"

"He said he would, but if he mentioned a time I've forgotten it."

"Maybe you should give him a call and let him know you're home now."

"Yes, I'll do that. Pat, I really appreciate you being here for me but I know you've got to get back to the school."

"Call the detective and we'll see if he can come by now." Pat fetches Judith's bag so she can get her mobile. She stares stupidly at the phone until Pat takes it from her saying:

"His name is Grant, right?"

Judith nods and listens while Pat conducts a very efficient phone-call with George Grant who says he'll be over right away.

"You just stay lying there on the couch and I'll wait to let him in when he gets here. I won't quiz him – tempting though that is! but when you're feeling better please give me a call and an update, okay?"

"Thanks, Pat."

The older woman smooths Judith's hair back from her forehead and finding an afghan folded over a chair she covers Judith up.

"Just close your eyes and nap, Judith."

Chapter 31

About an hour later, when Judith wakens, it's Grant sitting beside her holding her hand. She gives him a sweet smile to show how happy she is to see him, but he's looking anxious.

"Judith I am so, so sorry I wasn't there to protect you.. or at least to be the one to find you. Brian Penner, eh? Why was he even here?"

"I have no idea Grant," then noting his frown adds: "He's never been here before."

Grant's shoulders drop down, relaxing some of his tension, but his face still shows concern.

"How do you feel? Your poor head, all bandaged... Judith I feel awful about quarrelling with you–"

"Oh, don't. You were right, I should have told you. I felt my loyalties were torn between you and Lila but I did everything wrong and ended up making both of you mad at me."

"Why is Lila mad?"

"She feels I pushed her into this position of telling Arnie that he has to inform the authorities or she will."

"But that's the right thing – *the only thing* – to do."

"And she knows that, she even acknowledged it, but she still blames me."

"Well that's not fair. You only pushed to help her since she's been dithering about this for weeks. I re-interviewed her but had to cut our meeting short because she was so disconnected. She obviously needed like twelve hours of sleep! she couldn't focus well enough to answer my questions. I don't how long she would have continued but something would have snapped sooner or later."

"Yeah, Rev Robbie's death was like the final straw. Boy, that Arnie really did a number on her when he came out to visit."

"Didn't you or Lila mention, actually she mentioned at Christmas, that her family were all cops, right?"

"Not her immediate family, well a younger brother is in training or whatever. But not her Dad. However her uncles, some aunts, and her grandfather are all cops so, yeah she's got plenty in her family but I'd guess there's still a bit of an us-and-them attitude since neither of her parents are on the force."

"You're right, there would be. Both sides probably look down on each other a bit, privately of course, but yeah.

So what you're saying is that Lila blew you off and then I came over and basically did the same. Then you got your head bashed in."

"Pretty much! but I don't remember a thing about that. I was feeling pretty low that morning," Grant winces, recalling how he'd heard her sobbing when he left the night before, and she hastens to explain, "but I decided to do something positive, I was heading to The Centre with my thumb drive to see if I could help get the financials back on track.

I know Rev Robbie's computer was stolen, but there are plenty of other computers and lap-tops there. So, that was my plan and I was feeling better to actually be doing something when bang, I guess. I don't remember anything else until I came to in the ambulance.

I might remember more. I mean, Brian was there fighting with Andrea so subconsciously I must have been hearing things but I really don't care if that memory ever returns to be honest."

Grant leans over and kisses her forehead beside the bandage. Then he kisses her nose and when she smiles he bends to her lips and gives her a proper kiss.

"Why on earth would Andrea Seely want to harm you?"

Judith was surprised and struggled a bit to sit up: "You mean you don't know?"

"Do you?"

"No, not a clue."

"Me neither. Well, actually that's not quite true because we do have two clues. One is that according to Brian Penner Seely kept yelling *she knows* and *I've got to find her proof*' which sure sounds like she thinks you knew something that's compromising to her. And two: our financial forensics specialist found evidence of theft and fraudulent entries on your thumb drive. No indication by whom, but based on what's just happened I think it's a safe bet that Andrea Seely, in her position as Treasurer, was misappropriating funds. They'll track it all down eventually.

The very first time I spoke to her she tried to cast the blame on Rev Robbie but you know she's such a silly and annoying woman that I have to admit I was guilty of dismissing her. I felt she was just trying to make herself look important. I won't make that mistake with her again. When I interview her I plan to ask about the money, The Centre's financial records, and of course why she attacked you."

"You know, Grant, she has been clever enough to play everyone. I was thinking on... I'm not sure, a couple of days ago anyhow, I thought that maybe her chasing the boy Kyle-something was just a smokescreen."

"You never mentioned any of this, I don't know what you mean?"

"Then you're one of the few people who doesn't know! Even her daughter – you remember precocious Margaret?"

"How could I forget her!"

"Well, Margaret got into a fist-fight at school because some older student repeated the rumour that's been going around about how Andrea Seely is chasing after the young sports coach, called Kyle, from The Centre. She's made a laughingstock of herself but what I got to thinking was: what if that was deliberate? What if Andrea played up to be this character people ridiculed and dismissed as cover for something else?"

"Like stealing The Centre's money? Maybe..." He paused to mull over this idea for a few moments before asking: "But why?"

"That is a mystery because you saw their home, it's a mansion. The Seely's are very well-off."

"Except that looks can deceive, right?"

"Oh sure, all flash no cash, but Pat confirmed that Mr. Seely – I can't remember his first name – is a very successful businessman. So this means you haven't interviewed Andrea Seely yet?"

"I tried but she lawyered up immediately, and the first thing her lawyer did was ask for a psych evaluation so now I'm cooling my heels till I get the all-clear."

"I'd like to think about this some more because I don't see how Andrea Seely and the drugs and Rev Robbie can connect but my head is a little fuzzy. Maybe I'll just close my eyes again for a bit..."

"Yes, do that. Get your rest, Judith. I'm not going anywhere," Grant reassures her.

He shifts their seats so that he can put his arm around her shoulders and lay her head against his chest. Judith snuggles into his embrace and her slowed breathing indicates she'd fallen asleep. Grant is careful not to let his chin drop down on her head since she is bruised and bandaged.

He is planning to think through all they've discussed but soon his eyes are closed, too. He didn't sleep well the night before.

Judith wakes with her face pressed into Grant's shirt. She stays still for a moment listening to his heartbeat. He is stroking her arm and when she sits up he pulls her close for a slow, satisfying kiss. After an enjoyable interlude of kissing she draws back saying:

"I need coffee, food, and a pee."

"In that order?"

"Almost!" Freeing herself from his arms she heads to the bathroom. Grant stands up as well and stretches, his long legs have felt cramped caught between the coffee table and the couch but he didn't want to move and disturb her.

"I doubt if you want to go out for a meal," he says when Judith returns, "so what would you like me to order in?"

"Nothing," she replies. "If you don't mind I'm craving chicken noodle soup and a grilled cheese sandwich."

"Oh, wow, that sounds great!" he says with enthusiasm.

"Well, it's just tinned soup but it's comfort food and I enjoy it every now and then."

"Can I help? I'm an expert can opener..."

"No, there's not enough room in my kitchen for both of us but you can sit at the table and keep me company. First though, when we mentioned Margaret before you didn't tell me who is looking after her now while her mother's in custody?"

"She's staying with the Penners until her father gets back. We were able to get hold of him and he's probably already here by now. His name is John, by the way, John Seely. He was quite forthcoming with me, although shocked when he heard about the assault on you.

It seems Andrea was making it difficult for him to see Margaret – who is reportedly thrilled to be with her Dad. Andrea was withholding access in order to get more money from him. Anyhow, Margaret is being looked after.

But the important question is how are you feeling? and be honest!"

"I think I'm always honest, Grant. In fact, I've been told I'm *honest to a fault*. So I'm telling you the truth when I say you that although I'm a bit weak I'm not the least bit headachey – which is a surprise considering I just saw how bad my battered face looks in the bathroom mirror."

"You can never look bad to me, Judith."

The two are comfortable with each other and when Judith brings out plates and cutlery Grant sets the table. They drink their coffee while she cooks and in fifteen minutes are having their soup and sandwiches.

"So, any insights while you were napping?" asks Grant.

"Yes, as a matter of fact. It occurred to me that Andrea either moved really fast to seize the opportunity of Rev Robbie's death to clean out the safe, or, she'd emptied it already. If so, did she leave it open? is that why the Fentanyl was available to his killer? and what were the dates that the funds were stolen? That must have happened very close to the murder or Rev Robbie would have raised the alarm."

"I think Andrea Seely killed Rev Robbie."

"I realize she must have done, Pat said so too, but it's truly a shocker. I mean, I can imagine her stealing well, no I can't actually imagine that because it makes no sense, but murder? That's a huge leap from theft!"

"I agree, but it's my only conclusion. Here's my thinking:

Andrea Seely, for whatever reason, is going through large amounts of money. She's been elected or appointed Treasurer at The Centre which gives her access to the cash in the bank account. She also has the combination to the safe where the daily collections are stored. She transfers or withdraws the banked funds, and helps herself to the loose cash in the safe.

Rev Robbie either catches her in the act or accuses her. She makes up some story to buy a bit of time – but probably just a day at most – then arranges to meet with him to be counselled, or to discuss a repayment plan, or something like that. She has nothing to do with the drugs except that she's seen the Fentanyl in the safe or, somehow, knows it's there and she steals it.

I'm guessing that when she meets with Rev Robbie she arrives with coffees or more likely chai lattes knowing her, and she's doctored his. She probably used all of the Fentanyl because we only found the tiniest amount left behind. It's a highly potent drug and he dies quickly.

She's picked a time when there are lots of people about, especially young people who she hopes will fall under suspicion because of the drug angle, and that's why she left the safe open, too."

"Wow, that answers all the questions. Good work, Grant."

"It doesn't explain why she stole the money in the first place, though."

"Oh that's easy, Andrea Seely has a gambling problem."

"That would explain it... but how do you know?"

"Well I don't *know* but Lila and I saw her at the casino when we went for dinner with those tickets you gave me."

"Okay, but lots of people go to casinos. It doesn't mean they have an addiction and are stealing to feed their habit."

"True, but what about all her absences? Margaret is left at home alone a lot and even when her mother's there she often slips out late at night after Margaret's gone to bed. The casinos are open very late, aren't they?"

"Yes, they are and seven days a week. Judith, I think you might be on to something. There have been several cases in the last few years where gamblers – all women, actually – were caught embezzling large amounts of money from their employers and their defence was an addiction to slot machines and VLTs."

"What are those?"

"Video Lottery Terminals, a kind of slot machine."

"Oh. Did the embezzlers get off?"

"God no, they've all been convicted and either fined or jailed, and ordered to pay back the money. So far that defence has never been successful."

"Maybe that's what's caused the breakdown of her marriage? maybe her husband knew about the gambling and cut off the funds."

"We're not sure about the gambling–"

"I am," Judith insists, "And if Andrea won't talk maybe John Seely will? Maybe he's had enough of his wife and her using Margaret as a pawn to get more money out of him."

"We'll find out more when I actually get her into an interview room. At the moment we've only got her on assault. Oh, you will press charges, right?"

"Absolutely. Hey, it's becoming a bit of a habit with me... first Billy MacNeill and now Andrea Seely."

"I'll bet she's the one who broke into your car and stole The Centre's bookkeeping ledger. Especially if she has been looking for some sort of proof. As a parent she'd have a pretty good idea of the school routines and could pick the best time to do it unseen.

But since nothing was pointing the finger at her, specifically, why did she keep saying *she knows, she knows* to Brian Penner?"

"Oh that must be because of... oh, that's my fault. After Margaret got suspended for fighting Andrea demanded a meeting, the silly woman thought she could bully Pat into letting Margaret come back to class. I was present and she made some remark or something, damn that's something else I can't remember. Anyhow, I was annoyed, especially knowing that she kept leaving Margaret alone which might not be illegal but it's morally reprehensible. So I phoned but I got the answering machine and I had to be circumspect in how I worded my message in case Margaret heard. Andrea must have thought I was hinting and beating around the bush... oh, her guilty conscience filled in the blanks!"

They finish their meal and sit over another cup of coffee.

"Despite all this caffeine and my nap I think I'm going to have an early night," says Judith.

"I'm staying over," insists Grant. He notes her sudden blush and quickly adds: "On the couch. I just don't want to leave you alone, Judith."

"Thank you, Grant. That's very kind and reassuring, too. By the way, if Fentanyl is so deadly why is it available?"

"It's one of those products that turned out to be so much better than the hype! It's just about the best painkiller hospitals can use, about thirty times more powerful than heroin. So it comes into the country legally for medical use but too often it ends up in the hands of drugs dealers and their clients. It's caused a lot of deaths because it's easy to overdose."

"Oh, I wondered. I've never experimented with any kind of drugs, never had a sip of wine or beer or alcohol, and never smoked a cigarette. Pretty dull and boring life, eh?"

Grant stares into her eyes and she is drawn by the sparkling interest she sees in his. *Oh! He must have realized I haven't had any sexual experiences either!* Judith feels the heat of her blush flooding her cheeks and quickly glances away.

"I don't think you're boring or dull at all, Judith. But you know, you should probably get in touch with the Red Cross because I'll bet they'd love to have you as a Blood Donor."

Judith laughs, his comment having rescued her from embarrassment, and the tension that's built-up between them breaks harmlessly.

"I tried to give blood once but they wouldn't take it. There was a clinic set up for two days at the University and when the nurse said I looked pale and asked if I was sick I said *oh no, it's just my* oh! maybe I shouldn't, oh what the heck you said you've got sisters so I'm sure you know all about it... anyhow I said I was on *my period* so she said I couldn't. I later learned that's wrong and I could have donated, but I've never tried again. You're right though, I should. It's something we should all do if we can."

"Do you know your blood type?"

"A+, you?"

"A-, one of the rarer types. I can give blood to you but I can't take it from you. I can only receive blood from A- and O-. No B types."

"Same, I can't take blood from B types but the others are okay. So, we're somewhat compatible?"

Gathering up their used coffee cups Grant turns to the sink calling over his shoulder:

"I think we're very compatible, Judith. Now, let's get you to bed."

Chapter 32

True to his word Grant stays on the couch all night but in the morning Judith wakens to find him sitting on the edge of her bed. He's looking at her like she's a beautiful woman, and his look makes her feel like she really is. Without a word she opens her arms to him and then he's holding her, kissing her, and murmuring lovely words. The rest just happens naturally.

Judith has left him to start coffee and toast while she gets cleaned up. She's not yet ready for company in the shower, especially since she has to wear a shower cap to keep her head dry. *I wish I could wash my hair,* she thinks, *but that's a no-no right now.*

When she comes out of the bathroom, fully dressed but in comfortable clothes, he tells her her phone's been ringing and buzzing so she has a look and see missed calls and a *call me now* text from Pat Johnson.

"It's my boss sounding urgent so I'd better phone her right away," she says, hitting the button. Pat answers immediately:

"Judith, thank God! I need to tell somebody but there's nobody else I can really tell. Well, Samira, of course, but you need to know."

"Know what, Pat?"

"It's Lila! She just called me from Toronto. Judith, her husband has committed suicide! He's dead! Suicide! Can you believe it? Did you meet him when he was out here? I know he visited at the beginning of the year..."

"No, I didn't. We planned to but... omigod Pat, this is just awful, awful news."

Grant is staring at Judith with concern and she wants to tell him but doesn't want Pat to know he's still here so early in the day. Instead she just repeats the words:

"I can't believe Arnie has killed himself," and sees Grant's eyes widen in surprise just as a look of disgust crosses his face. "Poor Lila. What's she going... what are her plans?"

"Well first off, she is coming back so that's a huge relief. Apparently she has to stay over Saturday night to get a good price on her airfare–"

"What about the airline's bereavement discount? does she know about that?"

"Well it's really not much for domestic flights. Usually the sale price is better. Of course if it's an international flight then it really makes a difference... oh why are we talking about this?"

"Because the news is just so horrible we want to avoid thinking about it. Anyhow, does that mean she's coming back on Sunday?"

"Yes, the funeral is on Friday. They have to wait until then because the Coroner had to agree to release the body. Oh, Judith you're right, this is horrible. Anyhow, Lila's catching the first flight out on Sunday and we'll see her at school on Monday. Judith, Lila didn't say why Arnie did this and I couldn't very well ask her, but do you have any idea?"

"I might... but, I'm not sure. He's same age as Lila – and me – but I think there was a health thing or something. I was supposed to meet him but Lila and I didn't really talk much about his actual visit... I can't say for sure, Pat."

"Well, it's a very sad thing no matter what the reason behind it is."

"Yes, it is. Pat thanks for letting me know. Toronto time is two hours ahead of us, right? I'll call her now–"

"Oh Judith, Lila asked that I pass on her news because she doesn't want to talk to anyone herself."

"Oh! Okay, then. Well, still, thanks for telling me. Bye for now."

"Bye, Judith – oh wait, how are you feeling today? Better?"

Judith has been looking at Grant throughout her conversation. "I was feeling great until I got this news. Physically I feel... wonderful, thanks!"

She disconnects the call and he pulls her straight into his arms.

"I only heard half of that and it was bad, tell me what's going on."

"Arnie has committed suicide, no explanation from Lila why, she doesn't want to talk to anybody, the funeral is Friday and she's flying back on Sunday morning. She plans to come to school on Monday so that must mean she's going to stay, right? She's not just coming back to wrap things up here?"

"Well, I don't know, Judith. But I don't think she'd rush back just to quit her job, break her lease, and plan a move, do you?"

"No, you're right. She'd stay with her family and get most of it sorted out long-distance. I should call her. I know things didn't end well between us but... either she hates me even more or she needs my comfort. I have to try."

"Okay, but remember she'll be really hurting right now and might say things that are... well, meant to hurt you back. You have to be the strong one, right?" He gives her a hug that turns into a long kiss.

Judith finds Lila's number in her contacts and calls. Lila doesn't answer and Judith can't leave a message because the mailbox is full. She tries again, several times, but never gets a different result.

Later, lying in each other's arm, Judith confesses to Grant:

"I feel doubly guilty now. One, because I can't help but see Arnie's death as probably the easiest solution to Lila's dilemma which isn't a very kind thought; and two because I'm feeling so happy here with you."

"I'm glad you feel that way, Judith. I was worried that you might feel overwhelmed by the news. I have no sympathy with suicides, they do terrible things to the people they leave behind."

"I expect I would have felt differently if Arnie and Lila had been a happy couple. Then I'd be devastated for her loss but–"

"I know what you mean. This way there's no trial, no family shame, no torn-apart loyalties. I'm guessing he did it before telling the authorities, don't you think? that's usually the way since cowards don't want to face up to their actions and the consequences."

"Yes, I think he did it instead of telling the authorities. You realize Lila is going to blame herself for driving him to it. Oh, she's going to blame me even more for pushing her..."

"But you said she was going to tell her family, at least her non-police relatives so that would be her parents, right? before giving Arnie the ultimatum?"

Judith sits up, animated by her thoughts: "Yes, that's right! She wanted him to know that there was no way he could talk her round, that it wasn't just their secret because she'd already told her parents. Yes! they would have backed her up in her decision. They're a close family and their support would definitely have fortified her. So I'm not entirely to blame..." she sighs with relief then sinks back into Grant's embrace.

Chapter 33

Judith has to go back to the hospital on Wednesday for a check-up. The Resident she sees isn't happy with the state of her healing, saying the swelling should have gone done much more. He sends her for yet more tests. Judith feels a twinge of unease but consoles herself with the thought that Resident's are overly cautious, determined to dot every 'i' and cross every 't'.

She mentions that after getting bad news about a friend she hasn't been sleeping too well. He admonishes her that she needs to get her rest, it's an important part of healing. Judith smiles to herself thinking that the time she's been spending in bed lately isn't exactly restful... although it does feel healing.

She sends Grant a text knowing she'll be spending several hours at the hospital with her phoned switched off. Hoping he'll get it and reply right away she is delighted to hear the *ding!* of an incoming message. He wants to know if there is a problem and she replies:

JUDITH: no just tests

Grant goes on to say that Andrea Seely's lawyer has called and they are all meeting for an interview at 11:00 this morning. Judith wishes him good luck and ends the chat advising she'll check in as soon as she's finished, and can turn her phone back on again.

A couple of hours later, while waiting for test results, she spots Mark Johnson. Meeting up with him in the foyer she asks if he'll let her buy him a cup of coffee in thanks for the ride home he gave her on Monday.

"Oh no need for that, Ms. Taylor—" he begins, but Judith interrupts saying:

"Judith, please. And I'd like to have a coffee myself. In fact, I see this hospital has a mini Tim Horton's concession and I could go for a doughnut, too."

He smiles and agrees, giving her his order and saying he'll grab a table for them.

Minutes later Judith joins him at a high-top carrying a tray holding their drinks and snacks.

"Let's see, this is yours since the mug is marked Decaf," she says, passing it over to him. Sitting back to sip their hot drinks and take a bite of doughnut, Judith continues: "This is a busy hospital, isn't it? Is this the only one you drive for?"

"I mostly get calls for here, the Villages Hospital, because it's close to my home and I can get here fairly quickly, but I have been asked to take people to and from Calgary hospitals as well. I've been getting more calls than usual lately. Lots of people suffering bad cases of the flu."

"Well, I think it's a great service you provide, Mr. Johnson. I know I certainly appreciated it. I was beginning to think that nurse was going to keep me here!"

He chuckles at that, adding: "They love their policies, don't they? How did you get here today?"

"I drove myself... it never occurred to me that maybe I shouldn't? I feel fine, no faintness, headaches, or ringing in my ears. I just seem to tire more quickly than before but I'm sure I'll soon have my strength back."

They sit in companionable silence, eating and sipping.

"Normally I enjoy people-watching when I'm on the sidelines like this but a hospital is different, isn't it?"

"Yes, I understand what you're saying. It's different at airports and shopping centres because people might be rushed and harried but, for the most part, they're happy to be there. Whereas here, well nobody wants to be here except the staff."

"I guess they get used to the smell over time."

"What smell?" asks Mark Johnson with a sly smile.

Judith's name is paged so she gets up to head back to her section. Mark Johnson thanks her for the coffee, and she thanks him again for her ride and for keeping her company today.

This time the Resident is accompanied by a middle-aged doctor who explains that the amount of swelling is normal for the severity of the blow and the slow healing isn't a worry. The Resident had been concerned in case chips of bone had come loose which is why he brought it to her attention but she tells Judith there is no indication of anything like that.

"The scans show heavy bruising that goes down deep so the blow you took was harder than we originally realized. Based on that we've determined that the pace of your healing is normal, and you need to to stay off work for a few more days to get well-rested."

"When can I wash my hair?"

"Not yet, I'm afraid. But it doesn't look bad, you know, it's not greasy-looking." The doctor, whose own hair is pulled into a perfect french twist, has a good look and adds: "In another day or two you can try a dry shampoo but keep it away from the abraded area, okay?"

The Resident changes Judith's dressing then escorts her to the Out-Patients reception to make a follow-up appointment for Monday.

Back in her own car Judith switches on her phone to check for messages. Just the one, from Grant, saying the interview with Andrea Seely has been delayed until 3:00. The car clock reads 4:10 and out of habit Judith automatically checks the time on her phone to confirm it matches. It does.

Judith texts back her own message saying she's finally finished up at the hospital and everything is good. She plans to go straight home but *en route* changes her mind and instead drives to the Penner residence. She is curious, though very grateful, about why Brian Penner came to her apartment building on Sunday.

"By time I get there Beth should have gotten home from school," she spoke aloud. "And even if her Dad isn't home from work yet, she'll probably know why he came round to my place."

It's a short drive from the hospital to their home. Edgemont isn't a large village – just a wealthy one.

Brian Penner's not home yet but Beth is there and she welcomes Judith. The bungalow is homey and lived-in, with a bookmarked novel on the arm of an overstuffed chair, nail polish paraphernalia set out beside an open magazine on the coffee table, a sweater hanging from a doorknob... Judith figures they must have a cleaner come in on a weekly basis.

"I heard about what happened, Ms. Taylor. Look at your poor head! you're all bruised, too."

Judith refuses a hot drink, explaining she's had a coffee and doughnut at the hospital, but Beth's offer of a ginger-ale is appealing.

"Yes, I'll have a glass of that, thanks. Ginger-ale always makes me think of drinking it to get better, same with chicken noodle soup."

"Me, too!" exclaims Beth. "But other than the bruises and that big bandage you really don't look sick."

"No, I'm not. I'm a little tired, that's all, so I won't stay, but I did want to ask your father why he came over to my apartment and, of course, to thank him for saving me. Did you know it was Andrea Seely, Margaret's mother, who attacked me?"

"Omigod yes! Everybody's talking about it but nobody can believe it. Everyone thought she was just so... Anyhow, I met Margaret's Dad when he came by here to take her home and he's a really nice man. She'd been staying with us, you know."

"Yes, I heard."

"Well, it was a pretty upsetting time for her I mean first you get attacked and then it turns out it was by her mother! But once her Dad arrived everything was okay. Margaret had really been missing her father and he took her straight back to their own home, no hotel this time, so she's settled again.

I know she'll be glad to hear that you're up and about, too. She was worried about you... and worried about you not liking her any more."

"No, really? That's silly, Margaret's not responsible for her mother's actions." Judith thinks about her words and, as usual these past couple of days, her mind immediately travels to what happened with Arnie, and to Lila, and their friendship.

"Beth, have you heard anything about Ms. Morelli?"

"I heard she'll be back at school on Monday but that's all I know."

"Hmmm. Well, you can tell your Dad about this but no one else, okay?" Judith pauses to get Beth's agreement before continuing: "Lila's husband has.. well, he's killed himself. He's dead and Lila is now a widow. Committing suicide is a truly awful thing to do and she's going to be feeling very fragile. I just thought you should know."

"He killed himself? but he's old, I mean if he and Lila were married then he's gotta be like my Dad's age! I thought only teenagers killed themselves?"

"Well we don't know why he did it but..."

"Probably because she said she wasn't coming back, don't you think?"

"Well that's... possible. That would be a more likely reason for a teenage suicide but still... yeah, it could be. Anyhow, I don't want us to dwell on that, but I did think you and your Dad should know. Anyhow, Beth, your Dad might have saved my life, he's a hero."

"I know! I've always known that, though," smiles Beth. "And I'm kinda proud of myself too, see, 'cause I'm the one who made him go round to see you. If he hadn't well... who knows what would have happened?"

"What do you mean?"

"Dad really likes Lila – and I mean *really* likes Lila – so ever since she shut us out he's been moping around. When we found out that she went back to Toronto now instead of waiting until Easter he figured something was wrong or well... I 'm not sure what he thought, but anyhow I told him he should ask you. Do you know why she suddenly went back?"

"I have some ideas but I don't want to speculate. So you suggested your father come round to my place to ask if I knew what was going on with Lila?"

"Yes, that's right. You don't mind, do you?"

"In view of what happened? I'm thrilled he was there. Otherwise, well... yeah I guess it was okay. We do have to look after the men, don't we?"

The two smile at each other as if they are worldly-wise women. Judith finishes her drink and stands to go asking Beth to pass on what they've discussed to her father, including her thanks.

"I'll get your Dad a bottle of something, what type of liquor does he drink?"

"Scotch. Single malt but I think that's expensive so..."

"A bottle of single malt Scotch it is, then. Thanks, Beth. I expect I'll be back at school on Monday so will see you then."

Chapter 34

At 9:00 am Grant meets with the lawyer from the Crown Prosecutor's office to discuss strategy. He is ready well in advance of the 11:00 o'clock appointment when he gets the call about a delay until mid-afternoon. Since he has nothing else scheduled, having planned on being in an interview room, he decides to take a chance on getting hold of John Seely, Andrea's estranged husband.

"Mr. Seely is away from the office but will be picking up messages if you care to leave one?" says John Seely's P.A. Grant's call has been transferred three times to get this far and his renowned patience is wearing thin. Of course he hasn't said he is from the police, the matter only affects Seely indirectly so no point in causing talk, but he isn't willing to wait any longer.

"Yes, thank you, this is in relation to a family matter of Mr. Seely's so please have him contact Detective George Grant–" Seely's assistant interrupts to say she is aware of the incident involving Mrs. Seely and, as instructed, will give Grant Mr. Seely's cell number so he can reach him directly.

Grant thanks her again and makes the call. John Seely invites Grant to come over to his house for lunch saying:

"My cooking skills are pretty much limited to omelettes but if that works for you..."

"That sounds great, yes. I know roughly where your house is but I don't have the exact address."

John Seely gives it to him then mentions that "Margaret's been allowed to return to class but I've kept her home from school this week while things get sorted out. It's not a problem though, I've also spoken very frankly with her because, well... I can't get away with anything else."

"I've met Margaret so yes, I understand."

"Oh you're *that* policeman... Margaret developed quite a crush! Now I'm really looking forward to meeting you Detective Grant!"

Grant is greeted by Margaret on his arrival and dragged through to the kitchen. The house has an ultramodern design and furnishings to match in numerous shades of gray. Grant feels right at home.

They eat a delicious meal and Grant is interested to see how Margaret see-saws between joy at being with her father then glumness when thinking about her mother's situation.

"You and I are probably on different sides of the fence here, Detective. I want Andrea to be sent to a rehab facility to deal with her gambling problem and that means getting her off this assault charge. I know that she'll be incarcerated if convicted but what she really needs is treatment."

"Her addiction isn't a defence–" begins Grant but is interrupted by John Seely saying:

"Agreed, but then we're probably going to dispute the whole assault claim."

"I've seen the victim, I know her, and she most definitely was assaulted."

"Hmm, your knowing her might compromise the impartiality of your involvement in this case, Detective."

Grant sits back and surveys the man, acknowledging his intelligent and ruthless grasp of the point.

"I discussed this with the Crown Prosecutor's Office, just this morning as a matter of fact, and the decision is that since I'm the lead investigator in the Reverend Robert Wilcox murder – which overlaps – then I'll at least do the interview."

John Seely is quiet for a moment as the implications of this new information sink in. He shoots a sideways glance at his daughter who is all ears.

"Margaret, my love–" he starts but is met by the nine-year-old stubbornly shaking her head and refusing to leave the room.

"I don't care what you have to say, Daddy. It doesn't matter. I know all about what Mother did to Ms. Taylor and I know she hated Rev Robbie. Everyone else loved him but she complained and complained that he was too nosey and too sharp—"

"Margaret stop!" insists her father cutting off further comment.

Grant stands saying:

"Don't worry, Mr. Seely. Margaret's comments are hearsay and inadmissible. I wasn't sure how much you knew and well... you're right, we're on opposite sides so I'll get going."

"I don't know whether or not our marriage can be salvaged out of all this but Margaret here needs both her parents and I want both of us to be here for her."

There's a hint of defiance in his tone but Grant simply nods, saying: "Thank you agreeing to see me, sir. And thank you for a very tasty lunch."

Grant checks his phone as soon as he leaves the house but no message yet from Judith. At least there isn't a message from Andrea Seely's lawyer about yet another delay.

Chapter 35

Thursday, February 27, 2020

"Well the verdict's in on Andrea Seely and yup, she's crazy."

"Ahhh, an insanity plea. That's what came out from her psych evaluation?"

"Oh no, that's just my opinion."

Judith gives Grant a swat on the arm saying:

"Stop! this is serious stuff."

He pulls her close for a quick cuddle before continuing.

"No, I mean it. This afternoon? She had everything going her way with her high-priced lawyer, the expensive professional witness, and her well-connected husband, but she flipped out and couldn't or wouldn't stop talking. She was practically foaming at the mouth by the time she finished her tirade.

Actually, I think the lawyer will switch from the addiction defence to dissociative mental disorder, or psychotic break, or whatever the latest version of *temporary insanity* is called these days."

"What happened?"

"Well, we finally get everybody sitting down in the interview room which was like a game of Musical Chairs what with all the shuffling and stalling and nonsense.

I start laying out our case and all of a sudden she starts yelling – shrieking and swearing, actually – that I've got it all wrong. She started spitting out the words so fast it was impossible to

447

understand. It took me half-a-dozen listens of the recording to even get the gist of what she was saying. Let's see, it was:

Rev Robbie was a liar who was trying to defame her because he *knew* she was only *borrowing* the money and that's why she had to kill him. The school accountant – I'm guessing that's you – was trying to threaten her, or maybe blackmail her or extort money, and all over a misunderstanding – I have no idea what that means – and she was only trying to get the proof back when she accidentally killed you, as she thinks.

And let's see... oh yeah, her husband has cut off her allowance, blocked her from the bank accounts, and refuses to give her any money even though she needs money to raise Margaret. Everyone hates her, they're all jealous, oh and my personal fav she's figured out a pattern to the slot machines and if everybody will just leave her alone to do her thing she is going to hit it big and bust the casino."

"Wow. She said a lot."

"And pretty much all in one sentence. The only time she paused was to draw in a deep enough breath to keep going. And she was loud too, because she was struggling to make herself heard over everyone else trying to shut her up."

"What do you think about her using this insanity defence?"

Grant sobers up as he thinks for a moment before replying: "This afternoon I did feel like I was sitting across the table from a crazy woman."

"This confession she made about killing Rev Robbie–"

"Yeah, it's on tape and her lawyer was right beside her, trying to put a lid on it, and the psychiatrist-for-the-defence can be heard talking over her, but she said certainly said the words."

"What do you think will happen to her?"

"I think she'll be spending a few years under psychiatric care and I believe that's the right outcome. If her husband gets his way it will be an expensive, private clinic. If the Crown wins its case she'll be moved to the public healthcare system.

Maybe John Seely will quietly divorce her and relocate with Margaret to a new city, or maybe he still loves Andrea. I couldn't get a read on his feelings about her. Regardless, he is devoted to his daughter so she'll be well taken care of."

"You know Grant, that's two murders I've been peripherally involved with and in both cases the killers were insane, crazy, mentally unfit..."

"Well Judith my love, I think anybody who kills is mentally unfit. I've been in law enforcement for a long time and while I'd advocate for rehabilitation for most crimes, I do believe that some people do need to be locked away for the safety of everyone else."

"Did Andrea Seely have anything to say about where the Fentanyl came from?"

"No, but she knew about it because of something Kyle Danby let slip. Poor guy was trying to get away from her and blurted out that Rev Robbie needed him to witness how much Fentanyl he was locking in the safe. By the way, I'm sure you're right about her pretending to lust after that young man as a distraction."

"So Kyle does know the source of the drug?"

"He says not, and I believe him. I'm pretty sure he has his suspicions but he won't incriminate anyone. Especially now that we can link that Fentanyl to the fatal dose Rev Robbie was given.

It doesn't matter that the person who brought the Fentanyl to The Centre never planned on it being taken away from them and used as a murder weapon but that's what happened so, arguably, they share some culpability."

"That's hardly fair–"

"But it was their deliberate actions that resulted in a murderer getting his/her hands on the deadly drug. You can't help but wonder if Rev Robbie would be dead if the poison hadn't been available.

Anyhow, nobody's going to own up to being the original owner of the Fentanyl now.

Meanwhile, you need to get your rest so that swelling can go down and your wound can heal. Your bruises are just beginning to blossom so you'll have them for a few days. People will probably give me funny looks."

"Beth gave me a funny look when I saw her today."

"Beth? was she at the hospital?"

"No, I detoured over to her place – actually to see her father – when I left the hospital. I knew she'd be home from school but wasn't sure if he'd be home from work. He wasn't, but she was able to answer my question about why he was here on Sunday.

Turns out she told him to come and talk to me. He was anxious about Lila, especially since she changed her plans to go to Toronto now instead of at Eastertime. Luckily for me he listened to Beth and did come over and right in the nick of time.

Grant, Andrea might have kept hitting me when she didn't find this proof she was looking for. That's a scary thought."

"It is, so don't think about it any more."

"But Andrea Seely must really be sick, eh?"

"Judith don't you dare feel sorry for that woman! She stole and when caught she murdered to cover up her crime. She was negligent about her daughter, and she attacked you. She doesn't deserve anyone's pity, least of all yours."

"No, you're right. She killed a very good and worthy man. And, now that I think of it, she was careful enough not to wear perfume when she did so or we'd have smelled it in his poky little office."

"That's true. It definitely was a premeditated killing, and she came to your place with the intention of doing you harm."

"Oh, that reminds me. I asked Beth what her father liked to drink and she said single malt Scotch. I've never been inside a liquor store and I'm really not keen to start now... will you buy this bottle for me? Of course I'll give you the money. I seem to remember my mother saying they only take cash."

"Judith, of course I'll buy the Scotch for Brian Penner and I will definitely pay for it. I'm the one who's grateful for his timely intervention. I've reaped all the benefits!"

"That's very kind of you but honestly I can afford to buy the bottle."

"I'm sure you can but please, let me do this for you."

"Okay, but you've already bought me the most beautiful earrings in the world and... well, you've done so much for me, Grant."

"Oh Judith, there's so much more to come."

Chapter 36

Sunday, March 1, 2020

Judith is grateful for Grant's offer to go with her to meet Lila's plane but she wonders if she wouldn't be better off going on her own even though that would be a challenge.

"She might totally snub me and just walk right by," explains Judith.

"All the more reason for me to come along to comfort you," he replies.

"But maybe the sight of the two of us, together, will make her feel worse?"

"Then I'll wait in the car. Tell Lila that I'm just there as the chauffeur so that the two of you can concentrate on your conversation."

"That actually... that's a good idea. We can sit together and talk without the hassle of figuring out how to get out of the airport again and back here."

"It will give you and Lila a good chance to talk. And, if things don't work out well then, I'll be there for you, Judith."

It's always nice to be welcomed by a familiar face in the crowd. Coming down the escalator Lila spots Judith pacing back and forth while looking around anxiously. It occurs to Lila that her friend might never have been inside an airport before, reminding herself that Judith lives a very restricted, solitary life.

But Lila doesn't feel ready to meet with anyone today, especially not Judith. She's all knotted up inside with painful, conflicting emotions *and I'm just beat*, she thinks to herself. *I don't want to talk at all. Not to anyone.*

Judith turns around and that's when Lila sees the large white bandage covering the top side of her forehead. Both eyes are bruised with one being extremely dark, and her skin looks so pale, her face so pinched. Lila immediately feels concern for her friend wondering what on earth has happened? A car accident? a serious fall? a mugging?

Just then Judith finds Lila and her face lights up with delight. Lila's response comes right from her core and it's an answering joy, realizing that the two of them really do care about each other. She waves and laughs to see Judith bouncing on the balls of her feet in anticipation. They meet in a hug so tight that the next passengers just move around instead of trying to interrupt.

Then both of them are speaking at the same time, interrupting each other:

"Lila! it's so good to see you–"

"It was really nice of you to come pick me up–"

"Grant drove, I've never been to the airport before, but he's told me we can ignore him and just talk to each other."

Judith carries Lila's bag so her friend can get into her outdoor things. Spring hasn't arrived in Calgary yet although the temperatures are ping-ponging between well-below and well-above seasonal averages. There is no chinook warming the air today but at least there's no snow, although that can change quickly.

As soon as they come through the sliding doors Grant pulls up to the curb. He hops out and gives Lila a quick hug before putting her case in the front seat and opening the back door for the women to slide in.

"I'm sorry for your loss, Lila, but it's good to see you back home again," he says.

"Thank you, Grant, and thanks for the ride, too."

"Well, it would be irresponsible of me to let Judith drive while bawling her eyes out so..." He gets back in his seat and drives off just as a traffic warden heads towards them.

Judith sees a forest of signs and is glad she doesn't have to read them while trying to steer the car out of the one-way system. Grant drives confidently so she is able to concentrate on Lila.

The strain of the past days – weeks, actually – show in lines and tension around Lila's eyes and mouth. Judith's own mouth trembles and without thinking a moment further both women collapse amid tears in each other's arms. They sob, hiccup, and laugh at themselves. They stay wrapped up in each other, giggling, apologizing, and mildly arguing, for the whole drive.

"What's with this bandage? what happened to you?"

"I was attacked by Andrea Seely, Margaret's mother, can you believe that?"

"But why?"

"Omigod you don't know... Andrea Seely killed Rev Robbie!"

"No! that BITCH! I could kill her myself. Hey Grant? pretend you didn't hear me say that!"

"Say what, Lila?"

"Why did she kill him? and why would she attack you?"

"Because she thought I knew something – which I didn't – but he did know that she was embezzling money from The Centre."

"She killed a fine man like that over money?"

"Worse, we think she killed him to protect her reputation. Everything I know about Rev Robbie makes me think he would have helped her repay the debt – over time or something – but he'd insist on making the Board aware of the situation, right? as part of her penitence or something. He'd help her but he wouldn't let her get off scot-free."

"No, he definitely wouldn't. He believed in the importance of facing up to mistakes. For Rev Robbie acknowledging and atoning would go hand-in-hand. Wow, this is hard to believe. But her husband is rich, why did she have to steal?"

"Andrea Seely has a gambling problem. She's poured a fortune into slot machines until her husband finally cut off the funds. Now, either she downplayed her problem or he didn't really believe in it, I don't know which, but he thought she would just stop playing once there was no more money. Instead, she stole and then killed to cover up her crime."

"Plus she attacked you–"

"And basically abandoned her daughter, too. Margaret was being left alone a lot – even late at night."

"She was spending a lot of time with the Penners'–"

"It was Brian Penner who save me from her."

"What? Brian?"

"Yeah, he's really got a thing for you, you know." Judith smiles as her friend suddenly gets an evasive look but then returns her stare saying,

"I thought so, and I had to ward him off. I knew my marriage was over, but while I was still legally married I couldn't encourage him any further than the friendship we enjoyed. Really enjoyed, too! But now... everything's on hold right now. I can't even think of–"

"But you are staying here in Edgemont, right?"

"Oh yes, Edgemont is my home now."

Judith squeezes Lila's hand tightly.

"I know you're really tired and, frankly, I'm pretty drained myself so we're going to take you straight home. Before coming to the airport we stopped and picked up a few perishables, you know: milk, eggs, bread, so we'll carry everything inside and then leave you to get some sleep. Are you back at school tomorrow?"

"I'm planning to go."

Grant calls out that he's reached the Edgemont exit from the highway and he needs directions to Lila's place. She starts by giving him her address and he asks:

"Do you a fire station on your street? the only one that takes back hazardous household materials?"

"Yes, do you know it?"

"I've been there. Okay, I know where I'm going now. Carry on, Judith."

"I will. As I was saying, I've got a follow-up visit at the hospital in the morning but this time it should just be a standard check and remove the bandage so I expect I'll be at school for the afternoon. But I'm going to call Pat and let her know that you'll probably be late and I'm 100% certain that will be fine, Lila. You're entitled to bereavement days anyways. So sleep as long as you can."

Tears welled up again in Lila's eyes, this time over the kindness of her friends.

Chapter 37

Monday, March 2, 2020

Judith's hospital visit is a speedy affair so she is back at her desk mid-morning and Lila hasn't arrived yet. Judith checks in with Pat and confirms she feels well enough to return to work.

"Your bruises have faded but one still looks particularly nasty. I see they've removed the dressing."

"Yes, and the swelling has gone down in the back of my head and on Wednesday I can actually wash my hair! because I'll have waited the full ten days by then. What a relief that's going to be. This dry shampoo makes my scalp so itchy!"

"Why not skip the shampoo and wear a headscarf or a cute beret instead? Oh well, it's your decision. The students are pleased to have everyone back as well. They get unsettled when there are *goings-on*. "

"You've got a school full of drama queens, that's why!"

"True enough. They've made you a *Get Well Soon* card and a *Sorry For Your Loss* card for Lila. The whole school has signed them."

"Even Marta?"

"Okay, *almost* the whole school has signed them!" laughs Pat.

Marta Smith is the school's oldest teacher and the years have turned her into a bitter woman filled with spite and malicious gossip. Pat Johnson would love to end her contract but no one can complain about the quality of Marta's teaching.

" I'm so glad Beth Penner has taken Margaret Seely under her wing. Beth has become such a popular girl and everyone likes her so, by extension, they're now all being good with Margaret. Once the story started circulating about her mother, and Rev Robbie and the gambling, she could easily have become a target for bullies."

"On the other hand Margaret has shown that she's a fighter. Literally!"

"Let's hope there's no more of that. I'd like to get through the next four months of this school year without any more incidents or fussing or fighting."

"Amen to that," Judith agrees.

"Although..."

"What?"

"Well, what have you been hearing about this deadly Coronavirus? this Covid-19?"

"That's only a problem in China, right? I mean, at the end of December I read about an article in... let me think.. The Washington Post, I believe, stating that Chinese news agencies had just announced a pneumonia outbreak but there was speculation that it was much more than pneumonia. That is was some sort of respiratory disease, and highly infectious."

"And of course all the cruise ships."

"I heard something but, between Lila and Grant and Rev Robbie's murder, I've been pretty distracted and wrapped up in my own issues. What's the scoop on the cruise ships?"

"One of the Princess cruise ships has been quarantined in Japan for almost a month and they've had some deaths. Other cruise ships have had outbreaks too. In 2017 Mark and I took a Caribbean cruise, remember? and we really enjoyed it, but you are in awfully close proximity with all the other passengers and crew so I can easily understand how a virus could spread quickly."

"I guess, but they've contained it, right?"

"We haven't closed our borders so I suppose it's possible that travellers and returning citizens could bring infection with them... do you recall the SARS scare back about fifteen years ago? I bet Lila remembers it, even though she'd just have been in her teens. It was a big deal in Toronto, a few dozen died and businesses had to close. There were quarantine restrictions and everything."

"I remember now that you've mentioned it, but the whole thing just kind of fizzled out, didn't it? I mean I never heard of them finding a cure but the panicking just stopped."

"Oh I know exactly what you mean, I made the same comment to Mark afterwards and he told me it stopped because of something called 'herd immunity'. I'm sure Lila can explain this better but apparently when this herd immunity happens the disease dies off or something."

"That's a clear enough explanation, Principal Johnson," says Lila smiling from the doorway.

"Lila!" Pat hurries over to give the younger woman a hug. Judith is beaming with everyone being together and she's happy although she can't miss Lila's underlying sadness.

Samira hovers in the doorway announcing she has paperwork for both Judith and Lila to sign so the reunion breaks up and they follow the secretary back to her desk in the front.

Walking back to their respective offices the two women are welcomed with plenty of well-wishing greetings, and given their respective cards.

Chapter 38

The week ends on an unhappy note when Pat calls Judith at home Friday night to say Mark has tested positive for Covid-19 that day, so both he and she are in quarantine. She asks Judith to again step in as Acting Principal until they get the all-clear from Alberta Health Services.

"Is Mark very sick? and do you have it too?"

"Mark said it feels like he's got the 24-hour flu. The only reason he got tested is because the hospital admitted someone who later tested positive so then they tested all personnel – staff and volunteers. I don't feel in the least bit sick but we have to isolate for the ten or fourteen day period – we're waiting to hear back for more information."

"I'll get some groceries for you and any other shopping you need–"

"Thanks, but you can't. We aren't allowed to have contact with anybody. There are some volunteer services with people all fitted up with *Personal Protective Equipment* looking after stuff like groceries and medicines – again, we're waiting for more details – but thanks so much for thinking of us, Judith. I'll definitely let you know what's going on. Luckily I'm the type of shopper who stockpiles when things are on sale so we're well-set for canned, packaged, and frozen foods plus non-food items, too."

"Thank goodness. What a thing to happen! and all because Mark generously volunteers his time to help people who are sick."

"I'm just sorry to stick you with covering my job again so soon after the last time."

"At least there's no murder mystery to solve!"

"That reminds me... I've been meaning to ask how things are going with you and the handsome detective? Now that I've got all this free time I can indulge in a gossip session with you so tell me all... are you in love?"

"Pat! I can't tell you that before I tell him."

"Oooh Judith, you are in love! Why haven't you told him?"

"Because Grant has to say the words first."

Third book in the Village of Edgemont Cozy Mysteries series

A *Sinister Spring*
in Edgemont

Della North

A Sinister Spring in Edgemont

Della North

copyright 2023

publisher Lynda French

cover design by Dezynetek

Chapter 1

Tuesday, April 21, 2020

My life has changed and become so much better this past year, muses Barbie Nichols, getting out of the tub to apply moisturizing lotion. Her reminiscing occurs, as it usually does, while she's admiring her roomy, luxurious bathroom. They've only been in this house for a month and everything about it is still new and delightful to her. Winding down before bedtime she continues thinking back, and feeling grateful for this grand life.

On this day last year Greg injured his wrist at work and I was so worried about losing his income. I only made minimum wage hairdressing and we were already dodging calls from bill collectors. Then two weeks later I won the lottery. Well, I didn't win it all, but a 3-way split on $52 million worked out to be more than 17 million dollars. 17 MILLION DOLLARS! What a windfall, I still can't believe it.

According to the news this Covid-19 pandemic is changing the whole world, but the lottery money is protecting me from that too. It doesn't matter that the salon and the trucking company and the school all had to close, we're financially secure. Barbie savours that phrase, repeating it a couple of times, before settling into bed enjoying her thankfulness and wearing a satisfied smile.

John Seely likes living in Edgemont Village but feels Margaret, his daughter, will have a better chance if they move far away from the area. Edgemont is too small since the family's dirty laundry has become common knowledge. *And it's quite a bit more than just dirty laundry,* he reminds himself.

Properties here never stay on the market for long but even so he is surprised and pleased at how quickly he is able to conclude the sale. A cash offer makes all the difference: no conditions and no financing. The new owner is a local hairdresser who won the lottery.

Barbie Nichols never dreamed that someday she'd live in Edgemont's Executive Estates. Her goal has been moving up from renting the main floor of a bungalow to a mobile home in the Edgemont Trailer Park. Even that dream seemed impossibly out of reach. The lottery win makes such a difference. Everyone knows a win will change their lives but until it happens it's beyond imagination.

Too bad it's caused so much trouble in the family.

News about a lottery winner's tragic end is always featured as a top story. Whether it's because the public suffers from envy or *schadenfreude* the item gets plenty of attention, focusing on the downside of winning. The news anchors seem to gloat over rags-to-riches-to-rags tales, suicides, divorces, and even murders.

For most people winning the lottery is good luck, but although Barbie Nichols herself enjoyed every minute of her new-found wealth it turned out to be a curse. At least she died quickly enough not to have any regrets.

COVID-19 Update: An announcement is made that for the first time in its history there will be no Calgary Stampede Rodeo and Fair in 2020. Not even two World Wars shut down the famous parade. To date COVID-19 has claimed the lives of 68 Albertans and the province is in a state of emergency.

Chapter 2

Grant has come over to Judith's apartment but not for long, he's waiting on the call to handle the investigation into Barbie Nichols' death. Meanwhile she's made coffee and they're drinking it while nibbling on cookies.

"Who, and how, is your new partner?" Judith asks and Grant tells her all he knows about the man, and also gives her his impressions.

Detective First Class Reginald *call me Reg* Osborne, a recent transfer in from the Maritimes, is close to retirement. His age is the only concern Grant feels about his new partner.

Reg is a knowledgeable, even-tempered, affable man. He doesn't smoke, vape, or chew tobacco, and if he drinks there is never a whiff of alcohol sweating out of his system. His wardrobe is unexciting, but he always appears neat and professional-looking. His social life seems to revolve around family get-togethers with his four adult children and their families. He is divorced, and a widower, and a grandfather.

He isn't much of a talker, and doesn't volunteer personal information, but answers fully when asked. Grant and Reg have been partnered for three weeks now and are getting along fine. Reg is comfortable to be around, and he's a steady, easy-going driver which suits Grant who often gets impatient behind the wheel.

Reg explains that he's been learning his way around Edgemont and the surrounding villages adding:

"I like driving, I find it relaxing. And I'm starting to get my bearings. Someone once told me it takes three months to feel at home in a new place but I can tell already that I'm going to like living here."

Grant hasn't discussed retirement with Reg and he tries to sound the man out to get an idea about his plans.

"I've never been to any of the Atlantic provinces but I heard it's beautiful there, a popular destination for tourists and retirees."

"It is, especially tourism. I have no idea how folks will manage now they've closed the provinces down because of this virus."

"Oh right, I heard something about that. Actually, it was an article about someone in the middle of moving house being told they couldn't go into New Brunswick from Nova Scotia, or vice versa? I can't remember the details."

"It's crazy, that whole area is too interconnected to have closed borders."

"I guess the Premiers will just have to work it out – or maybe the Federal Government will get involved? The Maritimes has always been a Liberal stronghold so..."

"That's true. I make it a rule to never discuss politics at work or socially."

Grant took the hint and changed direction: "Whereabouts did you live?"

"Amherst. Pretty as a picture in summer and popular with artists and craftspeople. Lots of market-garden type farming in the community, and of course, great seafood. It's great having the ocean nearby although I find the Atlantic to be cold all year round. I really do not like the winters in Nova Scotia."

Grant huffs a laugh and asks: "Do you really thing the weather will be better in Alberta?"

"I do! Go ahead and laugh, but you'd know what I mean if you ever felt the bone-chilling damp that comes off the water in winter. And even though it doesn't get very cold, I mean -20 is generally the worst, we get huge, really huge, dumps of snow all at once."

"Winters here haven't seemed as cold as when I was a kid, but maybe everybody thinks that? however we usually stay in the high minus-twenties with a couple of weeks of -35 or so every year. February is our coldest month, March is our snowiest, and we have green Christmases fairly often, maybe that's climate change?"

"Minus mid-thirties sure does sound cold but they say it's a dry cold and that makes a difference."

"Yeah, expect to have badly chapped lips your first winter here. But on most days we have beautiful blue skies with tons of sunshine. Our weather always seems to be better than Edmonton's, probably because we're so close to the Rockies."

"Once I get settled in here I plan to do plenty of exploring in the mountains and all these Provincial Parks. I hope to end my days living as an Albertan, but not for some time yet!" Reg chuckles.

After Grant relates that conversation he'd had with Reg Judith comments: "He sounds like a nice man. I never thought Suzanne was a nice woman so I hope you and Reg will work well together."

"I think we will. He's got many years of experience but there's much more to it than *time served*. There's the intelligence necessary to process all the insights picked up along the way. One good thing, though, is that despite his age he doesn't discriminate."

"Oh, now you're discriminating, Grant. I believe that's called ageism–"

Judith doesn't get to finish her gibe before Grant half-wrestles her into a hug saying:

"You know what I mean. Lots of the older cops tell racist and sexist jokes or make assumptions that perpetuate systemic discrimination within the police force."

"Like profiling?"

"No, profiling is different, it's based on facts and statistics. Like insurance companies use when they charge young male drivers higher rates than females."

"Um, just because the insurance companies do the same thing doesn't make it right. Their self-interest is evident and they're all about the bottom line."

"And that's why profiling is only one tool in the policeman's tool-box, and it's fluid because the stats from six or seven years ago no longer apply. Don't get me started on the fairness of that argument, it's based on sound logic and it is flexible when it should be."

Sitting back up straight on the couch and finger-combing her hair back in place Judith announces:

"We'll shelve that discussion for now, then. So what's happening with Barbie Nichols?"

"What have people been saying? and did you know her? What can you tell me about her?"

"Her three daughters attend our school, they were subsidized but now well, now Barbie is the one offering financial help with her lottery winnings which is so nice. Well, it was. There is a fourth daughter, Brenda's twin, but there's something wrong, behavioural problems I think, and she's home-schooled.

There's also a son of Greg Nichols' from his first marriage, so he's Barbie's stepson, but I don't know anything about it except that he's older than the girls."

"Well, yeah," Grant says with a smile.

"Oh! I see what you mean. No, the twins are from Barbie's first... well, not a marriage and I'm not even sure if they were together long enough to qualify as common-law? Hmm, anyhow he's not in the picture. He's dead."

"So both Barbie and Greg Nichols brought children into their marriage and then had two daughters themselves?"

"Yes, that's right. Brenda is in her final year with us so she must be about seventeen. I believe her half-sisters are eight and eleven."

"You get a lot of mixed or I guess the right word is *extended* families nowadays, don't you?"

"We do, and It's fine. Our only concern is that no one has access to the girls in our school unless they're on an approved list. The onus is on the legal guardian to keep us updated but we still send out reminders a few times a year. People change romantic partners quite a bit, Grant."

His smile turns into a grin as pulls her close for a kiss.

"You just keep getting dragged into the big, bad, old world, eh?" he teases fondly.

Judith's upbringing was sheltered to protect the secret of her mother's alcoholism. She never had any close friends until recently, and Grant is her first boyfriend. She thinks the words boyfriend and girlfriend are silly at their age but there's no way she'll refer to him as her lover! Meeting his gaze with these thoughts in her head makes her blush. Grant's eyes sparkle at her but he says:

"Never mind distracting me, woman. I'm on call and I'll have to leave quickly."

Judith just shakes her head but she can't stop smiling. Bringing herself back to the topic at hand she explains:

"You know, some of the parents get quite huffy if we use the wrong names. I've found that most of the mothers keep the same surname as their children, at least in their dealings with the school, but not everyone. In fact, Barbie Nichols' oldest, Brenda, is called Nikovics and her two youngest are called Nichols."

"I'm just going to make a note of that," says Grant, typing into his phone. "Can you spell it for me?"

Judith does so explaining that Nikovics was Barbie Nichols' maiden name. She has no idea what the father of the girls is, or was, called.

"Same initials, that's convenient."

"I don't imagine the Nikovics ever had much, if any, engraved or monogrammed belongings. Still you're right when it comes to initialing stuff."

"So the family is what.. Eastern European?"

"Just Barbie's father. Her mother's an Irishwoman, Moira, and I've met her a few times recently. She's raised her granddaughters and they've now all moved here to live together with Barbie and her second family."

"That's very odd, isn't it?"

"Oh I forgot to mention! The father of Barbie's twins was an abuser. Shortly after the twins were born she dumped them on her mother and disappeared. He became violent with Moira and she had him arrested. He went to jail for awhile but when he came out he did the exact same thing again except he managed to escape custody and disappeared into the Kananaskis backcountry. He was pursued and there was a manhunt. It was on the news."

"I remember some of that. The hunt for him turned into a search-and-rescue and then a body retrieval because he was presumed to have drowned. He had a European name as well, but I don't recall it. I'll have to get someone to dig up the file for me. They never did find his body, right?"

"Oh, I don't know. But that would explain... hmm, that would explain why Moira Nikovics kept the girls instead of returning them to Barbie when she resurfaced."

"Where was she?"

"Apparently working cash jobs in the National Parks. Travelling from Banff to Lake Louise to Yoho, waitressing or housekeeping, stuff like that. She's a qualified hairdresser too. That's the work she was doing when her younger girls got enrolled in the school."

"And the family qualified for your subsidy?"

"Yes, because Greg Nichols works in a warehouse and drives a local delivery truck so he doesn't have a big paycheque, and Barbie just made minimum wage hairdressing. She worked with Dana Lezinsky, do you remember her?"

"Holly's mother, of course. I wonder if I'll be interviewing her again this time."

"What exactly is *this time* all about, Grant?" All I heard is that Barbie Nichols is dead and she was killed while asleep in her own bed."

"I don't know a lot more except that it's definitely murder. She was smothered with a pillow and died of asphyxiation. The pillow was still over her face, no effort made to hide it."

"Suffocated while she slept! That's horrible. She would have fought back, right?"

"There's a lot we don't know. If someone was pressing down with both hands and their body weight it would take about four minutes to fatally cut off the air supply. If Barbie Nichols was deeply asleep when the attack began she might not have struggled that much, and if she'd taken a sleeping pill or had a couple of drinks before bed, well... That information will all come to light after the autopsy."

The graphic description of Barbie's death has brought tears to Judith's eyes. Grant pulls her into a tight embrace and apologizes.

"No, no Grant. You can always tell me, in fact I want you to. I want you to know that you can confide in me, or use me as a sounding-board. I'm only crying because Barbie was such a nice woman. She really was. Always joking – even when she was complaining about something she'd still make you laugh. And she laughed a lot, too. Her life was difficult and I remember when I heard about her lottery win my first thought was *it couldn't have happened to a more deserving person.*"

Judith cries a little more before moving out of the comfort of Grant's arms. Wiping her eyes she asks if he wants another coffee or maybe a bite to eat?

"No, thanks hon. Those shortbread cookies were delicious. I can't believe I ate so many, did you bake them?"

"Don't be silly," Judith laughs. "Why would I bake when I can buy real Walkers Shortbread, imported straight from Scotland? I doubt if I could make them for what Costco charges. Do you know how much a pound of butter costs? and a batch of shortbread must take at least one pound."

"I'm joking!" he laughs. "I saw you open the package, remember?"

The sad moment has passed just as Grant's phone rings and he has to leave. Before he heads out Judith pulls him back to the kitchen where she's now placed a bar of soap by the sink, reminding him:

"Don't forget the new rule about disinfecting your hands when entering and leaving any place."

Brian really rocks the casual look of faded jeans and sweatshirt, thinks Lila looking up at the tall man walking beside her. They're on a short hike, one of the few activities still allowed these days.

Brian Penner has dark red hair, blue eyes, and the strong physique of a construction worker. She's very aware of his presence, especially since he's hovering over her in a protective manner. A recent widow, Lila is feeling fragile yet she's enjoying Brian's companionship and is having trouble reconciling those feelings.

She'd fallen out of love with her husband but would have stayed in her marriage if he'd behaved differently. The manner of his death destroyed any residual feeling she had left, but there are other losses and she is just learning how to cope with that.

Brian's wife had died ten years ago of cancer. His teenage daughter, Beth, had been encouraging him to find someone for awhile now but it wasn't until he met Lila Morelli that his interest was piqued.

Lila, with her bubbly good nature and gurgling laugh. Her pretty face and petite figure. Typical of Lila's personality that she adds streaks of pink or purple or blue to her lovely blonde curls the way other women will paint their fingernails to match their outfit. It's no surprise that Lila has caught Brian Penner's eye, she's the kind of person people notice – both men and women.

"Lila honey I know it's way, way too soon for me to say anything to you, but I just want to be sure that you understand I'm here ready and waiting for whenever you're ready. I hope that won't take too long, but whatever time you need is yours. I'm not going anywhere."

Lila was enjoying the low rumble of Brian's deep voice before registering his words and when she does realize what he's saying she draws in her breath with a gasp. He immediately puts his arm around her shoulders but holds it there lightly, gentling and soothing her.

"I'm sorry if I seem pushy, Lila. I just want to be sure you know how I feel. But you do know, right? You knew before you even went back to Toronto, didn't you?"

"I suspected as much, Brian and I'm flattered, truly, but–"

He touches his finger to her lips signalling her to hush, she doesn't need to say anything now. The look of concern leaves her face and is replaced by a sweet smile. It takes all of Brian's restraint to hold back from kissing those lovely lips.

"We'd better hurry and catch Beth up before we lose sight of her."

"Well we certainly won't lose her in the crowd!" quips Brian.

COVID-19 Update: Rules and regulations are being discussed and recommended by Federal, Provincial, and City governments and Health Authorities. There's so much uncertainty, and _two weeks to flatten the curve_ is now at five weeks and counting.

Chapter 3

Wednesday, April 22, 2020

"What the hell, Gary? what are you doing in my purse?" demands Brenda finding her stepbrother digging into her bag. She turns to Glenda saying: "You better check your money too, Gee, Gary might have stolen it."

The sisters have come into Brenda's room only to find their stepbrother, older by just a few years, already there.

"Hey, it's important. I gotta get out of here. The police will think I killed your Mom."

"Did you?"

"What? no way! what's the matter with you?"

"Then why are you running?"

"Duh, I'm the stepson who has no job, always broke... of course they're going to suspect me."

"They're going to suspect us all and I had thirty bucks in my wallet Gary, so give it back," says Glenda with her hand stuck out.

"Shit, no, I need it. I've really gotta go."

"Gary...:"

"Okay listen, your Mom and I had a big fight. Another one. She and my Dad fought about something and when he took off she was still pissed and took it out on me."

"About what?"

"The same stuff, as usual, I have to get a job or go to school, either/
or, otherwise I have to find someplace else to live. I mean, how the
fu, uh, hell am I going to do that with no money? So I asked if she'd
stake me some funds upfront, just to get me settled like, and she
laughed her head off. I mean, seriously, she's rolling in it. Would it
kill her to give..."

The three teenagers give each other scared looks.

"Yeah, good one. You're such a loser, Gary. Gimme back my money
now."

"No, I told you, I gotta go, they'll be after me."

"Oh you're so dramatic, Gary. You just react without thinking."

"Do not! Listen, how does this sound *oh yeah Officer, I was home
at the time but I didn't do anything to Barbie.* They'll take one look
at me and won't bother looking at anyone else. I mean I really was
here but that's no alibi. I spent almost every minute in my room
and didn't see nobody or talk to anybody–"

"I heard you. I heard your horrible music playing, very loudly."

"That doesn't prove anything, though."

"Well, I also heard you thumping about. I don't know why you're
always wearing your boots in the house but I heard you going
stomp, stomp, stomp as usual."

Smirking, her twin joins the conversation to ask: "Were you
dancing, Gary?"

"Just you shut up Glenda," the young man replies with a heavy
frown on his red face.

Ignoring him she turns to Brenda asking: "Have you ever seen him dance? He struts around like he thinks he's Mick Jagger. He even does the pursed-up lips thing," and the two of them start laughing.

"Geez, Gary, couldn't you imitate someone from our generation at least?"

"Yeah, instead of like... our grandparents?"

"Aw, to hell with you two," he snarls and, as Brenda had pointed out, stalks off with his uncommonly heavy tread.

"Hey! get back here, loser! You've still got our money."

After the twins successfully recover their cash they return to Brenda's bedroom since it's tidy, to talk out their thoughts.

"I fought with Mom too, you know."

"Oh we're all quarrelling with each other because of being cooped up together so much. Can't even go to the mall."

"No, I mean we fought-fought."

"Are you crazy? with that impaired driving issue hanging over your head you should be acting like the perfect kid until Mom agrees to hire a good lawyer for you."

"No thanks, one perfect kid in this family is enough."

Sighing deeply Brenda asks "What was it about this time?"

"She refuses to use my new name, my name of choice."

"Okay, I'll bite, what's your new name, Gee?"

"Well, it's not Gee anymore. It's Enda, and I want that to be your name too."

"Oh as if... Enda? what kind of a name is that? It's a made-up name and it's stupid."

"Actually it's an Irish name but that's not why I chose it. *Enda* will make it easier for all the lazy pricks around here to not have to say those two consonants distinguishing between you and me. I mean, how much simpler to just say Enda for either of us? We all know that if the voice is complaining, yelling, nagging, or criticizing then it's talking to me, and if the voice is all sweetness and light then it's directed at you."

"Gee, I'm not going to call you Enda and I'm not going to answer if you call me that, either. I sometimes think you're mental."

"Funny, that's what Mom said. Then she told me to shut up, that she chose our names and I'm stuck with mine until I'm eighteen. Then I can change my name legally if I want to. That's what she said. So I said, why Glenda? My father's name wasn't Glen. And she goes, you're a twin and I wanted two names that match. Brenda and Glenda. I was also thinking Tessie and Jessie but those would actually be Theresa and Jessica. This way the name I chose can't be turned into something else by someone else – not even an ungrateful brat."

"So I said that was effing lame and she–"

"No way!"

"I did! but I did say *effing* not, you know."

"And she grounded you, right?"

"No, actually I expected that, but she was already in a bad mood and just told me to go away 'cause she wasn't in the mood for my nonsense."

"Why? I mean, no one's ever in the mood for your crap, but you said she was already in a bad mood so what was that all about?"

"Do you know, I'm not sure... I mean Mom has been fighting with everybody. Gary, me, Greg, oh and she and Gran had a real blow-out too."

"Not again!"

"Oh and this was something. You know, Gran and Mom can really push each other's buttons... well, they could. Gran was so pissed off, I've never seen her like that. And whatever it was they were fighting about had something to do with us."

"What did you hear?"

"It's what I *didn't* hear... they both shut up as soon as they saw me. Just stopped mid-sentence, mid-argument, just stopped talking – didn't even pretend or try to cover up – just glared at me until I left."

"Yeah, I guess that was kind of obvious. Maybe it was just about you, not us."

"Dream on. They don't see you and I as anything but *us, we*'re just *the twins*. We're lucky we got separate bedrooms."

"I would have insisted, I mean honestly Gee you're such a slob. Like is there anything actually hanging in any of your closets?"

Glenda pulls open the door of first one of Brenda's closets and then the other. The clothes hang neatly, shoes line up on the floor, and miscellaneous items are handily stacked on the top shelf. She gives her head a shake and narrows her eyes at her sister, *the perfect twin*.

Brenda ignores that look continuing:

"Oh Gee, what are we going to do now? You know Gran has been wanting us to move back East, she fought with Mom about it all week, and after this, well. But I don't want to go. I know that's where Gran has her life and all her friends and stuff, and it wasn't fair of Mom to just disrupt things and move us all here, but I love it here. I want to stay."

"I hate it here."

"You hate it everywhere."

"True."

"So you might as well hate it here as anywhere else, right?"

"We're seventeen, Bee, I don't think we're going to get a say in the matter."

Grant has visited the victim's house before, in fact he'd had lunch there with the previous owner, and remembers it had an ultra-modern design. On that occasion he'd only seen the front entry and the kitchen but today he went to the upper floor to Barbie Nichols bedroom.

The architect probably considers the staircase a masterpiece but to Grant it's a monstrosity. In a house decorated in shades of gray, with a few black and white accents, the modular curving stairs in a fire-engine red acrylic, is an eyesore. *Damned difficult to walk on, too!* he thinks as he carefully navigates the slippery steps that seem to float they look so insubstantial.

He safely reaches the landing where he notices that access to the second floor up is via a normal set of stairs. That's where the three older kids have their rooms – each with their own en suite bath – and a communal den, according to the constable who's given him the layout of the place.

The hi-tech colour scheme extends to the halls and rooms but Barbie Nichols had imprinted her own style on the master bedroom. Half-a-dozen brightly coloured cushions featuring whimsical cats are scattered on the floor, knocked off of the bed. The bedspread is a violet and aqua mix that shouldn't work but somehow does. It's vibrant, rather than the blinding.

Flowers on the dressers, clothes tossed over a *chaise longue*, a selection of wigs draped over an antique-looking cheval standing mirror rebel against the sleek lines of the glossy black furniture. Lots of electronics too: an Alexa, desktop computer, iPad, wall-mounted flat-screen TV, and a Bang & Olufsen sound system that makes Grant drool.

Two open doors lead to a walk-in closet, rather sparsely occupied, and a full-size 4-piece bathroom. Traces of powder sprinkled on the floor give off a strong smell of honeysuckle from an overly generous application rather than spillage.

A shelf runs around half the bathtub and it's laden with fancy-shaped containers, colourful bottles, many candles, and more flowers. Obviously Barbie Nichols spent a fair bit of time relaxing in the oversized tub. A plush bathmat matches equally fluffy towels folded over a heated rail. A lot of luxury for the late occupant.

Grant considers that sobering thought as he turns to inspect the bed where the body was found.

COVID-19 Update: Evidence now shows the virus isn't as lethal as first believed. Antibody testing indicates about five times more people have been infected but they haven't reported any symptoms. This means the Infected Fatality Rate (IFR) is well below 1%, similar to the IFR of influenza, flu, in a bad year.

Chapter 4

Thursday, April 23, 2020

Grant and Reg are meeting Dr. Alexiy in his office, which Grant vastly prefers to the examining room itself, but the smells linger in every room of the whole morgue. The man arrives still wearing gloves but pulling off his face mask. He examines the article for a moment before muttering obscurely *good thing I'm used to wearing one of these.*

The autopsy report Grant is reading doesn't add any new information – just confirmation of the medical examiner's findings during the postmortem. Full analysis of stomach contents and tox screening are still to come but there is no indication of heavy enough drinking or drugging to render the victim unconscious before the attack.

Grant had already come to that conclusion when he visited the victim's home. Her body had already been removed but he'd seen the rumpled bedclothes at the scene. Studying the many photographs he saw that the bed sheets had been pulled right up to the victim's chin, trapping her arms, and it was only the rumpling of the covers where her hands and feet had lain underneath that showed her struggle.

The doctor opined that the murderer had held the pillow over the victim's face, pressing down with both arms and torso, to still any sounds and to contain the thrashing about. Grant shuddered at the horror of those four minutes or so that she'd suffered through, and from the look on Reg's face he felt the same revulsion.

"For a short time it's possible to breathe through the fabric of the pillow, there's always some air trapped inside, but eventually suffocation occurs," the pathologist explains.

"It would take a fair bit of strength wouldn't it? To hold down steadily while a fit adult woman is fighting against you?"

"If she was asleep when the attack began half the damage would have been done by time she woke enough to realize what was happening. So yes, it would take physical strength but maybe not as much as you'd think. Even more so, it would take great mental stamina to follow through once the struggling began. Off the record I would say the killer felt real anger, even hatred, towards Ms. Nichols."

"A crime of impulse and opportunity?"

Closing the file on his desk the man looks over his glasses saying, with a bit of a smirk:

"That's your job to figure out, Detectives."

"So what's your thinking about suspects?" Reg glances over at Grant from behind the wheel. He's in his comfort zone, relaxed and ready to talk, to speculate and hypothesize.

"Well, for starters there's the family. Within the 24-hour time period up to her death Barbie Nichols had quarrelled with her husband, her stepson, her–"

"Sorry to interrupt, but remind of who's who."

"Right. Husband Greg Nichols, stepson Gary Nichols, her daughter Glenda Nikovics, the *difficult* twin, and her mother,

Moira Nikovics. And I just found out about a sister of Barbie's, Bonnie something-or-other – even Moira doesn't know her latest married name – who is flaky, apparently."

"Why would Barbie Nichols' mother and her daughter have the same surname?"

"Because Barbie Nichols wasn't married to the twins' father. Barbie's maiden name was Nikovics so her daughters were assigned that name, the same name as their grandmother who raised them."

"All one big, happy, extended family?"

"No, apparently Barbie dumped them on her mother when they were only infants and she disappeared for years. According to Moira Nikovics, and so far we have no corroboration about this, she and her daughter had always been in touch, but Barbie was never in touch with her children. Apparently she was terrified of their father, and remained paranoid about him for years."

"And he isn't suspect number one because...?"

"He's dead."

"Sure about that?"

"No, but the authorities declared him dead nine or ten years ago, after he'd been missing for the requisite seven years."

"Damn, might have guessed that solution was too easy."

"Oh I'm a big believer in *Occam's Razor*, Reg, but so far there are no clear and likely answers, yet."

"Still, a dangerous abuser disappears and then his wife, or rather the mother of his children, turns up murdered. Unfortunately that's all too common an occurrence. What were the circumstances of the man's disappearance and presumed dying?"

"He's believed to have died of drowning due to hypothermia. He'd been in prison, got released, re-offended right away but escaped custody on his return to jail and fled into the wilderness. They tracked him for some distance but the trail grew cold – no pun intended! – at a lake.

The water in our mountain lakes is really cold all year round because it's fed by glaciers and snow-pack. The experts reckon about an hour tops and then hypothermia sets in. Even the best swimmers can't save themselves when their muscles can't move their arms or legs.

The Underwater Search Team, a group of divers – civilians who volunteer – searched but the lake in question, I looked this up, is about 65 metres deep and 21 kilometres long. So even with sonar images it's a difficult place to search.

In the last sighting of... hang on, I made a note of his name, yeah it's Anton Czerny spelled C-Z-E-R-N-Y and I'm probably not saying it right, anyhow the last sighting of Czerny was him in a wooded area on a trail that comes out at this lake and that was like sixteen years ago."

"And you said he'd been in prison so chances are if he did manage to safely escape from that area he would have re-offended sometime in those years and his records would have popped up."

"Another good reason for the presumption of death."

Reg is driving them back to their station and the two men are silent for the rest of the trip, thinking over the inconvenient fact of Anton Czerny's death.

I'm going to spare you the details, they're on the gruesome side," says Grant. He and Judith are sitting together on her couch and he had his arm around her shoulders but has shifted position to take a sip of coffee.

"Gruesome. That's a word you don't hear much these days. Same as ghastly," Judith replies.

"My grandparents kept a few books for me and my sisters at their place and there was one that I loved called *Beastly Boys and Ghastly Girls*, but I don't remember anything about it other than the name. I think it was funny rhymes."

"I never heard of it."

"No, it was an older book and probably no longer carried in the library by time you were learning to read."

"So, to get back to *gruesome*, you realize my imagination is conjuring up horrible images so you might as well just tell me."

"I get what you're saying it's just... well, you knew the woman and you liked her. It's hard to hear facts about her dying without feeling emotional. But, you're right. The truth might not be as bad as whatever it is you're imagining.

It was a bloodless death, of course, and the body had already been removed by the time the locals called me in but the scene showed where the sheets and duvet had been pulled aside in the struggle and it was a very telling scene. I can't explain it any better than that."

"Poignant?"

"Hmm, there's another of those old-fashioned words but yeah, that fits what I was thinking and feeling."

"Thank you for sharing that with me, Grant. I hope you know you can say anything to me, I'm not a fragile woman. I am naive about a lot of things, I know, but I can learn and I'm willing to do so. You've already taught me so much," Judith says with a shy smile.

"We aren't talking about criminal investigation any more, are we?" Grant answers with a smile of his own.

"Well... I just wanted to be sure you knew you could confide. Apparently it's the distancing and lack of communication that causes most police marriages to fail. You'd think it would be the hours but.. Oh! what's wrong, Grant?"

Grant stood up abruptly leaving Judith looking at him in surprise. He's run his hands through his hair, ruining the normally impeccable styling. He's frowning and looks anxious.

"Nothing's wrong, not wrong, but well... marriage, failed marriages, that's quite a leap. Anyhow, Judith I've got to get going. I shouldn't have ducked out today at all, but I did want to see you. I'll try to see you again tomorrow. I guess you're pretty bored stuck home on your own so much, eh?"

Judith frowns back at Grant trying to understand why his conversation is jumping all over the place. Obviously he needs to get going now so she simply stands up to walk him to the door.

"No jacket, right?"

"No, when I left I thought it was going to be nice out, real spring weather, you know? Oh well, it's coming. If I don't get to see you tomorrow I'll call," He gives her a chaste close-lipped kiss but she slips her hand behind his neck and makes him kiss her properly.

"I'm glad you stopped by," she says when they pull apart. He leans in to rest his forehead against hers and they just stand like that a moment, each thinking their own thoughts. He kisses her cheek, her nose, and her lips then says goodbye and leaves.

Judith feels puzzled by Grant's behaviour but shrugs it off as she locks up for the night.

COVID-19 Update: The few shops that are open, like hardware stores selling essential goods, will not take back any product for any reason. Once the item is in your home it's yours. The utility companies won't come inside either. They leave coils of cable wire at your front door and tell you to just keep what you don't use.

Chapter 5

The neighbourhood of *McMansions,* large homes with only a couple of metres of lawn separating them, soon becomes streets full of real mansions. Huge homes set well-back from the road. Most are fenced-in and some have ornate gates closing the world out. What they don't have are sidewalks, only a shoulder of fine gravel or in some cases, just a boulevard of brown grass between the property and the road.

Moira is the only person out walking today, same as yesterday and the day before that. No one walks here, they don't even jog. No infants in prams or toddlers in strollers, no seniors being pushed in a wheelchair, and no dogs on leashes. There isn't even a bus stop for the hired help to walk to and from. No one walking... except Moira.

With so many people stuck at home nowadays you'd think they'd enjoy getting out for a breath of fresh air, change of scene, stretch their legs... but no, thinks Moira. Certainly no one else is outside smoking. She hates living here.

Her life in Alberta has always been an unhappy memory for Moira. Widowed too young from a husband she'd deeply loved, raising Barbie and Bonnie on far too little money, and finally the painful violence of Barbie's boyfriend Anton.

She'd been happy and relieved to leave it all behind when she moved with her granddaughters to Toronto. There she'd built up a colourful life with her boutique in Yorkville and her lovely home on Avenue Road. A home with character, not like these soulless tributes to wealth.

Barbie winning the lottery is the worst thing that could have happened as far as Moira is concerned. It's caused fights in the family plus jealousy, bitterness, and resentment. It also resulted in Barbie demanding, after all these years, that her daughters be returned to live with their mother. Of course Moira has to come too, after all she's the one who raised the twins, and they are her girls.

As per their regulations the Lottery people demand photos of the winner. Barbie has rushed them all out here in order to play the part of a good and generous daughter, wife, and mother with her loving family gathered round. It was fun and so exciting at first – winning the lottery!

Moira knows how her daughter's family struggled with debt and now there'll be no more worries about *how will we afford it if the car breaks down?* or scrimping at the grocery store while waiting for payday, or dodging the creditors phone-calls.

Then there were the shocking number of begging requests – from individuals, charities, schools, churches – Moira has truly been amazed at the vast number of people willing to put pen to paper to ask for money from a stranger.

Plenty of sob stories but also many feeling that Barbie should *do the right thing* and share some of her wealth with them. Pleas soon became angry demands followed by vile hate mail and finally the threats of kidnap and of killing.

Once again Barbie's picture will be splashed all over the news but no grins from the family this time – they'll all look sad or grim because of her death.

Is it actually possible that the lottery win enraged some psycho to the point that he'd murder her daughter? The way their world has been turned upside down makes it possible for Moira to believe anything.

Anyone following Reg will think he's just driving aimlessly but in fact the man is alert to his surroundings while noticing and storing up details in his memory banks. He finds he does his best thinking behind the wheel but still, subconsciously, his cop's eye is always looking.

He drives past all of the schools and playgrounds, around the perimeters of the parking lots at the two malls, through the drop-off centre for recycling and donations, and over to The Centre which is bustling with activity as usual. He finishes his cruise with a drive through the trailer park where there had been all that trouble back in February.

In his mind he is considering the possibility that Barbie Nichols' killer isn't a member of her family. What is the likelihood of her murder stemming from a robbery or kidnapping gone wrong? Whenever there's a lot of money there's a lot to lose. The lowlifes are always on the prowl for opportunities. And of course there are always psychos on the loose.

Someone could easily have seen Barbie's picture on the TV news and decided either she was sending him a secret message, or that God/Satan/Spacemen had ordered him to kill her.

The do-gooders on the far left did a lot of damage when they *emancipated* the mentally ill from their incarceration in asylums, and the penny-pinchers on the right were only too happy to shut down the facilities and cross off that expense from the balance-sheet. The result? a lot of people who should be receiving care are wandering the streets without their medication.

When he and Grant discussed the suspect list they considered that the killer might have slain the wrong victim. Barbie Nichols has only lived in this house for a month. From the sounds of it the woman who lived there before was a piece of work, but it's an unlikely supposition. They put that possibility at the very bottom of their list.

The fact that Barbie Nichols has been murdered in her own home and in her own bed argues against a stranger killing. Family was at hand with no excuse required for being there. And use of a pillow makes the crime seem impulsive, but full of hate. A difficult way to die and a very difficult way to kill but no one can *push your buttons* like your nearest and dearest.

So yeah, the family members will be under a microscope and while the lottery money is probably the motive they have to keep their minds open to other possibilities. Maybe Barbie Nichols would have died even if she'd stayed poor?

Grant is having a hard time getting a handle on Greg Nichols. For a grieving widower he seems more angry than sad. That's fairly common, the survivor blaming the victim for being in the wrong place or doing the wrong thing or just for leaving them behind. But something's different, off, with Nichols.

Greg Nichols is such an average sort of man. No doubt he's accepted as *one of the guys* at work or the bar, but looking at him right now Grant is struck by the lack of distinguishing features, the bland personality, the physical description that could match most of the population's white men of Greg's particular age. Everyone talks about the vibrancy of Barbie Nichols so this marriage must be a classic example of *opposites attract*.

Or maybe it's just that I don't like the man, thinks Grant, then amends that thought to: m*aybe I'm the problem.*

"Okay, Mr. Nichols let me confirm what you've said so far. You and your wife fought–"

"No, it was just an argument."

"But you stayed out all night, right?"

"Well, I was pissed off and then I got pissed. I wouldn't drive like that."

"No, I expect someone who drives truck for a living has to be especially careful."

"You'd be surprised," mutters Greg Nichols.

"You said that the two of you started fi– uh, quarrelling during dinner and by time you left the house it would have been between 8:00 and 9:00."

"Yeah, something like that. We usually eat at 6:30, 7:00 but now that Barbie isn't out working any more sometimes we eat earlier. It all depends. Oh..." he stops for a moment as the realization hits him again. Grant sees tears in the man's eyes but he gets himself under control.

"So what did you argue over?"

"The usual, money. You know, when we were broke we argued about money – about having no money – all the time so you'd think that now, well everything would be great, right? Not! Seventeen *fricking* million dollars, it's just too much. It changes things, it changes people."

"You're saying that winning the money changed your wife?"

"Oh yeah. Barbie really changed. She'd never been the penny-pinching type, she was always up for a good time and would joke about champagne taste on a beer budget and then she'd roar out a laugh and say *damn good thing I like my beer*. But once she got all this money, it's like it was water running through her fingers."

"You mean she started splashing out," Grant winced at the unintended pun but fortunately Greg Nichols didn't notice.

"Yes and no. She wasn't a pushover, nobody's sob story was going to pry cash out Barbie, but she spent on big stuff. Like the house. She just went out and bought it, never said a word to me. And she paid cash so it all happened really fast."

"You don't like the house?"

"It's not what I planned on. See, I thought we'd get an acreage and build ourselves a nice place. Not too close to anybody, and with great scenic views. Maybe a log cabin, maybe river rock, or cedar you know, something natural."

"And instead you got an ultra-modern home full of granite and marble."

"A house, Detective. Not a home."

"Your wife didn't share the dream of peaceful, rustic living?"

"She said she wasn't about to camp out in a place that was under construction because it would take years to get it all done just right and she couldn't be bothered with the mess and the inconvenience."

"Why would you have to camp out?"

"We had to move out of our rental. You wouldn't believe how in your face people get when you have a big win. They act like you *have* to share it with them, that you should just be handing out money to anybody who asks. The other two tenants, the neighbours, the local church, the daycare, everybody wants a piece.

We ended up moving into a hotel. Barbie's mother got us a suite under her name so we could hide out. Barbie was mad it wasn't the best hotel in Calgary but it's still a really good, really expensive place. It's where the visiting NHL teams stay but I didn't see any hockey players while we were there."

"I see. You ended your lease where you were renting, moved into a hotel, and then into the Seely home in the Executive Estates. I know the home, I've been there a couple of times."

"So you know what I mean when I say it's not very homey at all. Have you seen that eyesore of a staircase? And the Executive Estates, well... let's just say that's not really our style.

We even had a moving company even though we didn't take much. Barbie bought most of the furniture that was in the house and me and my son could easily have packed up the rest in a U-Haul but no way, says Barbie. I told her she shouldn't worry about what the neighbours think because it's not like they're ever going to be friends with us. She didn't like me saying that. But it's true. We don't fit in."

"And there's a whole houseful of you too, isn't there?"

"Yeah, it's me and Barbie..uh, well. My son Gary, from my first marriage, our two girls, Shawna and Sheila, then there's Barbie's teenage daughters, the twins, Brenda and Glenda, and Barbie's mother Moira who raised the twins. So yeah, there were eight of us and we still have tons of room. The family we bought from only had two people, a man and his young girl. Well, I expect there was a wife but she didn't live there any more for some reason."

Grant is non-committal on the subject of Andrea Seely. He still bears her a grudge.

"Can you tell me specifically what the argument was about, please," Grant's words are more of a demand than a question.

"It was a stupid thing, well isn't that always the way? I can't believe those were the last words we'll ever speak to each other but I guess you hear plenty of people say that, eh? Lots of regrets in life."

Seeing Grant's impatient look Greg Nichols hurries to get his story back on track.

"It was actually over something that started before we moved to the new place. See I wanted to get some fitted shelving in for the new garage but I didn't know the exact measurements and I didn't feel comfortable coming over while the Seely's were still living here and I was kinda bitching about it and Barbie's like *we'll be there in a week, you can wait until then* but I couldn't. The building store was having a sale that was about to end and I wanted to catch it. 40%, that's a really good savings. But Barbie just laughed at me saying *it's nothing, get it through your head that we don't have to be nickel-and-dimed any more, we've got money* and I said *you've got the money, not me.*

Well, that turned into our usual argument with her wanting everything to be different and me having trouble letting go. I mean, I did have to quit my job. I didn't want to but everybody started acting funny. We couldn't even go out for drinks after work without someone going on about how lucky I was and how about a loan. It was easy enough for me to say *that's Barbie's money, it's not mine to give* but then, especially after a few drinks, guys would get belligerent and tell me I'm whipped and I need to let her know who's boss. Some wiseass said I should just cuff her one, to teach her a lesson like, and I'm *ha! yeah no, I really don't want to get charged with assault.* Besides, Barbie woulda killed me!"

They both stop and think about the unfortunate choice of words, then Grant motions for him to continue. They've already had this conversation, or parts of it, a few times but with each repetition new things come out and Nichols' body language and tone of voice are nuanced. Grant feels he is getting a fairly accurate picture of how day-to-day life has evolved for the lottery winners. For a start, it sounds like everyone now has way too much time on their hands.

"At dinner on Tuesday I mentioned how much more I'd had to spend on the shelving for the garage since I missed the sale and Barbie finally asked what I wanted the shelves for. I explained I needed space to put all my gear for working on the car since I couldn't do it in the warehouse at work any more 'cause of no longer working there, and she's like *you can't work on your car in our garage, there's probably something against doing stuff like that in the Homeowners Association rules.* Then I'm saying *I'll be damned if I'm taking my pick-up to some shop to get an oil change. No way am I paying for something like that, something I've always done myself because it's easy to do.* And she got all huffy about it saying *no, things are different now and we got to act different, too.* So, that's it in a nutshell. That's the kind of stuff we would argue about. Really stupid, I know but there it is."

"We're back to you leaving between 8:00 and 9:00 and going for a drink."

"I drove around a bit first. I really didn't want to see any of the guys, not when Barbie and me had been fighting. Plus they always expect me to pick up the tab when we're out and I can do that, I mean I can afford it now, but that's not the point. It's them just figuring they don't even have to ask, and ordering Jack Daniels, too instead of draft beer like they'd be doing on their own dime. I don't know, it's just... well, as I said, things have changed."

Grant gets up and moves around the interview room. He is finding it hard to be patient with Greg Nichols' rambling account. Grant knows he shouldn't be so impatient, the man is grieving his wife's death after all. And it isn't just a death, it's a murder. Lately though, Grant finds he's easily irritated.

Stretching his legs seems to help and when he sits back down his demeanour is much more relaxed. Greg Nichols has watched the detective anxiously, somehow sensing his annoyance without knowing what's caused it. Suspecting it might him delaying telling his story he hurries to explain:

"So I drove into Calgary and I just stayed on the Ring Road which brought me down to the southwest quadrant. I was in a mostly residential area, not much in the way of taverns, when I spotted the sign for the Indian Casino. I knew I could get a drink in the Hotel part for sure. So I go in and it's a nice place and I have a couple and get talking to some guys at the bar. They don't know me, they don't know anything about the money, we're just regular guys shootin' the shit, like how it should be. Anyhooo next thing I know is me and my new friends have gone over to the casino side."

"Do you have any idea what time it was then?"

"It was after twelve, just a little bit after. I know because one of the guys said he had to get up early for work next morning and it was Cinderella time."

"So you went into the casino, what did you do next?"

"Just kinda hung out. I'm not much of a gambler and nobody was waving around wads a cash to play with or I would have watched him play. I know one of the guys left to go home and another said he was going to play some slots. I just walked around looking at the people and the games and I ended up in the Poker Room.

I know how to play poker but I'm not very good at it. I bought some chips and lasted for awhile. No idea how long but I know I had two beers. When I lost all my chips I went and sat on one of the couches, planning to rest a bit before driving home and next thing I know some guy I've never seen before is waking me up and saying it's time for the free breakfast."

"Right, it's a 24-hour poker room," comments Grant.

"Yeah, and a real nice place, too," adds Greg Nichols.

COVID-19 Update: The closure of movie theatres, live events, pubs and bars, casinos, bingos, etc... means many people are turning to online alternatives like streaming TV and movie channels which might impact entertainment venues even after re-opening.

Chapter 6

Brian is flipping through the offerings on Netflix while Lila snuggles back into the sofa, comfortable and content. She's nibbling on popcorn and warns him that she'll have the bowl finished before he even picks out a movie to watch.

"Then I'll just have to make some more," he answers with a smile.

"I've heard that this microwave popcorn isn't good for you," Lila remarks.

"Actually it's not the popcorn, it's the bag. It's some stuff they put on it or in it. Something that causes a chemical reaction when it's nuked," explains Beth.

She's standing in the doorway sipping on some frothy concoction she's made with their fancy coffee machine that produces lattes and cappuccinos. Probably other types of coffee too but Lila has never touched anything in the Penner kitchen. In her opinion that would be making herself at bit too cozy in their home.

"What do you feel like watching, Beth?"

The girl takes a step back saying:

"Oh, I'm not watching TV with you two, I just came for a drink. I'm going online to find some friends to game with, not sure what I'm in the mood for yet."

Lila comments: "I guess with the lockdown everyone's having to resort to socializing this way."

"Beth always did so it's nothing new to her. Honey you won't be *in the way* if you join us, you know."

"Oh Dad, you and Lila might want to talk or something–"

"Beth, stop trying to be tactful. You know how I feel about Lila, and she and I have already talked it over. I've agreed to hold back until Lila is ready for the next step. In the meantime we're really good friends who enjoy having you with us."

"That's right, Beth. Never feel like *three's a crowd* or anything like that. I enjoy being here with both of you."

"Well thanks... but I really do want to get together with my friends tonight. By the way, the series *The Blacklist* is good."

"Oh Judith mentioned that. Grant told her about it and she's totally hooked. Lots of action and twists and turns."

"I thought you wanted to watch a movie?"

"Movie or TV show, I'm good."

"Oh well definitely a series, that way you'll have to come back to see the rest!"

"Yeah, just don't you be watching it without me or I'll make you watch the episodes all over again and you can't say a word about what's going to happen."

"Oh I'll totally be giving a running commentary like *oh this part is soooo good* and *you really need to pay attention to what he's saying here* you know, stuff like that."

"I will shove a handful of popcorn in your mouth to shut you up!" Lila threatens him with the popcorn bowl laughingly. Brian takes it from her and grabbing her wrists pulls her up against his chest and settles the two of them in a cozy embrace.

"There, I can hold onto your arms this way and I've still got one hand for the remote. And I've got the popcorn, too!"

He finds *The Blacklist* on the screen and they proceed to watch, sitting easily together, neither noticing when Beth slips out of the room.

After the first episode Brian asks Lila what she thinks about the show.

"I like it so far, and usually it takes me about three episodes before I can get into a series."

"Yeah, I know what you mean. Okay, ready to watch another?"

"Sure, if you hand over the popcorn."

"Ugh, hang on, I placed it out of reach because I couldn't stop eating it."

"It is good, eh? Extra butter flavour."

"And I've got to watch night-time snacking or I'll get a *Dad bod*."

Lila gently prods his waistline saying:

"I don't think you've got anything to worry about yet, Brian. I can feel your six-pack."

"Oh you'll have something to worry about if you keep poking at me like that..."

"Stop it. No seriously, do you have to work out a lot or something? Doesn't your job keep you fit?"

"It does, but I'm getting older and since I can't go to gyms right now I've got to keep an eye on my calorie intake. Nowadays I have to choose between enjoying a tasty snack, like a bowl of ice cream, or relaxing with a shot or two of Crown Royal."

"Whiskey doesn't have calories does it? I thought mix was the problem and you wouldn't add pop to Crown Royal."

"No of course not, it's perfect for sipping and savouring. But it still has calories. I suppose you have one of those super-fast metabolisms and never have to worry?"

"Of course I have to worry, I'm Italian! I live on pasta and rich sauces. Very little sugary stuff though so that helps."

"And the fact that you're ten or twelve years younger than me doesn't hurt either!"

"You keep talking about getting old Brian, what's brought this on?"

"Impatience, mostly. I always wanted to have a bigger family but after Mandy – Amanda – died, well it didn't seem like I'd get the chance. But now..."

"You would want a baby now? You'd be willing to live with diaper changes, feedings in the wee hours, teething, terrible twos... you've already *been there, done that,* would you really want to go through it again?"

"Sure, I mean you'd be the one doing all the work–" He tries to keep a straight face as he says this which Lila sees through, but she keeps up the pretense telling him he's full of macho crap.

"I am, it's true. I'd love to keep you at home barefoot and pregnant."

"I'd love to be pregnant. I've wanted to have a family of my own for so long now."

"I can help you with that," says Brian with a leer.

"Never mind waggling your eyebrows at me, mister!"

"What can I say? I'm a very focused guy. I enjoy a drink, but I don't do drugs or gamble or chase women or overindulge in anything. Really my only vice is that I'm driven and ambitious. Not to make a lot of money but to achieve my goals, to have the life I've envisioned. And I'd love to have children with you, Lila."

His expression is serious and his gaze probing as he looks into her eyes. She stares back and they both enjoy a wordless communication of promise for the future.

"And Beth has told me often enough that she can't wait to be a big sister."

"She's a lovely girl, Brian."

"I know and I'm so lucky. Whenever I think about how I almost lost her—"

Lila hears the emotion in his voice and leaning in gives him a closed-mouth kiss on the lips and a hug. Again they share a moment full of unspoken feelings.

COVID-19 Update: Travel agents and airlines are dealing with ever-changing rules for every arrival and every destination point. Canadians can get very cheap flights to Europe but on return have to quarantine. Policies established at the end of March have changed several times but violators can still face up to six months in prison.

Chapter 7

Judith is relieved to get Pat's phone call. She didn't hear back from Grant after he left and not a word all weekend, either. He's been a bit withdrawn and distant lately. Judith hopes he hasn't caught the virus.

Pat wants to discuss the province-wide lockdown. Edgemont School for Girls was made to close, same as all charter and public schools, by the government on March 16th.

"You're not out of the house, driving or anything are you?"

"Pat I never talk on the phone when I'm driving. Actually though, you'll probably laugh, but I'm luxuriating in a bubble-bath of all things. I mean, who ever had time for this before?"

"Judith I actually baked bread! First time in years and years, in fact long enough for me to forget that when the yeast blends with the water I get all woozy and have to lie down unless I hold my breath while stirring. Anyhow, back to our plans for the school–"

"First though, how are you feeling now? You and Mark are the only people I know who have actually had Covid-19."

"I've fully recovered, but Mark's still a bit wonky. He got it worse than I did, and now we're wondering if he might have that long-haul Covid condition."

"I haven't heard of that, what is it?"

"It seems quite a few people who had the disease and recovered still have lingering effects. The symptoms range through extreme shortness of breath, tiredness, overall weakness, basically an inability to function the way they used to even though they're over the virus.

Even when we had it we both felt mostly okay, but then after a week Mark's temperature suddenly skyrocketed. I called the 8-1-1 Healthline and they said to take him to the hospital but there's new rules about that. You get to the hospital and then you phone when you arrive, they gave me the number to a direct line, and wait in the car in the parking lot for instructions. It felt so strange, like we were in some sci-fi pandemic movie or something.

Anyhow, we did what they said and as soon as I called a doctor came right out, all masked and gloved up, and he examined Mark in the car. He told us he wouldn't be admitting Mark because he believed the fever would break that night so it was better – healthier – not to go into the hospital. But if Mark's temperature didn't drop we were to come back again next day. Well, the doctor was right because at some time in the wee hours Mark's temperature dropped down to normal so he avoided the hospital and respirators and intubation and all that horrid stuff."

"But he's still feeling some side-effects?"

"He just doesn't have any stamina. He used to be on the go all the time but now he has to keep taking breaks to catch his breath and rest up. It's been over a month and he still hasn't shaken this frailty."

"Oh, I can't picture Mark like that."

"I know, it's not like him at all. I tease him that he's far more restful to be around now but honestly? I hate to see him this way."

"Does being Black make a difference in the effects of the disease?"

"It might, but nobody knows anything for sure."

"I'm really sorry to hear this Pat. What's the prognosis, what are the doctors saying?"

"Not much. Again, it's all too new. Mark will probably end up being a test case or something. They're learning more about the disease every day and knowledge is being pooled in an international collaboration which is good to know. Johns Hopkins has an interactive map online tracking known cases throughout the world. We check it at least once a day, it's very informative."

"Well tell him I hope he's back to 100% soon."

"I will do so. Meanwhile, we need to discuss the situation at the school."

Judith gives the hot water tap a turn with her foot. She's thinking she should have soothing baths more often.

"Yes! it's unprecedented and the news from both the school board and the province changes daily and they certainly don't seem to be in sync. Parents need to know what's going on."

"Oh I know, I'm hearing from them and from our Trustees. It's frustrating not to have answers. However, what I want to say, Judith, is that I will continue as is until things get sorted and settled but then I'm stepping down. I've decided to retire and am recommending that you take my place."

That news makes Judith sit up so abruptly a bit of sudsy water splashes over the side of the tub but she doesn't even notice.

"What? You're leaving?"

"After getting sick with the virus, and all the worry that that entailed, Mark and I realized it's time to make some changes. As they say *YOLO: You Only Live Once* and we're not getting any younger. Oh listen to me, I'm full of cliches but I guess I'm feeling a bit awkward about this conversation. Not about you," she hastens to add, "You are the perfect choice as my successor and I'm sure the Board will agree, but just talking about retirement well...

Actually I've been thinking about it for some time and I finally decided I need to set a date and put this in motion. So, when the new school year starts I'll have my feet up sipping sangria or some fruity drink with an umbrella stuck in the glass enjoying the discounted holiday rates of the off season."

"I'm not sure if I want your job, Pat. I mean, Principal? that's a big step."

"Judith nobody really wants the job – the prestige, yes, I can certainly see Marta Smith wanting that – but the actual job of dealing with students, parents, boards, government, budgets, isn't exactly a barrel of laughs."

"You're not selling it well, you know!"

"Ha! no, but you know what I mean. It's not a glamourous job, despite the title, but you need a change, Judith. You're an excellent Bursar but you've settled into that position and it's time you took on a new challenge. You have the brains and you're not a pushover and that's what's needed to do this job."

"But I'm not qualified as a teacher–"

"You don't have to be for our type of school and besides, we have teachers with less university education than you have."

"Sure, but mine's in accounting."

"And that's an excellent basis for a leadership role. There are too many starry-eyed individuals who think they can just throw money at a problem. Not true! and you know that. You're a sensible, level-headed, intelligent and tough..."

"Oh cool, so when I apply and they ask for my qualifications I just say what? that *I don't suffer fools gladly* and that's my strength and my weakness?"

Pat lets loose with her booming rollicking laugh replying: "Yeah, that pretty much says it all, that's perfect!"

COVID 19 Update: Police are ticketing people for violating COVID-19 protocols while in public, and citizen journalists posting video clips of these interactions have turned sentiment again law enforcement. Homicides, particularly shootings, have increased and domestic violence calls are way up.

Chapter 8

Monday, April 27, 2020

Brian Penner lifts up his hard hat to wipe the sweat off his forehead. They've put in a busy morning's work. The cool air on his head feels great so he takes the helmet right off and tilts his face up. The temperatures are still cooler than normal for this time of the year but the warmth of the sun is a blessing. After drawing in a couple of deep breaths he opens his eyes to see the new guy watching with a half-smile.

Brian heads over to chat with the man, Andy he'd said his name was, to tell him he's doing a great job. This is a pleasant surprise because Brian very rarely resorts to picking up day labour from Calgary's *Cash Corner*. Lately though the pressures of this virus, causing illness and fear of infection, have negatively impacted the available workforce. Understandably Brian's client has been pushing to complete the project before everything gets shut down altogether.

Andy looks to be Brian's age, early forties, but the men hiring themselves out by the day usually live a rough existence and are often much younger than their appearance. Andy is a tall man with long limbs and a big man's build except he isn't filled out and his clothes hang loosely. But he wants to work and is healthy and strong enough to keep pace with Brian's crew. Of course his men aren't being friendly towards the newcomer. Andy wandered off on his own when they broke for lunch and no one called him over to join them or offered to share their food.

"Andy," calls Brian, walking towards the man, "I can use you again tomorrow if you're available?" Andy nods *sure* and Brian gestures to him to follow. They get in Brian's pick-up and drive a couple of blocks to a 7-11 where Brian tells Andy to *get a sandwich or hotdog or something* while he grabs coffees and a dozen bottles of water to take back. When his employee shakes his head Brian is firm saying:

"I'm offering to pay for your lunch because I need you to be able to work. If you're going to be coming back tomorrow ask the hostel or shelter where you're sleeping at to pack you a meal. I can sign a voucher or whatever you need."

Andy doesn't smile but he ducks his head in a quick nod then studies every offering in the snack selection before choosing roast beef and Swiss cheese. Brian is relieved Andy hasn't picked an egg salad sandwich because the odour he carries into the truck is bad enough without adding the strong smell of eggs and mayo.

If Andy does show up tomorrow, he thinks to himself, *I'll hire him for the rest of the week. Assuming he doesn't take today's pay and overindulge, that is.*

"Sorry I didn't get back to you last night, hon. Probably just as well 'cause I wasn't in the best of moods anyhow."

"Last night? I've been expecting to hear from you since Thursday, Grant. But nothing.

"Judith–"

"Is that why you've been avoiding me lately, Grant? because of what you're doing in your job?"

"No, it's not–"

"Oh, I see. So then it *is* a personal issue, hmm? Yeah, I've heard about this sort of thing."

"What are you talking about? I'm not avoiding–"

"Really? and here I thought couples got together – or at least spoke to one another – on weekends. Especially since they don't usually see each other during the week."

"STOP INTERRUPTING ME!"

"Ah, I'm an interruption am I? No worries."

Call ended. Grant stares at his phone wondering what just happened.

Judith isn't sure herself. She didn't even get a chance to tell Grant about Pat's proposal. Sitting in her office at the school she suddenly bursts into tears.

That startles her out of the peculiar mood she's been in. Judith draws a deep shuddering breath and manages to stop crying. She quickly wipes away the evidence but gets up to close the door anyhow. She needs to verbalize and doesn't want anyone to hear her talking out loud to herself.

"I can't act this way, I need to get to the bottom of this – whatever it is." Still standing by the door she starts to pace around the room but immediately starts counting her steps and that distracts her thoughts. "Dammit, I need to get outside."

It's been a cool April this year with temperatures in the low teens but the forecast is better for the week ahead. Judith hasn't put her coat away in the staffroom because she only planned on a quick visit to the school to go through the halls opening doors to check that everything looks okay. She can't concentrate on doing that until after she gets her head clear so she bundles up again and heads outside. There's no one to see or hear her marching around the wet grass on the field quietly muttering her thoughts.

"It's no use pretending everything's okay or normal or fine. It's not. It's got to have something to do with the sex, or maybe this is typical of the dynamics of men and women? I've heard of men pulling back when they start feeling things too deeply and saying they get frightened. I always thought that was one of those excuses that sound good but are meaningless. But what do I know?

The first time we made love, my first time ever, is a blur and mostly unremembered. For a couple of days I'd been expecting that we'd *do the deed* soon, but it didn't happen, and then the next night again it didn't happen, but when it finally did it was spontaneous, completely unplanned. I'd worried over stuff like *who undresses first?* but that wasn't even an issue. I was already in bed wearing a nightie, and it wasn't night time it was morning.

Grant had insisted on watching over me my first night home from the hospital. Like a gentleman he slept on the couch but when he came into my bedroom to check on me next day I just reached out my arms to him and we consummated our... hmm, less than marriage, but more than friendship. Our liaison. And that's pretty much all I recall, other than we made each other happy.

Lovemaking for our second time is a memory I'll never forget. Nothing hazy about that connection, not at all. Grant took charge of everything first by undressing me and lying down with me out on the bed, then setting the pace of our caresses and directing our um... foreplay. He used his body in ways that teased and tormented me in well, extraordinary ways, until I realized that his pale blue eyes weren't icy at all but instead flamed with blue fire. He showed me both gentleness and passion and throughout it all I was bathed in the comfort of how deeply he cared.

I'm having trouble reconciling the man he was then with the man he is now. In the space of a few weeks he's changed, or at least his feelings towards me have changed. I can feel him withdrawing from me and being evasive in our conversations. Is this what people mean by over-familiarity? moving on when there's no more *thrill of the chase?* I didn't feel like I was being used then, but I sure feel like I'm being discarded now.

I can't get Grant to tell me what's going on, but maybe Lila can give me some insights? When I go back inside I'll call her."

Judith is also enjoying the warmth of the sun on her skin. It lightens her mood and she realizes she has to call Grant as well to apologize for hanging up on him. With a sigh she heads back to the school to finish her chores and make her phone calls.

Judith isn't able to reach Lila on the phone but she sends a text asking her friend to call when she gets a chance.

Instead, Lila has dropped in for a rare visit. Lila never invites anyone to come to her place because she's very conscientious about carrying Covid germs to her er elderly landlady. However as she said, *this is an in-person conversation and I've been looking forward to having it.*

"I know you're a private person, Judith, and lovemaking is the most private act but do you want to talk about it?"

"Oh yes! First of all it was a wonderful experience. Grant is very good, well I have no one to compare him to, but as far as I can tell he does everything right."

"Oooh, I like the sound of that!" Lila teases.

"The first time was good but the second time, oh my! it was great."

The two women collapse in giggles.

"I was just thinking about this earlier," says Judith. Her smile is huge and it's obvious she's enjoying a happy memory in the privacy of her own thoughts.

"That's all I'm going to get out of you, isn't it?"

"Yeah, 'fraid so. I'm very happy but..."

"Uh-oh, why is there a *but?*"

"Because the last couple of days Grant seems to be, I don't know how to describe it – and maybe it's all in my head – but he *seems* to be pulling away from me."

"What do you mean, exactly? Give me an example."

"Okay, well he's a pretty reserved guy but once we got intimate it felt like he was always reaching out and touching my arm or stroking my hair, and kissing me a lot, but now it feels like he's avoiding any physical contact."

"Hmm, could it just be he's really wrapped up in this new case he's involved in?"

"That's what I wondered. I mean, he is very intense when he's focused on something and I guess, maybe, I'm just a bit resentful that his single-minded focus isn't on me. Oh, listen to me I sound like a spoilt child!"

"No, Judith. You're just a woman who is *finally* indulging and enjoying her first sexual relationship. You want him all to yourself right now and that's understandable. I'm really happy for you, hon."

"Thanks, Lila."

"Unfortunately though..."

"Yes I know, and when I think of poor Barbie Nichols, I just can't believe it."

"Have you spoken to him about it?"

"Not really... he did phone but I don't know, I was just in a mood, I guess, because I was snapping at him, wouldn't give him a chance to talk and then I hung up on him. I need to call him back."

"Well, yeah you do."

"I know, I know. I did send a text saying I was sorry and I'd phone later. Lila I'm too old for this nonsense."

Lila just laughed and said that her parents and her grandparents *still* go through *this nonsense.* It's all about being human and being in love.

"So how are things going with you and Brian? You've been seeing him a fair bit, eh?"

"Yes, we have, but just as friends. "

Judith snorts out a laugh and that makes Lila laugh too.

"Seriously, I think things will develop but we're going slow right now, I'm still feeling bruised by... well, you know."

"Yeah, I know. But Brian's friendship helps, right?"

"It does, it really does. Beth, too. I really like being in their company. We watch movies, chit-chat a lot, have a meal, I'm giving her some basic cooking lessons, that sort of thing."

"Wow, if you're sharing family recipes then things are heating up!"

"Oh stop, I'm just showing her my Nonna's way of making spaghetti sauce because it's too expensive to keep buying jars of the stuff."

"I don't know... sounds pretty serious to me," Judith teases.

"If it gets serious you'll be the first to know. Anyhow, I've stayed too long so I've got to go now. It's been good seeing you face-to-face. Keep me posted and I'll do the same."

"Actually, call me later on when you've got some time to chat, okay? It's nothing ominous but I have news I'd like to talk over with you. Today or tomorrow."

"I'm having dinner with Brian and Beth but I'm intrigued! I'll call you tonight for sure, but it might be late if that's okay?"

"Totally fine. It's not like either of us has to get up and go to work in the morning."

Brian Penner is enjoying peaceful contentment watching Lila teach Beth a safe way to quickly chop vegetables. The realization strikes him that it's been a long, long time since he felt this way. He'll be happier if he can claim Lila as his girlfriend soon-to-be wife but he accepts that only time will resolve that situation. Meanwhile he should savour what he has and he does.

Lila is such an attractive woman inside and out. Her personality is vibrant, she has a pretty face and a sexy figure, and her heart is huge.

She has a great sense of humour, too, thinks Brian. He's a few years older and Lila told him with a perfectly straight face that she appreciates him making his move while he's still healthy enough for her to believe he isn't just after her for her nurse's knowledge of gerontology. He quickly looked up the word on his phone then told her she's a sassy brat who should be spanked. Beth then assured Lila that her father had never punished her like that. The face he makes behind Beth's back implies he has different intentions towards Lila who sticks out her tongue at him when Beth isn't looking. Brat indeed!

After they've eaten dinner Beth is excused from kitchen clean-up so she can complete her online homework assignment. Chatting while they work Brian tells Lila about Andy, his new day labourer.

"I'd guesstimate he's in his late thirties or early forties and I don't know what caused his downfall, but he's a good worker. I hope he stays clean and sober tonight and is ready for another shift tomorrow."

"Clean and sober?"

"Sometimes people talk about their troubles but usually only when they figure they've got the problem beat. Or if they've accepted that it will never be beat and they need help to abstain forever."

"Oh! I wonder what's happening with AA meetings? I guess they'll just have to limit the number of attendees?"

"I heard there are some online meetings through Zoom or something."

"It seems sad that for some people the advice about *all things moderation* just doesn't apply."

"No, like your friend Judith, she doesn't drink at all, right?"

"That's true, but Judith doesn't have a problem with it, she's never drank. She can't even bear the smell of booze, but that's because her mother was a drunk. I guess I should pretty that up and say *alcoholic*."

"Pretty it up?"

"Well, I have to confess I'm not convinced alcoholism is a disease."

"But you're a nurse!"

"And that means I know what disease looks like. Disease is children born with their mother's syphilis, it's thirty-five-year-old men shockingly keeling over from heart attacks, it's young people battling cancer, and old folks suffering from dementia. Drug addiction, alcoholism, and STDs are largely preventable."

"What about AIDs?"

"Same thing. Infected people know they have it and need to take precautions and to warn their partners about the risk. Same with herpes and other STDs."

"But some people got AIDs from blood transfusions so–"

Lila interrupts saying: "But not these days. Yes, tragically people were given blood from infected donors but blood is thoroughly screened now."

"That's good to know. I don't know anyone that that happened to personally, but I know of a family whose child with leukemia got AIDs from a blood transfusion and they were hounded out of their small town. Everyone sympathized, but no one wanted their kids in the same classroom or swimming pool. Everyone was afraid they would get sick, too."

"Ugh, I can understand both points of view. AIDS seemed to come on the scene so quickly and so dangerously because so many people dismissed it as *only a homosexual thing,* but that was like 40-plus years ago. Brian, our conversation has certainly come a long way from your new employee, and that's probably my fault. If there's a side-road or a byway you can count on me to be racing down it."

"Good to know, I'll keep that in mind when you start to ramble."

"God yes! otherwise I forget the original topic," she laughs.

She's been handing him the dirty dishes and approves the way he's placing them to maximum effect in the dishwasher.

"Well talking reveals so much. I now know that you're pretty inflexible when it comes to self-induced or preventable trauma."

"True, but I'm not unsympathetic, I'm just a bit more ruthless in prioritizing. For example, I was a smoker for years and if I got lung cancer I would know that my actions contributed – probably even caused – the disease. But that doesn't mean I think I, or any other smoker or ex-smoker, *deserves* to get lung cancer. I'm so thankful that I was able to finally quit and I understand the difficulty because I found it really hard. But if I had to choose between a lifetime non-smoker versus a smoker to get a lung transplant I'd go with the non-smoker."

"Isn't that kind of like playing God?"

"No, the issue isn't between young or old, mentally-challenged or brilliant student, male or female, or anything like that, it's between victim of circumstance and victim of risk-taking."

"Wow, I'm seeing a new side of you, Lila."

"Uh-oh, I hope I'm not disappointing you."

"No, not at all. I was just thinking you have like the biggest heart but you're practical with it. I think that's a great way to be."

"I think that compliment deserves a kiss," she says, leaning in. Brian is a wonderful kisser: tender, considerate, and with just the right amount of passion. They kiss for a couple of minutes before Lila pulls back with a smile saying,

"Okay, let's get back to your new employee."

"Who?"

"Ha-ha. Andy."

"Oh yeah him... actually he's not an employee he's just casual labour. A good worker, as I said, but a man doesn't reach his age without some history. What his story is remains to be seen and I might never know. If he doesn't volunteer I sure can't ask."

"Aren't you curious?"

"Sure, but not enough to intrude."

Lila gives an exaggerated sigh saying: "Men!"

Brian leans in close saying:

"I'm perfectly willing to satisfy your curiosity about *this* man–" but Lila interrupts him with a kiss that he returns with passion.

Grant interviews Glenda but the girl is sullen and unresponsive. Big sighs between each answer and then it's only to give a *yes, no,* or *I don't know* response. Glenda is under eighteen so Moira is present, sitting quietly, but eventually she loses patience and tells her granddaughter to *smarten up and just admit she was home all night* .

"I know, I saw you here. You didn't go out."

Grant notices a mere flicker of a glance exchanged between the two. Is Moira protecting Glenda? or giving herself an alibi? More questioning and Moira admits she's the one who went out that night.

"Okay I was out, but just briefly, just 30 minutes... 45 tops, while I walked to the store and then came straight back."

"You walked at night? On a Friday night?"

Moira gives him an amused look as she continues saying:

"No one's going to bother me. At my age the boys looking for trouble aren't interested, and it's obvious I'm not worth mugging."

"But still, it's risky to be out walking on your own at night."

"She has every right to go walking at any time of day. Women shouldn't have to live by a curfew just because men can't control themselves!" bursts out Glenda, showing some animation for the first time. "If it isn't safe for her it's because you're not doing your job."

Neither Grant nor Reg have an easy answer to that accusation but before they can even try Moira responds:

"Well I don't drive so I don't have any choice, do I?"

Choosing to ignore Glenda's outburst Grant asks:

"Where did you go to shop?"

"Just the 7-11, I needed cigarettes. Barbie decided we should all quit smoking and bought those nicotine puffers instead of getting me my smokes. I told her I have no intention of quitting, I *like* smoking, but of course she argued and there's no changing her mind once she's set on something so I just went out and bought them myself."

"So you and your daughter had an argument that evening, and later that night she was killed."

"What are you trying to say!" shouts Glenda on her feet with her fists clenched.

"We're just asking questions, Miss, and we're asking everyone connected to your mother. Your grandmother is answering helpfully but not you. Why is that? Why aren't you trying to help us?" Reg sounds annoyed which surprises Grant. In the short time he's known the older man he's always found him to be easy-going, calm, and professional. He wonders if this is an interrogative tactic?

"I don't have to help you. Stop picking on my gran and stop picking on me!"

"Detective Grant I think we should take Miss Nikovics to the station where we can ask our questions in a formal interview."

"Officer I really don't think that's necessary—"

"I'm sorry Mrs Nikovics, but I think it is. Glenda is being obstructive and her answers are evasive. Maybe she'll take the questioning seriously when she's under caution and on tape and video. We would like you to come with us, too, as Glenda's legal guardian." Both men have stood during Reg's statement and are now waiting on Glenda, who is looking defiant, and Moira who is exasperated with her granddaughter.

"You'll have to drive us then, she's only got her Learner's Permit, well had it... anyhow, she can't drive at night."

Grant suppresses a smile when he replies:

"Yes, we were planning to drive you. And, of course, we'll bring you back home afterwards."

Reg has started the police car while Grant gets the two women settled in the back seat. He is just getting in himself when a Smart Car with an Uber sticker draws up alongside them on the driveway. Brenda Nikovics jumps out crying:

"What's going on? Where are you going?" and turning to Grant asks: "Where are you taking them? and why?"

Grant explains that Glenda is going to the police station to answer questions and gets in the passenger seat, closing the door in Brenda's shocked face. He sees her rush back to the Uber and get in it again, obviously directing the driver to *follow that car!*

It's late when Lila phones Judith and they've barely gotten past their *Hellos* when Judith says:

"Oh, hang on. There's my buzzer. I can't imagine who it could be at this time of night, I'm not expecting Grant but... hold on while I check," Judith presses the *Talk* button on her intercom saying

"Hello? who is it?" then she presses *Listen* and hears a young, desperate-sounding voice in tears crying:

"Oh Miss Taylor, I really need your help. It's Brenda Nikovics and something terrible has happened with my sister, Glenda. Can I talk to you?"

"Yes of course, I'm coming down now," answers Judith, grabbing her keys and hurrying out the door. "Did you hear all that, Lila? I don't think you've met Brenda, she only just came to the school when she moved into her mother's new home. I know you know about her mother being found murdered–"

"Yes, but now it sounds like the problem is with the sister. Judith, deal with this and call me back as soon as you can."

They disconnect just as Judith comes into the lobby to let the distraught teenager inside. She flings herself into Judith's arms and is awkwardly held while she sobs. Judith leads the girl back up the stairs to her place but only long enough to grab her coat and purse. As they head back down the stairs to the parking garage Judith instructs Brenda to tell her everything.

"The police have arrested Glenda, my twin, for killing Mom but she didn't do it and you have to help me convince them."

"Me? but I don't even know Glenda and–"

"No, but you solved cases before, I heard all about it at school, and you know the policeman in charge. We don't know anybody, Miss Taylor, you're my only hope!"

COVID 19 Update: The province recommends restricting your household to family members only, but if essential visitors need to come in they should stay no more than 15 minutes. Both indoor and outdoor gatherings are only allowed limited attendance. Violations can result in a $1,000 fine.

Chapter 9

Tuesday, April 28, 2020

"I don't mind a long conversation on the phone," begins Lila, "but I'd love to get out of this place for a couple of hours. What are we allowed to do?"

"We can pick-up coffees or food to-go so long as we stay back six feet and use sanitizer when we enter and when we leave."

"I could go for a pizza, what about you?"

"Sounds good, but where will we eat it outside? We're not allowed to sit at picnic tables or on park benches and all the playgrounds are shut down."

"The school! We can go sit on the steps round back. They don't face the road so no one will see us. They won't even see our cars in the staff lot."

"That will work. I'll grab the pizza, you get coffee and doughnuts."

Division of labour sorted, the women, happy to get out of their homes for a while, complete their tasks and meet up as planned.

Judith keeps a blanket in her trunk – along with other breakdown-in-cold-weather supplies – so she lays that on the steps and they spread out the food.

"This is delicious pizza," says Lila around a mouthful.

Judith laughs and answers: "You had a great idea."

They eat their lunch and finish with a coffee and dessert.

"I want to start with my story, mine and Pat's, and then I'll tell you what happened with Brenda."

"Last night's text was reassuring, especially now that there's no urgency."

"Yeah, sorry about not calling but I was just too tired to talk any more."

"Never worry about sending me a text!" Lila chuckles, "Believe me, it's my preference."

"Anyhow the original conversation I wanted to have with you like 24-hours ago? is that Pat is going to retire and she wants to nominate me as her replacement."

"Wow, I'm really surprised about Pat retiring, but not wow that she's choosing you as her successor. That makes perfect sense. I mean, you're Acting Head now and you've handled that job several times in the past. Even during a murder and kidnapping investigation, so that's a no-brainer. But why is she retiring?"

"I think them getting sick with Covid was like a wake-up call or something? Like a *this is it, this is all you get for a life so make the most of it* kind of thing."

"Is she even 65 yet?"

"I don't think so, but I'm not sure. Mark is past 65, I remember when he had his retirement party–"

"You went?"

"God no, all those strangers? Not a chance."

"That's the Judith I know–"

"And that's the problem," Judith interrupts in an anxious tone of voice. "I'm not sure I should even consider applying for the position of Principal. It's such a people-oriented job and dealing with people is not my forte."

"How do you know?"

Judith gives Lila a quizzical look as if to say *that's a stupid question.*

"I'm serious. You've never really given yourself a chance. I'm not blaming you, avoiding and even hiding away from people because of mother's problem—"

"Alcoholism."

"Yeah, okay, your mother's alcoholism was a fact of life for you growing up, but now? who knows what you can do?"

"But I don't even like people and I can't talk to them."

"Of course you can! I watched you handle a difficult school assembly and a parents' meeting and both times you were *calm, cool, and collected.* Judith you just need the confidence to spread your wings."

"I didn't have a choice about either of those things, it just had to be done."

"And you stepped up to do it and you did it well. You have natural poise and an air of authority. Besides, you know Marta Smith will want the position so you have to take it. I can't possibly have her as my boss."

"Eww, you're right. I'd report to her as well. Oh, she'll really hate it if I move up from Acting to Permanent Principal. Hey, if I get the job maybe that will finally push her into retiring!"

"Well I think that's being a little optimistic but who knows? Anyhow, Pat thinks you're the right choice and so do I. What does Grant say?"

"Pffft. I haven't told him yet, we haven't spoken at all. I'm annoyed at him for frightening those girls, imagine arresting a teenager for matricide."

"Right, but he didn't actually do that, did he?"

"Well, no. Brenda got the wrong end of the stick there... but he really gave her a scare. That much is true."

"What exactly happened?"

Judith goes on to relate how she'd brought Brenda up to her apartment but only long enough to grab her purse and a jacket. Entertaining a student in your home was an absolute no-no, no matter what the reason, so she'd ushered the girl down to the parking garage to drive her home.

"I'd once driven Margaret Seely home so I knew the house but couldn't remember what street it was on. Brenda gave me directions but said she didn't want to go home, she wanted to go to the police station. I had to explain that I couldn't possibly take her there at that time of night. The only place we could go was to her home but we could sit in the car in the driveway to talk if she didn't want to go indoors."

"Your text said Glenda was already back home when you got there."

"Yes, thank goodness. Of course we didn't know that, not until Glenda came outside. Then it was tears of joy and twin-speak. At least that's what I call it – when they talk to each other but half the words are left unsaid? Anyhow, I still don't know the whole story of what happened. I guess I do need to talk to Grant."

"Yeah, I think so."

Lila stands and starts packing away the garbage while Judith folds up her blanket.

"I'll take that stuff," she says, adding that there's a dumpster at her building.

"Brenda did say something that only struck me as odd later on, I wish I'd asked her to explain but..."

"What was it?"

"Well, I was trying to make conversation during the drive, you know something to distract her from her worries and her crying. Anyhow, I asked how she and Glenda liked being here, in Edgemont. She's a smart girl because she answered that she appreciated me trying to make her feel better, but I didn't need to. Then she went on to say:

Everything is great, she loves her home, her school, her family is wonderful, and once they get past the jealousy it will be perfect. After all, it's only natural that they want to spend time with their mother and same with her buying them presents, they've never lived together before so yeah, they're enjoying most of her attention and that's normal. It won't last forever, some people just need to learn patience."

"Huh! I see what you mean because who was she talking about? The grandmother might be jealous that the girls want to spend time with their mother, the husband might be jealous that she was spending money on them, her siblings might be jealous about the attention the twins are getting... but they're too young to do anything. Hmm, I wonder who needs to learn patience? Could it be jealousy between the twins themselves?"

"I don't know. I wish I'd asked her to be specific."

They walk to their respective cars but before getting in Lila says:

"So, *One:* you're going to tell Grant about Pat's offer and we know he's going to support you so can then call her to say you'll accept; *Two:* you'll find out what happened with Glenda and why Brenda thought she'd been arrested, and who is jealous?; and *Three:* you're going to let me know what everyone said, right?"

Judith sighs deeply but agrees to Lila's plan.

"Well there's no time like the present so go take care of business."

Lila gives her a wave and drives away in her sporty little car. Judith remains for a moment longer looking back at the familiar brick building that is Edgemont School for Girls. She's worked there for a number of years but is now looking at it with different eyes and from a viewpoint of much more responsibility.

"So do you have family in the area? or know folks from 'round about here?" asks Brian.

"My girls," replies Andy. "But I don't see them. I'd like that to change, though."

"Is their mother keeping them from you?"

"No, she's not a problem. Not now. She's with another guy and she's been married to him for years. No, the problem was me being unable to settle down and travelling around a lot. I did stay put in Banff for a few years, but it was just a menial job I was doing. Living there, enjoying the scenery and the outdoors, made up for the boredom of the work but in the end I gave it up."

"So your girls live in Calgary?"

"Mmm. I'm not sure there's a place for me in their lives after all this time. I'm still trying to decide if I should even bother."

Brian nods, but realizes Andy's lack of detail and sidestepping of the direct question means he doesn't want to continue the conversation. Tactfully, he changes the subject.

"I'm having a barbeque at my place. Just a few of the single guys because we aren't allowed to have many people at gatherings, right? and you're welcome to join us."

"A backyard barbeque with a few guys sounds really good... great, actually. Thanks."

"Where the hell is Gary?" demands Greg as he comes stomping into the kitchen and interrupting his stepdaughters' conversation with their grandmother. The three women just look at him and when he doesn't give a word of apology Moira just shakes her head, saying:

"I haven't seen him and we *were* having a conversation here, a private conversation."

Hearing their father's voice the two younger girls come in and soon the kitchen is crowded with women all talking at once. At least that's how it seems to Greg who is suffering with a hangover. He can't complain though, he was out with his friends and who does that when their murdered wife isn't even in her grave yet? It's not like he was drowning his sorrows although that was the original pretext for the trip to the bar.

"Gran are you going to stay here and take care of us like you did with the big girls?" asks Shawna, her voice a bit whiny. Before Moira can reply the girl continues: "Daddy can't look after us, even if he is at home all the time now. And Gary's always here, but we don't like him, do we Sheila?"

Her younger sister is busy nibbling the skin around her thumbnail and giving that task all of her concentration. She's chewed the area raw and will soon draw blood which will give her the excuse to suck on her thumb without being reprimanded that at eight years of age she is far too old to be thumb-sucking. She knows all that, but her mother's death and everything that's been going on these past few days have given her plenty of reason to need comfort.

"Why don't you like Gary?" asks their father, clearly surprised at this statement. He would never admit it out loud, but personally he finds his son to be a non-entity, too boring to be offensive.

Brenda leans forward and takes hold of the youngest girl's hand, pulling it away from her mouth and drawing Sheila into a hug. Shawna gives her sister and her half-sister a scowl. She wants the focus of attention to be on herself. It's no fair being stuck in the middle between much older twins and the baby of the family. Gary doesn't count because he's a boy.

"I don't like him 'cause he doesn't like us. He never hangs out with us, he just stays in his room and we aren't allowed in there. It's not fair."

Those last three words punctuate almost every utterance Shawna makes. Her life is just one inequity after another. There is no justice in this world for eleven-year-olds.

"So he's in his room now? I knocked but he didn't answer and I didn't hear anything."

"No, he's not there now. Or... I don't think so but I'll go look, okay?"

"Fine, fine." The unspoken words *just go!* hang in the air. Greg rubs at his temple trying to stave off a headache he feels lurking.

"Come to think of it," says Moira, "I haven't seen Gary for a couple of days now. What about you girls?"

Brenda doesn't hesitate, saying: "Nope, I must have seen him at some point over the weekend but I don't remember when."

"Well, we were a little preoccupied, what with me getting the third degree at the police station," replies her twin.

"What, again?" Greg winces at his own raised voice.

"No, just the one time–"

"Oh, that was hardly an interrogation. God, girl you do love to dramatize, just like your mother does..."

The ensuing silence is uncomfortable but no one rushes to break it. Each reflects a bit on their missing wife, mother, daughter. The sound of Shawna's feet flying down the stairs brings them each back to the here-and-now.

"He's not in his room and his bed hasn't been slept in, not for days," Shawna announces with a ghoulish flourish.

"What? How would you know that?" demands her father.

"Because the bed is made and Tilly hasn't been here since last Friday."

"But Friday's almost a week past!" exclaimed Greg. "Where has he gone?"

"It could even be more than that because I remember the last time I saw him and that was on Wednesday."

"You haven't seen him since a week Wednesday? are you sure, Glenda?"

"Of course I'm sure! we had a fight."

"What about?" asks Shawna, all curiosity, while Greg asks the same question angrily.

"We fought about him being in my bedroom stealing my money."

"What?! No way would he do that!" insists Gary's father.

"I'm afraid so, Greg. He stole out of my purse, too. We caught him and we quarreled about it," adds Brenda in a gentler tone.

"He had no business being in your bedrooms and no right to be taking money from you girls!" says Moira indignantly.

"But why would he?" Greg is sounding plaintive.

"He said he had to get away, to run away before the police arrested him."

"Oh for godsakes why would the police arrest Gary?"

"Because he and Mom had a big fight. He said she kicked him out."

"Oh this is crazy, running away just makes it look worse!"

"Greg, we're going to have to let the police know. They'll have to find him and bring him home."

They all exchanged looks before Shawna asked in a high-pitched voice:

"You mean he killed Mom? I told you I didn't like him."

COVID-19 Update: Meat-packing plants are suffering viral outbreaks but the forecast of more than 400 in hospital by this date is, thankfully, way off with just 82 hospitalizations, 21 in intensive care.

Chapter 10

Wednesday April 29, 2020

Judith sends Grant a text inviting him over for dinner. Actually what she's written is:

Judith: made a stew, ready whenever u get here

and Grant replies right away with the thumbs-up emoji and

Grant: 7ish???

but Judith doesn't bother to reply. She doesn't want to look eager. In fact, she's already a little annoyed with Grant and they haven't even spoken yet. She doesn't like the way she's been feeling: anxious about him, about their relationship, and now this job offer... not even an offer, just a proposal to put her name forward. Her getting the school presidency isn't a sure thing.

Oh great, she thinks, *now I have something else to worry about, just what I wanted!*

Lila has just eaten a huge meal of borscht, roast pork, perogies and cabbage rolls all prepared by her elderly landlady. She's still chuckling remembering the expression on Mrs. P's face when Lila asked: *No Chicken Kyiv?* Lila is quite certain she'll be served that dish within the week.

Putting a coffee pod in her machine she calls Brian who answers right away.

"My landlady has fed me so much food I can hardly move! I am so stuffed."

"Wish I'd been there, I love an authentic Ukrainian meal."

"Oh I have leftovers, and pretty much enough to make up a dinner for the three of us. You've got the barbeque tomorrow so we'll have these on Friday night."

"Looking forward to that! We'll probably have leftovers after tomorrow as well. Lots to look forward to, especially to seeing you, as always, Lila."

"That's sweet. Anyhow I'm curious, did your new guy Andy show up again for his third shift?"

"He did, and he worked just as hard as the last few days. I'm still not sure if he'll want to sign on with us, he hasn't said anything about that, but I definitely will hire him."

"And still no idea why he's picking up cash work?"

"Nope. It might not be addiction issues, though. Some of these guys owe a lot of money which they either don't want to pay – like to an ex – or they can never pay it so they don't even bother trying and just drop out."

"Plus the mentally-challenged, some of whom shouldn't even be on the street–"

"And some who are perfectly capable – and willing – to put in a good day's work but their personal hygiene and clothes keep them from getting a job."

"I thought the shelters had programmes at their facilities for showers, shaving, grooming, even new clothes, to help people get back into the workforce?"

"They do, and they do a good job, but the shelters fill up quickly."

Sighing, Lila comments that it's all very sad, and Brian agrees adding that it's also very common in the cities these days.

"But you'll get to meet him and decide for yourself because he accepted my invitation to the staff party."

Lila is pleased to be helping Brian host this party for his workers. She's wondering what he'll be like and how he'll treat her when everyone is watching how they interact. Is he the type to show her off? or act all possessive? She's looking forward to finding out.

"Detective?" the speech is hesitant but Grant recognizes Moira Nikovics from her raspy smoker's voice.

"Yes, Grant speaking, and it's Ms. Nikovics, isn't it?"

"It is. I'm glad I got hold of you but I can't talk for long. My..." she pauses, thinking, then continues saying: "My son-in-law, Greg Nichols, he didn't want me to call but his son, Gary, is missing."

"How long has Gary been gone?"

"Well... we're not sure but... well, days apparently."

"I'm on my way–" Grant begins, but Moira interrupts asking:

"Can you please not tell Greg that it was me who called you?"

"No worries. I'll see you all shortly."

Ending the call Grant looks up to see Judith's worried expression.

"I guess you're able to piece that together from what you heard. Do you know Gary Nichols?"

"No, I've never met him and I'm not even sure if I've ever seen him... oh wait! yes, once but just from a distance. He was standing outside Barbie's car while she came into the school to pick up Brenda. He was having a cigarette but quite openly, not trying to hide it or anything."

"The grandmother... well, she's not his grandmother, but she's a heavy smoker, too."

"Barbie was as well. I've never seen or smelled tobacco on the girls but I don't know about Glenda, the other twin."

"I'd like to discuss her further with you but I've got to go now. Ms. Nikovics is concerned about her Greg Nichols finding out she called us. I think I'd better head over there right away."

Grant is walking towards the door as he speaks but stops and turning asks: "Can I come by later?" and seems very surprised when Judith answers:

"No, not tonight. We'll talk again," and then she is opening the door and giving him a polite smile as she stands well out of reach.

Grant wants to stay and try to figure out what's wrong with Judith but work has to take precedence. He calls up Reg who says he can be at the Nichols' home in the Executive Estates in about ten minutes. The older man is waiting on the driveway, his car parked on the street, when Grant arrives. After quickly bringing Reg up to date the two men head to the front door and ring the bell. It chimes.

"They could do with a roof overhang here," comments Reg looking up. "Especially in winter, or when it's raining."

"That would ruin the *clean, spare lines of the house*," remarks Grant dryly. Reg just snorts a soft laugh.

The older of the two youngest girls pulls the door open saying: "Yes?"

Grant has heard an urgently whispered *You're supposed to ask who is it first!* and spots the youngest girl hovering behind her sister.

"Sheila is absolutely correct, Shawna, especially at night," he says. Both girls just gape at him but Shawna recovers her belligerence and demands to know *how did Grant know their names?*

"I'm a detective," he replies with a straight face. He hears Reg's cough poorly attempting to disguise a guffaw.

Faced with the two big men the girls step back. At that point Moira Nikovics comes into the hallway, nervously asking what their business is. Grant catches a glimpse of shadow in the room she just came out of and figures they are all being watched and listened to.

"Mrs. Niko..."

"Nikovics."

"Yes, pardon me. I'm here to speak to the teenagers, all three of them please."

"Why? What can they tell you?" she asks but before Grant can answer Greg Nichols step through the doorway saying:

"Gary's not here, and I'm not sure if the twins are around. What do you want to see them about, anyway?"

"That's police business, Mr-"

"Uh-uh, they're teens. You can't talk to them without one of us present."

"Your son has reached the age of majority, Mr. Nichols. We don't need your permission."

"But the girls–"

"Are apparently orphans. I can ask Social Services to appoint an *Appropriate Adult* if you aren't willing to work with us, Ms. Nikovics."

She waves her hand at him exclaiming that of course she will co-operate with the police, they are investigating the death of her daughter.

"And your wife!" she snaps at Greg Nichols who sighs and gestures for everyone to come inside. They all move into the living-room although Greg and Moira try to shoo the two girls upstairs.

"We should stay here, Gran," insists Shawna, "We might know something important, right Sheila?"

The younger girl doesn't give any indication she's even listening but Shawna continues undaunted:

"We might know the fact or find the clue that cracks this case wide open!" she says with excited relish.

"Shawna, stop that!"

"If you must stay then sit down and keep quiet. The sooner the police finish here the quicker they can be out there looking for the bad man who hurt Mommy," says Greg, emphasizing *out there*.

"You mean the killer who murdered our mother," comments Glenda, coming into the room with Brenda just a step behind. They seat themselves on the love-seat with Sheila choosing to sit on the floor between their legs. Shawna perches on the arm, alert and not in the least bit chastened by her father's words.

Seeing the identical twins together Grant is struck by how their attitudes let him differentiate between them. On Glenda her dark colouring, emphasized by Goth-style make-up, gives her a tough, bad-tempered look. Her poor posture and dark clothing add to her sullen, disinterested air. But Brenda's dark hair bounces with waves that catch the light and her dark eyes sparkle. Her good-natured smile shows white teeth set off by soft red lipstick, and her sallow skin is brightened with blusher.

"What time did Gary leave?" asks Reg and Grant gives him a mental thumbs-up for not asking the easier-to-answer *Where did he go?* Now Greg is put on the defensive.

"I don't know, he's a kid always going out and about..."

"You didn't speak to him before he went out?"

"No, no I didn't get the chance..."

"When is the last time you spoke to him?"

"Look what are you getting at?"

"Getting at?"

"Well, with these questions and your tone and your insinuations..."

"I apologise if you find my tone offensive Mr. Nichols, that's certainly not what I want, and I'm not sure what mean by *insinuations?*"

"Well, asking questions like I'm supposed to know the answers and if I don't know then why don't I? it's like you're implying something."

"Hmm," Reg ponders a moment as if giving Greg's half-hearted complain serious consideration. "First, if that's how I sound to you then please let me apologise again. Secondly, if I *do* seem to be implying something's wrong then I guess I must *think* something is wrong. Like, why would Gary leave without touching base with at least somebody, I mean as you said, Ms. Nikovics, this is a murder investigation. Gary's step-mother has been murdered and her killer is still on the loose. I think concern for Gary's whereabouts and well-being *should* be a priority, don't you?"

"Well yes, of course, but he hasn't been abducted or anything–"

"How do you know?"

"Well, why would he be? I mean..."

"When is the last time you saw Gary, Ms. Nikovics," cuts in Grant as he turns to the woman. "You're probably in the house and aware of who else is here more so than any of the others."

"I've been thinking about that, ever since Greg asked me, and I don't remember. But the girls said they last saw Gary to speak to on Wednesday."

"Wednesday! that's a week ago. Do you mean to say no one has seen Gary in a week?" He looks from one face to the other and sees evasiveness tinged with shame.

"We might have seen him but not spoken to him. Or we might have heard him in his room. I just can't remember," explains Brenda.

"Yeah, like we've kinda had a lot on our minds, eh? You know, Mom dying, and catching Gary stealing money from my room, and me being dragged down to the police station..."

"Dragged? Ms. Nikovics?"

"Well, that's how it felt,"

"And what were you saying about Gary stealing your money?"

"That was a misunderstanding, Officer. Glenda, you've got to be careful with what you're saying in case you give somebody the wrong idea. Gary wasn't stealing."

"Taking it without permission and then trying to cover his tracks so he wouldn't be found out? Hmm, sounds like stealing to me." Glenda turns sullen and doesn't want to speak anymore.

Grant decides not to push it. The room is already filled with tension and it's late for the younger girls to still be up. Turning to Reg he asks if he can get things in motion at the station and gets a confirming nod in return.

"I'll head back there now and get started on the Missing Persons report. I'm thinking I should date it *last seen Wednesday April 22nd*, agreed?"

Before Grant can answer Greg Nichols once again intervenes, trying to downplay his son's disappearance:

"It probably hasn't been a week, that's just all we can remember. The girls remember Wednesday because of the incident... the mix-up, that's all. I bet we've all seen him since but just can't remember because it was normal, nothing remarkable."

Grant shares his look from one face to the next until he'd checked in with everyone as he asks:

"Have you seen Gary since last Wednesday?"

No one replies.

COVID-19 Update: A second state of emergency has been declared in Fort McMurray because of flooding from ice jams forcing thousands to evacuate. Emergency protocols are in place for the weather and the virus.

Chapter 11

It's perfect weather for an outdoor get-together. There's enough of a breeze to keep most of the mosquitoes away and the smoke from the firepit takes care of the rest.

Judith and Lila arrive together, Judith having driven them both. She knows Brian will see that Lila gets home safely.

Although it's only a small group, due to the regulations about gatherings, it's all men which makes Judith draw back, feeling shy, but Lila marches right into the group giving greetings and asking for introductions. Her bubbly social manner puts everyone at ease and there are smiles all round. Judith nods hello here and there knowing she'll never remember all the names. It doesn't matter, she won't be initiating any conversations.

She just gets seated when a tall man, a few years older than herself, asks what he can get her to drink offering beer or wine or... but just then Beth calls out:

"Ms. Taylor, Judith, I've made you some lemonade."

"Oh that sounds lovely, Beth, thank you," then turning to man she adds: "I don't drink alcohol so it's very considerate of Beth to accommodate me."

"I don't drink either!" he exclaims. "By the way I'm Andy, and you are Judith, did she say?"

"Yes, Judith Taylor. Pleased to meet you, Andy."

He looks at her expectantly and then Judith notices he's holding out his hand to shake so she quickly takes it with a nervous smile.

Andy's answering smile is a bit more calculating. He sits in the next lawn-chair and scoots it closer to hers. This allows him to speak in a lower voice that makes their conversation seem far more intimate than it is. Judith is slightly taken aback, she isn't used to men paying attention to her because she isn't used to socializing period.

She gives him a quizzical look and says uncertainly: "We've met before... haven't we?"

"Oh, I would never forget meeting you, Judith. Maybe you saw me in passing? At a mall, a bank, driving by in your car?"

"Maybe.. I don't remember meeting you, but you look awfully familiar."

"Ah, perhaps you saw me and liked what you saw?" He laughs pleasantly and Judith blushes in answer.

Lila looks on with amusement having already noticed that Andy is quite a good-looking man. She begins to wonder what Grant will think of the cozy tableau the two of them make. *If he shows up,* she thinks with a frown.

"What's up, hon?" Brian is right there, spotting her sour look. He follows her gaze to where Andy is monopolizing Judith. Turning back to Lila he asks: "Is that a problem?"

"Oh no, " she smiles. "I'm just being a troublemaker, but only in my own mind! speculating about how Grant will interpret that little *tete-a-tete.* "

"Ahhh, well I know what I'd be thinking if I were him."

"Boy, you sure know how to throw a party, eh?"

"That I do," Brian chuckles, adding: "The secret is to let the guests create their own fireworks."

Once the food is ready to dish up Andy makes a point of helping Judith fill her plate by reaching, fetching, suggesting, and serving. Lila looks on with an amused smile noting Judith's slightly shell-shocked expression. Andy is coming on strong but with extreme courtesy which makes it hard to dissuade him. Along with plenty of compliments, something Judith isn't used to hearing.

Both Brian and Lila exchange a smile when they overhear Andy say:

"But of course you have to have to dessert! With your slim figure you can have two. No need for you to count calories, you are perfect as is!"

And Lila almost laughs out loud when she sees a square of carrot cake and a slice of lemon meringue pie on Judith's plate.

Brian spent quite a bit of money on the party by buying good quality meat for the grill and ready-made fixings – including a variety of desserts. He is in charge of the barbeque while Lila and Beth fetch cold drinks and circulate among the guests. Everyone is having a good time and complimenting their host for picking the perfect day.

Grant spots Judith the moment he arrives but she is engrossed in her conversation and doesn't notice him. She had been glancing at the gate into the backyard with some frequency earlier on but once the meal was served she'd stopped looking, having given up on Grant coming to the BBQ. She certainly understands that his work has to come first and that means it will get in the way of social engagements and she's okay with that. She isn't so sure about the coolness that she's felt entering their relationship, though.

Andy is aware of being watched. Looking up he catches Grant's eye right away and senses antagonism. When Judith follows his gaze her face breaks out in a spontaneous grin and Andy finds himself resenting the newcomer. Grant isn't the type to expect Judith to jump up and fix him a plate, but he does think of her as his lady and is somewhat disconcerted when all he gets is a big smile as acknowledgement.

Lila smooths over the awkwardness with an enthusiastic greeting while drawing Grant by the arm to see Brian at the BBQ and Beth at the tables spread with food. Grant knows both of them and they quickly settle into a *Sorry I'm late* and *Glad you could make it* conversation before commenting on *so much food! great weather! everyone is looking well...* and then *quite a crowd, who is that talking to Judith?*

Brian suppresses a smirk at Grant's poorly disguised rivalry. He and Lila don't really discuss their friends much, they are more her friends than his, but he knows something has been going on... some rift between Grant and Judith. He doesn't know the details, but Brian is sure Grant is a jealous man, even if he keeps his feelings well-hidden.

It was Grant and Judith together who had delivered a big bottle of expensive Scotch to Brian as a thank you for rescuing Judith from an attacker. Brian knew then that while Grant truly was grateful he also resented the other man's heroism, thinking he should have been Judith's knight in shining armour. *And so he should have!* thinks Brian even though the thought is unreasonable. He understands where Grant is coming from.

Now the man is trying to be nonchalant while focussing, intently, on the man leaning possessively over Judith's lawn chair.

"Oh that's Andy, one of my workers. Good guy. He just recently joined the crew and hasn't really made any friends yet."

Again he has to struggle to keep a straight face when Grant snorts over that *friends* comment. Beth has filled up a plate and Grant takes it from her with absentminded thanks.

He forks up the food without paying attention to it, his eyes never leaving Judith. She tilts her head and gives him a quizzical look. Grant immediately closes the distance between them and bending down kisses her lips. He looks at Andy who introduces himself but with one hand on the back of Judith's neck and the other holding a plate of food Grant simply nods, unable to shake the man's hand. Grant feels a moment's satisfaction when Andy narrows his eyes, insulted by the Grant's casual behaviour.

"Sorry I'm late but I got held up on the Nichols case, otherwise I'd have been here much sooner." Grant doesn't even bother to include Andy in the conversation. That courtesy falls to Judith who says:

"No worries, I know you're busy. Andy has been keeping me entertained, and fed! He keeps fetching me different things to eat," she laughs. "I've had two desserts!"

Standing over by the grill Brian is occupied talking to a couple of the men so it is Beth who Lila shares her giggles with.

"What's going on?"

"Well, Judith does not flirt – not at all – she's always 100% upfront and sincere, she doesn't hold back. Right now, even though she's not being coy the way she's acting is pushing Grant's buttons and she isn't even aware of it. Most women would be playing it up, flattered by the attentions of two men, but Judith just doesn't think that way."

"But Detective Grant is her boyfriend, right?" asks Beth.

"Oh yes but lately Grant has been living up to his name..."

Beth looks puzzled before bursting out with a giggle of her own: "Grant is taking her *for granted*."

The two of them collapse in laughter which catches Brian's attention. He finds it heartwarming to see how well the two females in his life get on together. Excusing himself from the employees he's been speaking with he joins Lila and Beth asking *what's the joke?* and they simply nod their heads in Judith's direction. Grant is trying to monopolize her while she politely keeps drawing Andy into their conversation. Andy speaks in a loud voice, attracting attention, while giving Judith intimate looks and smiles. She's starting to look flustered.

"Lila, go be a good hostess before our guests come to blows over there."

Lila controls her chuckles and makes her way into the tension surrounding the threesome.

Judith catches herself in a yawn and, apologising for it to the two men, stands up preparing to leave. They both stand as well and Grant manages to edge Andy behind him with his shoulder. He takes Judith's hand saying:

"When I saw your car here I had Reg drop me off if that's okay...?"

"Of course I'll give you a ride," replies Judith, removing her hand and mentally shaking her head as she thinks *men are so strange.*

Stepping around Grant she says goodbye to Andy thanking him for catering to her, and saying it's been a pleasure to meet. He takes her extended hand and holds on to it for a beat too long saying:

"It's been my pleasure to meet you, Judith. I really enjoyed our conversation and hope we can continue it. I'd like to call and maybe we could get together for a coffee? but I'm still getting settled in right now."

Judith just smiles. She wants to say goodbye to Lila, and also to thank Brian and Beth for their hospitality. Turning she finds Lila at her elbow and gives a little *Oh!* of surprise that makes them both laugh. Lila takes her arm and asks what is happening with Grant. Judith explains that she is taking him home.

"Sweet."

"Oh you! just never mind. Brian and Beth thank you both so much for inviting me today. The food was delicious, I'm absolutely stuffed, and I really enjoyed being out in the nice weather, and meeting everyone."

Brian leans in to give Judith a peck on the cheek telling her she is always welcome. Judith feels a shiver – a creepy feeling as if someone is watching her – and turning discovers Andy staring intently for a moment before he grins and waves goodbye.

While they walk to the gate she turns to Lila quietly says: "Andy mentioned he'd like to meet for a coffee but if he asks for my number please don't give it to him."

Lila squeezes her arm saying, "I would never do something like that."

"Well, you did give it to Brian, in fact you saved it in his Contacts list."

Laughing, Lila exclaims: "That's right, I did! Oh that was ages ago," and her expression sobers as she says, "So much has happened since then."

"Yes, for starters you've kept Brian all for yourself!" Judith smiles and joins Grant who is waiting for her on the driveway.

When they are seated in her car Grant leans over to give her a kiss. Judith responds with closed lips then pulls back, giving him a quick smile. Starting the car she reminds him to buckle up.

Once they get going Grant lets his head fall back and closes his eyes with a deep sigh.

"Long day for you?" asks Judith.

"Mmm, and unfortunately things are getting murkier. Tomorrow I'm seeing a family member I only just found out is actually here. I knew she existed but thought no one had seen or heard from her. Did you know Barbie had a sister, Bonnie? Although no one has, apparently, seen or heard from her for a few years she's been living in the area for some time."

"I never knew about her... Barbie really wasn't one to talk about her past much. It really is a shame you never met her because it's hard to explain the effect she had. Words don't do her justice but vibrant, alive, funny, sparkling are the closest I can come. She talked a mile-a-minute, her laugh was practically a yell, and although she wasn't pretty she attracted everyone around her. Like she was a magnet and they were all in her orbit.

I know that sounds fanciful but honestly, photos can't possibly show you her vitality or clue you in about who she was. It's just so sad that she's gone... and so hard to believe."

Grant opens his eyes to look at Judith when he hears the emotion in her voice. His concern is obvious and he wants to reach out and take hold of her hand but knows she wouldn't like that while driving. Judith's hands are always in the *ten to two* position on her steering wheel. He'd told her that nowadays new drivers were being taught *nine and three* and she'd simply said *Hmmm*.

Sitting upright Grant notices they aren't heading to Judith's apartment.

"Are we going to my place?" he asks.

"Yes of course, I said I'd give you a lift home."

"Oh! I thought we'd go... no problem, my place is tidy enough for a guest."

"I'm not coming in Grant, it's already getting late, you're tired, and you've got a busy day tomorrow. There, that's three good reasons for me to just drop you off."

"I can think of one excellent reason for you to come in with me," he murmurs, leaning in as closely as the seatbelt allows.

Judith only smiles and turning into the driveway leaves her car running as she tells him *good night*.

Grant knows he shouldn't say anything but his mouth refuses to shut up and his tone is belligerent when he asks: "So is *Andy* going to take you out for a coffee, or...?"

Judith narrows her eyes at him, the hurt confusion she'd experienced over the past several days morphing into anger, as she quietly says: "Or what?"

"Oh, I don't know Judith what do you think? What do you think a man like that wants from you?"

"He might just enjoy my company, like me as a person, want to be around me and spend time getting to know me, but you're right – he probably just wants what you already had."

Grant grabs her hand off the steering-wheel and brings it to his lips answering quietly but with feeling: "Have, Judith. What we had and still have."

She removes her hand from his grasp, but gently, and giving him a speculative look replies: "Why are you only interested when you think some other man is?"

"I'm not! That's not true, Judith. Don't say that. You and I, we... we have something special. At least it's special to me and I thought you felt the same."

She tilts her head and in that movement the light from the garage door picks out the glint in her eyes, wet with unshed tears. Turning her face to look straight out the windshield, away from him, she repeats:

"Goodnight, Grant," and refuses to look at him again.

<u>*COVID-19 Updates*</u>: By May 3rd with less than 100 cases of COVID-19 the first wave has ended in Alberta. The plan is to re-open with *Stage One* on May 13th.

Chapter 12

Grant has been replaying last night's conversation with Judith in his mind all day. It doesn't make sense, he can't understand why she acted the way she did.

Reg notices that his partner is distracted but senses Grant isn't keen to discuss his personal life. Figuring Grant will say something if and when he wants to, Reg doesn't ask any questions. When they part company for the day Reg simply reminds Grant to call him if anything comes up.

Driving home Grant finally comes to a decision. He doesn't want this divide between him and Judith to grow wider so he has to get together with her to sort things out. He didn't sleep well – he hated the way they left things – and that's not good, he needs to be alert and focused in his job. They need to talk.

He can't take her out for a meal because restaurants are closed for in-person dining. He thought of offering to cook at his place, but after the cold shoulder he got he thinks she might take that the wrong way. *And she'd be right to think that,* he tells himself.

He's not even sure if she'll talk to him on the phone, never mind planning a *tete-a-tete* in his bachelor pad. He chuckles to himself over that outdated phrase but Judith is a bit old-fashioned or at least not *au courant* with modern thinking. That's one of the things he likes about her. Really likes.

Feeling cowardly he taps the Message icon on his phone and sends her a text:

Grant: 2nite?

Judith: 6 my place

Grant: great *[grinning face emoji]*

Judith: *[thumbs up emoji]*

He's glad they're meeting early. This way they can have their talk, figure out something for a meal and then, well... Feeling his chin Grant decides to shave. His beard grows in heavily for such a fair-haired man and it comes in several shades darker which he thinks looks scruffy. He wants to look and feel good for Judith tonight. Thinking that, he decides he should change his clothes and if he's going to do that he might as well shower, too. He's got enough time.

He needs this busyness to occupy his mind. He doesn't want to be scripting scenarios for their talk, that never goes right and this is too important to... that makes him pause to think. This thing with him and Judith is really important to him. Judith is really important to him. He didn't think he'd been taking her for granted but maybe? Well, he'll fix all that up tonight.

Putting her phone down Judith tells Lila to call Brian and ask him to come over before six. She wants company when Grant arrives. She also wants to gauge his mood when he sees they're not alone. Judith still feels resentful about his possessive behaviour at Brian's barbeque. It makes her wonder if he'd have been quite so attentive if Andy hadn't been sitting so close flirting with her?

"Sure, I'll give him a call."

"Oh sorry, you guys don't have plans tonight, do you? I mean it is Friday night..."

"And we're in the middle of a pandemic where everything is closed. Can't go to the show, can't go to a restaurant, certainly can't go nightclubbing... oh hey, can you just imagine Brian under the strobes on a crowded dance-floor bopping along to techno-pop club music?" Lila's laugh is musical.

"No, I definitely can't!"

"That's for sure. Omigod I'm gonna have to share my mental picture with Beth. She'll pee herself thinking of her Dad in a hot room crammed with screaming, sweaty twenty-something's high on Ecstasy and puking up shooters as fast as they knock them back!"

"Ewww, gross! but you're right, there's plenty of binge-drinking going on with the younger crowd."

"Yeah, but I heard that drinking has dropped out of popularity with thirty-year-olds. Not sure if they've had enough, or if they're all smoking pot. Anyhow, Brian told me Beth was going to watch TV at a friend's place, a show on some subscription channel he doesn't stream, so we were just going to hang. I have a ton of leftovers from Mrs. P in the car that I was taking over there, and I know Brian's still got food from last night that I'll tell him to bring and we'll make it a pot luck supper. We can't stay late though, he'll want to be home when Beth gets back."

"He's a good Dad, eh?"

"You know, he really is. He's pretty much raised her all by himself and she's a great kid so yeah, he's been a good father to her."

"She is great and it's so nice to see you three getting along so well together. I mean, I've heard girls can get jealous if their fathers start dating–"

"Not Beth," laughs Lila, "She's the one playing matchmaker! Anyhow, what's the scoop for tonight?"

After a filling and varied meal the foursome are sitting in Judith's living room with coffees.

"I know you can't talk specifics about the case you're working on, Grant," says Brian sitting comfortably with his arm draped over the back of the couch, hovering near Lila's shoulders. "But this woman who was murdered left behind a family, eh? and I heard it's an extended family type of thing with a mix of blood and non-blood relatives so I can't help but feel sorry for those kids."

"Oh pffft, Grant can tell us stuff. When the legal community trots out that official line it's either to prevent a lawsuit or hide incompetence. Believe me, back in Toronto at my family get-togethers, which means lots of cops present, everything is openly discussed and opinions are given and debated. It's not natural to be all hush-hush about your work and it's probably not healthy either."

Grant chuckles at Lila's forthright comments. Taking Judith by the hand he says: "As a matter of fact, I have discussed cases with Judith. She's a great listener with a sensible attitude and helpful insights. You've been my sounding-board a few times now, haven't you?"

Judith returns his smile, but withdraws her hand disguising the gesture by reaching for the coffee pot and offering refills before saying: "But now Grant has Reg so I've been sidelined."

"Whose Reg?"

"My new partner. Bit of an odd situation, actually. He transferred here from the East Coast because he's really close to retirement and wanted to get settled in Alberta where his adult children live. Oh! that's an oxymoron, right?"

"I guess, but I don't know how you'd say children-that-are-adults in any other way."

"And when did you become a Grammar Expert?" laughs Lila.

"Stop interrupting Grant," teases Brian right back at her.

"Yeah, or I'll lose my train of thought. I've been suffering a bit of brain fog lately."

Grant is replying to Brian, but he glances up at Judith as if sharing something with her.

"I haven't met Reg but I'm sure he must be an improvement on Suzanne – we all met her, remember? she sent you on a wild goose chase, Brian, and her actions might have put Beth in greater danger and all because she resented Grant's friendliness towards me. Which was just professional courtesy anyways."

"Maybe to be begin with..." murmurs Lila. Judith gives her a look and Grant coughs to cover up a laugh.

"Okay anyhow, yes Reg is a great improvement. Given that I'm guesstimating him to already be at retirement age, or nearly there, I don't know how long he'll stay, but the experience he brings and his no-ego attitude is fantastic. I hope he sticks around for a good while yet.

Suzanne is well, frankly, her behaviour is often inappropriate. She has a good brain and she knows the law but her brash aggressiveness is just... I don't know how to explain it but with Reg it's calming just to be around him.

But, I still rely on having you to talk to, too, Judith. And you two as well, Lila is right – there are no state secrets in this case. However, my thoughts really are too muddled and I'd kind of like to have a night off from it all. I know I've been neglecting Judith and..." he raises his voice when she tries to interrupt, "It's not just because that guy Andy was all over you at the barbeque."

"He wasn't *all over me,* Grant."

"He was trying... okay, okay. I'm dropping the subject. Instead I will say, Brian since you mentioned the kids, that one thing about this case that has stayed with me is how many have now lost a mother.

Barbie Nichols was a wife, daughter, and sister, but most of all she was a mother. Even if it appeared she gave up the twins. Well, never mind appeared, she really did do that, but Moira explained that Barbie feared for their safety and her own, too. And rightly so, as it turned out because the ex-boyfriend was violent with Moira as well."

"I wonder if the older girls resent the fact that their mother raised their half-sisters?"

"Barbie was always broke. I think the twins had a better lifestyle with their grandmother. That's not to say they shouldn't have been with their mother but... sometimes you don't get to choose," put in Judith.

"So Barbie had four daughters."

"And a stepson, Gary."

"Ah, she and Gary's father are married?"

"Yes, she had the first two girls with a boyfriend which is why she was able to leave them with her mother, she was their sole guardian – they didn't even have their father's name. It's different now, I hope, but back then? I doubt if he would have even found a lawyer willing to represent him if he had tried to get custody."

"Okay so at some point Barbie married a man who was divorced? widowed?"

"I don't know... hmm, that could be important. Thanks, Brian."

"Oooh you mean a jealous, murderous ex?"

"Uh no, Lila, I didn't mean that at all. I was just thinking that if the first Mrs. Nichols is alive maybe that's where Gary is."

"Oh that's right, he's missing. Is there a search going on?"

"A BOLO has been issued—"

"I thought that was just an American thing from cop shows on TV," interrupts Brian.

"No, we send *Be On Look Outs* too," answers Grant with a smile. He continues saying: "And there's a Missing Person post on Crime Stoppers but there are issues. First of all he's an adult, and secondly there's some dispute about when he was last seen. Plus, his father's insisting that he isn't actually missing,"

"His *father* is saying that?"

"He's afraid we're going to think Gary has run away because he murdered his stepmother."

"But isn't the flip-side to that the fact that one family member has been murdered and another is missing so that's cause for concern – even alarm? Believe me, I've been there and I know what an awful feeling it is when your kid is missing. Especially when... well, that's all in the past now, and it all ended well."

Grant feels a momentary shame remembering the incident with Beth. Judith's gaze is sympathetic but he isn't sure if that look is for him or for Brian.

"You've had to be both father and mother to Beth so it affects you strongly," says Lila adding: "And a missing twenty-year-old male is way different from a missing thirteen- or fourteen-year-old girl."

"That's true, but we are concerned about Gary, nevertheless. I'll follow up with Greg Nichols about Gary's mother."

"There's a lot of missing mothers in this case, aren't there?" said Judith. "Brenda and Glenda grew up with a missing mother who is now dead, Gary's mother is well... we don't know yet but certainly not part of his day-to-day life, and the two younger girls have lost their mother. Barbie's mother stepped up to take in the twins but then she moved them away."

"You think the case revolves around Barbie as a mother?"

"I don't know, it's just... well look at us. My mother is gone and she wasn't very present even when she was alive. Beth lost her mother when she was quite young wasn't she, Brian? Oh! I'm sorry, maybe I shouldn't mention that..."

"Not at all, Judith. I was devastated when Mandy, Amanda, died. She left such a huge hole in my life and for a long time I didn't like to talk about that, but now that I've met Lila I feel I have another chance."

The two exchange smiles and Lila explains: "Mandy died of lung cancer."

"Right, and she actually lived three months longer than the doctor's predicted. I mourned Mandy, but we knew what was happening and were able to prepare somewhat. My big fear was raising Beth who at age six needed every bit of attention I could give her and more.

My mother lived nearby, she's still alive but now they're down in Florida, however at the time both she and Dad were wonderful supports to us. Family makes a difference."

"That's true. I've got sisters and they've all got families but my father's in a nursing home, not senile thank God, but very frail, and my mother passed which really left a gap."

"I didn't know that," says Judith. "I can tell you really miss her, too."

"I do. You know, when things go bad people want their mothers, they want *mommy* to comfort them and *make it all better*, but what I found was how much I miss Mom when something good happens. I mean, she was my biggest fan so any good thing in my life always gave her so much pleasure and I loved bringing her good news. She was always on my side and certain I deserved everything I ever got."

"Huh, that's true Grant, but I never thought of it before," says Lila. "When bad things happen I tend to shield my parents, not telling them because I'm hoping I can make things right and maybe they'll never have to know, but something good? I can't wait to share with them, especially Mama. And yeah, you're right about mothers being our number one cheerleaders."

"Unfortunately not all mothers, but we survive. What cliche can I think up? umm… oh yes, *we have to play the hand we're dealt.*"

"Oh Judith, I forgot. Sorry, I hope I didn't upset you." Lila looks concerned.

"Not at all, but speaking of upsets I'm not sure I've forgiven Grant for the upset he caused Brenda."

"Brenda? the good twin, right? what did I do to her?"

"You arrested Glenda! and she's not the *bad twin* she's just a girl who has difficulties with school–"

"Not just with school, she's got a bug up her butt against the police and that's entirely her own fault. She got picked up for an impaired driving charge and–"

"But she's not old enough to drink," interrupts Judith.

Lila replies saying: "That makes it worse. She doesn't have to have any particular amount of alcohol in her bloodstream, you know how it's .08…"

"Sometimes .05," puts in Brian.

"Yeah, well if the driver is underage even a sip of alcohol will result in an impaired charge."

"So do they bother to measure it? like with a breathalyzer?"

"They did, and got a blood alcohol reading of 0.02 which would mean nothing for you, Judith, but for an underage drinker behind the wheel it means an impaired driving charge."

"Why did she get stopped, was she driving erratically like all over the road or something?"

"No, nothing like that. She got caught in a spot check and her mistake was she answered honestly when the officer asked if she'd had a drink. She said *yes, one beer about an hour ago.* He was ready to let her go when he noticed she had a Class 7 licence, a learner's. Even if she wasn't underage that means a zero alcohol tolerance and automatic 30-day suspension."

"So she's penalized for her honesty?"

"No, Brian. She's penalized for breaking the law. Even if she hadn't had a drink once the officer saw the licence classification she was in trouble for driving on her own, first of all, and also for driving at night. That's two more violations including fines and the car, it was her mother's which she'd taken without permission, was impounded for a week."

"When Glenda messes up she goes all out!"

"She's also a very unpleasant girl, with a huge grievance against the world, sullen and sarcastic with a permanent scowl and a foul mouth to go with it."

"So a typical teenager then," puts in Lila.

Brian turns to her saying: "Beth's not like that."

"Exactly! Beth isn't typical, she's a sweetie," patting Brian's arm Lila adds, "Good job, Daddy." He quirks an eyebrow and smirks at that appellation which Lila quickly amends to *Dad* with a giggle.

"And I didn't arrest her–"

"But Brenda didn't know that when she arrived here in tears late at night. I was on the phone with Lila when the buzzer just rang and rang and it was poor Brenda in a panic saying you'd arrested her sister for the murder of their mother. She said she saw you take Glenda away to the police station."

"Well yes, but Glenda wasn't under arrest. She wouldn't co-operate and wasn't taking it seriously so Reg suggested a formal interview and he was right, that did the trick. Her grandmother was with her the whole time."

Grant is looking aggrieved but Judith still feels angry on behalf of both girls.

"Brenda was beside herself and I couldn't let her come in, I had to turn right around and drive her back home. She cried the whole way and was still crying in the car in their driveway when Glenda came out of the house saying you'd had to let her go."

"Oh that's just misrepresenting the facts!" Now Grant is annoyed but can't help noticing how attractive Judith is when her colour is high. She's drawn herself up with her shoulders thrown back and her chin thrust out, and he just wants to take her in his arms and kiss her. Lila and Brian are watching the argument with amused interest. As Grant advances Judith stands her ground.

"To even *think* about accusing a seventeen-year-old of matricide!"

"I did no such thing as you very well know. I can't be responsible for what you thought happened. I'm having trouble right now trying to figure out what's going on in that head of yours."

Judith narrows her eyes and thins her lips and stares long and hard at Grant. He refuses to back down and just holds her gaze with an expressionless face. As if she suddenly remembers they aren't alone Judith breaks away and apologizes to Lila and Brian for the argument adding:

"What a terrible hostess I am!"

"No, no it was my fault for bringing the subject up in the first place," says Brian.

"No, I overreacted but Judith, it's only because I don't want you to think badly of me," confesses Grant.

"I don't, Grant, really I don't."

He grins at her and gets a grudging smile in return. Beth takes hold of her and Brian's coffee cups and stands up saying they have to be on their way. Judith makes a halfhearted attempt to keep them longer while Grant is already shaking Brian's hand and giving Lila a cheek-kiss goodbye. The couple are out the door in a matter of minutes leaving Grant and Judith alone to face up to their situation.

Lila awakens slowly thinking she is far too comfortable to have to open her eyes and get up. She feels warm and cozy as she snuggles deeper into the soft blanket. Soft blanket? that does make her open her eyes. *This is Brian's couch,* she thinks, looking around the room. She's in the den, covered up by the plush fleece blanket he keeps on the loveseat and she is wrapped up in his arms. Lifting her head from his chest she meets his gaze.

"Is it good morning?" she asks. He smiles and answers *not yet*. Straightening up Lila realizes she's fallen asleep sitting in Brian's lap. Sliding over to the side she immediately finds herself missing the warmth.

"What time is it?"

"The clock just chimed so it's just a couple of minutes past eleven."

"Ha! It's your grandfather clock that probably woke me."

"I should set it to sleep mode. Then it only chimes from 7:00 in the morning I think it starts, until 10:00 or 11:00 at night."

"Did you sleep?"

"No, I was too busy enjoying myself watching you. You made a lovely bundle in my arms."

"Oh God, did I drool?"

He laughs in surprise adding:

"No, but I might have. You're beautiful, Lila."

"And you are a very sweet man who just happens to be extremely handsome yourself."

"Handsome, am I? Hmm, what about *hot*?"

"Oh very, very hot. No worries in that department, mister."

Brian pulls her in for a kiss, a long passionate kiss, and Lila feels her body respond. *No, it's too soon!* she thinks. *Arnie's funeral was only two months ago.*

But then a voice in her head reminds her that she and Arnie had separated almost ten months ago.

Their marriage had ended last June, at the start of the summer. She left and Arnie let her. She moved 2,000 miles away and it was more than six months before he even came to see her – having changed nothing and seeing no reason to do so. She was prepared to divorce him, but then he died. That wasn't the reason he was dead but she kept blaming herself.

Although her thoughts are far away she continues staring into Brian's face. Yes he is very handsome – and hot – but he is also a kind, caring, and serious man. And he wants her. He wants to make her a permanent part of his life and give her a second chance at happiness. Marriage, a stepdaughter, a family of her own, finally, and maybe a child of her own, their own.

Lila places her hands on either side of Brian's face and leans in to kiss him back, returning his passion, deciding the time had come to stop mourning.

After all, it wasn't from losing Arnie because that had happened long ago. No, she'd been mourning something she and Arnie could have had but let slip away. She had been mourning a life that might have been and it was time to start living the life she could have now.

The look Brian gives her is hopeful, but he isn't pushing, he's patiently waiting. He's giving her time to think her thoughts and come to a decision. Lila decides to choose him.

COVID-19 Update: Attendance at indoor and outdoor wedding ceremonies is limited to 10 people including the bride, groom, officiant, witnesses, photographer, and guests. Since no food or drink or dancing is permitted there are no wedding receptions.

Chapter 13

Saturday, May 2, 2020

I should be annoyed with myself for letting Grant stay the night, thinks Judith, but this morning has brought such lighthearted happiness she can't regret a thing.

Last night, after Lila and Brian left, she and Grant returned to the couch and their coffee and their conversation but... he'd suddenly pulled her to him in a crushing embrace and kissed her hard on the mouth. It was a very determined kiss, passionate and claiming, and it served to melt Judith's doubts and worries away. Next thing she knew they were in her bedroom and she was pretty sure they'd been lip-locked the whole way there.

He really is awfully good-looking, she thinks, studying his face while he sleeps. *I guess I'll just have to see how he behaves going forward.*

Grant opens his eyes, a pale blue that Judith finds very attractive, and with a smile rolls on top of her with a kiss.

"Morning, beautiful," he greets her when they finally break apart.

"I'm no beauty, Grant."

"You are to me, and I don't care what other people think. In fact, I'd be happier if I thought other men didn't find you beautiful but, beauty isn't just an arrangement of facial features, Judith, it's you."

"I would never have figured you to be the jealous type."

"Me neither, 'cause I never was before. Not until you... you're wrecking me, woman!"

"You know, when we're out I see women give you admiring looks and then they look at me as if they're trying to figure out *why her?* I mean, it's not surprising because you are a very handsome man. I was just thinking that when I watched you wake up, and I know Lila thinks you're hot. And Suzanne Mirteau certainly did..."

Grant rolls over onto his back and flings an arm over his eyes saying:

"Ugh, don't mention Suzanne when I'm feeling so relaxed and happy. She makes my skin crawl."

"I think most men would put up with a lot from her because of her looks and her sexy behaviour–"

"A lot of men are welcome to her, just not me. Now come here, I know a great way to get you to stop talking nonsense...'"

Lila is singing along with ZZ Top as she navigates her sporty Mazda into the Visitors Parking area at Judith's apartment. Her car is only a couple of years old but she racked up plenty of mileage when she drove here from Ontario. Since then she's made numerous drives around Kananaskis Country to explore the surrounding Provincial Parks.

Even after switching off the engine and silencing the music she's still loudly humming the tune as she sends a text to Judith.

Lila: u free for a visit

Judith: always

Lila: good im here

Grant is in the shower but it's not like Lila doesn't know about the two of them so... Judith opens her apartment door to greet Lila just as Grant calls out:

"Judith? can I keep a razor here? I hate this scruffy look. Good thing I shaved last night before I came over, but still– oh! Lila!"

With a big grin the blonde answers:

"Hiiiiiii Grant, fancy meeting you here."

Judith just shakes her head and pushes her friend towards the living-room. Giving a pointed look to a shirtless Grant suggests he finish dressing before joining them.

"Don't bother on my account," Lila shouts out with a cheeky laugh, "I'm enjoying the scenery."

"Ha-ha," says Judith but with a smile. "You're in a good mood, what brings you by so early on a Saturday?"

"Well, I didn't think we'd have an audience but I don't care, I have to tell you, I slept with Brian last night!"

"Wait, what!? Really?"

"Yeah and omigod Judith, it was wonderful." Lila lowers her voice but the apartment is small and both women figure Grant can overhear. Judith drops her voice as well to say:

"I can't believe it, I didn't think you were planning, well I know you've been seeing a lot of each other, but with Beth around, and.. oh wow. This is so exciting... such juicy gossip!"

"I know, I certainly hadn't planned on it and neither did Brian. I mean, he told me a while ago that he wanted us to get serious but was willing to wait until I was ready. I knew we'd get together at some point I just didn't think I was ready yet, but last night it just hit me that I was ready and it was time."

"Okay, give me a minute to untangle that sentence… Okay, I figured it out and I'm so happy for you!"

They didn't realize they'd grabbed hold of each other's hands until Grant enters the room saying:

"You two look so girly, what's going on?"

Judith doesn't speak, she just looks at Lila, who answers Grant saying:

"Well, you know how you woke up here this morning? Well, I woke up at Brian's place," then sits back with a satisfied smirk.

"Oh, you mean you fell asleep on his couch watching TV?" enquires Grant with a dead-serious expression but Lila knows he's teasing so she tosses a cushion at him which he easily catches. "So you two want to have some girl-talk time, eh? Well, I can make myself useful in the kitchen."

"Coffee's in the carafe, Grant," says Judith, turning to Lila and offering a cup.

"No, not for me thanks. I'm not really staying. Brian's coming over to my place so I'm going to swing by the grocery store and then clean my home. Beth's having a friend in for a sleepover tonight so Brian doesn't have to rush back home or anything."

"Look Grant, Lila's actually blushing!"

"Yeah well… Grant go in the kitchen so we can talk without me blushing 'cause you're around."

"I can take a hint. I'll get breakfast going."

As he leaves the room Lila confides to Judith that she really doesn't care if Grant knows, she just prefers to talk to Judith alone.

"So you're getting together at your place this evening and you're cooking dinner?"

"Yeah, I haven't decided what I'll make, I'll just see what meat looks good at the store and then I'll plan my meal.

Judith, Brian is so... well, he's only the second guy I've ever been with and, it's funny, but I felt kind of shy with him. I mean me and Arnie were together for twenty-odd years and I was never self-conscious or anything, but..."

"But everything was okay, right?"

"It was perfect. Really, absolutely perfect. Brian is..." she grins, "a great lover. Very um.. attentive, and considerate, and just wow."

"Oh Lila, that's so good. I'm really, really happy for you."

"I knew you would be! and this, Grant here, I'm glad you guys got over whatever that thing was?"

"Well, we still haven't talked about it, but yes, our feelings for each other are as strong as ever."

Grant comes back in with a cup of coffee and announces that he's taking Judith to the McDonald's drive-thru for breakfast.

"You do realize that if you didn't take milk in your coffee you'd have a completely empty fridge, right?"

Judith frowns, thinking, before acknowledging that she hasn't shopped. Actually, except for Brian's barbeque, she hasn't left the apartment for a few days.

Lila stands up and says she has to get going. At the front door she gives Judith a hug and her friend, always slightly uncomfortable with expressing herself, returns it while Grant smiles at them both.

"Put your shoes on hon, and we'll walk down with Lila. I'm starving."

"I need my purse."

"Don't worry, I'm buying. Let's just go, if I have to wait until you comb your hair and then decide to change your top I'll just faint from hunger."

Both women laugh at his exaggeration with Lila adding:

"Hmm, you managed to work up *quite* an appetite, Grant."

"Ha! we'll probably see Brian in the take-out line."

Lila laughs even louder and the three of them leave together.

COVID-19 Update: Stores allowed to open for in-person shopping have strict capacity limits. Customers lining-up to get in have to follow social distancing of 6 feet. Only one family member is allowed to enter. Arrows on the floor designate one-way aisles, along with markings at the check-outs that maintain appropriate spacing.

Chapter 14

Saturday, May 2, 2020

Judith unpacks the containers of take-out food and sets the table with plates while Grant fetches cutlery and condiments. He's bought lots and Judith relishes every bite. Although she avoids fast food as a rule, visiting drive-thrus are going to be part of her *new normal* during the pandemic, she realizes.

Munching on their meal Grant begins by telling her: "I've hashed this out once already with Reg, but you know some of the people involved so I think you'll have good input. I've got plenty of suspects, too many actually, and I'm looking at someone in the family."

"I'm happy to be your *sounding-board* as you called it, Grant. Plus, I do know about these people, even the ones I haven't met, from past conversations I had with Barbie.

You know, I honestly don't believe I'm a vain woman but having my hair done has always been my personal pampering treat. Just having someone else wash and brush it feels wonderful. Good hairdressers take the time to make the whole process a relaxing, enjoyable experience and Barbie wasn't good she was great. In addition to being completely open about her own life, her own feelings, and opinions, she was a great listener who never hesitated to give advice. I remember her telling me that I'd be a fool to let you slip away."

"I never met her!"

"No, but she'd seen and noticed you when you were at the trailer park interviewing Dana Lezinsky about Holly. They were friends as well as co-workers.

That reminds me, Dana told Barbie that her daughter Glenda had been hanging around the trailer park. There was that bad element, well, you know all about that because of what happened there... anyhow, she thought Barbie should know. Barbie was pretty pissed off about it, too. I had an appointment with her a couple of days later and she was still mad. She said she and Glenda had had a big fight where she told her daughter, and I quote, that she'd *beat her ass if she didn't stay outta that place.* Of course that was before the fire so none of them could have had anything to do with Barbie's death."

"I'm not so sure. I mean, it wasn't that long ago, and frankly if Barbie was causing trouble one of those lowlifes might have tried to shut her up. No one wants their business messed with when there's huge money to be earned, and Barbie might have been seen as a credible threat."

"I know about the money they make, I've seen *Breaking Bad* on Netflix. I realize that's just a show but–"

"But nothing, the money is unbelievable. Hmm, that's another non-family possibility to consider... gee thanks, Judith. You've done this to me before."

"Yeah, yeah that's why I'm here. What do you mean by *another* non-family possibility?"

"One option is that it could have been an attempted robbery. It doesn't look like anything was taken so maybe she interrupted the robber and he panicked? Another possibility is a botched kidnapping. $17 million is a lot of money and the Nichols have no security system in place."

"That surprises me. I would have expected the Seely's to have all the available protections in a sophisticated system considering John Seely travelled so much."

"You're right, the Seely's did have an alarm system, cameras, the works, but the Nichols household kept forgetting to switch them off. After emergency services started charging for all the trips for false alarms they cancelled the contract. So, that makes it possible that someone was going to be kidnapped that night but... well, the argument against either the robbery or the kidnapping scenarios is that Barbie Nichols was murdered in her bed while sleeping. She was hardly a threat to a thief or an abductor if she wasn't even conscious.

The only other non-family scenario, well until you brought up the drug dealers, that is, is a crazy person. Someone who learned about the lottery win, or just saw a photo of Barbie and decided she needed to die. That *could* have happened although they were extremely lucky to first of all find her house, sneak through it despite other people being home, locate Barbie's bedroom, and catch her alone *and* sleeping. The argument against is that the *modus operandi* isn't violent enough. Usually that type of killer repeatedly stabs or brutally batters their victim to death."

"Ugh, it's scary to imagine someone she might not even know having this whole evil obsession about her then stalking and murdering."

"Thank God it's a rare type of killing because it's really hard to find the perpetrator in those cases."

"Well, let's move on from thinking about that, then. Tell me about the family. First off, what's the story with Barbie's sister Bonnie?"

"Oh, let me tell you that one's a character, all right. They're only ten months apart, Bonnie being the eldest and–"

"*Irish twins,*" Judith interrupts with a nod.

"Well, yeah their mother is Irish–"

"No, it's an expression. Oh! it's probably not nice, certainly not politically correct to say that, it's just that the Irish aren't exactly renowned for birth control. I don't even think abortion is legal there yet."

"What are you talking about?"

"When babies are born within a year of each other the expression describing them is *Irish twins.*"

"Oh, I get it. No, you probably shouldn't say something like that these days. Anyhow, the two girls were extremely close growing up, did everything together, dressed alike, led a lot of people to believe they were natural twins apparently. But once puberty hit the trouble began. The girls had the same taste in men and, according to Moira, spent their teens stealing each other's boyfriends.

It didn't end until Bonnie *had to get married* and she moved out of the house. One day, about six months into her pregnancy, she discovered her husband and Barbie having intercourse. A huge fight occurred and her loving hubby hit her so hard blood started gushing and she was rushed to hospital. In the ambulance the paramedics handled an emergency premature delivery but the baby didn't make it. Bonnie recovered but was never able to have children after that."

"That's a horrible story. Barbie must have felt so guilty for her part in it."

"Yeah well, Barbie's guilt gets worse: the father of her twin daughters is that same brother-in-law who beat up her sister."

"Oh no. Oh, what a burden for everyone. So Bonnie must really have hated Barbie all these years..."

"Not to hear her tell it. She goes by Nikovics because *there were too many husbands to remember all their names*. Sounds like Bonnie jumped from bed to bed but managed to visit the altar each time, or at least a lot of times. She thinks it's eight but said she'd have to figure it out and why bother, what's the point? the men are all out of the picture now. Although I'll bet she's collecting alimony from someone.

Anyway, she was very calm when she related the story of the rift between her and Barbie, saying she's sure not having children turned out to be a blessing because what kind of mother would she have been? I'm pretty sure my mouth was just hanging open by this time. Especially if the look on Reg's face was anything to go by! She saw our expressions and said:

Detectives, what can I say? I was born to late to be a hippie but I fell for the romance of the free love culture. I'm too selfish to be a good mother or wife and too inconsiderate to care. I was never fussed about getting married, it's the men who always thought giving me their name would give them control. As for children? well... I'm not even sure I have a heart. If I ever did it got broken in the back of an ambulance and that was a long, long time ago... too long to count."

"I don't know what to say. I think it's just such a terribly tragic story and oh my... do Barbie's daughters know their history?"

"According to Moira no, they don't. By time they were old enough to start asking about their father he'd been declared dead. At that point Barbie could have safely retrieved her girls but they were happy with her mother and financially were living a better life than Barbie could provide. It wasn't until the lottery win that Barbie was determined to reunite her family or, as Moira puts it *buy her daughters' love.*"

"That is how it looks, isn't it? But I know Barbie wouldn't think she was buying them, she'd be happy to know she was sharing *with* them, Still. So how come Bonnie is in the area now? did she say?"

Grant has a real knack for storytelling. He's able to convey the various speakers' emotion so well it's like watching a play. Leaning forward he relates Bonnie Nikovic's story:

At forty-something Bonnie, with her long strawberry-blonde hair, bright blue eyes, and curvy figure, could be a real *cougar* except she doesn't play up her sexiness. Her make-up is discreet and her style of dress is modest. She does have a lively, vibrant personality – just like people say about her sister Barbie.

Bonnie's interest is in living a life that's fully engaged and active. No one's story is too long to listen to, it's never too early or too late or too far to travel somewhere for a good time, and she's never bored. Her excitement and enthusiasm make her very attractive.

Having spent a little bit of time in Europe and a lot of time travelling in the US Bonnie has decided to return home. She feels the need to *reconnect with her roots* and hopes to *find some much-needed grounding*. Aging makes her crave stability, and she sees settling in the Alberta foothills as the next step in her journey.

She doesn't want to try to transform and re-make her physical self to compete with younger women, she wants to explore this phase of her life and enjoy it as a new adventure.

Bonnie talks about the *realness* of the people who live in farming communities and small towns, and how she's discovered her *true home* here. She's been hired on as a hostess in the kind of restaurant the locals attend for *special occasions* and the hours don't keep her working too late or starting too early. She's found a place to rent, has a car, and is certainly making plenty of friends if the non-stop texts and calls she gets on her phone are any indication.

She confirms when Grant asks that yes, settling things with Barbie was her plan. She believed it was time for the sisters to reunite as a loving family. Leave the past where it belongs and celebrate the here-and-now. The future? no, it's not promised and, well look what's happened.

Bonnie is comfortable as she answers their questions without hesitation or evasion. Her reasons for seeking out her estranged, but suddenly wealthy, sister might be insincere but there's no indication of that.

Barbie and Bonnie didn't actually meet but they spoke on the phone after Bonnie convinced her mother to pass on her sister's number. No, they hadn't texted so she had nothing to show about their conversations except her call history testifies to several lengthy chats. They were working towards getting back to the closeness of their childhood – at least according to Bonnie.

"Do you believe her?"

"Right now I don't have any reason to disbelieve her except, as Reg pointed out, her general flaky behaviour. We can connect the dots and surmise why aging Bonnie suddenly wants to make amends with newly rich Barbie but that answer isn't necessarily the right one. So Bonnie remains in the game but on the sidelines for now."

"Ah! even someone as unsporting as me can figure out that analogy," comments Judith.

"You're not *unsporting* you're just not a sports fan, but I haven't given up on you in that regard," Grant replies.

"In any regard?" she sounds challenging but her voice trembles slightly.

"No, Judith, not at all."

Their discussion goes on hold while they enjoy a kissing break. Grant pulls away first although his eyes linger on Judith's lips now soft and rosy.

"You're a terrible distraction, woman!" he says, pretending to be annoyed.

"Thank you," is Judith's pretend-meek response.

"So, the sister is down near the bottom of the list. I would have said the same about the stepson, Gary, except that he's gone missing, or run away, depending on who you speak to."

Grant pulls his cellphone from his pocket and, apologizing to Judith for the interruption, fires off a text message. She notices he uses his thumbs and comments on how quickly he types. He tells her his speed improved once he got plenty of practise.

"It's such a convenient way to communicate. I mean, if I phoned Reg to speak to then I might be disrupting his day, but a text is something he can deal with when he's ready. It's quick, too, because you get to skip all the polite courtesies like *How are you? Hope I'm not disturbing you?* that sort of thing. Brian asked a good question about Gary's mother and her whereabouts. If she died and Greg was a widower then it's possible Barbie raised the boy. Her and Greg's oldest daughter is eleven I think–"

"Shawna? yes, she's eleven and Sheila is eight."

"So, Gary's twenty now which means he would have been around nine when his Dad remarried. If Barbie had the raising of him from that age, and if his real mother had passed away, he'd have a much closer relationship with her then we first thought."

"The first Mrs. Nichols doesn't have to be dead, either. They could have gotten a divorce and shared custody, or he could have gotten sole custody, and their wedding didn't have to happen immediately before Shawna came along, they could have been married for a few years meaning Gary could have been much younger when Barbie came into his life."

"Yes, you're right. Well, I've asked Reg to get in touch with Greg Nichols and he'll find out what's what for sure. Now, getting back to Gary himself. He's twenty years old and sounds aimless. He doesn't have the grades for university, no interest in college, and yet he doesn't have a job."

"He'll be collecting CERB, and I bet he doesn't qualify for it either."

"I don't know much about that programme. I've had no need to look into it since I'm still working."

"I've investigated because the school might lay everyone off and tell them to collect this. The initials stand for Canada Emergency Response Benefit, administered by the tax department so the Federal Government can quickly get funds into the hands of workers who are unemployed due to the lockdown. It's a real help to people, with none of the waiting and jumping through hoops you sometimes have to go through when collecting EI benefits."

"Why don't you think Gary qualifies for it?"

"First of all you have to lose income and if he was already unemployed he hasn't lost anything. That's why seniors can't collect it because their pensions haven't stopped.

Secondly, you have to have made a minimum of $5,000 net the previous year and filed a tax return. Even if he had a part-time summer job at our $15.00 minimum hourly wage he probably wouldn't have made that much money over two months. Barbie complained that he was lazy, sleeping late every day then hanging out in his room on his computer. I remember asking if he played video games and she answered *probably, but a boy is just as likely to be watching porn.*"

"Then he won't get those payments."

"Oh he will if he applies, because everyone who applies gets it. Nobody is checking up, although Canadians have been told they're on the honour system and to keep in mind that Revenue Canada will be following up eventually. And since there are no deductions – it's $2,000 deposited monthly into your bank account – most people are going to owe income tax."

"So you or I could just apply and get $2,000 a month for how long?"

Until this Fall, I believe. It started at the beginning of April and I guess it could end sooner if all the lockdowns are lifted and everyone goes back to work right away. And yeah, you and I could go online right now and answer the two or three questions they ask and we'd get the money. I'm sure Gary would have done that."

"That is... wow. I mean it's great for people in need but how many are going to cheat the system?"

"Lots. And when they get caught I'm sure it'll be *I can't afford to pay that back* or even *I can't afford to pay this tax bill.*"

"That must be costing a huge amount of money."

"It is for sure. There are other programmes too for employers to collect a portion of wages or something. Pat and I discussed the *layoff-and-CERB* route and she, well both of us, I guess, will implement whatever package works out best for the school. We still have no idea when we'll re-open. There's also talk about going to online learning so nothing is firm yet."

"Both of you? Oh, right, as Bursar you handle all the financial stuff–"

"Grant! I never told you, no I guess we haven't had a chance to sit down and talk until now, but Pat wants to retire and she's putting my name forward as her replacement."

"You as Principal? that's great news! Congratulations, Judith. Oooh, I'm going to have to call you Ma'am."

Judith laughs saying: "I'm not the Queen! and nothing's definite but we'll talk about that later, let's continue discussing this family of suspects."

"Okay well, again at the bottom of the list – despite you jumping to conclusions and getting all mad at me–"

"Hey, I'm not the only one who's been overreacting lately..."

"Not my fault, I never knew I'm the jealous type. Anyhow, at the bottom of the list is the twin daughters. I can't rule them out entirely because both means and opportunity are perfect fits. An unplanned murder, weapon grabbed on impulse, both girls at home for some part of the evening."

"But what about motive? There's no motive."

"As I'm sure you're aware from all the TV shows and books you read that police don't concern themselves with motive. We simply establish the facts: who, what, when, where; then present whatever evidence we've gathered to the Crown Prosecutor. It's the defence and the prosecution who have to worry about motive because motives aren't facts.

Sure, if someone's heavily in debt and they knew they'd inherit a lot of money if so-and-so died then we can *surmise* a motive for them but it's only supposition. That being said an apparently motiveless crime is going to be a hard sell to any jury so sure, we give it *some* consideration."

"You've shown that either of the twins, or even working together, could have committed the crime but since the crime in question is the murder of their mother I sure can't get my head around that. Even I never wanted to kill my mother although...

"Although what? you can tell me, Judith. You can tell me anything."

"No, it's too horrible. I mean, I'm sure you've figured out what I'm going to say so let's just leave it at that, okay? No need to air all the dirty laundry."

She hates that her voice is shaking as though tears aren't far off. Grant senses this because he doesn't enfold her in his arms – a surefire way to force her pent-up feelings to burst free – but leans in closer and rests his palm on her hand. Her hand is cold and he presses down gently, transferring his warmth to her.

"Judith, please talk to me."

"Well... when I was going through all the angsty emotional rollercoaster of teenagehood there were a few times that I wished she'd just hurry up and drink herself to death. I mean, I always knew that was going to happen someday, as it did, and I got impatient and frustrated at being held back, trapped, by her neediness. At that age everything is *so unfair*. But now, looking back, I feel, well, guilty."

"I don't have to tell you that you shouldn't, you already know that, but I can understand the guilt feelings that mix and mingle in your head after a death occurs. Really, I do. That's another conversation we'll have later, okay?"

"So long as you don't think I'm some horrible freaky person then yes, it's okay."

"Wellll, I didn't say you weren't freaky..."

Judith punches his upper arm and laughs loudly at his remark.

"Anyhow, when it comes to teenage girls I'm deferring to you since you work with plenty of them every day so you're my *resident expert*."

"Plus, I was one myself once upon a time."

"Exactly! So what could a mother do to enrage her daughter to the extent she kills her?"

"Well... that does take some thinking about."

Judith blows out her breath in a gust, her eyes unfocused as she considers. Grant doesn't rush or interrupt her contemplation.

"Smothering with a pillow is, probably, impulsive but not in the same way as grabbing up a sharp knife off the kitchen counter and stabbing is impulsive."

"Yes, that's very true. The pillow killer had to time it just right, waiting until Barbie was in bed and sleeping, or at least dozing, before creeping in silently, and moving into position quickly. The kitchen knife killer could just as easily have grabbed a meat-pounder or a rolling pin or a glass bowl and struck out with any of those objects, meaning to hurt and harm but not necessarily kill. There was no ambiguity in the pillow killer's intention. Although they may have regretted the act soon afterwards."

"Okay, so having figured that out I'd say the girl had to have a fairly long-standing resentment that just kept building. She would see her mother as an obstacle blocking her from achieving... something. Or, if the girl was fearful for her life but too frightened of her mother to challenge her, then she might believe this to be her only solution."

"So possibly resentful, thwarted, and angry which pretty much describes all teenage girls at some point during any given week, or desperate, deeply unhappy, and scared. Neither of the Nikovics twins fits well into either category. Glenda's sullen grumpiness isn't enough, and Brenda is emotional but very open with it.

"I agree with your assessment."

"Good to know. The remaining children, the younger daughters, are simply too young. I know children can kill but neither of those two are strong enough to smother a grown woman, not even if they acted together."

"But, unfortunately, the bickering and even fighting that's been going on in that home over the lottery win, everything from how to spend the money to pulling all the family together under one roof, will have affected the girls. If they're acting up, and I seem to recall that Shawna is quite a dramatic young lady, then they might be saying things that put thoughts into somebody else's head. Children are always upset when there's tension between their parents.

"Meaning they might unwittingly be the catalysts that made someone react?"

"Yes, but I think that's a remote possibility."

"Let's hope so, because next up is their grandmother Moira. Let me tell you about my interview with her."

"Okay but let's take a break. I really enjoyed those french fries and my cheeseburger, but I ate too much and now I need a nap. Ever since I stopped going to work I've developed a really bad habit of daytime napping, every day around this time."

"That sounds like a really great idea!"

Judith is yawning, she really does want to sleep for a bit, but looking at the smile on Grant's face she suspects nap time will be delayed for a bit... and that's okay.

COVID-19 Update: If ordered to self-isolate you must stay indoors. If you share a bathroom or bedroom wear a mask, open a window, wash your hands often, and disinfect all surfaces.

Chapter 15

Saturday, May 2, 2020

Having woken from their nap neither Grant nor Judith is in a rush to get out of the cozy bed.

"I meant to tell you, Judith, this bed is really comfortable to sleep on."

"Thanks, I haven't had it long. It's one of those mattresses that come in a box and I just unrolled it and put it on top of my old box-spring. It's got that memory foam plus two layers of some other stuff. I'm glad you like it, I think it was a great buy."

"Well, it's certainly comfortable enough to stay in while we talk."

Judith gets up, pulling the duvet half off the bed with her to cover up. She grabs Grant's shirt off the floor and slipping into it says she'll grab them each a cold bottled water.

When she returns Grant casts a critical eye over her saying: "That shirt looks better on you than on me."

Judith smiles at the compliment, commenting: "Well, you are the fashion police, Grant. Always perfectly turned out to suit the occasion."

She gets back under the cover but keeps the shirt on.

Grant frowns, saying: "It will get all wrinkled–"

But Judith interrupts to assure him she does own an iron and ironing board.

"Also, why are we drinking bottled water? Isn't your school into all the environmental sh-stuff?"

"I'll let you in on my little secret. The water is in a bottle but it came out of my tap. Maybe you didn't notice but I have one of those purifying filters on the faucet so I just refill my empty water bottles and keep them in the fridge."

"Hmm, I don't know if you're clever or cunning..."

"Why not both? Now continue telling me about your suspects. I love how you turn the interviews into stories, so go ahead."

Grant begins: "Moira is a study in contrasts. Here in Edgemont she is a grandmother and mother but at home in Toronto she's a successful businesswoman running a large Media and Communications company with a dozen permanent employees plus numerous freelancers. As well as acting the role of *mother* to the twins. She's more comfortable in her big city life than here in suburbia.

Working with creative professionals might account for the touches of flamboyance in her own appearance. She's let her dark red hair grow out while the gray is coming in so it's like half her head is covered with a scarf. She wears dark eye make-up, her eyebrows are tattooed on, and her skin owes its youthfulness to *Botox* injections.

She's a chain-smoker who wears the smells of nicotine and tobacco the way some women do with a cloud of perfume. Waving the ever-present cigarette draws attention to her hands with their professionally manicured nails worn long and fancifully decorated. The backs of her hands show her age. She dresses her slim figure in shirt/sweater/legging ensembles in bright colours but at work prefers Chanel-style fashions from the Sixties.

This trip back to Alberta is not a welcome homecoming for her. Barbie wanted her daughters to come live with her and Moira came along to settle them in – or fight for their choice if they prefer living in Toronto. She's had the raising of the girls since they were infants, but she's giving them options.

Barbie is her daughter so it's not an either/or choice, they'll all still be in touch no matter what. Their curiosity about their mother and her family, the novelty of a new place, and the possibilities of a wealthy life are hugely attractive. But as teenagers what they want now might easily change in six months time. Part of her will be hurt if the twins want to stay here but Moira decided to keep that a well-hidden secret. Barbie knew though, and in their frequent arguments kept pushing at her mother, trying to get her to admit it.

Barbie's disappointment in her mother for not jumping at the chance to give up her current life was well-known to the whole family. Barbie longed for gratitude but only got resentment. It seemed just about everybody was envious of her win."

"If she was telling you the truth Barbie's mother really had no good reason to kill her daughter. Obviously she'd resent Barbie bringing this disruption into their lives and breaking up the close relationship she has with her granddaughters but it sounds like she acknowledged and accepted that the girls would, naturally, want to explore this option and she wants the girls to be happy."

"That's true, but I got the distinct impression that Barbie wasn't willing to let her mother go back to Toronto. She probably suspected that having an out, a place to escape to, would make it harder to keep the girls where she wanted them. A bit like the children of divorced parents playing one off each other to get their own way. So long as her mother was here the girls would have to stay here.

Moira may have resigned herself to returning to Toronto on her own but she certainly did plan to return, that's where her life is, and that's what was causing conflict."

"Once when we were chatting – poor Barbie must have had a real struggle with me and my lack of small talk – she asked if my parents lived near. When I said no, I'd been orphaned in my teens, she said her Dad was dead and she'd never got on with her mother. She mentioned that quite casually and I remember being envious at how easy she was about it. I always got all bristly if questioned about of my mother."

"That's because your mother put the burden of her secret on your young shoulders. I never met her but I wouldn't like her just because of what she put you through. There must have been times when it was really stressful for you to answer questions, not understanding the nuances and minefields of adult conversation."

"It was exactly like that!" Judith said, marvelling at his understanding. "Although I couldn't have put it into those words then. But yes, there were a few women who used to poke their noses into our business, asking questions about how my mother was, what she was doing? where was she today? and I always ran in the opposite direction if I saw them coming because I just dreaded talking to them. Looking back now I realize they were concerned, and rightly so, but at the time I just thought they were nosy busybodies and I was afraid of them.

Grant, all of these mother-daughter relationships are getting entangled. There's Barbie and Moira, Bonnie and Moira, Glenda and Brenda with both Moira and Barbie... do the twins know Bonnie?"

"Yes, the girls knew of her, Bonnie was still in touch with Moira off-and-on over the years, but I'm not sure if they ever met. No one has said."

"Maybe her feelings towards them are tainted by the fact they're the result of her husband's cheating? I realize that's not the girls' fault but.."

"Could be, but I think it's more likely that Bonnie is too self-absorbed to bother with anyone unless they're in her immediate field of vision."

"You really didn't like her, eh?"

"No actually, there's not enough to her to like or dislike. When you're sitting in front of her she's animated and bubbly and just wide-eyed with interest but at the slightest distraction, a text, an ambulance siren, anything, her attention snaps away and you're left wondering how she fooled you into thinking she was paying any attention in the first place."

"Oh that's weird. I'd like to meet her sometime and see for myself what she's like. Maybe she'll come to a school event to cheer on Brenda."

"She'd probably be thrilled to do that... just as soon as someone pointed out who Brenda is."

"Okay, moving on. Where does Moira fit in your list of suspects?"

"I think she's a likely candidate. Means and opportunity are the same as her granddaughters so those are covered, and I think she has enough passion to fight for those girls, and for herself. If she saw Barbie as an insurmountable problem well... I think she'd want and be able to deal with her."

"But her own daughter..."

"Who has basically been a stranger ever since she grew up and used her mother to raise her own children. Now she wants to take everything away and in return is offering a place at the family table."

"A 17-million dollar table."

"Except Moira Nikovics owns her own home in Toronto, has a thriving business, large circle of friends, and a variety of interest. Why would she want to retire from that life and move to a place where not driving means you can't get around?"

"A compelling argument, sir. Leave her near the top of the list."

"The only other one left on the list is Greg Nichols. I find him odd, or rather his behaviour is what I find odd. He told me himself that he resents Barbie winning that money because everything changed, she changed."

"I expect that's normal, don't you think so?"

"Yeah, but like most people who buy lottery tickets I've never really given much thought to what I'd actually do if I won, have you?"

"I don't buy lottery tickets."

"Of course you don't," he gives her a quick kiss on the nose to show he isn't criticizing.

"But you're right, because when they interview the winners they're very vague about what they'd like to do. They just say stuff like *quit my job, pay off the mortgage, do some travelling.*"

"I'm sure the actual claiming of the prize takes some time and then they'll be getting advice from their bank, a lawyer, maybe they'll hire a money manager of sorts... and of course the begging letters and calls and visits from strangers and friends and family will have started and, no doubt, overwhelmed everybody."

"It could be a very stressful time even while they're happy – ecstatic – about their good fortune. I can see that it would be a huge adjustment. And maybe even more so for a man to adjust to his wife having all that money. No matter how open-handed and generous Barbie is he'd still be wishing he was the winner."

"I'm not so sure that she was open-handed with her *largesse*. He complained that she laughed at him for wanting to get a sale price at the hardware store but then refused to settle allowances on the kids. He didn't mind that she wouldn't give money to her daughters, but he felt Gary should have been treated better."

"If Glenda was caught hanging out with the dodgy element at the trailer park I'm not surprised Barbie wouldn't give her money. I mean, drugs – right? but Brenda's a good, responsible girl. Oh, I guess she couldn't very well treat one but not the other. Yeah, and she's certainly not going to hand over money to her stepson if she's not giving it to her own girls. But unless someone had a pressing need I'm sure they could have worked it all out satisfactorily given time. I mean, it all comes down to the fact that it's Barbie's money to do what she wants, and Barbie was the type to want everyone to be happy."

"Absolutely true, but that doesn't really make it any easier, does it?"

"Right, but Greg Nichols is not going to murder his wife because she won't give his son spending money. I mean, in the overall plans for their future—"

"But that's the problem. Sorry to interrupt hon, but Greg does think small. He's not looking at the next ten years, not even next year. Not beyond thinking about going on a vacation and for him the ideal would probably be a cabin by the lake with a speedboat, or a camper and a couple of dirt-bikes or quads. Planning down the road? probably just some vague idea about paying for university if anyone wants to go. So, no he's still top of my list of suspects but I haven't made up my mind or anything. We're still methodically checking alibis and bank accounts and phone records."

"And you might have a new line of enquiry when Reg finds out what happened with Gary's mother, Greg's first wife. Let's hope she's not dead from an unsolved homicide."

"Judith! don't even think about stuff like that, can you imagine?"

Catching sight of her mischievous smile he pulls her onto his lap for a cuddle growling sexy threats in her ear while her grin turns into a squeal and a chuckle.

COVID-19 Update: No pet adoptions from the Calgary Humane Society until further notice. Animals are being looked after by shelter workers, while volunteers have been sent home.

Chapter 16

Sunday, May 3, 2020

The aroma of coffee in a mug placed on her bedside table rouses Judith. "A lovely, lazy Sunday morning," she says with a stretch and a smile for Grant. He's moved back to stand in the doorway, sipping at his own coffee and telling her getting any closer will tempt him back into bed and somebody needs to think about breakfast.

"Yesterday you acted like I have no food but actually there's plenty for breakfast. There's milk and there's cereal, there's bread and buns in the freezer along with peanut butter and jam and marmalade in the pantry. I can feed you, you know."

"What kind of cereal?"

"Chocolatey kiddie stuff or tasteless-but-healthy organic stuff, take your pick."

"I pick you, Ms. Taylor, breakfast can wait."

"Don't jump on the bed 'til I put my coffee down!" she exclaims then shrieks and giggles as Grant starts tickling her. "Let me drink my coffee in peace, you brute."

He stretches out on his back, arms behind his head, and watches her retrieve her coffee.

"I could just lie here and watch you all day," he says.

"You've been doing that for two days now."

"No, I haven't... oh wait a minute, you're right! I've been here since Friday night, dammit Judith I don't know why I'm paying rent when..." he pauses and for a long moment they just look at one another. Then he stands saying:

"Have your shower, get dressed, I'll get the cereal and fixings on the table and then you and I need to have a talk, or rather there's something I need to tell you."

Judith gives Grant a curious look but doesn't ask questions as she chooses her clothes for the day and heads to the bathroom.

Grant watches her, enjoying the view, then catches sight of his unshaven face in the mirror and grimaces. While some men seem to rock the heavy stubble beard Grant despises that look on himself, feeling grubby and scratchy. And since his chin hair grows in dark it makes his head hair look dyed.

He'd been teased mercilessly as a boy over his platinum locks and always wore a buzz cut. It was his high-school girlfriend, Jenny Wong, who persuaded him to let it grow out.

It's Jenny he needs to speak to Judith about. He's not sure why, but he needs to do this now. The timing is right. Grants feels a great pressure in his chest that's making it difficult to take a deep breath. *Is this anxiety? or a panic attack?* he wonders.

He sets the table and lays out the cereal choices and a couple of blackened bananas that turn out surprisingly well once he's peeled them. He knows Judith likes to add fruit to her cereal: banana, grapes, or berries in season and apples or raisins in the wintertime.

He smiles at her fresh-faced appearance when she sits down at the table a few minutes later. Wearing minimal make-up and having a no-fuss haircut means she's always able to get ready quickly.

"Mmm, this looks delicious and I'm hungry," she announces, pulling her chair up close. She chooses the kiddie cereal and slices the banana into it before looking up at Grant and saying: "Oh! let me look at this shaggy face for a moment, I'm not sure what I think."

"I know it looks awful, so unkempt and messy–"

Judith leans forward, stretching her hand out to rub against his hairy skin, commenting:

"It feels a bit softer than yesterday."

"Well it's grown a little bit longer. You know I can't believe some men, actually a lot of men, choose this style. I just want to scratch all the time! and when my fingers do brush against this I hate it."

"In that case, yes you may store a razor in my spinster's bathroom."

"You're not longer a spinster, Judith," Grant smiles at her. Her cheeks colour up as she replies:

"I'm not longer a virgin, Grant, but I am still a spinster. Just as you're a bachelor."

"Huh! the only time you hear that word is when someone's talking about that TV show."

"I know what you mean but I haven't seen it. I don't care for reality TV, even though I'm sure it's scripted, it just doesn't appeal."

"Something else we have in common then."

"If you'd like, how about taking a walk while we have our talk? It looks like a nice day out and it will be good to feel the sun on our faces."

Grant thinks for a moment before agreeing adding that what he has to say is going to be difficult so he prefers privacy and could they just wander in that local playing field rather than following the popular biking/walking paths?

"The story I'm going to tell you is from my past but I realize it's shadowing my present, and our future, so I need to get it out in the open."

The expression on Grant's face belies the confidence of the words and listening closely Judith can detect a slight tremor to his voice. Whatever Grant has to say it's obviously something he feels deeply. At Judith's apprehensive look he is quick to lift her hand to his lips and plant a reassuring kiss on her knuckles, telling her she has nothing to worry about.

By mutual consent nothing more is said until they've tidied away their breakfast things, slipped on light jackets, and locked up the apartment. A solitary dog walker steps off the sidewalk onto the boulevard to maintain the 6-foot social distancing rule as they approach. Judith and Grant nod their appreciation of his gesture. Less than five minutes later they are walking the perimeter of an empty soccer and softball field.

Although they'd been hand-in-hand Grant now pulls away a bit and shoves his hands in the pockets of his jacket. Looking down at his feet he begins by saying:

"Ever since I can remember I've been called *good-looking, handsome, movie star, heartbreaker...* all the flattery that women bestow on little boys. I grew up hearing that and it continued when I reached puberty because I didn't suffer with acne or braces or gawkiness from growth spurts. I had girls crushing on me even while the boys all made fun of my *peroxide blond* hair and called me Ken Doll."

Judith tilted her head to study him and encouraging him to go on said:

"Yeah, I can see that. Were you bullied?"

"No, as I said I skipped the scrawny stage so I was big enough to avoid getting picked on. But I had absolutely zero self-confidence. I was only an average student, same with sports, and I didn't have any special musical talent, or chess skills, or anything like that. All I had going for me was my looks so naturally I figured anyone who showed an interest only wanted me as *eye-candy*."

"Wow, I've never thought of that happening to guys. Give me a moment to consider this... yeah, wow. As you know I didn't have any close friends growing up but of course I would hear the others girls talking and complaining about how they got treated because of their looks. They'd say stuff like *they think I'm stupid because I'm pretty* or even worse, *just because my body developed quickly doesn't make me easy* which were attitudes they'd encountered.

But for men... I guess it's the same with movie stars, with people falling in love with your looks even though they don't know the first thing about you."

"That's how it feels. Like I don't even have to open my mouth, they already figure they know everything about me. So anyhow, I didn't get a chance to pursue girls because they chased me. Girls would phone me and ask for a date, I wasn't interested and I didn't like it. Until Jenny came along.

Jenny, Jian Wong, was my first and only girlfriend starting from the end of Grade 8 until she went to University. She was smart enough to act like a buddy and when we did kiss for the first time our lips and eyes were tightly closed! Being around her constantly became the norm and halfway through high-school I realized that Jenny had claimed me as her boyfriend and kept the other girls at bay. But I'd never actually *chosen her* to be my girlfriend.

If this was a movie-of-the-week at this point I'd have sneaked out on a date, got caught, broken up before an emotional reuniting when I came to my senses. Nothing like that happened, in fact, nothing happened at all, we just went on as we had been.

As you might have realized from her name Jenny was Chinese, but born in Canada. Her parents had come from Hong Kong years before. They spoke English well, and both seemed to accept me. Partly because I never tried to go out with Jenny on weeknights, which was a thing they frowned on.

They had a very full regime for her of studying, piano and violin lessons, swimming and ice-skating, and Chinese language classes. On Friday or Saturday nights we would go to a show, or a school dance, or stay home and watch Hockey Night in Canada. And, of course, we spent lots of time just talking.

Things continued without really progressing until our senior year of high-school when we had to start applying for University and that's when it all fell apart between us. I had no interest in continuing with higher education, I had known for years that I wanted to be a policeman.

Jenny argued that the job was beneath me and I explained that it wasn't a job to me but a calling. I remember being confused because I'd always said I was going to become a cop. I felt a bit hurt when she dismissed the idea saying it was a boy's dream and I was a man now."

"Since you didn't marry Jenny and you did become a policeman that means you two broke up."

"Mmm, sort of."

Judith bumps him with her shoulder, She has a wry look on her face when she says: "You're going to have explain that a bit better, Grant."

He smiles in return but his facial muscles are tight. He'd told her it was going to be a difficult conversation and now that he is getting to the crux of the matter his concern is obvious.

"Judith, I.. um.. okay I'm going to jump ahead a bit and then I'll come back and explain."

Wearing a serious expression herself Judith stops and pulls one of Grant's hands out of his pocket and wraps it in both of hers. She doesn't say anything, she's already connected with him and now waits patiently.

"Right, here goes. Jenny went to UBC, that was the only university carrying all of the courses she needed for the degree she wanted, and before the first semester was over she killed herself. An intentional drug overdose, prescription drugs not recreational. She never touched anything illegal."

Judith is thinking she should probably be giving Grant a hug but it feels awkward, she's not spontaneous with affection. Instead she squeezes his hand tighter and stares into his eyes, willing him to go on.

"I didn't realize that Jenny had made plans for both of us to move to BC for school. Vancouver is really, really expensive but she'd been counting on us living together and pooling our student loans with her parents subsidizing the rest. Did I mention they have a lot of money? They're really well off and Jenny is, was, their only child."

Grant pauses for a moment while a spasm of pain flashes across his face. It was evident to Judith that he truly had cared about Jenny and about her parents, too.

"Even though I told her, over and over again, that I wasn't going she just didn't take me seriously. She got my high-school transcript, submitted my application, and applied for funding. When she went to get the airline tickets, about a week before it was time for her to go, I had to stop her. I was sure I could get through to her parents, even if I wasn't getting through to Jenny, and I had to try.

See, I don't know if this is still the case but back then when it came to cancelling or refunding airline tickets it was the person whose name was *on* the ticket, not the person who paid, who got the money. There was no way I could let Jenny buy a ticket in my name, it would have turned an awkward situation ugly. Well, I guess that was always going to happen.

So, I went to her house and she wasn't home, she'd run out to the pharmacy, so I was going to wait but then I thought no, I need to talk to her parents. And I did. I told them that under no circumstance was I going to university, and certainly not UBC.

They were so shocked, they thought Jenny and I had just had a fight or something, so it was really hard, but I had to explain to them that I had never planned on going. Worst of all, I had to tell them that Jenny had known this for a year. They were completely bewildered and Mrs. Wong was crying and Mr. Wong was angry, but he couldn't figure out who he should be angry with. Then Jenny walked through the door.

I can still see her, clear as day, wearing her faded denim jacket and brown cords, brown loafers, the typical collegiate look except instead of books she held a white paper bag from Shoppers Drug Mart. She looked from one of us to the other asking *what's wrong?* and when her father repeated what I'd said and demanded an explanation she.. she just waved her hand as if she could swat away my words. And while I was standing right there she told them *He doesn't mean it, and even if he doesn't come out now he'll be there, with me, before the end of the month. You'll see us when you come visit us for Thanksgiving.*"

"Oh no, oh that's... she was–"

"Delusional, yeah. The prescription was for antidepressants. Her doctor had written her a large prescription, well a large number of refills, to last her until she could get on a doctor's list in Vancouver. He had no hesitation to do so because Jenny was always a responsible girl.

After she flew out she phoned me a lot and it's a relief to me now to be able to say I never avoided her or lied to her. It didn't matter though, she just blithely went on and on about what she'd been doing and how much she'll enjoy showing me around when I get there. I would try to tell her about my training with the police but she wasn't interested. She treated it like it was my little hobby.

So there you have it. Even without ever making a committment I managed to break one, and break the girl's heart and mind at the same time, *and* drive her to suicide. I can only imagine how you feel about me now."

Judith has started walking again, there are lots of thoughts, feelings, and unfamiliar emotions that she needs to unpack. Some of the things she will need to talk over with Lila to try and gain some insights and get some guidance. Meanwhile, Grant's longer strides overtake and pass her so she jogs a bit to catch hold of his arm to slow him down.

"So our growing closer has made the threat of committment loom large and that scares you. Okay, Grant, I don't have the words right now but I will, later, when I process all this but for this moment in time I need you to stop," after a couple more steps he complies.

Judith takes his face in her hands and stepping on her tiptoes finds his mouth to let a hard kiss convey what she feels. He doesn't respond at first but she won't let go and soon they're tightly wrapped in each other's arms, comforting with a warm embrace.

"You must see me differently–" he begins but she interrupts saying:

"I do, of course I do, and what I see makes me love you even more. I know we haven't used *the L word* yet Grant but I don't care. I love you, and I hope you love me too, but if you don't that doesn't change how I feel. I feel closer to you than ever and I want you more than ever."

When they finally pull back and stare into each other's eyes she sees his are shiny with unshed tears while her cheeks are wet from her steady stream. She swipes her hand under each eye, flicking tears away, before sniffing and declaring *this is all way too emotional and now it's her turn to talk.*

Grant tells her to *go ahead* but his look is wary.

"Okay I told you a bit of this, about Pat retiring and proposing me for her job, but we didn't discuss how I feel and what I should do and what this means and, well, let's talk about me for a bit."

Laughing, Grant gives her a loud smacking kiss on the mouth and agrees:

"Yes, thank God, Judith, let's talk about you."

COVID-19 Update: No decision has been made whether or not schools will re-open for the rest of this semester, about two month's worth of classes. The Public Health Authority will advise the Premier.

Chapter 17

Monday, May 4, 2020

Judith surprised herself by falling asleep quickly and dreamlessly last night. After Grant's revelation she'd expected to toss and turn with her thoughts until the wee hours. Grant had gone back to his own apartment so she had plenty of opportunity to think, and she had plenty to think about.

She badly wanted to talk to Lila but she wasn't ready to share Grant's past just yet.

This morning, Judith wakes feeling calm and refreshed. As she goes through her morning routine of shower, toe-touches, making the bed, drinking hot water with lemon, her mind re-caps the conclusions she came to last night. Nothing has changed, what she'd figured out then still feels right.

Although Grant and Jenny were a couple for years they couldn't have been in love. Not with her being so obsessive and him being too compliant.

Jenny's lack of understanding about his goals showed she wasn't attuned to his needs. And, it sounded like Grant drifted into the relationship and then just *went with the flow*. No evidence of a strong character back then, but maybe he was neither interested nor ready for a relationship? Maybe he used Jenny, hopefully subconsciously, to keep the other girls away? choosing Jenny as the safe option.

"If any of that is true then after she died he'd have been carrying a huge burden of guilt all this time," Judith says aloud to her empty kitchen as she fixes cereal for breakfast. "Especially if his heart

622

wasn't broken... if Jenny's death only underlined the lack of depth to his feelings for her."

Judith is immersed in her thoughts when the 4-minute timer on her phone signals the coffee is ready in her French Press. With a steady hand she presses down the plunger but her mind is still distracted. She realizes that sometime after Grant's unadventurous teens he must have been thoroughly indoctrinated into the joy of sex and she's wondering how that came about... exactly.

There's nothing hesitant, shy, or passionless about Grant's approach so did he have a wild time in his twenties? He didn't go to university but the police must have some sort of academy or training centre, and then there's the job itself with its strong *manly-males* vibe. Plenty of female co-workers, and even cop groupies, and if he ever worked Vice... Judith's imagination goes into overtime. Now her mind is running through shows of varying explicitness that she's watched on Netflix and HBO.

"But, that's not my business," she declares. Pausing a moment to think it over she's pleased to realize that that's truly how she feels. She repeats: "Grant's past is not my business. I'm very glad he shared what happened with Jenny and how that affected him, but there's no need for me to voice an opinion on that. And I definitely don't need or want him to share his sexual experiences with me although..." she smiles as she concludes: "I'm always happy to benefit from the expertise he's acquired."

Reg is already at his desk drinking coffee from a mug with the slogan *World's Greatest Granpa* when Grant arrives carrying a take-out order.

"You made coffee? Here? Nobody ever makes coffee."

"Well, I want to drink it so I guess I'm gonna make it."

"Good to know, and did I tell you yet that you're my favourite partner ever?"

Reg laughs pointing out that *someone's in a good mood today.*

"Yeah, and thanks for putting up with my moody nonsense on Friday," Grant replies.

"Happens. Anyhooo, I got hold of Greg Nichols last night and got the scoop on his ex."

"Ex? Divorced then, not widowed."

"Oh yeah, and the first Mrs. Nichols sounds like a real piece of work, too. But before we get into that I did promise to pass on his question: *when will his wife's body be released for the funeral?* and when I told him that's not up to us he pointed out it's almost two weeks now."

"Let me give a quick call to find out."

"Good idea, because once you hear about the first wife we'll probably be heading out right away."

Grant raises a quizzical eyebrow as he places his call. Reg finishes his coffee in a couple of big gulps then stores his mug inside the desk drawer.

Standing up to put his suit jacket back on he hears Grant winding up his call saying: "Okay, thanks. Please just make sure somebody from your office notifies the family so they can make their arrangements. Yeah, 'bye."

"Grab your to-go cup, we might as well have this talk in the car on the way."

"On the way to...?"

"To maybe find Gary at his Mom's place? You know that trailer park on the east side?"

"All too well, I'm afraid."

"Hi Mark, it's Judith Taylor, how are you doing?"

"Judith, hello! I'm doing great, thanks. Took a long while but I'm definitely on the mend now."

Judith isn't sure if that's really true but knows some men like to play down their illnesses. "Oh I'm glad to hear that. We were all concerned about you and Pat."

"It's a funny illness, first you don't feel sick at all, then you're mildly ill, and just when you figure it's run its course wham-bam your temperature spikes and you can't breathe. Awful! Anyhow, enough about me. I know it's Pat you're phoning for, so let me get her."

"Thanks Mark, it's been good talking to you."

"You, too. Hang on..."

Judith can hear the handset of the phone clatter on a hard surface. The Johnson's prefer to be called on their landline, reserving their mobile phones for emergency use. In fact, Pat had told her that Mark keeps his in the glove-box of his car where, of course, the battery is always running down.

"Judith, good timing! I'm just about to head out the door."

"Hmm, that's actually my definition of bad timing, Pat!"

"No, I can stay long enough to hear you say *Yes Pat, put my name forward for your job.*"

"Okay then, consider it said!"

"Really? That's terrific news. I'm really glad you're going for it and I'm like 99.9% sure you're going to get it."

"I like those odds," laughs Judith. "So where are you hurrying off to?"

"We're going to get some new plants to have them ready to put in at the end of the month."

"Oh are garden centres still open?"

"Well, you can get plants at Costco and probably Canadian Tire too, but this is something new. We're going to a *wholesale pop-up garden centre*. I just heard about this on the weekend and there are several in town. We're going to check out the one at McMahon Stadium and I hope they've got a good selection."

"I won't keep you then, and I hope you find what you want."

"Thanks Judith, I'll give you a call this evening or tomorrow. Oh before I forget, Samira said to tell you she'll be right by your side, supporting you all the way."

"Oh that's wonderful news, Pat! I mean, we both know your secretary is the one who really gets things done..."

"Ha-ha, but probably true. She said it's good I'm retiring so I can spend more time with Mark and enjoy life to the fullest."

"And she's right, Pat. Bye for now."

"Bernice Jantz, the ex-Mrs. Nichols, walked out on her husband and toddler when she got a better offer from a flashy car salesman. It wasn't a fling, she made it clear to Greg that she wasn't coming back.

In those days you had to be separated for three years to end a marriage on grounds of *irreconcilable differences.* After that time period was up the divorce went through–"

"But Nichols could have divorced her for adultery so why didn't he? thought they'd get back together maybe?"

"Maybe, but he said it's because he couldn't afford the lawyer and court costs. Or he might have just not wanted to make thing easy on her. Anyhow, I don't know if the waiting had anything to do with it or not, but the salesman never did marry her. They continued *living in sin* as I've always enjoyed calling it, for about ten years before splitting when each of them met someone else. Reading between the lines I think they'd both been looking for awhile."

"And she never took Gary back to live with her?"

"Nope, and Greg told me that every time little Gary showed up on his mother's doorstep, which happened way too often according to her, she packed him into her car and brought him straight back home. Kid didn't even get a sleepover."

"I hate to hear stuff like that. But I guess it makes it easier on us, obviously Ms. Jantz wasn't gunning for Barbie Nichols."

"Nooooo, but she did recently file a lawsuit against Greg Nichols for alimony and child support."

"Child support? she never had custody of Gary."

"True but she wanted it... at least that's her story *now*. She's got a lawyer who's ready to negotiate a settlement rather than *put everyone though all the unseemly publicity of a trial of public opinion.* People are envious of lottery winners and might be all too ready to vilify Barbie Nichols for unlawfully keeping Gary and his mother apart."

"I'm guessing the lawsuit was launched shortly after the lottery win hit the news?"

"Yup."

"But people can see right through that–"

"True, but lots of people want to think the worst. I think it's what they call a *nuisance suit* where the plaintiffs are hoping for an offer of cash to make them go away."

"Wow, she's a real peach."

"Bernie, as she'll tell you she prefers to be called, is lazy, stupid, and self-centred. Greg told me how for years his little boy would sob his heart out after yet another of his mother's rejections. When Greg and Barbie married the boy was eight, I think he said, and after the initial cold-shouldering Gary soon settled down although he always called his stepmother *Barbie* which she seemed to prefer anyhow."

"No, she wasn't particularly maternal either. Maybe it's a type Greg Nichols goes for?"

"He's a big of an odd duck," agrees Reg.

They pull into the Edgemont Trailer Park and wander around the looping road at its 15km speed limit until arriving at a trim home. There's a recently washed Rav4 in the driveway so it looks like someone is home. Bernice Jantz has heard their car and gets the door open before they climb up the two stairs.

"Come in, both of you. I figured you'd come by so I've been waiting. I can have coffee ready in a jiffy or there's beer in the fridge if you'd prefer a cold one? Hell, there's vodka in the freezer if you'd like something really frosty!" and the middle-aged hennaed redhead rattles off a machine-gun laugh.

She's wearing a bottle-green velour tracksuit that is just a shade too bright for her colouring, and more than a shade too tight for her figure. The top is unzipped low enough to show off a generous amount of sagging, freckled cleavage.

Grant thinks she presents a sad picture before considering that her banter and innuendo is probably a big hit with the right kind of company, both male and female. Although her looks aren't to his taste she's certainly made an effort to achieve them with heavy eye make-up, strong musky perfume, long nails painted several colours, high-heeled slip-ons, and a lot of flashy jewellery.

When I describe her to Judith I'll say she's trashy and loud, but I bet she's the life of the party at her local bar or Legion or whatever club she and her husband attend, Grant decides. He keeps his expression friendly as he accepts her offer to *sit down and take a load off.*

"Oh I almost forgot this damn thing, here stick out your hands," she instructs before spritzing them with a large bottle of sanitizer. "Gotta follow all these new laws, right boys?" and she winks outrageously causing the men to chuckle along with her.

Both Grant and Reg decline the alcohol: *not on duty,* and the coffee: *already coffee'ed out this morning, but thanks!*

"I know when Reg called, Ms. Jantz, he–"

"Oh Bernie, pleeeeez," she insists with a toothy smile that shows off a diamond, or maybe it's just a rhinestone, stud in her incisor.

"Bernie it is, then. Well, Reg wouldn't have wanted to alarm you but we are growing concerned about Gary's continued absence."

Bernie Jantz thinks about – but just as quickly discards – making a theatrical gesture when faced with the sober and serious faces of the two big men crowded round her kitchen table. Neither one has sneaked any admiring glances at her, nor have they responded to her flirtatious moves. She figures she'd better play it straight and get rid of them before she gets bored. She'll enjoy playing up the interview to an appreciative audience later.

"Gary made a habit of running away over the years. I guess he could only take so much of Greg and that Barbie. He'd come here, well I wasn't always living here, but he'd come to me but I always had to let them take him back. Greg was his legal guardian, after all." Her deep sigh elicits no sympathy. "But at his age it's no longer *running away* so why are you looking? He's an adult, right?"

"True, but only just. He's still a teenager and he's been gone for a number of days now."

"How many days?"

"No one is quite sure when he was home last–"

"Huh! that's typical. Gary got shunted to the side now that they've got kids of their own. He was always a very jealous little boy, always clinging to me and demanding my attention, but I guess he learned to keep it hidden. Hard enough being odd man out without drawing extra attention to himself."

"Well, he's certainly slipped under everyone's radar now. And his stepmother's been murdered so we want to find him."

"Why? You don't think Gary had anything to do with that, do you?" she is avidly interested, as if discussing a character in a daytime soap opera instead of her own son.

"At this point our concern is that there's a killer on the loose. We don't know why Ms. Nichols was murdered–"

"Oh it'll have something to do with that money she won, I'm sure of it."

"You're probably right, Ms... uh, Bernie. So, just to keep our records straight–"

"Cross your i's and dot your t's, eh?" she cackles at her own wit.

"When is the last time you saw or spoke to your son?"

"Oh boy, now you're asking... let's see it would have been... hmm. What's the date today?"

"Monday, May 4," supplies Reg.

"Oh well then, not for ages. My birthday is April 1st but believe me I'm nobody's fool," she winks. "Gary always makes a big deal out of it, phoning, wanting to come around. I managed to put him off this year but he definitely would have called so I'm going to say April 1st."

Both of the policemen maintain their bland expressions as they thank her for the information and for her time. Grant isn't surprised when Bernie Jantz doesn't ask them to keep her updated on news of Gary. He's almost tempted to pretend-innocently ask *would you like us to keep you informed?* but he's been well-schooled in dealing with the public.

Later, speaking to Judith on the phone is like fresh air has swept away the lingering disgust he felt in his meeting with Bernie Janz.

"Did you call Pat?"

"Yeah, I did and she's really glad I accepted. I appreciate your support as well, you know."

"Judith, I've only known you for... five months, is it? wow, seems like more, but in that time you've changed a lot. I don't know if you used to be shy or if you were just withdrawn, an introvert, but you're so much more outgoing now, and friendlier, too."

"Most of that's down to you, Grant. You built up my confidence. Both you and Lila have been such good friends to me."

"Lila, right... I've been meaning to talk to her. Listen, I gotta go, I'll call you back, okay?"

Grant realizes he's ended their conversation abruptly and briefly worries how Judith will interpret that but he'll call her later and explain it all then.

COVID-19 Update: No one is supposed to be shaking hands in greeting or saying goodbye with a hug, but people forget. Families are warned to keep small children away from grandparents and older relatives since the 75+ age groups are suffering the most fatalities.

Chapter 18

Tuesday, May 5, 2020

Judith and Lila are chatting on the phone. Lila is sprawled over her couch with an espresso in hand and a box of chocolates spread out on her coffee table.

Judith has stepped out on her tiny balcony to get a breath of fresh air. It's hard being cooped up day in and day out. She regrets not adopting a cat while she could. Unfortunately the animal shelter is now closed for the pandemic.

Instead she's enjoying a starry sky on a clear night. Calgary is often cloudy at night, and its light pollution stretches near Edgemont.

"Grant phoned me yesterday," states Lila. "I was surprised to hear from him and really surprised when I found out why he called. I assumed it was to talk about you, but it wasn't."

"You mean he's not planning a surprise party for me? I knew he was going to call you so I just naturally assumed..."

"When did you develop a sense of humour?" laughs Lila.

"When I changed. Grant commented yesterday about how I have changed even in the few months he's known me. Neither of us can believe it's only been a few months."

"Every change I've seen has been for the better, Judith."

"Aww, thanks! I told Grant that your friendship, and his too, has really made a difference. Now, what did he call you about?"

"His exact words were *how did you move past the guilt of your husband's suicide?*"

"WHAT?!"

"I know, eh? I said *Gee, Grant let's just jump right in at the deep-end.* And he apologized but said he'd told you about his high-school girlfriend killing herself and now that he's actually faced up to what happened and discussed it, he wants to move on.

His ongoing guilt over her act, despite knowing that she was being treating for depression, has always made him leery of committment. He's afraid of hurting someone else and he's afraid of getting hurt again himself, but he's more afraid of losing you."

"I would never kill myself."

"And I'm sure he knows that, knows that he isn't going to break you. You have a strong will and you're gutsy, and you have backbone. Grant wants to overcome his issues because he really wants to hang on to you."

In a quiet voice Judith asks: "Do you really think so?"

"Judith when is your birthday?"

"August 13, I'm a Leo."

"Well, lioness, I won't be surprised if Grant gives you an engagement ring."

"I sure would! It's only been a few months and—"

"And Grant's old enough to know his mind, to know what he wants. He wants you, Judith."

"Is all this because of that guy Andy paying so much attention to me?"

"That might have been the wake-up call. By the way, Andy did ask Brian for your phone number. I'd already given him a heads-up, after the barbeque, but then things improved between you and Grant so Brian didn't hesitate to tell Andy *no*. Plus, Brian says that although Andy has proven to be a good worker he wouldn't like to see you involved with someone like him."

"Meaning what, exactly?"

"Well, Brian said he might live in a homeless shelter but Brian thinks it's far more likely that he's in a halfway house. You know, for released prisoners? Of course he's only guessing, but Andy still doesn't let anyone pick him up or drive him to his home, it's always *drop me off downtown* so he's probably hiding something. Brian says he couldn't care less for a manual labourer but he draws the line at arranging a date with a friend of his."

"Yet he had him to his home..."

"To a backyard barbeque where Brian was present the whole time. He doesn't think Andy's a problem, but he's certain Andy has a past."

"I see. Hmm, he did tell me he was hoping to re-connect with family he has in this area."

"Yes, he's been estranged from his two daughters–"

"Omigod Lila, that's it!" Judith's excitement is evident even over the phone.

"What did I say?"

"Two daughters. Brenda and Glenda Nikovics, I'll bet you anything. I've been puzzling in my mind where I knew Andy from because he looked so familiar yet I didn't think I'd ever met him. I mentioned it to him and he said he was sure we'd never met but still... it nagged at me. Now, it makes perfect sense. I've only seen Glenda in passing but I've spent time with Brenda, her identical twin, and yes, I'm sure they're Andy's daughters."

The two women speak practically in unison:

"But the father of the twins..."

"Was supposed to have died years ago."

"And Barbie didn't raise the girls herself because she was in hiding from her abusive ex, their father."

"Then the lottery win meant her picture was in the paper and on the evening news. That must be how he found her!"

"Do you think he killed her?"

"Oh Lila, I wouldn't have thought it of him... but what do I really know about him? I've got to tell Grant about this right away."

"This is... wow. I'm going to call Brian, too. Wait, what time is it? Oh damn, he'll be in bed already, his day begins at the crack of dawn. I'll text him. If he's asleep and Beth's home he'll have his phone turned off so it won't disturb him."

"Oh that's a good idea because even if my phone's on vibrate I get woken by the ding of incoming messages."

"Who sends you messages when you're sleeping?"

"Spammy stuff, either it's scheduled by a bot or they know it's late night and hope I'll click the links before I'm fully awake."

"Huh, I never get stuff like that. Anyhow, I am going to text Brian to warn him that he needs to be on his guard around Andy just, you know, just in case."

"I'll ask Grant what he thinks about that too."

"Okay call me as soon as you know anything."

Gary's been couch-surfing with some friends in the Trailer Park but they've gotten fed up with him still hanging around. They were okay when he arrived with a case of beer and a carton of smokes saying he needed to hide out for a couple of days, but the money he'd scrounged from the house soon ran out and so did his welcome.

His mother lives in this very same place but Gary knows better than to drop in on her. She's never had any time for him, she's never been the maternal type. It's nothing to do with him, that's just the way she is. Once he'd come to that conclusion he felt much better about things.

At least she never had any other kids so Gary knows he hasn't been dissed in favour of some younger child. No, his mom simply doesn't have a motherly drop of blood in her whole body, she isn't interested in kids or family. Not like Barbie Nichols who made such a big deal of it.

Gary acknowledges that Barbie always treated him better than his own flesh-and-blood mother but still... It was bad enough having to accept it when his two half-sisters came along but the sudden introduction of two grown stepsisters, and their grandmother, well... filling up the house with all those females was too much. Especially when he found his new *sisters* hot, and the idea of twins phew, even hotter!

At least that's what all his friends say, and say it with all the salacious drooling of healthy teenage males. But to Gary they're just one more shitty thing in his shitty life. Just when things start looking up something always comes along to bite you in the ass.

But he'll have to head back pretty soon. He's been hoping the police would have arrested somebody by now. They're always asking for help from the public meaning rats. But he can't hide out forever, what if CrimeStoppers puts up his photo and he ends up getting turned in by his so-called friends? Not that he'd blame them, they only live in a single-wide trailer which got pretty cramped with all of them there. And if a reward was offered? Huh!

He's having to go to a lot of trouble to make a call to his father. He'd forgotten to bring his charger and none of his temporary room mates have iPhones, just Androids, which no one will let him borrow. He wanders around the trailer park trying to find someone he knows and ends up in the laundromat. This building still has a pay-phone but it only takes calling cards, not coins. Not that that matters since Gary doesn't have any change.

He finally approaches the woman who works there explaining he needs to call his Dad. She isn't willing to help until he hands over his iPhone as collateral. She makes a big deal out of cleaning it off with a *handiwipe,* then loans him her flip-phone which he has to study for a minute to figure out how to use. When he has to ask the woman for his phone back so he can get his father's number from his contacts she refuses, telling him to give her his pin so she can unlock the phone and look it up.

Gary huffs over this, he isn't happy about letting his phone out of his hands to begin with, but then he reasons he can change his password. He doesn't like that idea though, he likes what he's got and hates change, then he thinks *maybe I don't have to...* it's not like he'll ever see this woman again.

Gary gets hold of his father and asks if he'll come pick him up. First off Greg says no but then asks his location. Feeling aggrieved and annoyed by now Gary snaps that he's at the trailer park.

"You mean you've been at your mother's place? Huh, well you can walk from there."

"Dad c'mon, I've been at my friend's place, not Mom's, and he doesn't have a car. Can't you come get me? If it's okay for me to come home, I mean."

"Why wouldn't it be? Oh! you mean because of the police? Nobody's made any accusations or anything. You're just gonna have to talk to them, that's all. Anyhow, you're a lot closer to home than I am, even walking, so I'm not coming all the way out there to get you. Come home and we'll talk things over later."

"Walk? I don't wanna..." but his father has already disconnected the call.

The woman had heard everything and now she just smirks at Gary, holding her hand out for her phone before she returns his.

"You're welcome!" she hollers after him but the sarcasm goes right over Gary's head. He's too wrapped up feeling sorry for himself to spare her any consideration.

When he gets back to his friend's trailer an impromptu party had broken out with a few cars pulled up and a bunch of people his own age sitting on lawn chairs or sprawled on the grass. Some girl hands Gary a beer which he accepts with a grin, deciding he'll go home later or maybe even wait until tomorrow.

Maybe his old man will feel bad about not coming to get him. He can't push him too far, though, because his father is going to end up with a lot of money pretty soon.

Honestly, sometimes he treats me like I'm an irresponsible child, fumes Judith after a very unsatisfactory conversation with Grant. Her news, the connection she's made, is a revelation. She's pumped up to share it but is Grant appreciative? no, of course not. He immediately dismisses any idea of collaborating, planning or plotting. *He's such a… a CHAUVINIST,* she decides.

"And I'm sure Grant's acting like this because it's Andy. Grant's got a real grudge against him just because he showed me a little attention at Brian's party. Anybody else and we'd probably still be discussing ways and means but with Andy? no way, I have to butt out because *it might be dangerous.*"

Judith's phone rings, interrupting her monologue, with a call from Lila. She's fared no better.

"Hope you got further with Grant than I did with Brian, because I got no joy from him whatsoever. Here, I'll read you what he texted back:

Brian: the professionals can handle it so let the cops do their job

What did Grant say?"

"Pretty much the same thing except with him instead of amateur versus professional it feels more like silly woman versus sensible man. Aarrgghh! I get so frustrated with that attitude."

"Tell me about it! I basically ran things with Arnie but Brian? different story altogether. Don't get me wrong, I love that I can't push him around but hey, where's the harm in a little nudging," Lila says with a laugh.

"Oh I agree. I don't want someone who can't even decide where to eat dinner, but this *laying down the law* can go too far."

"Well, law kind of is Grant's thing, right?"

"Lila," warns Judith, "I can hear you holding back a giggle! and I'm too annoyed to laugh."

"You're such a newbie at relationships! Listen, ever heard the expression *it's better to ask for forgiveness than permission*? Weeeeellll, just because the guys are telling us what to do doesn't mean we have to do it."

"Oh! you mean we could–"

"Could and should. So, let's plan!"

COVID-19 Update: Businesses are incurring costs to meet the re-opening requirements. Reduced capacity means seating is removed or areas closed off with signs post on doors. Plexiglass dividers are installed to separate staff from customers, 6-foot social distancing markers are placed on floors and sidewalks, and sanitizer and cleaning wipes must be provided at every entrance and cash register.

Chapter 19

Grant is well-aware that Judith us angry with him – again – but it can't be helped. If Andy really is the father of Barbie's daughters then he is a dangerous man. Not necessarily a murderer, but that's something they have to consider.

Today is going to be all about getting factual information. Anton Czerny was officially declared deceased so they'll have to jump through hoops to get an arrest warrant because dead men can't commit crimes. The law is often blinkered.

Grant is meeting with the Crown Prosecutor's office to discuss this unusual situation. He's pretty sure he'll come out of that meeting with his hands tied. First, though, he wants to bring Reg up-to-date with this new information, and then they'll go see Moira Nikovics.

"I don't think you should bring this to Moira yet."

Grant is taken aback at Reg's opposition to his plan.

"But she's the only one we know who could identify Anton Czerny."

"*Might* be able to identify him you mean. There's no guarantee. That's one of the reasons I think it's a mistake to involve her until you have more information. Another reason is the fear and worry this will cause and maybe – probably – unnecessarily, too."

"Really? you don't see this as a likely scenario?"

"No, of course not. Grant, what have you got? besides a very persuasive girlfriend, that is."

"Judith is not fanciful, nor does she dramatize herself," replies Grant stiffly.

"I didn't mean to imply she was but.. okay, let's re-cap what you've told me. A guy named Andy has returned to this area to reconnect with daughters he left behind. He bears a resemblance to the twins whose father disappeared many years ago. And...?"

"And the missing father was called Anton, and this Andy has served time and is the right age and has no money or job or home yet he's confident the girl's mother *won't be a problem*. Look, I know it's not enough to get an arrest warrant or anything but if Moira Nikovics can give us any kind of identifying information like height, build, eye colour, age, then I want to hear it and maybe we'll really luck out and she's got a photo."

"Grant, put yourself in the woman's shoes. One, her daughter has just been murdered, and two, you're asking if the man who terrorized her before blessedly dying a decade ago might still be alive and back here now looking for her granddaughters. Do you really thing that's fair?"

"Fair? Reg, how *fair* will it be if Andy *is* Anton and he's killed Barbie and is now on his way to find his girls?"

"Oh, so you've pegged him as the killer, too?"

"Are you so sure he isn't? If there's even the slightest chance then I think Moira, and Greg Nichols, and those girls deserve a heads-up."

"Even considering the emotional cost..."

"She's a strong woman, I believe she'd want to know."

Reg shakes his head but doesn't argue further.

"You're the boss."

"No, the office of the Crown Prosecutor is actually our boss at the moment. No sense both of us being alternately bored then ridiculed so I'll go get lectured and will meet you back here.

"As I said... you're the boss." Reg repeats with a snarky grin.

Gary's temporary landlord kicked him out of the trailer after a quarrel late that night. The girl he'd been flirting with had left and too many beers made him morose and argumentative. He ended up finding refuge on top of a picnic table. The air turned chilly in the early morning hours and Gary awoke dry-mouthed and miserable. He staggered away to take a whizz against a tree before stumbling back and flopping down on the table again.

He's lain there, sprawled out, all day. At 5:00 pm a resident calls the manager, Jerry Bennett, to complain. He says he's just sat down to his supper but will check things out as soon as he finished. The lady assures him it certainly wasn't worth interrupting his meal, adding that hopefully the bum will be gone before he gets there.

So it's about 5:45 when Gary is roughly shaken awake by a big man with a red face and a small, odd-looking moustache. His colouring is the result of a two-month-old burn and the pared-down facial hair is all that remains of Jerry's once-luxuriant Fu Manchu. He's determined to grow it back, though.

In the meantime Gary finds the big man intimidating, not laughable, so he doesn't argue when he's told to go to his trailer or get off the property. He sits up with a groan from his uncomfortable makeshift bed on the picnic table and absently starts scratching at the mosquito bites dotted along his forearms.

He turns towards his friend's trailer before remembering their fight and instead aims for the road out. Jerry Bennett stands watching until Gary is out of sight.

The sunshine is still bright and shines hotly on the back of Gary's neck as he trudges with his head hanging down. He's suffering from a pounding hangover headache. The walk home really isn't that far but he's in no rush to arrive. In fact, he doesn't want to see anyone at all and sure doesn't want to answer questions. He just wants to go back to sleep in his own comfortable bed. After downing a couple of bottles of water or cola.

He'll go in the kitchen door, grab what he needs from the fridge, then quietly sneak up to his room and lock himself in. He's done it before.

Judith and Lila have made their plan but it doesn't start till end of the afternoon and Judith is getting antsy. She calls Lila to invite herself over so they can hang out until it's time to leave.

"Yeah sure, drop in, are you hungry?"

"Why? is your landlady cooking?"

"Mrs. P is *always* cooking or baking something and I've got a fridge full of her dishes. Come over and raid it."

"I'm on my way!"

Twenty minutes later Judith has texted her arrival and Lila is waiting for her at the back door. As soon as they walk down the stairs to Lila's basement suite Judith smells the wonderful aroma of home cooking.

"I've gone ahead to heat up a couple of platefuls. Mrs P doesn't think much of microwaves so her re-heating instructions are always for the oven which takes longer."

"I'm drooling it smells so good!"

"I am so lucky with her for my landlady. I took Brian up to meet her and she's ready to adopt him. Right in front of him she says to me *so handsome, you better watch out for the hungry girls* and he reassures her that I keep him well-fed and of course I'm turning all shades of red because I know what the two of them are really talking about. They got on soooo well."

"He does seem to be an easy-going guy but, as you've discovered, he's just as good as Grant when it comes to the macho crap."

"Oh Brian's better at it than Grant is because he's had years of being *Daddy* with all of the overprotective behaviour that involves."

Lila puts a couple of padded placemats down then brings the hot plates out of the oven. Judith helps herself to a bottled water from the fridge and asks:

"What do you want to drink?"

"I've got a water going – do you want a glass with lemon?"

"No, this is good thanks. Mmm, and this food is excellent!"

The two women eat their meal with shared enjoyment. They tease each other about their *boyfriends* and giggle over jokes and innuendo. Judith is experiencing the giddy foolishness of having a *bestie* to confide in, something she missed out on back in high-school.

Lila's kitchen doesn't include a dishwasher so she fills up the sink with hot soapy water but Judith moves her aside saying: "You dry because I don't know where anything goes."

After they get the place tidied up again Judith suggests popping upstairs to thank the old lady for the food. Lila agrees it's a good idea but wants to check first because her landlady often takes a nap around about this time. Judith doesn't have long to wait before Lila is back and waving for her to follow.

Mrs. Piernitsky is sitting at her kitchen table drinking a glass of cranberry juice. She gestures with the glass saying:

"Terrible taste but doctor says I need it for my plumbing. Maybe too many babies, eh?"

The younger women laugh at her outrageous wink and Lila admonishes:

"Don't be naughty Mrs. P. I'm still blushing from Brian's visit and the things you said..."

"I only talked about good cooking!" she answers with a cackle. "Do you know Brian too, Judith?" She pronounces the name *Ju-deetz*.

"Yes, his daughter Beth is a student at our school. I met Brian last December. Well, that's really when Lila and I became friendly too."

"Ah, too bad for you that Lila sees him first huh? He's such a handsome boy with that lovely red hair... shows he has the passion in him."

"Don't worry about Judith, Mrs. P. We all met because of a police investigation and Judith snagged the top cop for herself!"

"Oh-ho, the two of you both have men so now you'll be settling down?"

"Well December was only a few months ago–" begins Judith but the senior waves away that objection saying:

"With my Zoso, God-rest-his-soul, I knew right away and so did he. You two girls are pretty but you can't wait too long. If you start your family too late you'll be too old to enjoy your grandchildren."

"Wow, now we're talking grandchildren."

"Mrs. P does not mess about when she wants to make a point," says Lila with one arm around the lady's shoulders to give her a squeeze.

"Well you certainly can cook a delicious meal. That's the second time Lila's fed me with your cooking and both times were mmmm, so good!"

"If your man wants Ukrainian or Hungarian food you tell me and I teach you how to make a couple of things."

"Thank you! I'd like to learn."

Lila and Judith leave soon after having scheduled a date for a cooking lesson.

Mrs. Piernitsky warns Lila not to say anything to her children since she's been rationing her time with them explaining: "Lovely grandchildren and great-grandchildren but too much germs from the little ones."

They all exchange goodbyes and the two friends head back downstairs to Lila's suite.

"Soooo... you've told your landlady about Brian but how about your parents?"

Lila screws up her face in a grimace saying she doesn't have the nerve yet.

"I mean, I've told them about him and how I spend quite a bit of time with him and Beth so maybe they've read between the lines but nobody's said anything."

"Hmm, but if you've introduced him to Mrs. Piernitsky then, well, it's obviously serious."

"You mean because I told my substitute Mom, or because I'm sleeping with him?"

Judith's eyes widen at Lila's frankness then she smiles and answers: "Both!"

"To tell you the truth I can really see us making a life together. I mean I know it's super-sudden and everything but we're adults and we know what we want and, we both want the same thing: a family."

"Yes, you'd be getting a ready-made family with Beth..."

"And, hopefully, children of our own, too."

"Brian wants more kids?"

"So much so that when I told him I would make a doctor's appointment to take care of the birth control situation he asked if I would consider not doing anything preventative, just let nature take its course."

"But.. what.. what did he mean?"

"He means to get me pregnant. And Judith? I love the idea!"

"Oh, oh I see. So if you do fall pregnant that would force the committment thing between the two of you, right?"

"Pregnancy would mean us getting married, yes."

"OMIGOD! Marriage, kids, and you love him?" Judith asks the question with a little hesitation, it seems such a personal thing but Lila just grins back and answers *Yes! Oh, yes!*

Judith hugs her friend and they're both surprised at her making such an impulsive gesture. Now it's time for the two friends to begin their tailing and surveillance but once they're buckled into the car Judith brings up the subject of birth control again, asking Lila what she was planning on.

"You being a nurse, you'll know what's best to use."

"Especially me being a nurse in an all-girls school full of adolescents."

"Oh right, I hadn't thought about that."

"Well Acting-but-soon-to-be-permanent-Principal Taylor it's something you better think about. Oh, we could make *recommending that the students get the HPV vaccination* as your first point of contention with the parents and the Board."

"Lila, let's save the controversy for another day, hmm?"

"Spoilsport. Anyhow, at our age I recommend an IUD."

"Okay I've heard of that..."

"It's a small device your doctor inserts and you can forget about it for like ten years, or is it five? No, I think I read it's good for ten years now."

"Sounds creepy."

"No, it's perfect, a drug-free solution, and you won't even know it's there. Seriously, make an appointment with your doctor to get it put in. Then tell Grant he owes me big-time," laughs Lila.

Grant begins their meeting with Moira Nikovics by explaining he has no new information about Gary or about Barbie's killer. He then apologizes in advance for broaching a subject that might cause her concern, possibly even distress, before asking if she'd ever had any reason to believe the girls' father was still alive.

Moira responds with a loud laugh of disbelief, saying *of course not,* and then scoffs at them for *grasping at straws.*

"That Anton was a nasty piece of work who died years ago and good riddance. Look, I know no body was ever found but as they told us at the time it was a very, very deep lake. Maybe the Rocky Mountains have their own version of a Loch Ness monster and it got him? That would make me smile, a monster devoured by a bigger monster."

"Well it was something we had to follow up. He was actually your son-in-law, right? say you don't have a photo of him by any chance, do you?" Grant's enquiry is made casually but Moira isn't fooled.

"Look just tell me what's going on? I don't have a photo but you do – you've got a mug shot, he was arrested and went to prison."

"Yeah, I'll look into that." Grant is careful not to meet Reg's enquiring look. The file Grant had requisitioned should have had a mug shot and when it didn't he immediately looked at the charges and the suspicion he had was confirmed when he saw *Resisting Arrest*. Whether or not Anton Czerny had actually resisted he was almost definitely beaten up by the arresting officers and his face was too messed up for a photo to go in the official record.

Things used to be handled quite differently – wrongly – but the uniformed thugs should have been terminated by the nineties. Obviously not all were.

Reg speaks up then, surprising Grant considering how he'd disagreed earlier, saying: "I think you better come clean with Ms. Nikovics, Grant. I realize it's only supposition but tell her what's brought us here and then she can give us her opinion."

Moira gives Grant a skeptical but interested look so taking a deep breath and cursing himself for feeling foolish he plunges right in.

"A couple of the employees at Brenda's school, the bursar and the school nurse, are friends and they heard a story that has them connecting dots and called me with a possible tip. There's a man, early to mid-forties, called Andy, working as casual day labour for construction crews. He's newly arrived in Calgary mentioning that he has daughters here who he'd like to reconnect with after many years."

"Well sure, the age is right and Anton was a hard worker, a builder, but that's quite a stretch–"

"Thing is, these women met this Andy and they insist he bears a very strong resemblance to Brenda and Glenda."

"No."

"You're probably right, but as I said–"

"No, No! NO! Oh God, no-no-no, it can't be." Moira's fear fills the room startling both men with its intensity.

"Ms. Nikovics, Moira, please–"

"If anyone could come back from Hell it would be him, he's always been a devil. Omigod the girls! We have to get out of here!"

Reg grabs the woman's hands, easily covering them with his own big hands, and speaks to her in his soothing, calming voice.

"We don't know if it's him and frankly it's really, really unlikely so don't panic. We know where this Andy will be working tomorrow so we're planning to talk to him and we'll get a photo to show you. It's probably no use me telling you not to worry about this tonight but try."

"I am really sorry to have upset you like this, Ms. Nikovics. We never want to worry people, especially since as Reg says this is a real long-shot, but *what if?* I believe you're a strong woman who can handle knowing what we're investigating, so I think it's important to give you a heads-up. You should be on your guard for yourself and the girls because even if there's nothing to this Andy-Anton idea there still is a killer out there."

Moira reaches into her pocket and pulls out a pack of cigarettes. Her hands shake so badly she can't hold the lighter steady so Reg helps out. After Moira inhales deeply they can see her visibly relax. It is still a full minute before she speaks and when she does it's to thank the men for their honesty.

"Anton Czerny being alive would be the worst possible thing that could happen. Barbie couldn't fight him back then, neither could

I, and the thought of him anywhere near the girls is just sickening but... no point getting my stomach in knots worrying about the possibility. Still, I'll make sure the house is locked up and everyone is careful of strangers. I'll say you told me a suspicious character was reported hanging around. I don't have to explain any more than that."

Both Grant and Reg approve this plan, with Grant adding that as soon as he has more information and a photo he'll be back.

"Tomorrow, yes?"

"Yes, we'll see you sometime tomorrow."

COVID-19 Update: Workers forced to self-isolate, or care for someone ill, can apply for the Employment Insurance benefit. If they don't qualify for EI the Federal Government will pay them up to $450 weekly for 15 weeks. The Province is paying to cover the usual 2-week waiting period.

Chapter 20

Wednesday, May 6, 2020

"Brian? Hi, it's Grant, George Grant. I got your number from Judith, do you have a few minutes to talk?"

"Sure, I just got home from work. I never knew your first name was George, I just thought it was Grant something."

"Yeah well, Grant's what I've always gone by so..."

"Learn something new every day."

"Speaking of which... has Lila said anything about your employee Andy? What's his last name, by the way?"

"I don't know his last name because he's not an employee, just casual labour I pay in cash at the end of each day. Lila did send me a text about her and Judith figuring Andy might be the long-lost father of these girls from their school, the girls whose mother was recently murdered. Anyhow, I texted back that she needs to keep her nose out of it."

"Oh thank God. The last thing those two need is any encouragement to be amateur sleuths like that young woman... you know her, it's a TV show but... nah, I can't remember her name. Anyhow, I'm glad you and I are on the same page about warning them off from getting involved. So, getting back to Andy, what's your take on the guy?"

"Good worker. Punctual, skilled, capable, strong, and he gets along okay with the rest of my crew."

"I guess I'm a bit biased about the guy..."

"Oh I'm not advocating for him, I know there's gotta be something wrong with the man. You don't get to be that age with nothing to your name unless you threw it away via a bottle or crime or any of a dozen reasons, I guess. He doesn't talk about his past except for mentioning he's estranged from his daughters who live in this area. Oh, and he said their mother wasn't a problem, she'd remarried or something."

"Or something... hmm, I wonder."

"Do you know anything about these girls' father?"

"Yeah, he's supposed to be dead but no body was ever found."

"Oh."

"Yeah, *oh* is right. The story is Barbie dumped her twin daughters on her mother soon after their birth and then disappeared to get away from their abusive father, who was also her brother-in-law. He ended up in jail for a couple of years, bar fight I think it was, and as soon as he got out he made a beeline for the mother's place where his girls were.

After that confrontation the mother, Barbie's mother, sold up everything and left Alberta, moving to Toronto. The girls' father had gotten violent with her and she had him arrested but he escaped custody and ran into Kananaskis country where he vanished, presumed drowned. This happened more than a dozen years ago. Eventually he was declared dead, and no one's ever heard from him, but... Andy's age is right and the abusive Dad was called Anton."

"Shit."

"So, you can see why I told Judith to back off and I'm glad you said the same thing to Lila."

"Yeah, geez I had this guy at my home, around my daughter, I just.."

"Brian, Andy might not be Anton. It's only supposition based on a few offhand remarks. I did talk to the girl's grandmother, she's certain she can identify Anton Czerny if it is him. At this point I can't pull him in for a line-up but there are ways...

My next step is to talk to Andy but he's not obligated to answer any of my questions. I mean I can ask for his ID and do a records search which might lead me somewhere... I was hoping you had his full name and an address."

"No, as I said if he was an employee then yes, I'd have that information, and if he works for another four days I'm going to get it from him for payroll tax and WCB because he'll have moved into a casual/part-time situation but until then, sorry."

"How does he get to work, do you pick him up somewhere?"

"I get him at *Cash Corner* do you know it?"

"Yeah, I do, what time do you get him?"

"Uh, Grant, this is starting to get awkward."

"Brian, I get it. Obviously he's going to know this came from you, but he already knows we're friends and he probably knows I'm a cop–"

"I've never told anyone that."

"No and thanks, but with ex-cons you don't have to, we recognize each other. This is better than me showing up at your job-site in front of your crew, right? If there's no connection, if the guy's innocent, well I can't say *no harm done* because he might not be willing to stay working with you but I definitely need to talk to him."

"Yeah, okay, I can see that. Damn, he was a lucky find, a really good worker, you know? But that in itself means that there's something hinky about him hanging around *Cash Corner.* Anyhow I told him I'd see him about 7:10 so we could be on site by 7:30."

"I'll be in place before 7:00 then. There's no need for you to come by."

"I think I will, though."

Unknown to the two men is the fact that Judith and Lila are already executing the plan they've defiantly put in place.

"I remember that the job site is really open, a new subdivision under construction, so no cover and Brian knows your car as well as mine, Judith. When he talks about Andy he says he always picks him up and drops him off back at *Cash Corner* so that's why we're hanging out here. We can stay well back, Andy doesn't have a car of his own so he won't be travelling too quickly. Anyhow, we just want to see where he goes, just to get an idea of what he does, where he lives..."

"And we're bored to tears stuck indoors during this pandemic so..."

"Oh look, right on time, that's Brian's pick-up." The two women slump down a bit in their seats although no one's looking in their direction.

"Yup, there's Andy. Looks like they're talking about working again tomorrow."

"Okay, and there goes Brian. He'll head home, grab a shower, find out what Beth's plans are, and then give me a call."

"You better turn your ringer off, just in case he calls at a bad time."

"Really? Why do you think...oh never mind, it's always somebody's ringing phone that screws things up in the movies. I'll put it on vibrate now so I don't forget if we get busy later."

"It doesn't look like we'll be busy at all, look Andy's just standing there. How are we supposed to follow him if he won't go anywhere?"

"Judith, impatient or what? Relax."

"Yeah, yeah. I just want something to happen, you know."

"Of course I know, you want to be able to have an *I told you so* moment where you tell Grant something startling, something he hadn't known or couldn't have figured out for himself."

"So maybe it's a little childish..."

"No, it's a lot childish but 100% understandable. So, give it a chance."

"But why is he just standing there?"

"Omigod Judith! it's a bus stop, see?"

Judith screws up her face in self-disgust and her expression makes Lila laugh heartily. Lila's laugh always sets Judith off and soon the two are gasping for breath. The overreaction is due to nerves and excitement.

Luckily the bus pulls up then so they begin the tedious yet anxiety-inducing process of following a city bus at rush-hour, ignoring the honking horns and rude gestures of the other drivers.

After about forty minutes the bus reaches the city limit and the remaining passengers all get off to go their separate ways. Some are met by waiting cars, and some go into the Tim Horton's. Andy stays on the road and starts walking.

"Well that sucks," says Lila. "We can't follow him in a car while he's walking, we'll look like curb-crawlers."

"What's that?"

"That's what they call the guys in cars who go trolling through red light districts checking out the working girls."

"It's hardly the same thing!"

"No, at least they're potential customers. We're just stalkers."

"No we aren't, we're... okay I guess we are. Well, so much for that idea. I wonder where he's going?"

"Home, I mean our home. This is a secondary road leads into the west-end of Edgemont."

"I wonder if we should grab a coffee? we can kill fifteen minutes or so drinking it here in the parking lot. That should give him a chance to get near where he's going, then we can drive by and pick up his trail?"

"I suppose we could.. I can always drink a cup of coffee and oh look! he's just hitched a ride from that SUV."

"Lila, I've always wanted to say *follow that car*," says Judith with delight.

"*And step on it*, am I right?"

<u>*COVID-19 Update*</u>: To reduce the risk of the virus entering prisons no classes or group therapies or visitations are allowed. Outdoor time and activities have been curtailed or suspended because maintaining social distancing of 6 feet is impossible.

Chapter 21

Wednesday, May 6, 2020

Grant isn't unduly surprised when his call to Judith goes straight to voice-mail, just a little disappointed because he wants to update her on what actions he's taken about Andy. He wants to get back on her good side, not liking it when she's mad at him.

He decides to leave a message: "Hey sweetie, lots to tell you about that lead you found so call me when you get this. Kisses."

At the same time Brian is puzzled at not being able to reach Lila. They don't have firm plans for tonight but he was expecting to see her. He's sure she would have called or texted if something came up unexpectedly, and hopes nothing's wrong. He worries about her being a nurse and getting exposed to the virus.

Lila has already discussed a possible job change, temporarily, that is. She told Brian that if the number of hospitalizations jumps she suspects all of the nurses working in the province will be called to front-line duties. She also said that with the school shut down she would feel obligated to go help. He hopes that doesn't happen. The lack of concrete information about the disease makes everyone nervous.

If he knew what Lila was up to right now with Judith he'd have good reason to be annoyed... and worried.

"This is the worst possible neighbourhood to try to hide," whispers Lila.

They've followed the SUV at a respectable distance until it stops at an intersection and Andy jumps out. They're forced to go through the light but manage to turn around in the lot on the corner, a 7-11 convenience store.

Andy is easy to spot, there's no one else around, so they drive past him with Judith exclaiming *that's Barbie Nichols' home!* and park the car a couple of houses down. Since the properties are so large they have quite a ways to walk back.

They're sneaking along the edge of the sidewalk on this dark, quiet street feeling incredibly conspicuous. They don't dare step on lawns because of motion-sensing lights or patrolling dogs. The houses are so well-concealed behind walls and shrubbery you can't even tell if anyone is home. With nothing to see or hear the atmosphere weighs down on the two women, but they remain alert.

Andy isn't on the Nichols' driveway or at their front door so he must have gone around to the side or back of the house. Judith and Lila creep as quietly as they can and follow his path. They duck down when passing windows but the rooms are dark. The last window on this side shows a light but it's muted since the drapes are drawn.

Both women hesitate to round the corner into the back of the property. It's so dark, and leaving the protective cover of the wall is scary. Judith is in the lead on the walkway and reaching back she grabs hold of Lila's hand. Her friend's answering squeeze gives her the necessary courage. With a deep breath and a silent prayer that they aren't about to come face-to-face with Andy Judith steps out.

Being hyper alert after meeting with the police Moira is on the lookout for anything out of the ordinary. She hears a scuffling down the path along the side of the house and immediately phones Grant. He tells her he's on his way but she must keep everyone inside and call 9-1-1. They'll keep her on the line until the police arrive. He calls Reg as he runs down the stairs from his apartment to get his car.

"Might be a false alarm but Moira Nikovics just called to say someone's on the property so I'm heading out there now."

"I'll call 9-1-1 and meet you the house," Reg replies and disconnects before Grant can tell him Moira has already called the emergency services.

When Greg came home that afternoon from wherever it is that he's now spending his days – a bar, from the look of him – Moira told him about Grant's visit. Greg is utterly disbelieving and because he's never known Anton Czerny he can't understand the frightened reaction of his mother-in-law. Moira makes him promise not to say anything to the girls, neither the big nor the little girls, but to make sure they stay safe inside.

Once dinner is over Moira finds herself restless, unable to settle, and goes wandering through the house checking in on everyone. Then she makes sure all the doors are locked, something she usually doesn't bother about until bedtime.

Now, after phoning Grant, she goes in search of Greg. She finds him sitting with the girls watching some new-release movie on the huge projection screen TV. They are all relaxed and safely accounted for so she backs out of the room without interrupting their show and comes back to the kitchen to call 9-1-1.

The lawn spreads out before Judith and Lila, just a smooth expanse with darker shapes along the edges denoting where a lot of trees and bushes grow. Turning her head to the left Judith sees a brick patio leading to sliding doors, the room behind them dark, and then views of lit windows on the upper floors.

The reflected light from one of those windows shows movement near the top of a tall elm. Straining to see Judith hears Lila's gasp as an echo of her own when a jean-clad leg disappears from the tree through an open window into a dark room. They have an anxious whispered conversation about the urgent need to stop Andy versus the wiser course of calling for help. After a few moments they agree that immediate intervention is required.

Neither of them has climbed a tree in years.

"I'll go up and you call 9-1-1 and knock on the door, telling them what's happened."

"No, I'll climb it. I think I'm in better shape than you, I go to the gym."

"Stop wasting time, Lila!"

"I'm not letting you to go after him alone, Grant would kill me if anything happened to you."

"Oh he's already going to kill both of us for coming this far!" their nervousness makes them giggle at that remark.

Judith jumps to grab hold of a low branch and swings herself up, already reaching for the next. The bark is rough under her hands and curiously wet. Sap? or something coming off of the crushed leaves? Lila is right behind and she can hear her saying she needs the police for an intruder and no, she doesn't know the address but can't they just trace her call?

The further up they climb the more difficult it becomes. Having just seen Andy scale the tree they know there is a way through but he's taller and has a longer reach. They struggle onwards and up, pausing to assess their route.

"What kind of tree is this anyhow?"

"It's an elm."

"Can't be, they all died out from Dutch Elm Disease."

"Not in Alberta, the province took measures to prevent that happening."

"Really? that was a–" but Lila is interrupt by Judith's hissed command to *keep quiet, we're here.*

They crouch together in a vee of branch and trunk, straining to see inside the dark room. There's enough ambient light to show that the screen has been pushed aside. They saw Andy come through here just moments before they arrived so they're also straining to hear any sounds from him.

Grabbing hold of a smaller branch above her head Judith lifts up her right leg and stretches it to the window sill and then over into the darkness. Her foot gropes for purchase finally touching a surface – a night table? no, too soft, a couch or a bed. With Lila steadying her hips she manages to get one hand on the window ledge and the other at the side, enough to swing her body in. She lands on a sofa and almost tumbles off but after a wobble keeps her balance. Turning back to the window she reaches out for Lila who has already got both legs on the ledge ready to slide into the room.

They've made some noise getting here so now they pause, breaths held, to listen. They hear stealthy movement in the next room. Then the connecting door is flung open and they're momentarily blinded by the bright fluorescent light of a bathroom but they can still see a tall silhouette.

"Stop!" yells Judith.

Just as Lila warns: "Police are coming!"

All that the dark figure, Gary, hears are cries of *stop! Police!* and he races out of the room. Judith and Lila are right behind him and Andy, having followed the women up the tree, has now jumped into the room in pursuit.

The hallway is dimly lit but Gary knows his way and goes thundering down the stairs. His pursuers have slowed slightly, none having ever been in the house before, and that hesitation means the subsequent injuries are less severe than they might easily have been.

Gary has stopped on the landing and when the women close in on him he grabs and then pushes them out of his way. They fall right down that treacherously slippery staircase to the main floor.

The crashing of bodies and the high-pitched screams draws everyone into the great hall, including Grant and Reg who've just followed the 9-1-1 responders through the front door.

Standing just past the door Grant is stunned to see a tangled heap of bodies including Lila, moaning in pain, and Judith unresponsive and deathly pale.

Gary, landing on his knees, now scrambles up and runs out the door. Andy chases after him. He freezes for a split-second when Moira's shriek of *Anton! no!* startles everyone, but then he's gone.

Reg and the two uniforms speed after the two men, one of them calling into his radio for an ambulance, and for back-up to capture suspects fleeing on foot.

Grant drops down beside Judith gently laying his hand on her throat, relieved to feel a pulse but afraid to move her. Beth painfully scoots backwards until she's propped up against the wall. There she relaxes some of the pressure on her upper body. When she meets Grant's eye she explains, through gritted teeth, that she's dislocated her shoulder.

Sirens announce the arrival of several more police cars and the ambulance. That crew, a man and a woman, immediately demand everyone clear the area citing the authority of COVID-19 protocols.

Grant is ready to protest but a uniformed cop pulls him outside so the EMTs can do their job. The family members are finally dispersed from the hallway. After a few minutes of chaotic milling about the techs load both Judith and Lila onto stretchers and wheel them into the ambulance. There's no room for Grant despite him claiming to be Judith's fiance. Lila, already enjoying relief from the painkiller she's been given, smiles to herself thinking *I'll have to remember him saying that so I can tell Beth and Brian.*

COVID-19 Update: All pensioned seniors will receive a non-taxable one-time payment of $300 to help offset added costs. 9 million in Federal funding goes to agencies providing delivery services for groceries, medications. toiletries, etc... to seniors.

Chapter 22

Anton Czerny, *aka Andy*, easily catches up with Gary Nichols but now that the police are involved instead of tackling the youth he runs right past him. Escaping lawful custody means he's guilty of an indictable offense and there is no statute of limitations on prosecuting that charge. So he continues to run, determined to get far away as quickly as he can.

Ever since Barbie's photo appeared in the news, a picture that included her family and specifically his girls, Anton has been surveilling the house. All the information included in the headline item made it easy for him to track them to their fancy new home in this rich suburb.

He's been enjoying glimpses of his daughters, and keeps watching in the hopes that one or both will come into the back garden to give him a chance to meet them. It doesn't occur to him that the sudden appearance of a stranger in the privacy of her own yard would drive any female away screaming.

While lurking in the shrubbery he's seen the new husband, the stepson and the younger girls, Moira, and even heard Bonnie's voice on speaker during a call with Barbie which really surprised him. But on that fateful Tuesday he didn't see any stranger enter or leave, so he knew that Barbie's killer belonged in the house.

The police would like his testimony about those vital hours but Anton, successful in living on the run for more than a decade, continues to excel at evading capture. His daughters, having grown up in fear of their violent father, don't want a re-union. Neither of them are interested in finding out anything about the man who ran after Gary.

In the aftermath of the arrest Grant sits down with Moira to discuss the Anton Czerny situation. The Crown does not want him to *return to life* after an official declaration of death, and Moira decides that she really can't be certain it was Anton after all. Grant knows she is 100% certain it was him, but a dead man can't fight for custody and she only has a couple more years of having the girls at home. She isn't worried about their estranged father finding them back at home in Toronto.

Two police cars corner Gary who surrenders when faced with armed officers. Reg arrives as the handcuffed young man is bundled into the back of a cruiser. Sobbing that he didn't mean to kill her, but she made him so mad and he wasn't thinking straight or he'd have realized it was a dumb thing to do. Reg advises Gary of his rights under the Canadian Charter.

"I want to talk to my Dad," insists the youth.

Reg points out that Gary is legally an adult but kindly adds that he'll let Greg Nichols know about the arrest and where they've taken his son.

Returning to the house he does notify Greg who appears utterly stunned by the news.

Shawna, in the hallway jumping up and down with excitement, shrilly cries: "Me and Sheila always knew it was Gary, I said so, too. We never liked him and we were right!"

Her half-sisters shepherd the two younger girls upstairs, while Moira takes Greg by the arm and leads the shattered man to sit down.

Judith, still unconscious, is admitted to the hospital but Lila is treated in the back of the ambulance. Only emergency patients are allowed inside Alberta Health facilities. The paramedics did the job of wrenching her shoulder back in place and putting her arm in a sling to keep the painful area immobile, but need a doctor to sign off on the treatment.

During the twenty-minute wait in the parking lot Lila calls Brian to come pick her up. She'll worry about getting her car home tomorrow. Tonight she has to worry about Brian's angry disapproval of what she and Judith were up to, but hopes to play the injured victim card for some sympathy and tender loving care.

"You've been very lucky – again!" admonishes Grant. He's speaking gently because it's such a relief to hear Judith's voice. He has to be content with a phone call since no one's allowed inside the hospital.

Tomorrow morning at 10:00 he'll be waiting in the parking lot to pick her up after she's released.

Judith is suffering from a mild concussion but fortunately there is no swelling or brain damage, and no broken bones from the fall down the stairs.

It turned out to be the same doctor who'd seen her back in March and the woman just shakes her head about Judith being accident-prone. No one bothers to correct her.

"Luckily I have a really hard head, I guess," answers Judith.

"Hard-headed as in stubborn? For sure! Oh, Judith," Grant pauses a moment and she can hear him take a deep breath. "It's pretty obvious that I'm going to have to take care of you from now on."

"Hmm, that sounds awfully bossy unless... Grant, is that a proposal?"

"No... but it's a promise."

COVID-19 Update: City parks and children's playgrounds are closed off with yellow tape and can't re-open until they had on-site safety inspections. Signage will be added promoting healthy best-practices.

About the Author

Della enjoys mysteries that won't keep her up at night, have a hint of romance, and a satisfactory ending. Preferably in a series.

She and her partner live with a tuxedo cat in the sunniest city in Canada, nestled in the foothills of the Rocky Mountains.

In November of 2022 Della undertook the National Novel Writing challenge to complete a 50.000 word first draft and the Village of Edgemont series began.

Books in this series:

1 - "**A Deadly December in Edgemont**"

2 - "**A Fatal February in Edgemont**"

3 - "**A Sinister Spring in Edgemont**"

A portion of sale proceeds will be donated to NaNoWriMo.org in appreciation.

Read more at dellanorth.ca.

www.ingramcontent.com/pod-product-compliance
Lightning Source LLC
Chambersburg PA
CBHW030737030726
47497CB00001B/24